SACRIFICIAL PRINCESS AND THE KING OF BEASTS

1

contents

D0124805

Sacrificial Princess and the King of Beasts

1

Yu Tomofuji

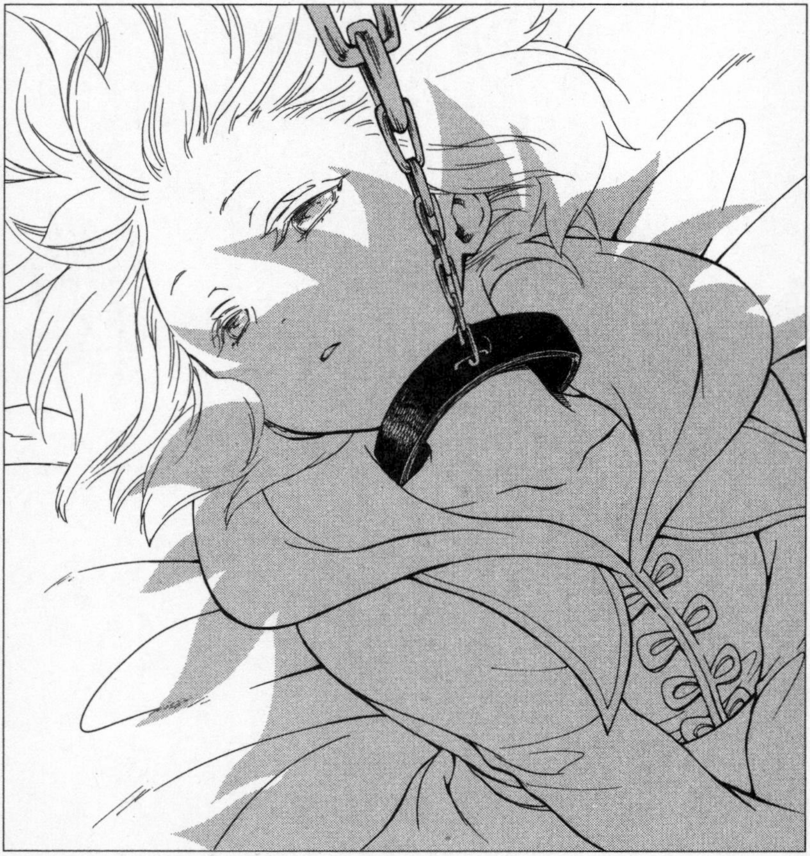

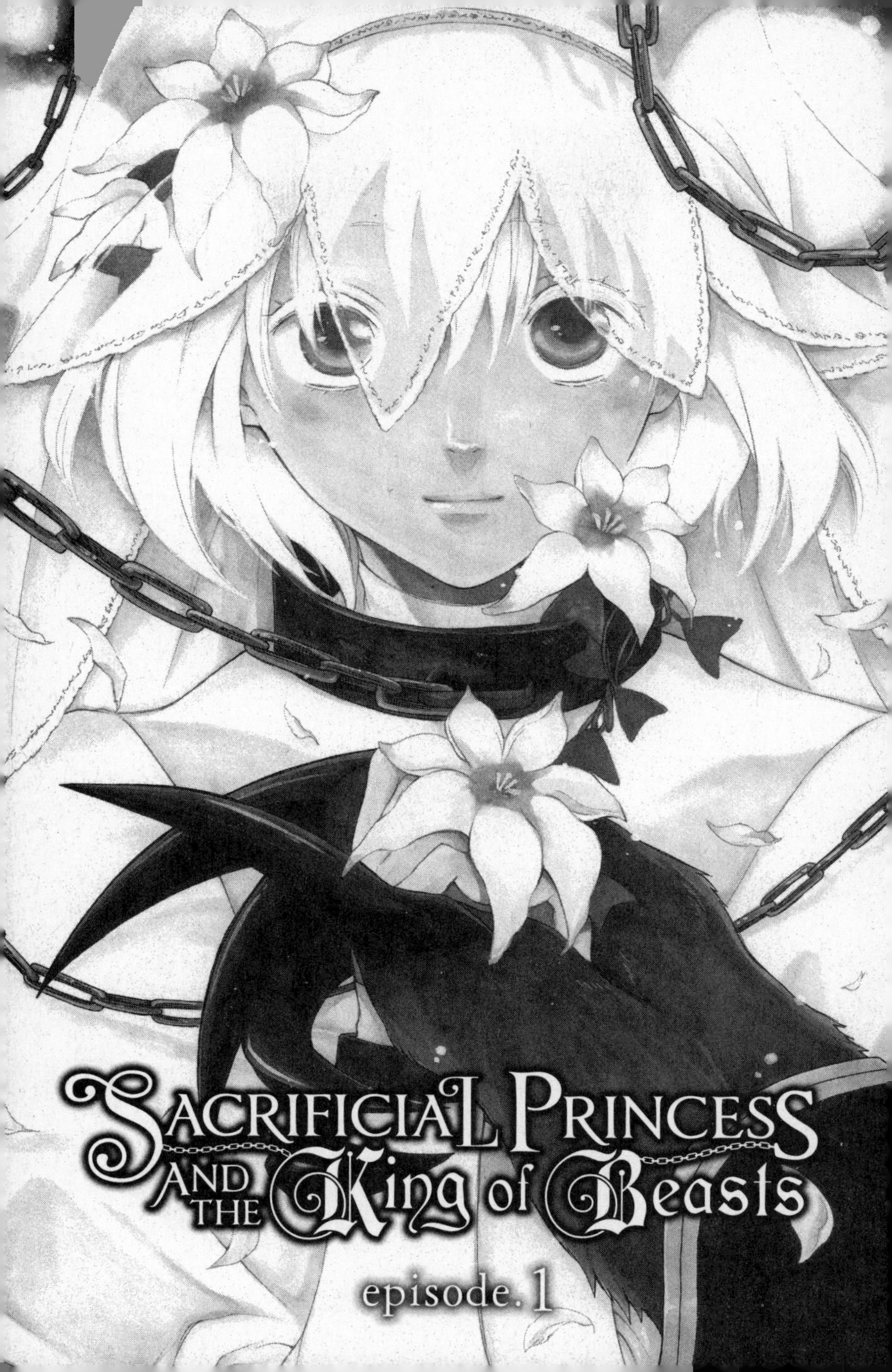
SACRIFICIAL PRINCESS AND THE King of Beasts
episode. 1

HELLO!
IT'S VERY
NICE TO
MEET YOU!
I'M YU
TOMOFUJI.
THANK YOU
SO MUCH FOR
PICKING UP
*SACRIFICIAL
PRINCESS
AND THE
KING OF
BEASTS!*
IT WAS A
LOT OF FUN
DRAWING A
STORY WITH
ENTIRELY
BEAST(-LIKE)
CHARACTERS,
ASIDE
FROM THE
PROTAGONIST,
SARIPHI.
I HOPE YOU
ENJOY IT.

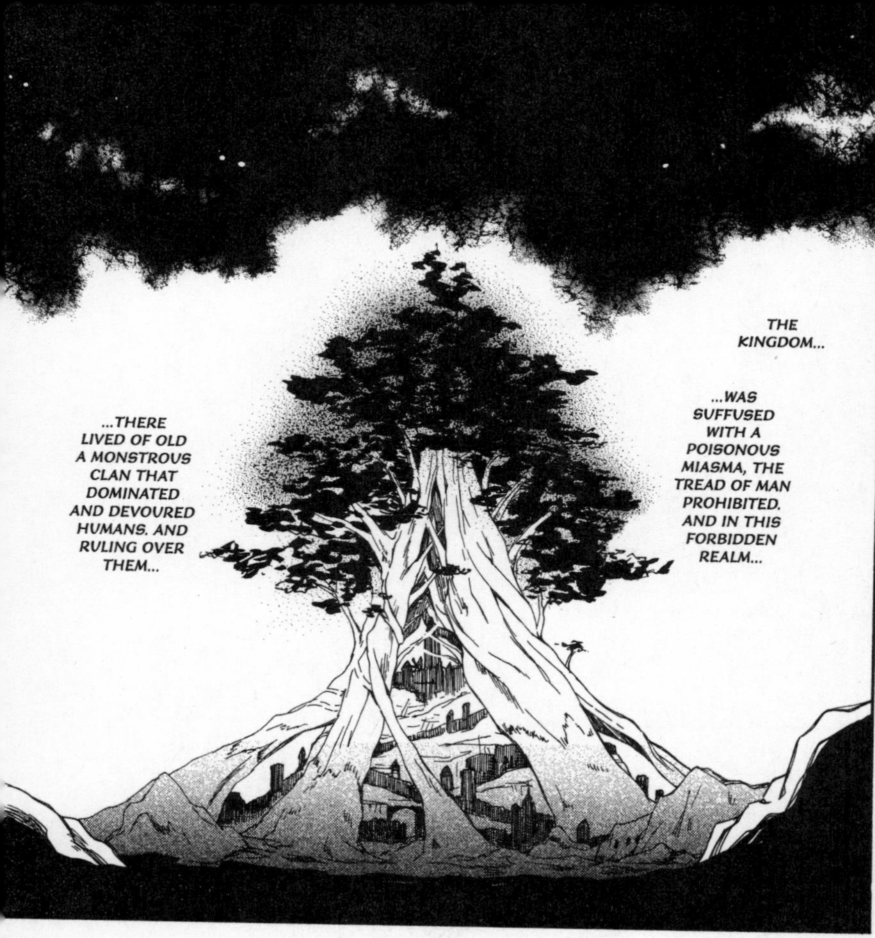
THE KINGDOM...
...WAS SUFFUSED WITH A POISONOUS MIASMA, THE TREAD OF MAN PROHIBITED. AND IN THIS FORBIDDEN REALM...
...THERE LIVED OF OLD A MONSTROUS CLAN THAT DOMINATED AND DEVOURED HUMANS. AND RULING OVER THEM...

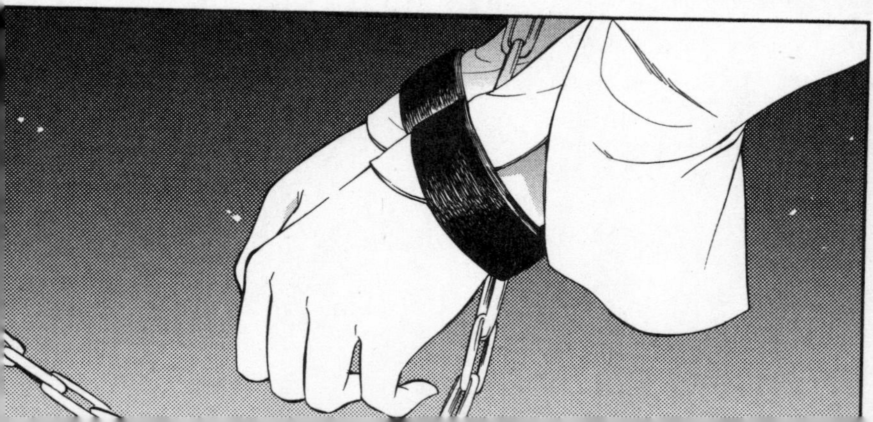

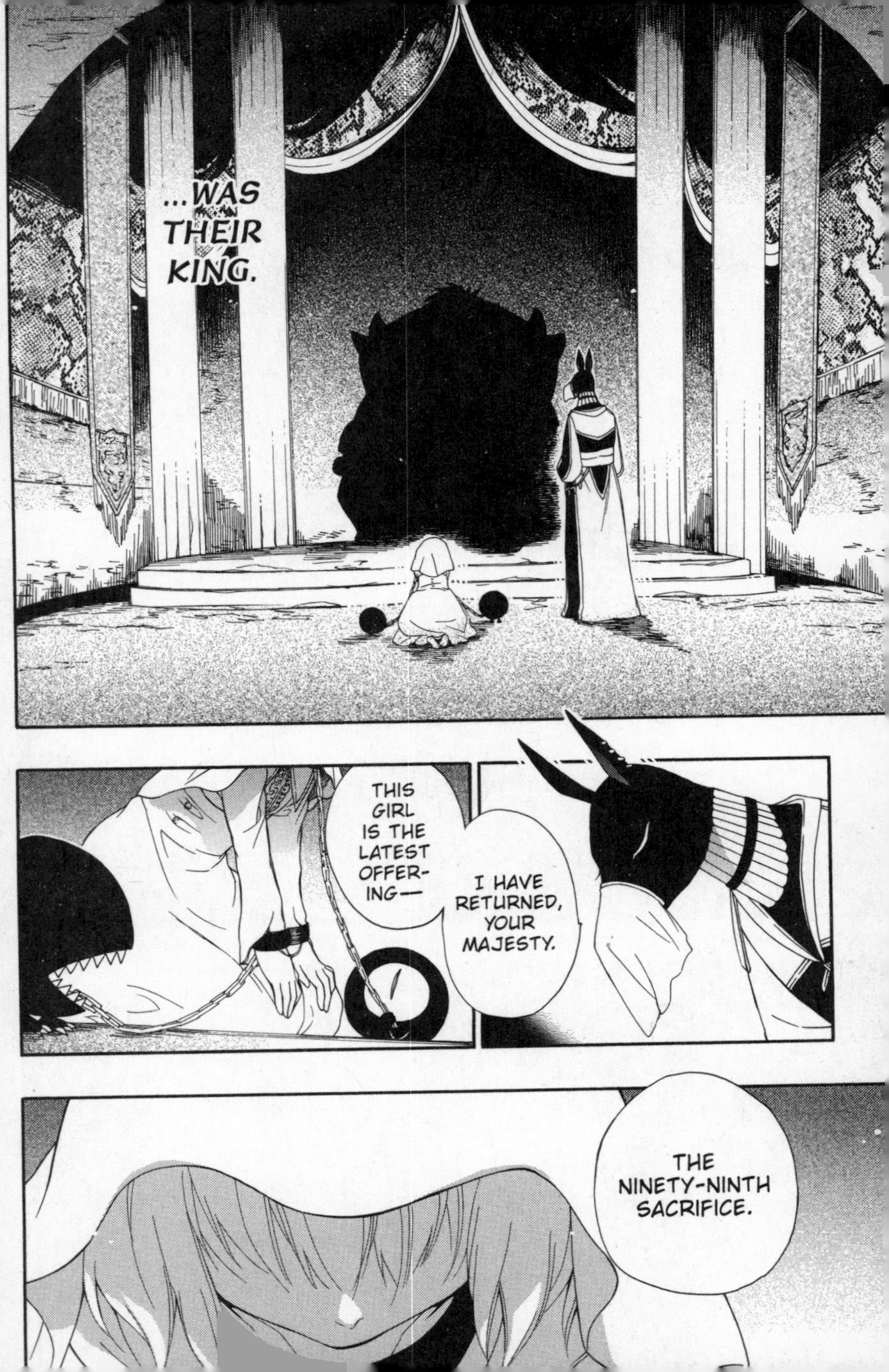
...WAS THEIR KING.
I HAVE RETURNED, YOUR MAJESTY.
THIS GIRL IS THE LATEST OFFERING—
THE NINETY-NINTH SACRIFICE.

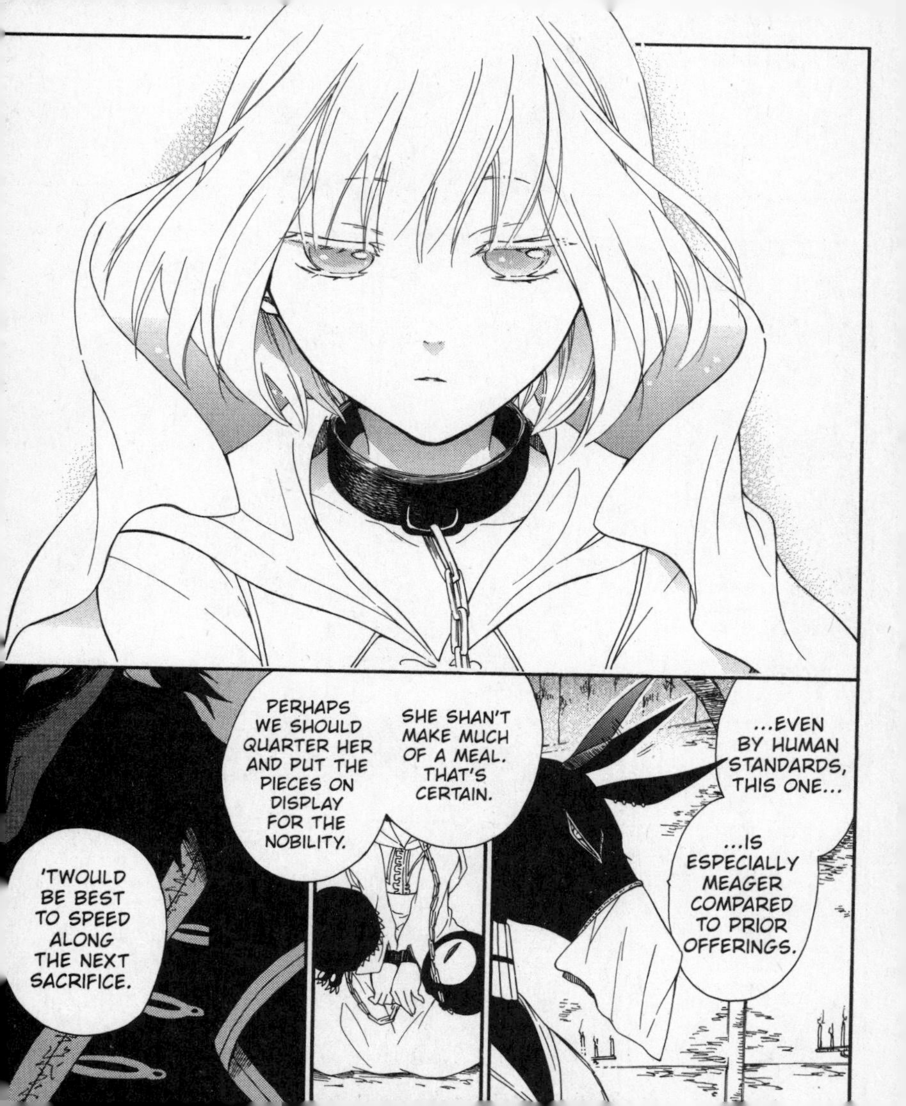
...EVEN BY HUMAN STANDARDS, THIS ONE...
...IS ESPECIALLY MEAGER COMPARED TO PRIOR OFFERINGS.
SHE SHAN'T MAKE MUCH OF A MEAL. THAT'S CERTAIN.
PERHAPS WE SHOULD QUARTER HER AND PUT THE PIECES ON DISPLAY FOR THE NOBILITY.
'TWOULD BE BEST TO SPEED ALONG THE NEXT SACRIFICE.

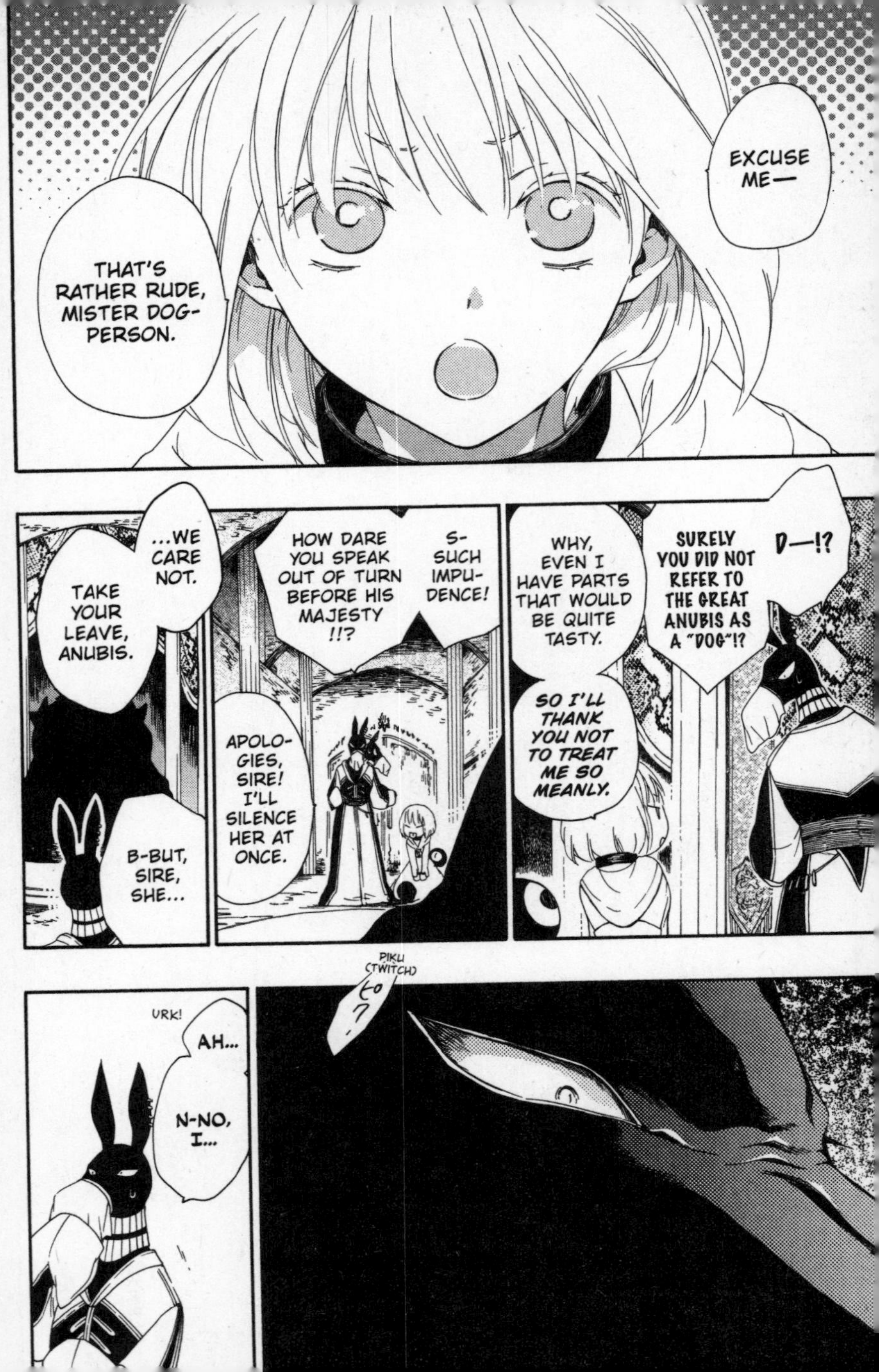
EXCUSE ME—
THAT'S RATHER RUDE, MISTER DOG-PERSON.
D—!?
SURELY YOU DID NOT REFER TO THE GREAT ANUBIS AS A "DOG"!?
WHY, EVEN I HAVE PARTS THAT WOULD BE QUITE TASTY.
SO I'LL THANK YOU NOT TO TREAT ME SO MEANLY.
S-SUCH IMPUDENCE!
HOW DARE YOU SPEAK OUT OF TURN BEFORE HIS MAJESTY!!?
APOLOGIES, SIRE! I'LL SILENCE HER AT ONCE.
...WE CARE NOT.
TAKE YOUR LEAVE, ANUBIS.
B-BUT, SIRE, SHE...
PIKU (TWITCH)
URK!
AH...
N-NO, I...

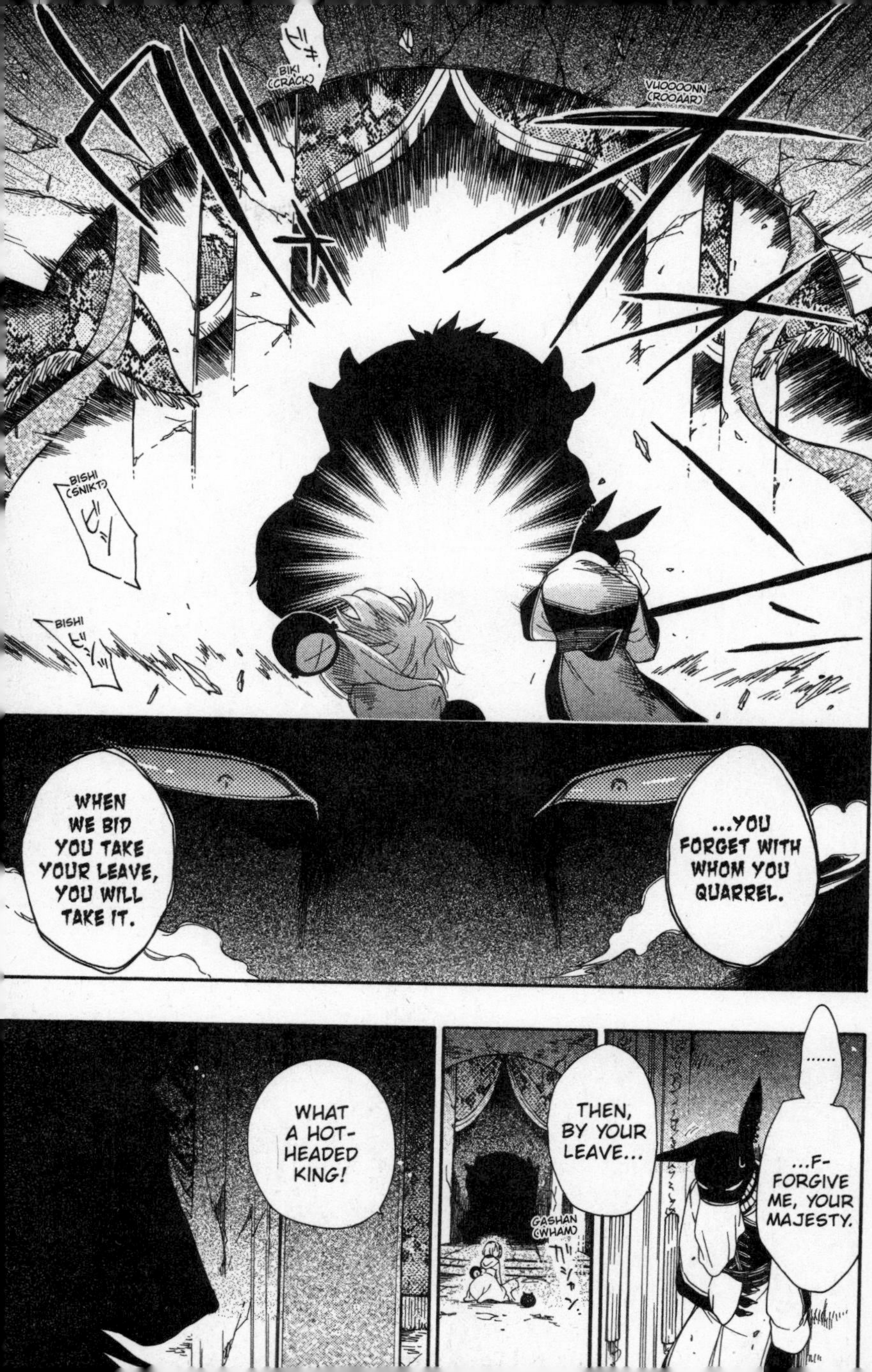
VUOOOONN (ROOAAR)
BIKI (CRACK)
BISHI (SNIKT)
BISHI
...YOU FORGET WITH WHOM YOU QUARREL.
WHEN WE BID YOU TAKE YOUR LEAVE, YOU WILL TAKE IT.
......
...F-FORGIVE ME, YOUR MAJESTY.
THEN, BY YOUR LEAVE...
GASHAN (WHAM)
WHAT A HOT-HEADED KING!

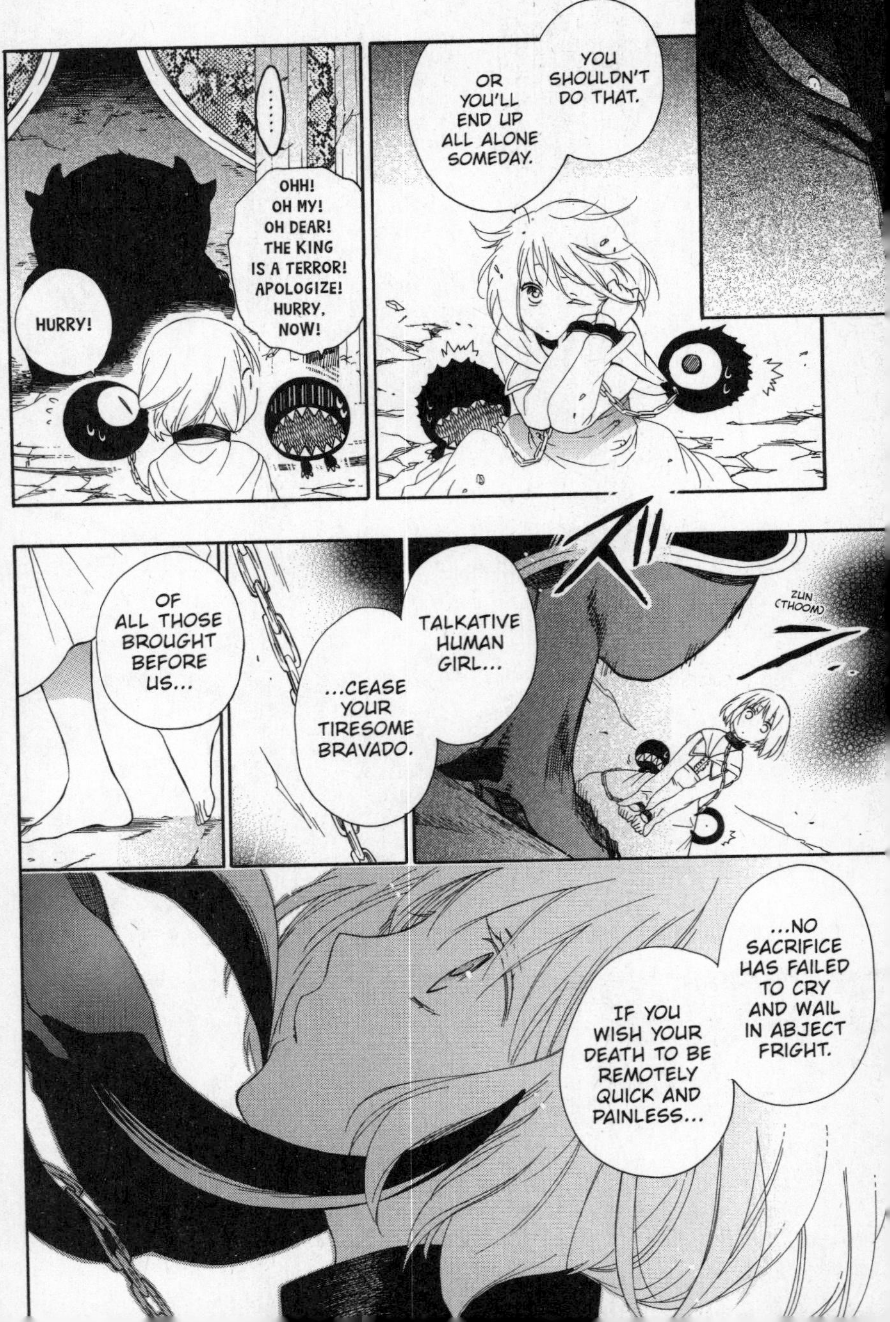
YOU SHOULDN'T DO THAT.
OR YOU'LL END UP ALL ALONE SOMEDAY.
......
OHH! OH MY! OH DEAR! THE KING IS A TERROR! APOLOGIZE! HURRY, NOW!
HURRY!
ZUN (THOOM)
TALKATIVE HUMAN GIRL...
...CEASE YOUR TIRESOME BRAVADO.
OF ALL THOSE BROUGHT BEFORE US...
...NO SACRIFICE HAS FAILED TO CRY AND WAIL IN ABJECT FRIGHT.
IF YOU WISH YOUR DEATH TO BE REMOTELY QUICK AND PAINLESS...

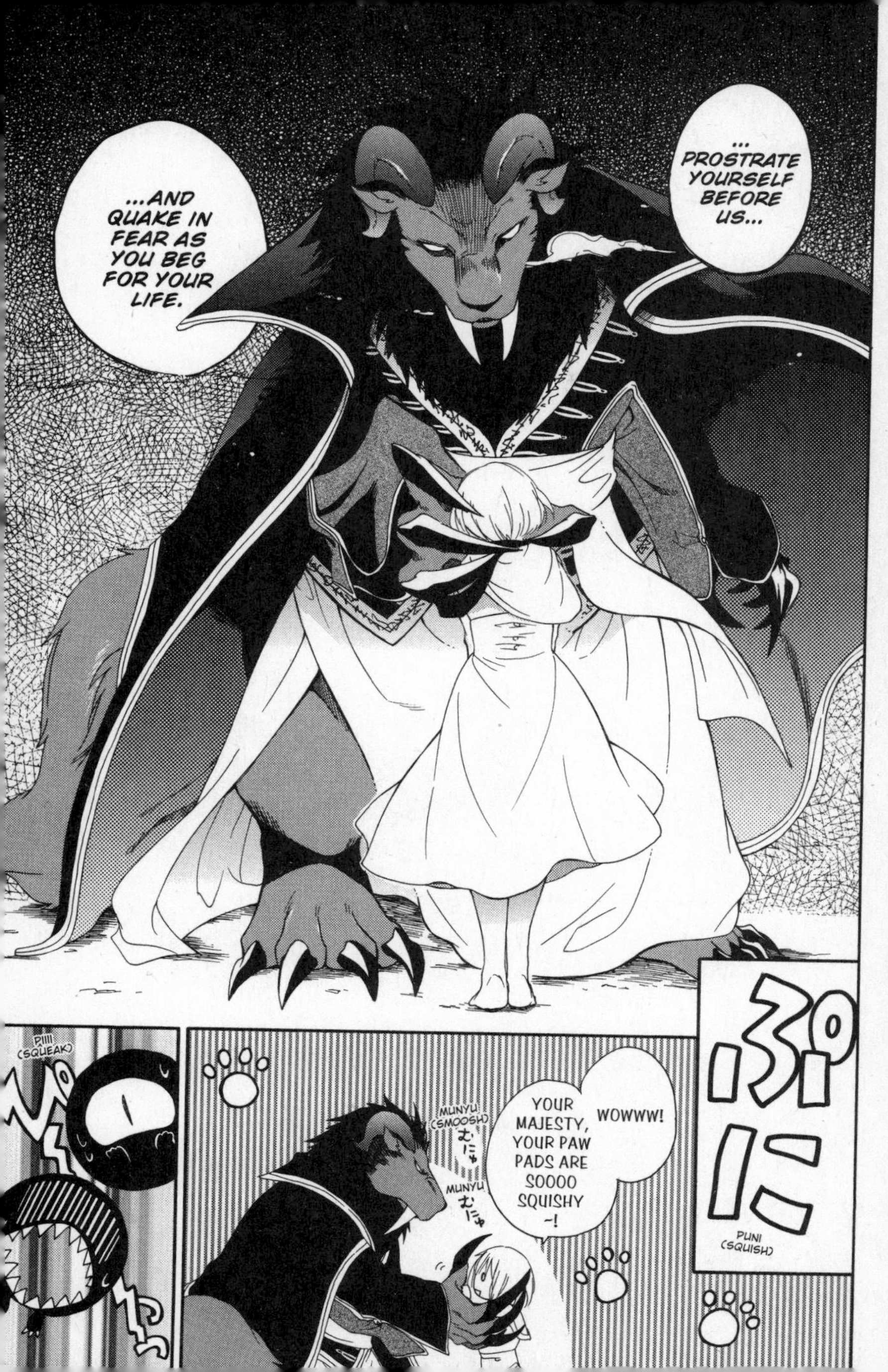
...PROSTRATE YOURSELF BEFORE US...
...AND QUAKE IN FEAR AS YOU BEG FOR YOUR LIFE.
ぷに
PUNI (SQUISH)
WOWWW!
YOUR MAJESTY, YOUR PAW PADS ARE SOOOO SQUISHY ~!
MUNYU (SMOOSH)
むにゅ
MUNYU
むにゅ
PIIII (SQUEAK)

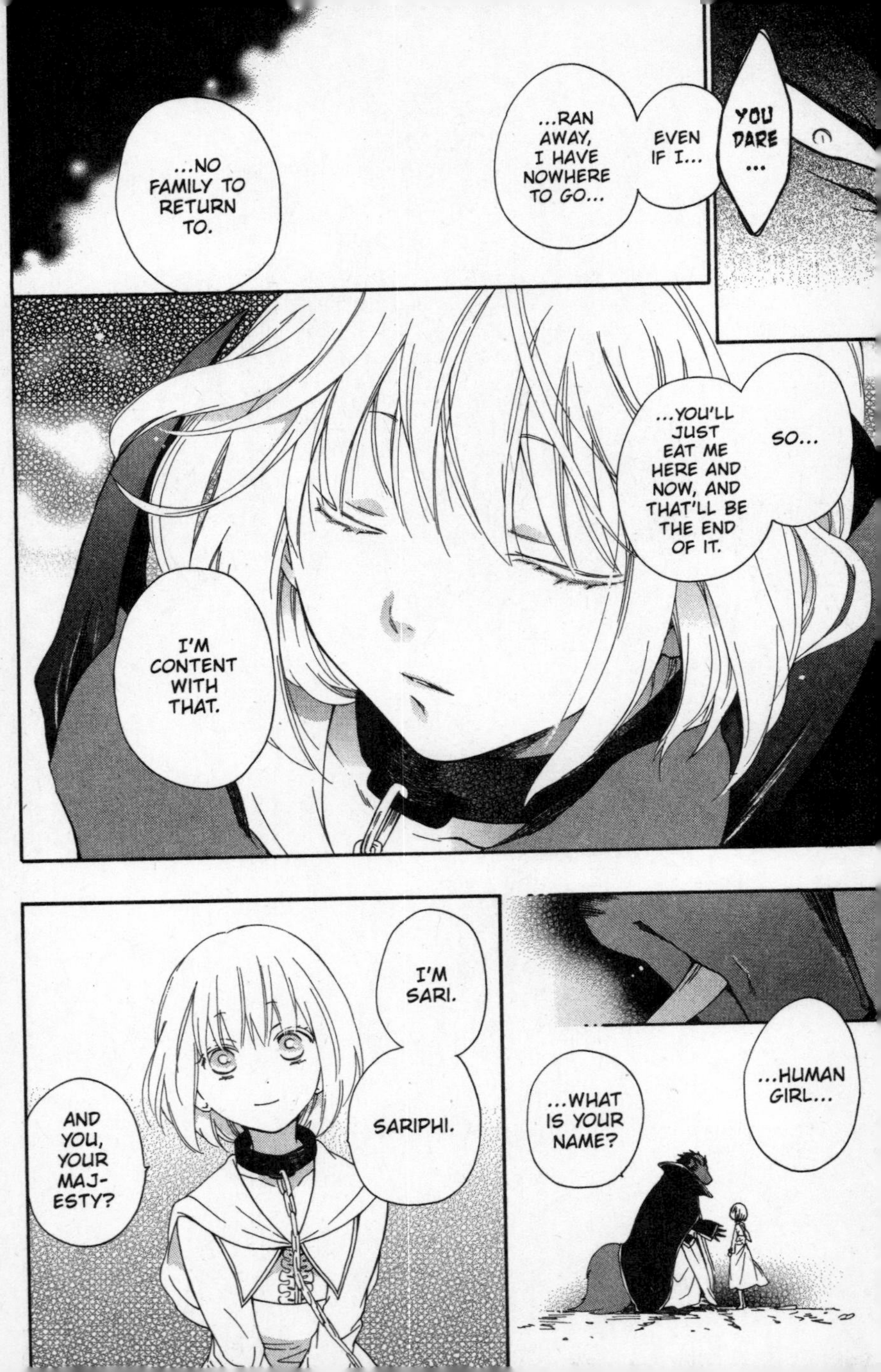
YOU DARE...
EVEN IF I...
...RAN AWAY, I HAVE NOWHERE TO GO...
...NO FAMILY TO RETURN TO.
SO...
...YOU'LL JUST EAT ME HERE AND NOW, AND THAT'LL BE THE END OF IT.
I'M CONTENT WITH THAT.
...HUMAN GIRL...
...WHAT IS YOUR NAME?
I'M SARI.
SARIPHI.
AND YOU, YOUR MAJ-ESTY?

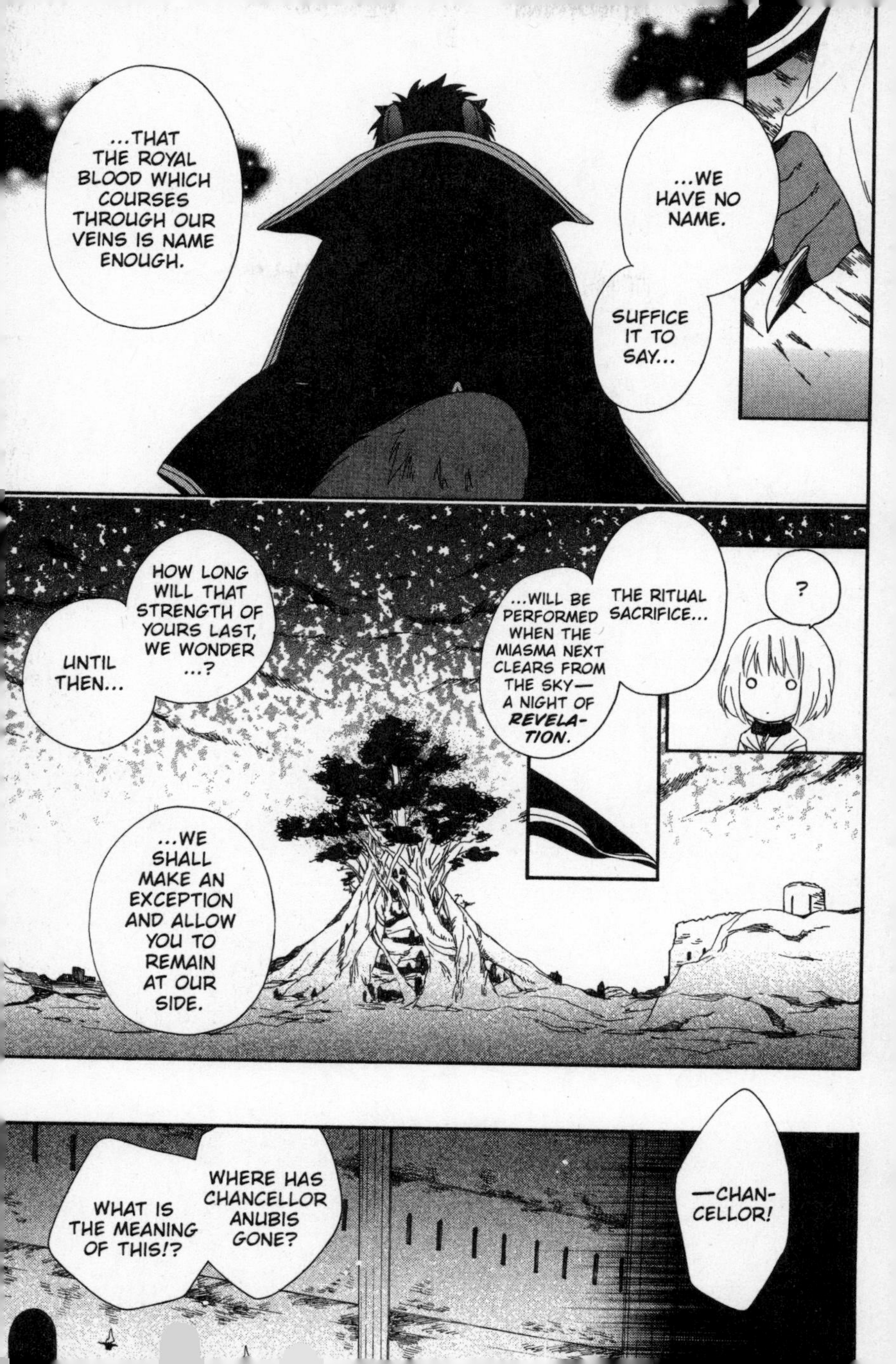
...WE HAVE NO NAME.
SUFFICE IT TO SAY...
...THAT THE ROYAL BLOOD WHICH COURSES THROUGH OUR VEINS IS NAME ENOUGH.
?
THE RITUAL SACRIFICE...
...WILL BE PERFORMED WHEN THE MIASMA NEXT CLEARS FROM THE SKY— A NIGHT OF *REVELATION*.
HOW LONG WILL THAT STRENGTH OF YOURS LAST, WE WONDER...?
UNTIL THEN...
...WE SHALL MAKE AN EXCEPTION AND ALLOW YOU TO REMAIN AT OUR SIDE.
—CHANCELLOR!
WHERE HAS CHANCELLOR ANUBIS GONE?
WHAT IS THE MEANING OF THIS!?

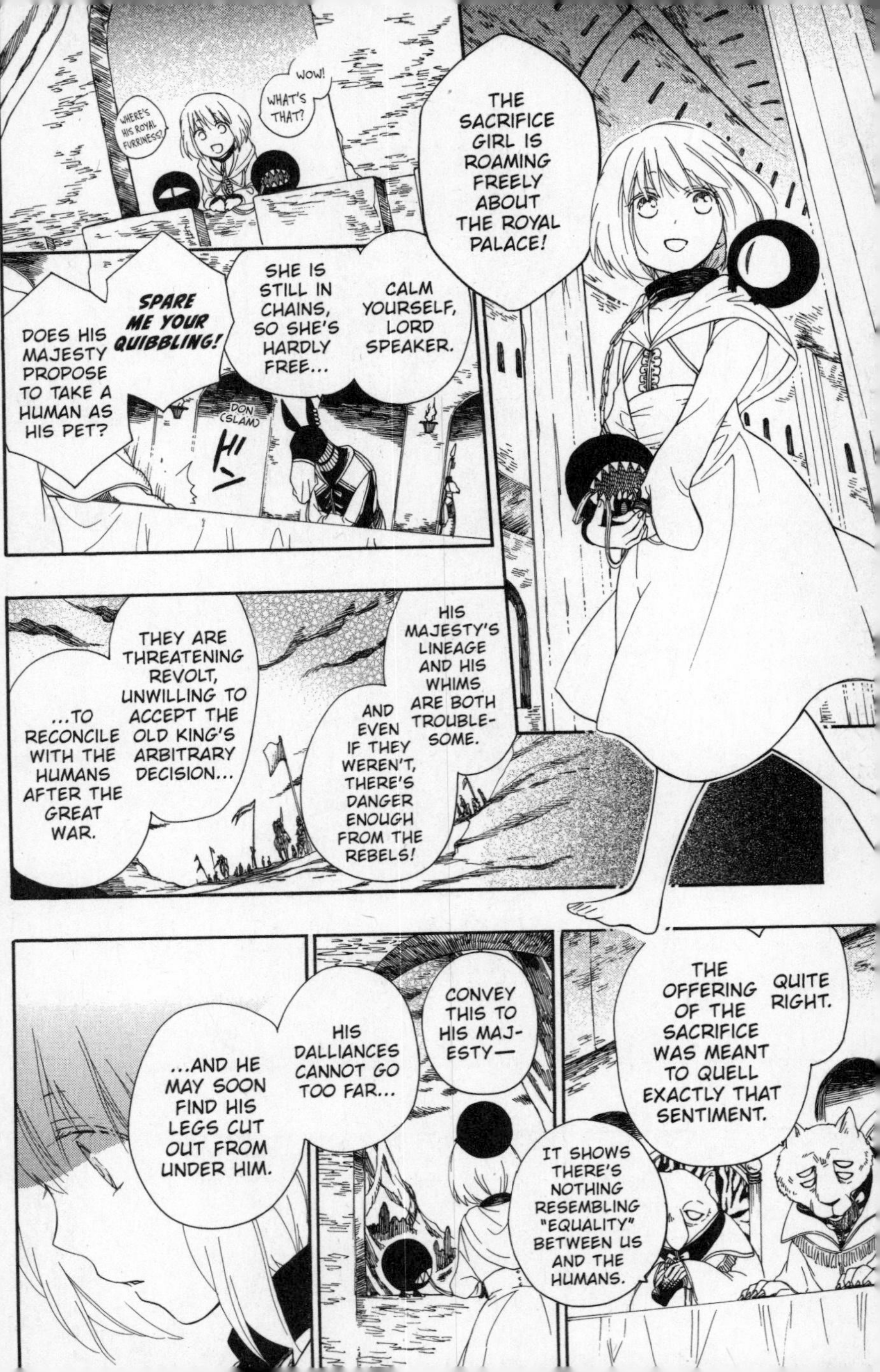

THE SACRIFICE GIRL IS ROAMING FREELY ABOUT THE ROYAL PALACE!
WOW!
WHAT'S THAT?
WHERE'S HIS ROYAL FURRINESS?
CALM YOURSELF, LORD SPEAKER.
SHE IS STILL IN CHAINS, SO SHE'S HARDLY FREE...
SPARE ME YOUR QUIBBLING!
DOES HIS MAJESTY PROPOSE TO TAKE A HUMAN AS HIS PET?
DON (SLAM)
HIS MAJESTY'S LINEAGE AND HIS WHIMS ARE BOTH TROUBLESOME.
AND EVEN IF THEY WEREN'T, THERE'S DANGER ENOUGH FROM THE REBELS!
THEY ARE THREATENING REVOLT, UNWILLING TO ACCEPT THE OLD KING'S ARBITRARY DECISION...
...TO RECONCILE WITH THE HUMANS AFTER THE GREAT WAR.
QUITE RIGHT.
THE OFFERING OF THE SACRIFICE WAS MEANT TO QUELL EXACTLY THAT SENTIMENT.
IT SHOWS THERE'S NOTHING RESEMBLING "EQUALITY" BETWEEN US AND THE HUMANS.
CONVEY THIS TO HIS MAJESTY—
HIS DALLIANCES CANNOT GO TOO FAR...
...AND HE MAY SOON FIND HIS LEGS CUT OUT FROM UNDER HIM.

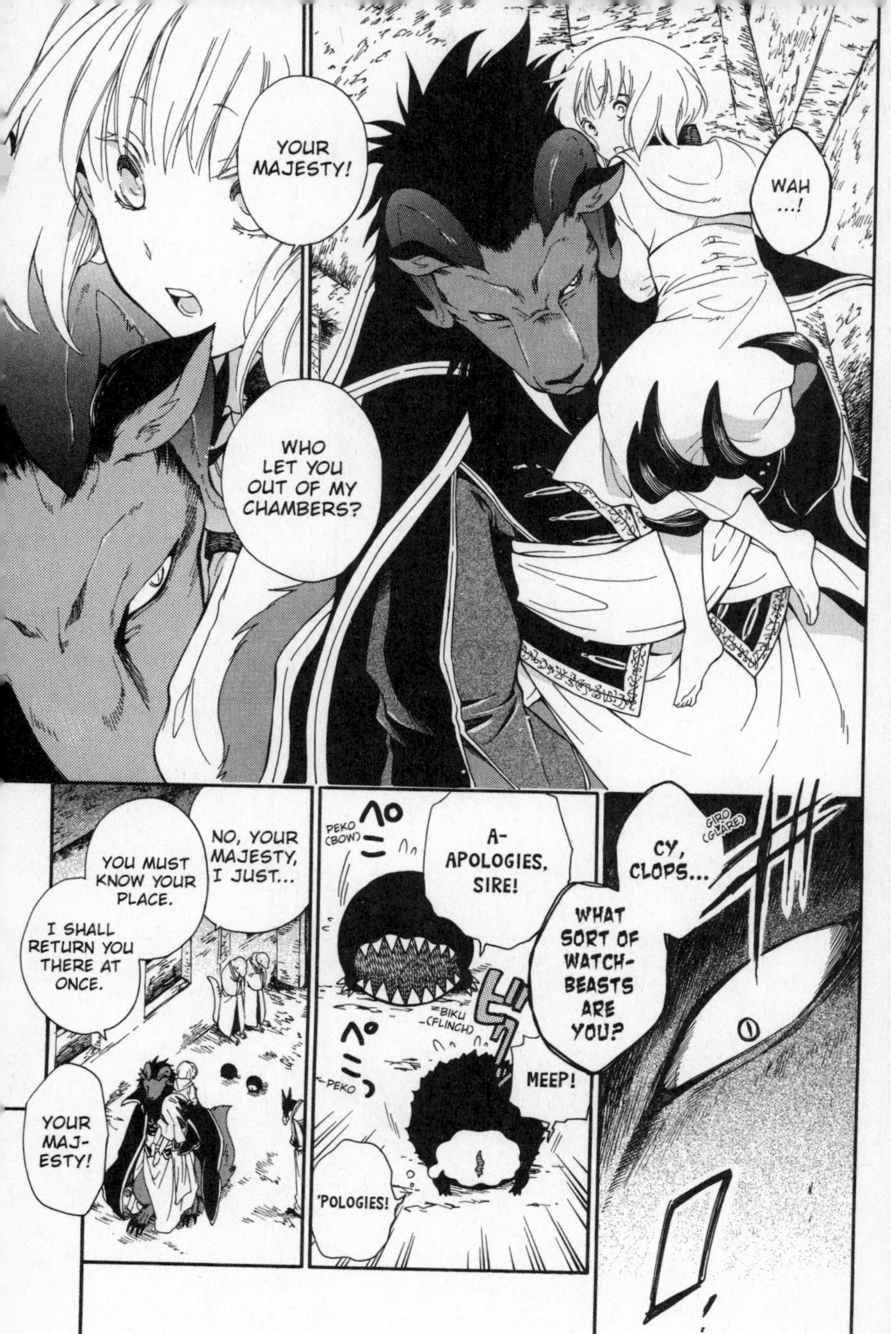
WAH ...!
YOUR MAJESTY!
WHO LET YOU OUT OF MY CHAMBERS?
GIRO (GLARE)
CY, CLOPS...
WHAT SORT OF WATCH-BEASTS ARE YOU?
A-APOLOGIES, SIRE!
PEKO (BOW)
BIKU (FLINCH)
MEEP!
PEKO
'POLOGIES!
NO, YOUR MAJESTY, I JUST...
YOU MUST KNOW YOUR PLACE.
I SHALL RETURN YOU THERE AT ONCE.
YOUR MAJ-ESTY!

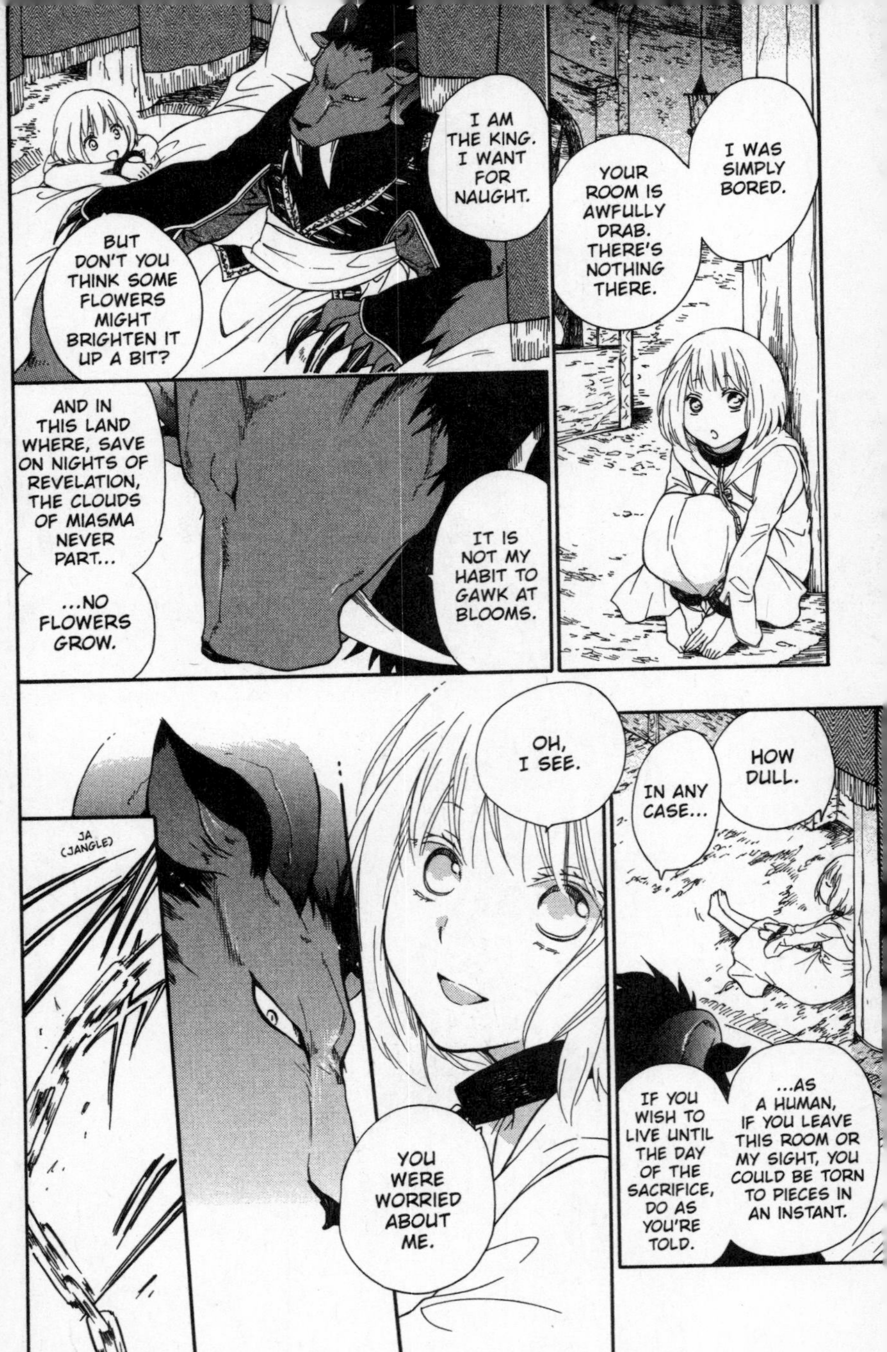
I WAS SIMPLY BORED.
YOUR ROOM IS AWFULLY DRAB. THERE'S NOTHING THERE.
I AM THE KING. I WANT FOR NAUGHT.
BUT DON'T YOU THINK SOME FLOWERS MIGHT BRIGHTEN IT UP A BIT?
IT IS NOT MY HABIT TO GAWK AT BLOOMS.
AND IN THIS LAND WHERE, SAVE ON NIGHTS OF REVELATION, THE CLOUDS OF MIASMA NEVER PART...
...NO FLOWERS GROW.
HOW DULL.
IN ANY CASE...
...AS A HUMAN, IF YOU LEAVE THIS ROOM OR MY SIGHT, YOU COULD BE TORN TO PIECES IN AN INSTANT.
IF YOU WISH TO LIVE UNTIL THE DAY OF THE SACRIFICE, DO AS YOU'RE TOLD.
OH, I SEE.
JA (JANGLE)
YOU WERE WORRIED ABOUT ME.

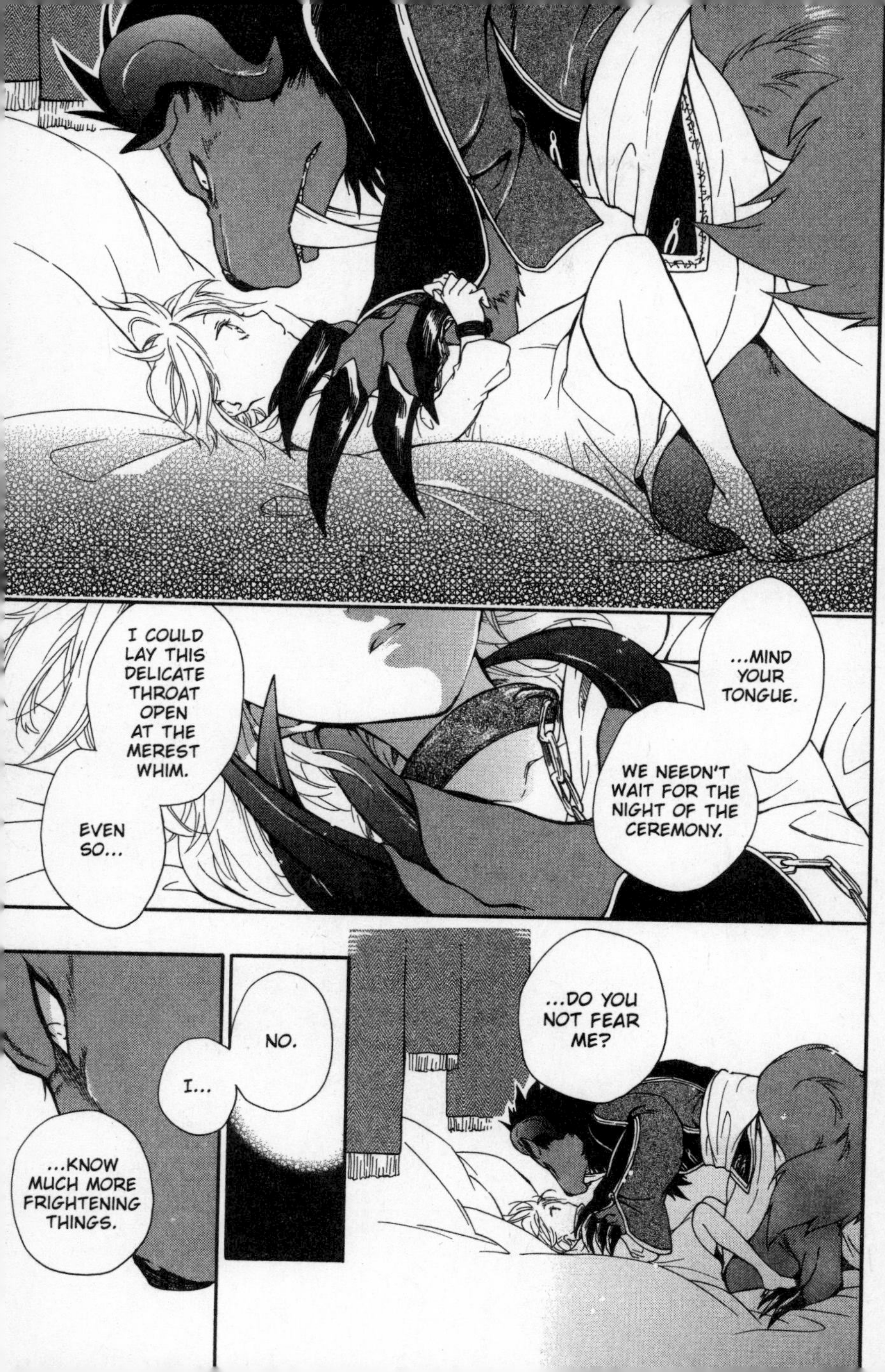
...MIND YOUR TONGUE.
I COULD LAY THIS DELICATE THROAT OPEN AT THE MEREST WHIM.
WE NEEDN'T WAIT FOR THE NIGHT OF THE CEREMONY.
EVEN SO...
...DO YOU NOT FEAR ME?
NO.
I...
...KNOW MUCH MORE FRIGHTENING THINGS.

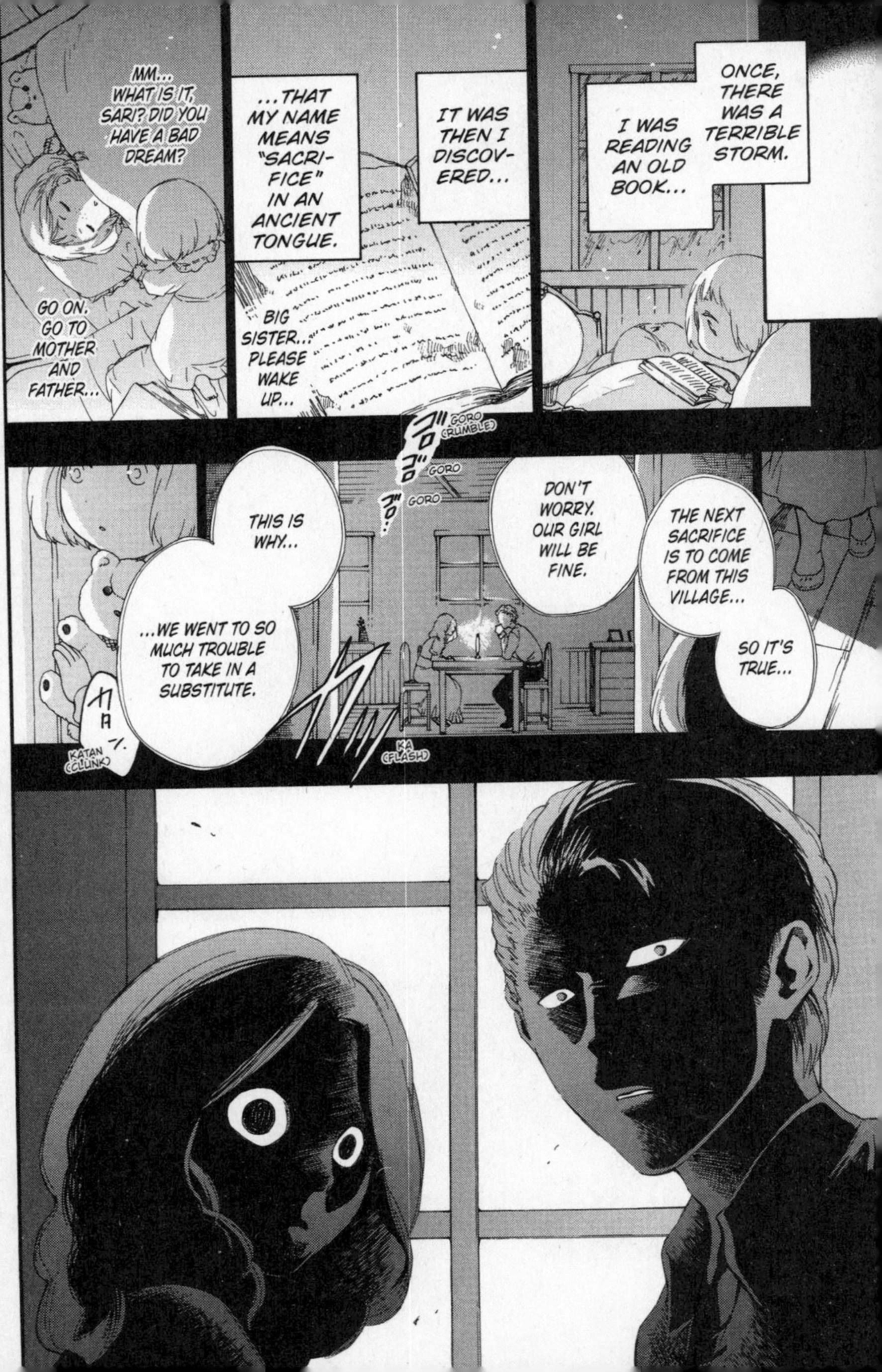
ONCE, THERE WAS A TERRIBLE STORM.
I WAS READING AN OLD BOOK...
IT WAS THEN I DISCOVERED...
...THAT MY NAME MEANS "SACRIFICE" IN AN ANCIENT TONGUE.
BIG SISTER... PLEASE WAKE UP...
MM... WHAT IS IT, SARI? DID YOU HAVE A BAD DREAM?
GO ON. GO TO MOTHER AND FATHER...
GORO (RUMBLE)
GORO
GORO
THE NEXT SACRIFICE IS TO COME FROM THIS VILLAGE...
SO IT'S TRUE...
DON'T WORRY. OUR GIRL WILL BE FINE.
KA (FLASH)
THIS IS WHY...
...WE WENT TO SO MUCH TROUBLE TO TAKE IN A SUBSTITUTE.
KATAN (CLUNK)

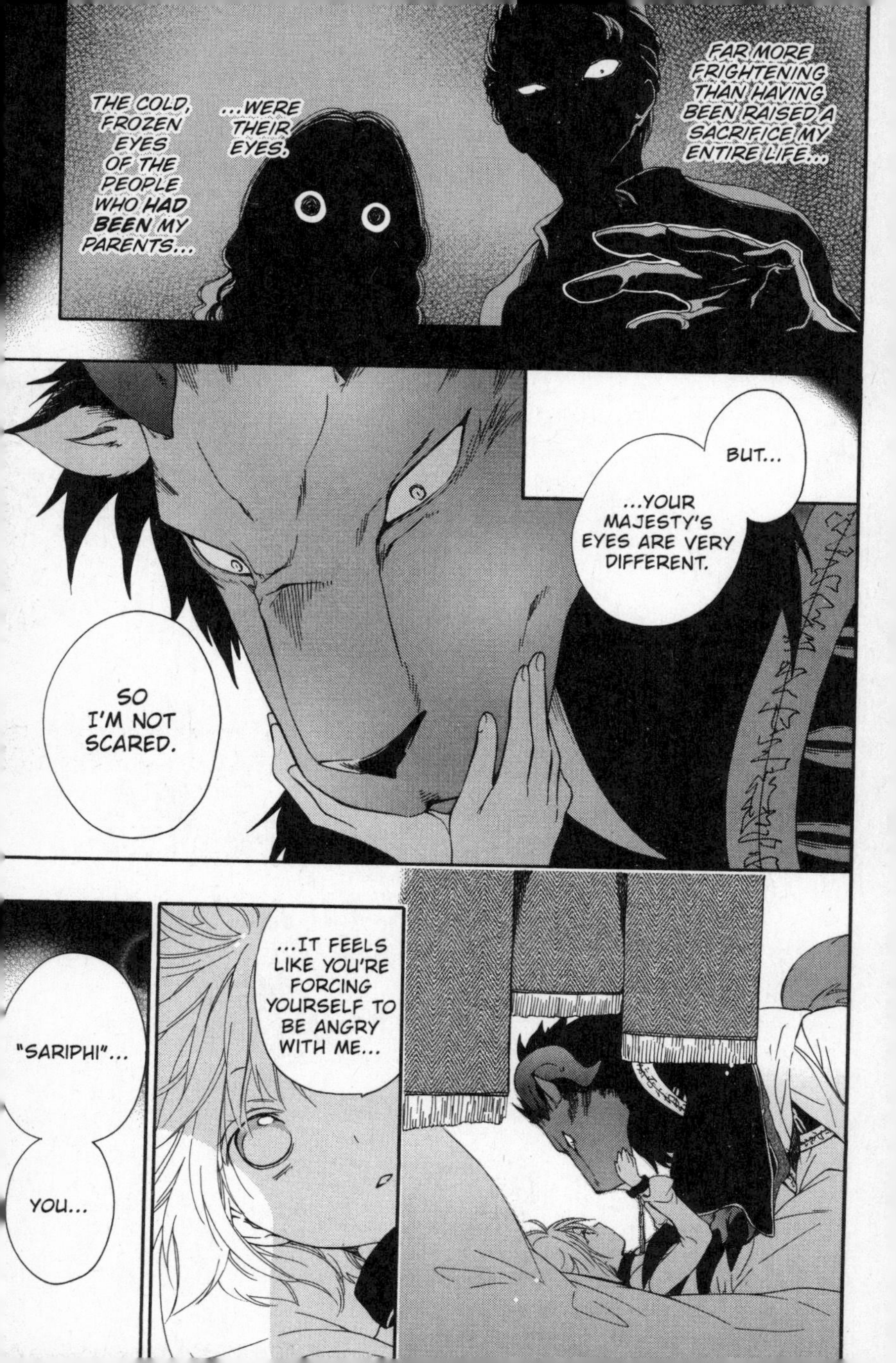
FAR MORE FRIGHTENING THAN HAVING BEEN RAISED A SACRIFICE MY ENTIRE LIFE...
...WERE THEIR EYES.
THE COLD, FROZEN EYES OF THE PEOPLE WHO HAD BEEN MY PARENTS...
BUT...
...YOUR MAJESTY'S EYES ARE VERY DIFFERENT.
SO I'M NOT SCARED.
...IT FEELS LIKE YOU'RE FORCING YOURSELF TO BE ANGRY WITH ME...
"SARIPHI"...
YOU...

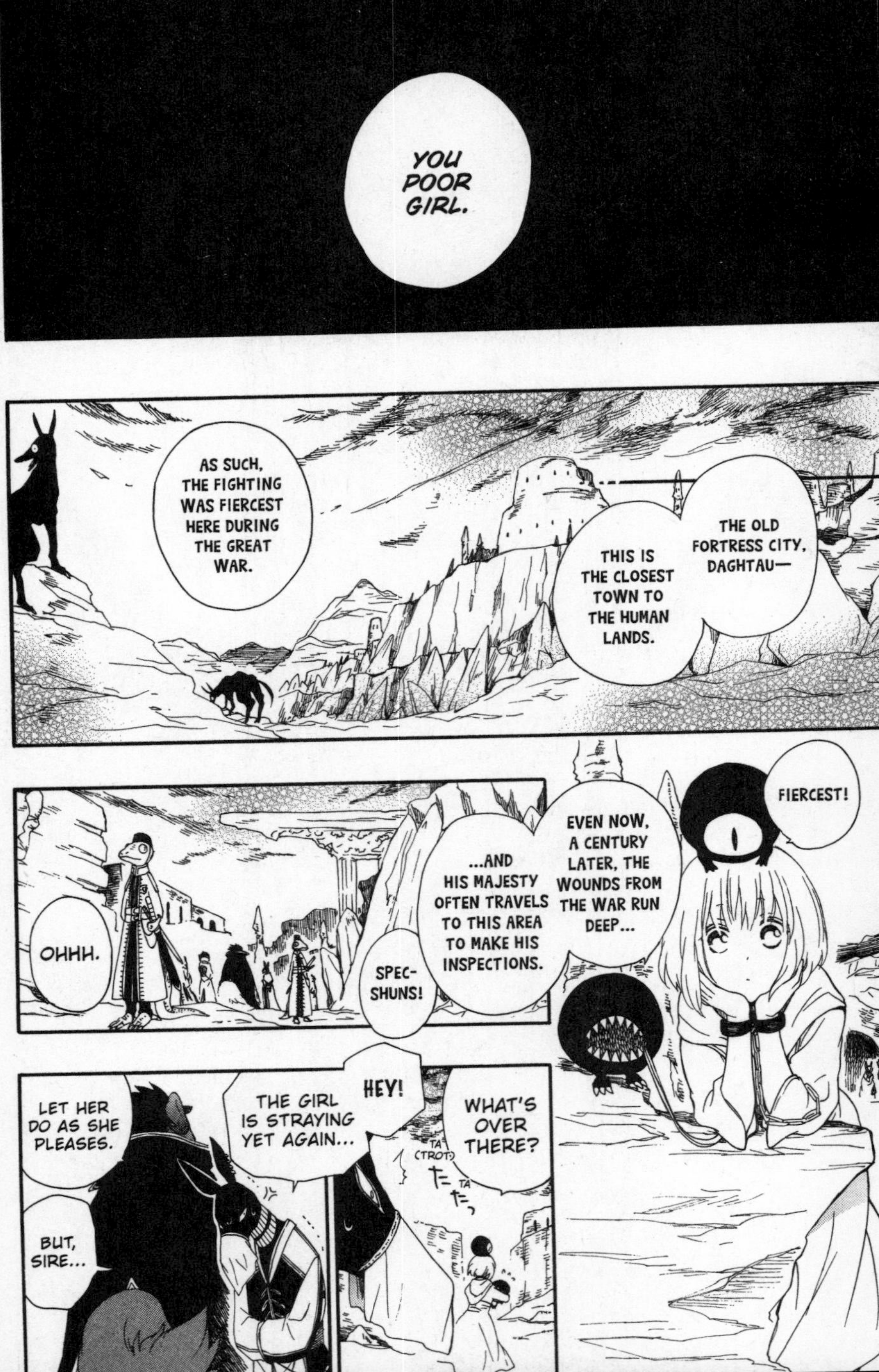
YOU POOR GIRL.
THE OLD FORTRESS CITY, DAGHTAU—
THIS IS THE CLOSEST TOWN TO THE HUMAN LANDS.
AS SUCH, THE FIGHTING WAS FIERCEST HERE DURING THE GREAT WAR.
FIERCEST!
EVEN NOW, A CENTURY LATER, THE WOUNDS FROM THE WAR RUN DEEP...
...AND HIS MAJESTY OFTEN TRAVELS TO THIS AREA TO MAKE HIS INSPECTIONS.
SPEC-SHUNS!
OHHH.
WHAT'S OVER THERE?
TA TA (TROT)
HEY!
THE GIRL IS STRAYING YET AGAIN...
LET HER DO AS SHE PLEASES.
BUT, SIRE...

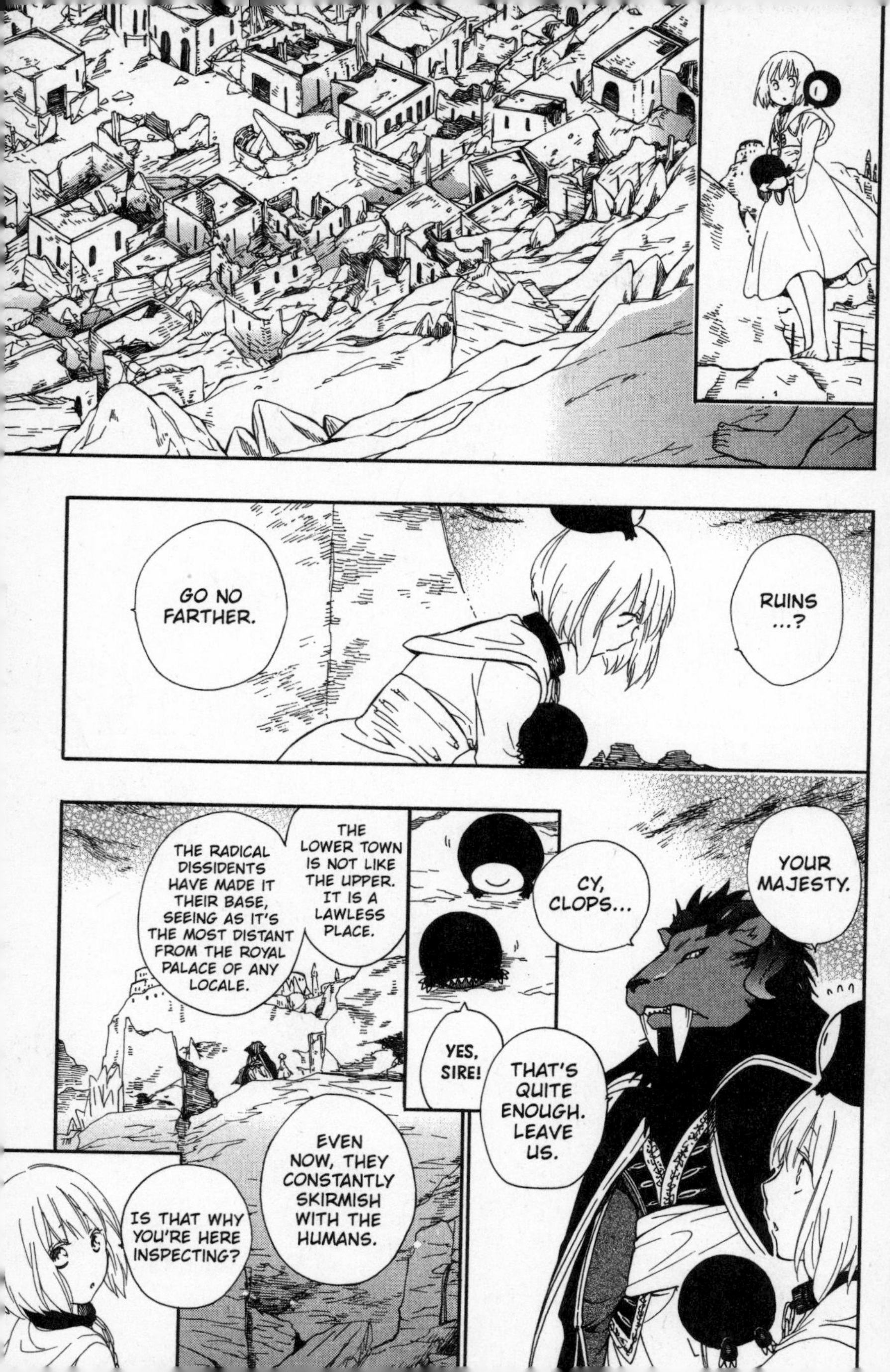
RUINS ...?
GO NO FARTHER.
YOUR MAJESTY.
THAT'S QUITE ENOUGH. LEAVE US.
CY, CLOPS...
YES, SIRE!
THE LOWER TOWN IS NOT LIKE THE UPPER. IT IS A LAWLESS PLACE.
THE RADICAL DISSIDENTS HAVE MADE IT THEIR BASE, SEEING AS IT'S THE MOST DISTANT FROM THE ROYAL PALACE OF ANY LOCALE.
EVEN NOW, THEY CONSTANTLY SKIRMISH WITH THE HUMANS.
IS THAT WHY YOU'RE HERE INSPECTING?

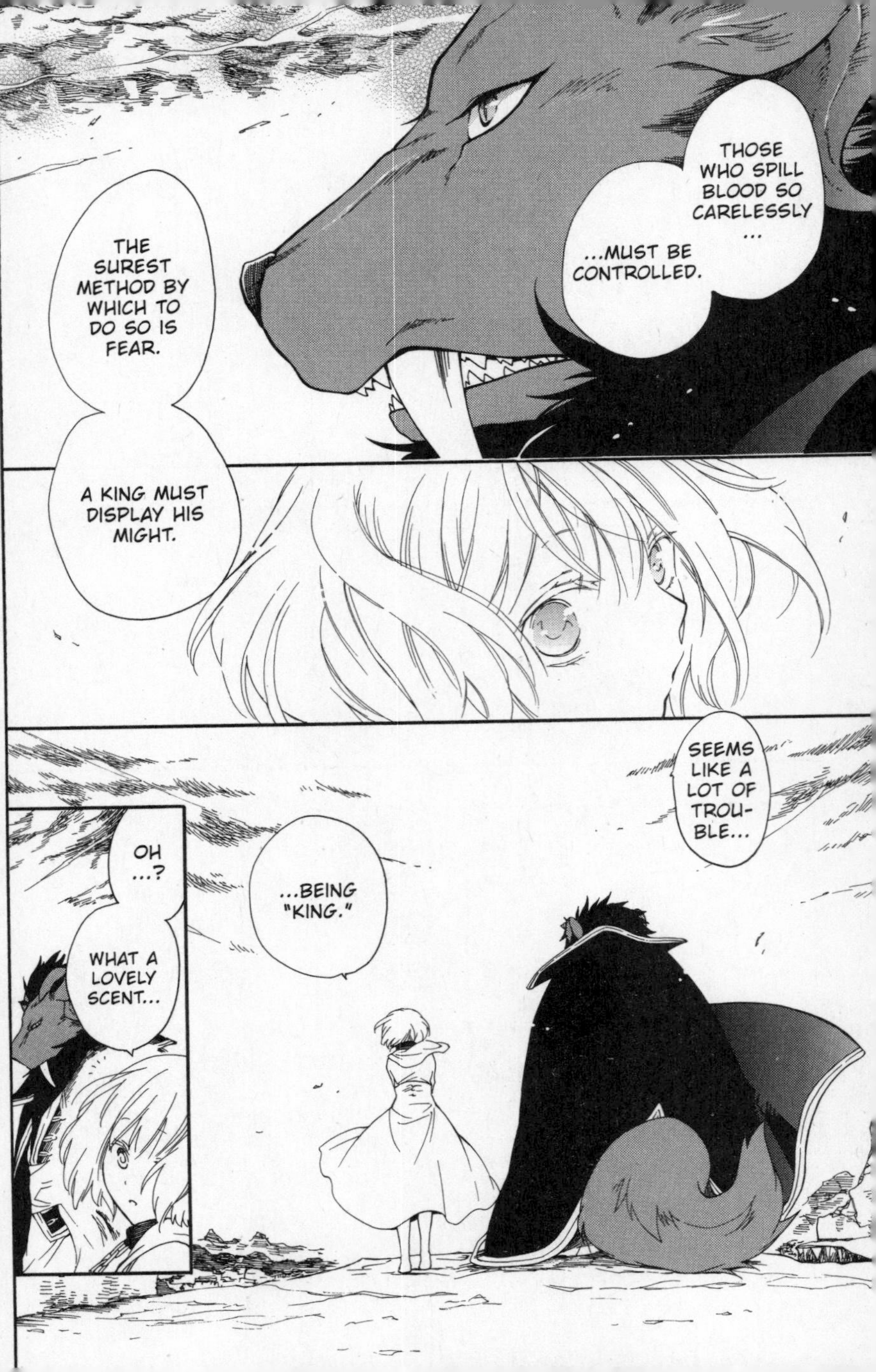
THOSE WHO SPILL BLOOD SO CARELESSLY ...
...MUST BE CONTROLLED.
THE SUREST METHOD BY WHICH TO DO SO IS FEAR.
A KING MUST DISPLAY HIS MIGHT.
SEEMS LIKE A LOT OF TROU-BLE...
...BEING "KING."
OH ...?
WHAT A LOVELY SCENT...

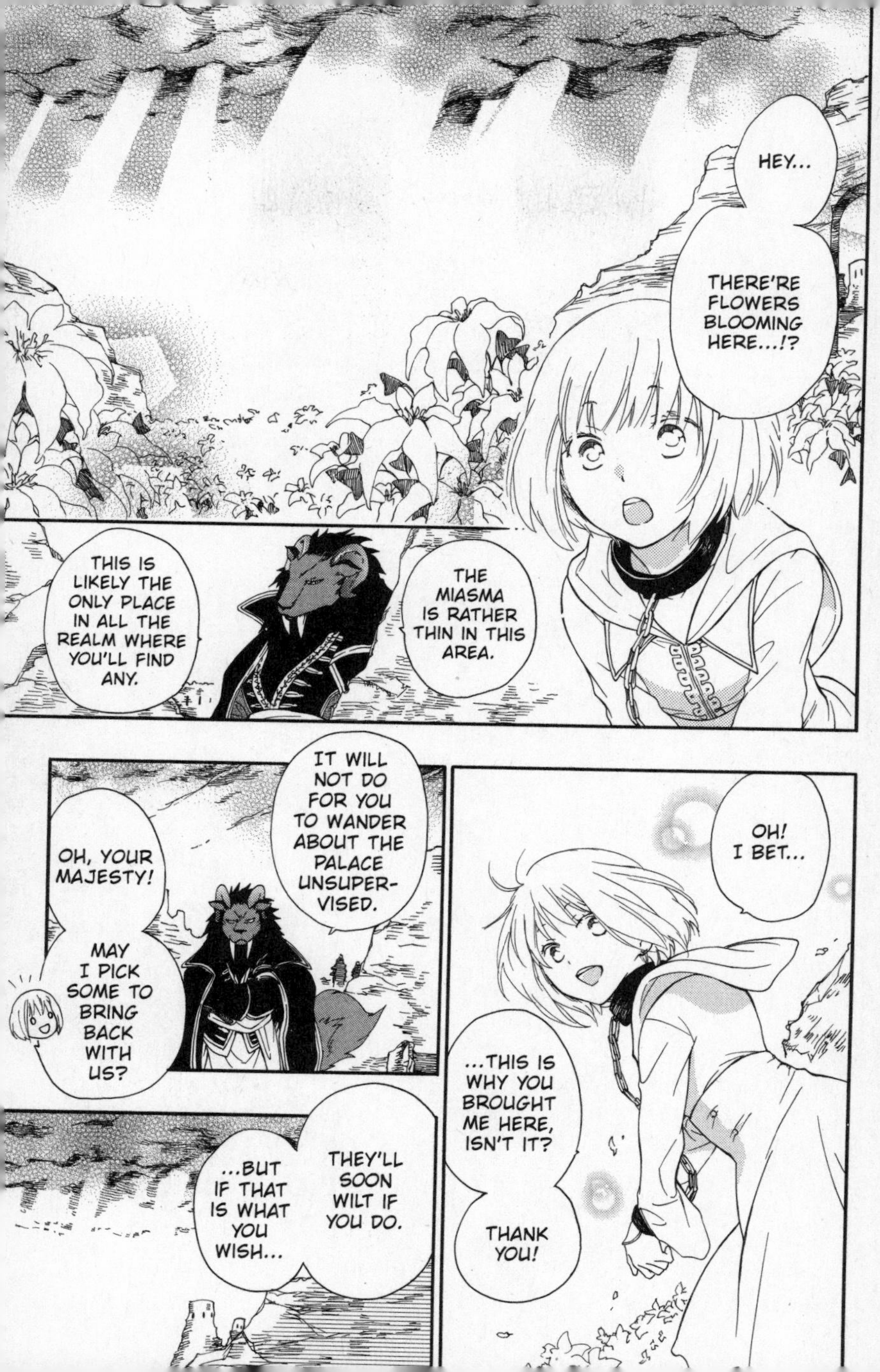
HEY...
THERE'RE FLOWERS BLOOMING HERE...!?
THE MIASMA IS RATHER THIN IN THIS AREA.
THIS IS LIKELY THE ONLY PLACE IN ALL THE REALM WHERE YOU'LL FIND ANY.
OH! I BET...
...THIS IS WHY YOU BROUGHT ME HERE, ISN'T IT?
THANK YOU!
IT WILL NOT DO FOR YOU TO WANDER ABOUT THE PALACE UNSUPERVISED.
OH, YOUR MAJESTY!
MAY I PICK SOME TO BRING BACK WITH US?
THEY'LL SOON WILT IF YOU DO.
...BUT IF THAT IS WHAT YOU WISH...

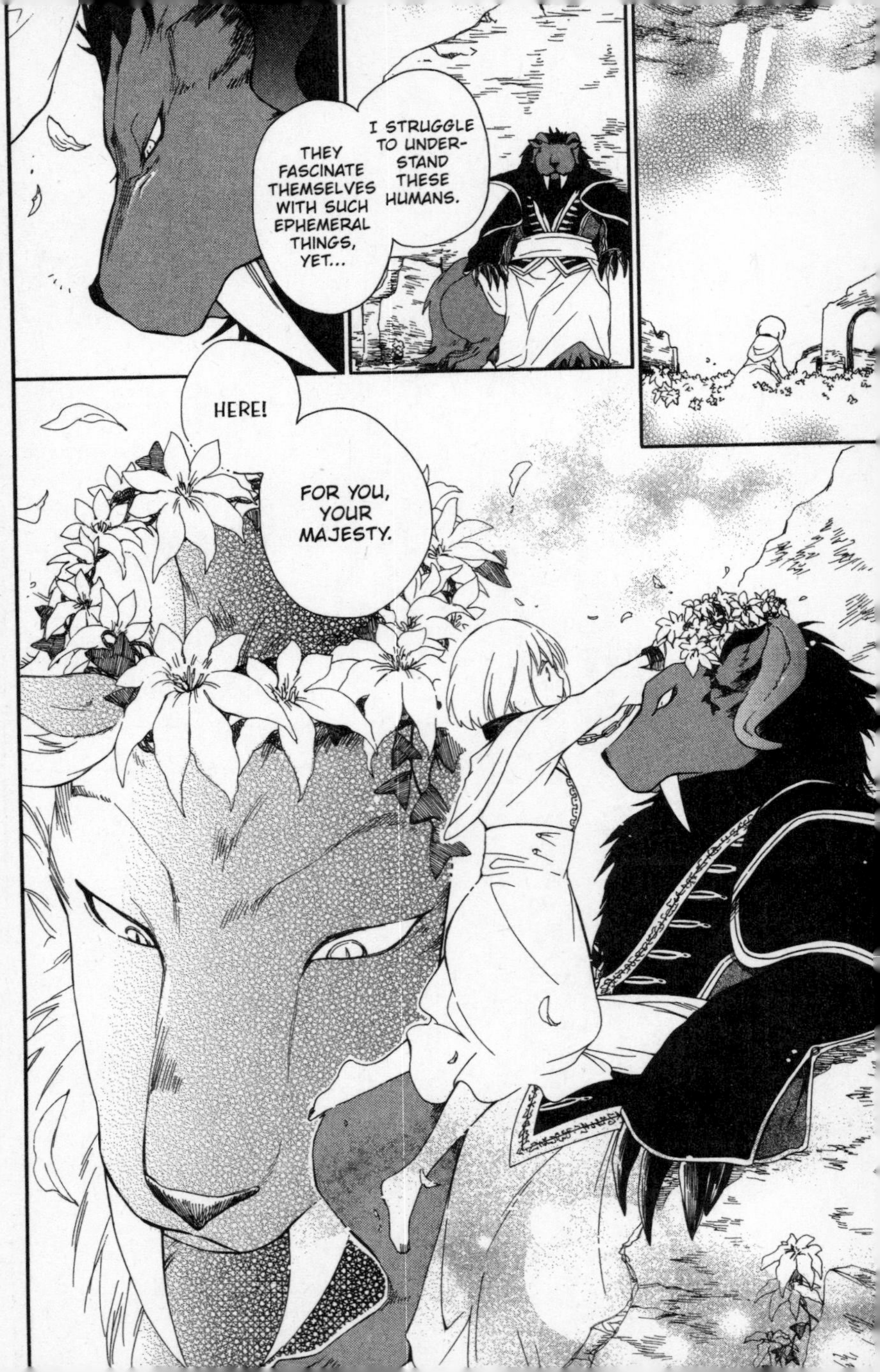
I STRUGGLE TO UNDER-STAND THESE HUMANS.
THEY FASCINATE THEMSELVES WITH SUCH EPHEMERAL THINGS, YET...
HERE!
FOR YOU, YOUR MAJESTY.

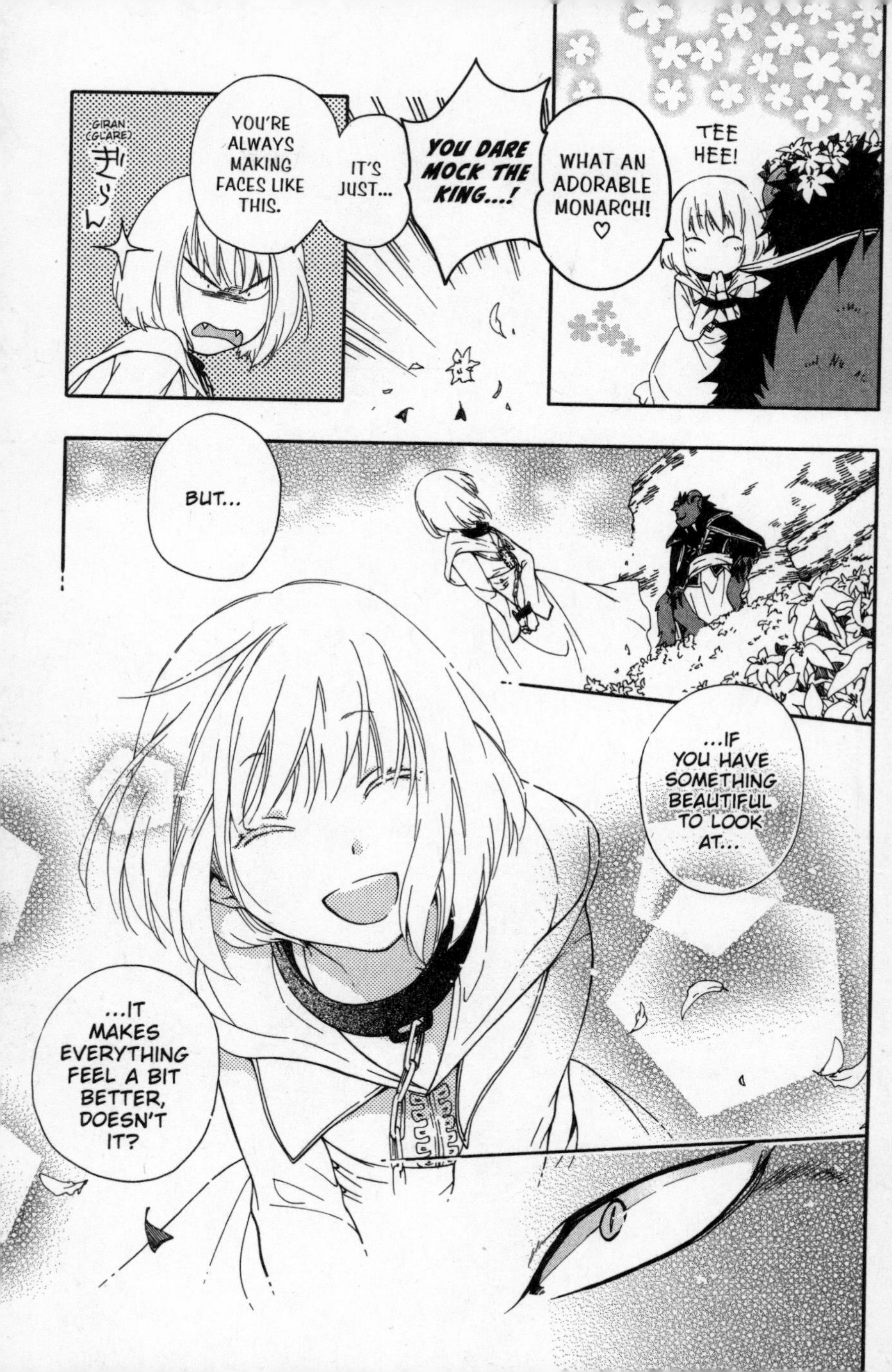
TEE HEE!
WHAT AN ADORABLE MONARCH! ♡
YOU DARE MOCK THE KING...!
IT'S JUST...
YOU'RE ALWAYS MAKING FACES LIKE THIS.
GIRAN (GLARE)
BUT...
...IF YOU HAVE SOMETHING BEAUTIFUL TO LOOK AT...
...IT MAKES EVERYTHING FEEL A BIT BETTER, DOESN'T IT?

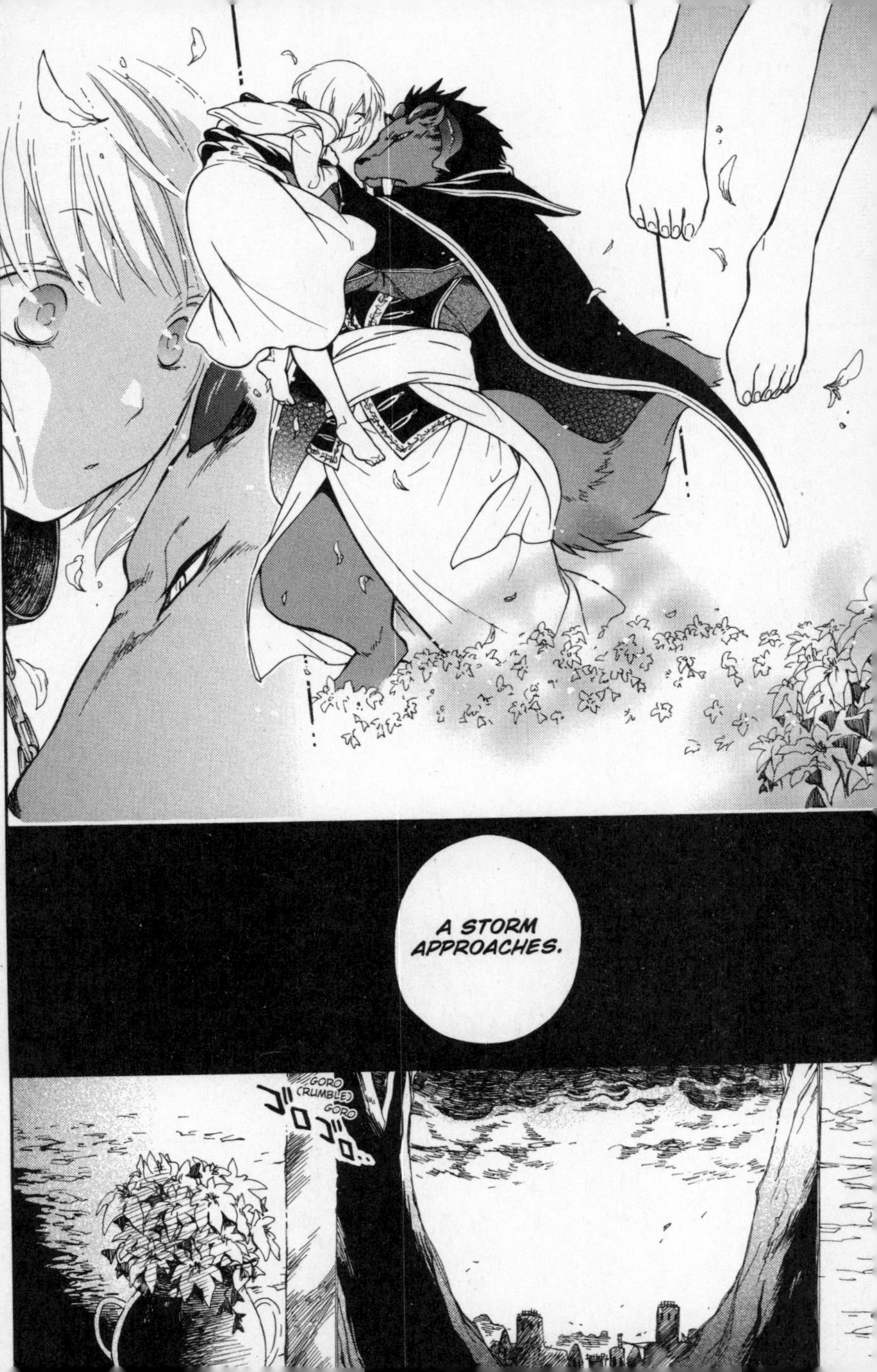
A STORM APPROACHES.
ゴロゴロ..
GORO (RUMBLE) GORO

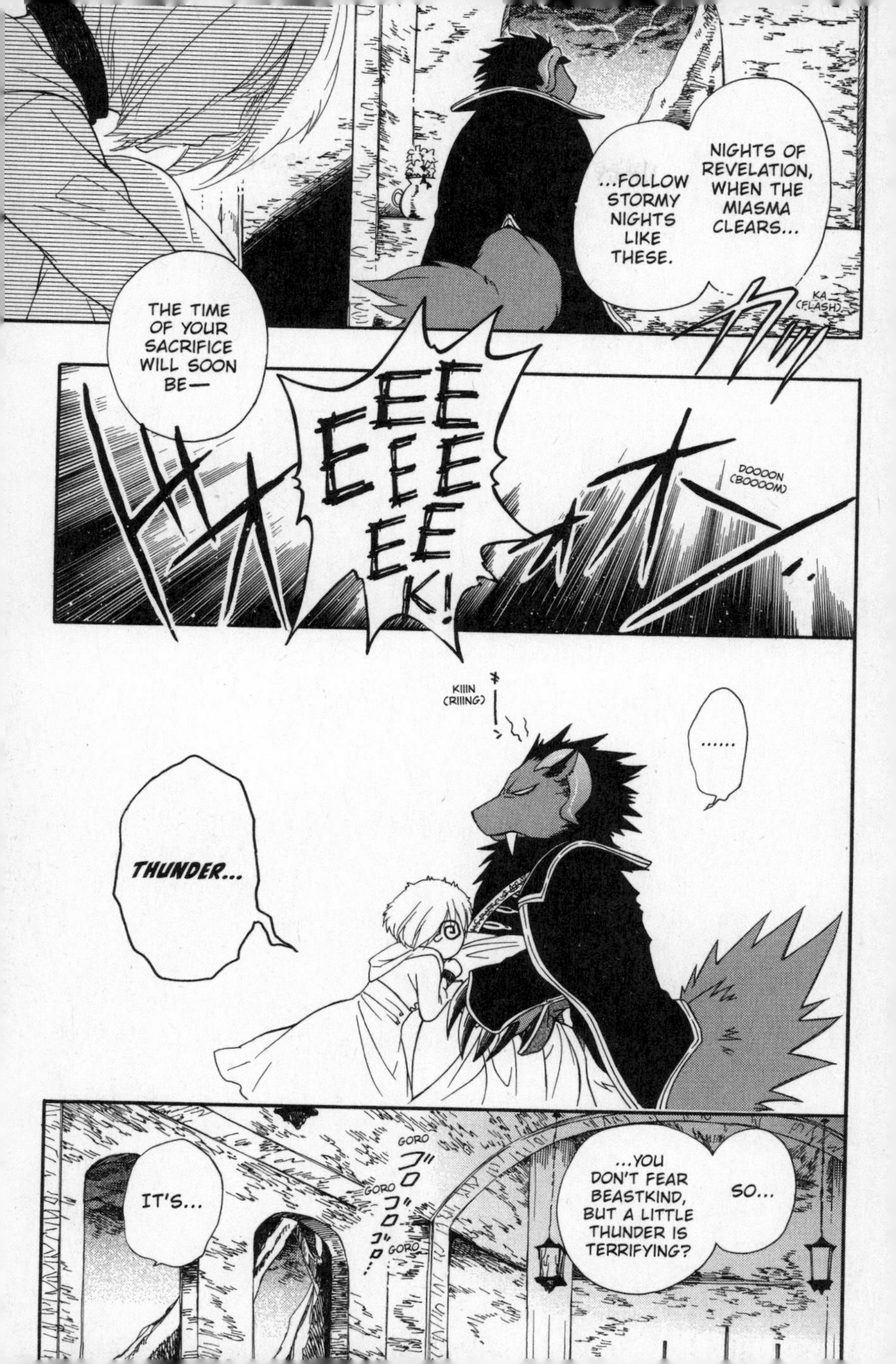
NIGHTS OF REVELATION, WHEN THE MIASMA CLEARS...
...FOLLOW STORMY NIGHTS LIKE THESE.
KA (FLASH)
THE TIME OF YOUR SACRIFICE WILL SOON BE—
DOOOON (BOOOOM)
EEEEEEEEEK!
KIIIN (RIIING)
......
THUNDER...
SO...
...YOU DON'T FEAR BEASTKIND, BUT A LITTLE THUNDER IS TERRIFYING?
GORO
GORO
GORO
IT'S...

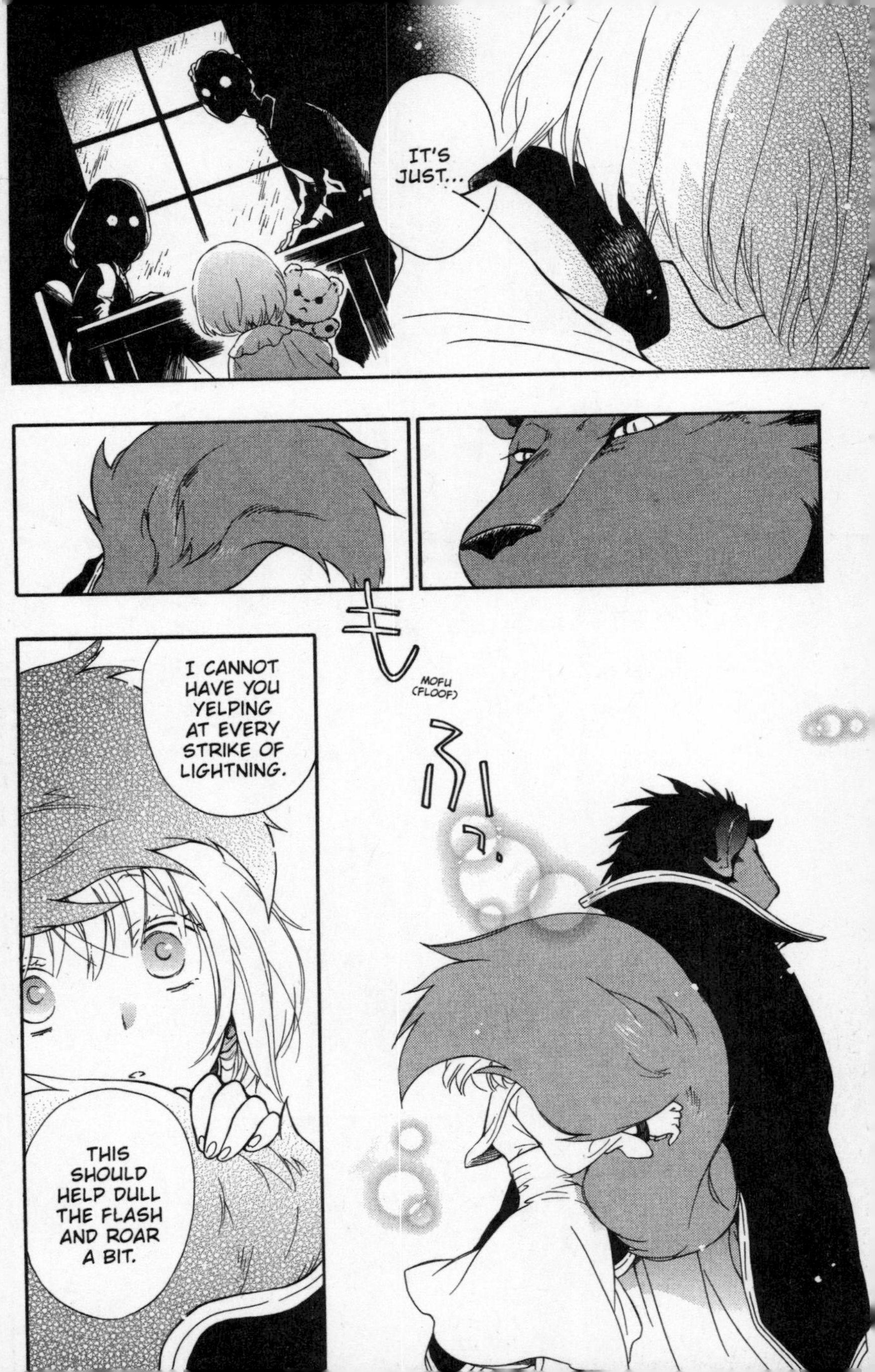
IT'S JUST...
MOFU (FLOOF)
I CANNOT HAVE YOU YELPING AT EVERY STRIKE OF LIGHTNING.
THIS SHOULD HELP DULL THE FLASH AND ROAR A BIT.

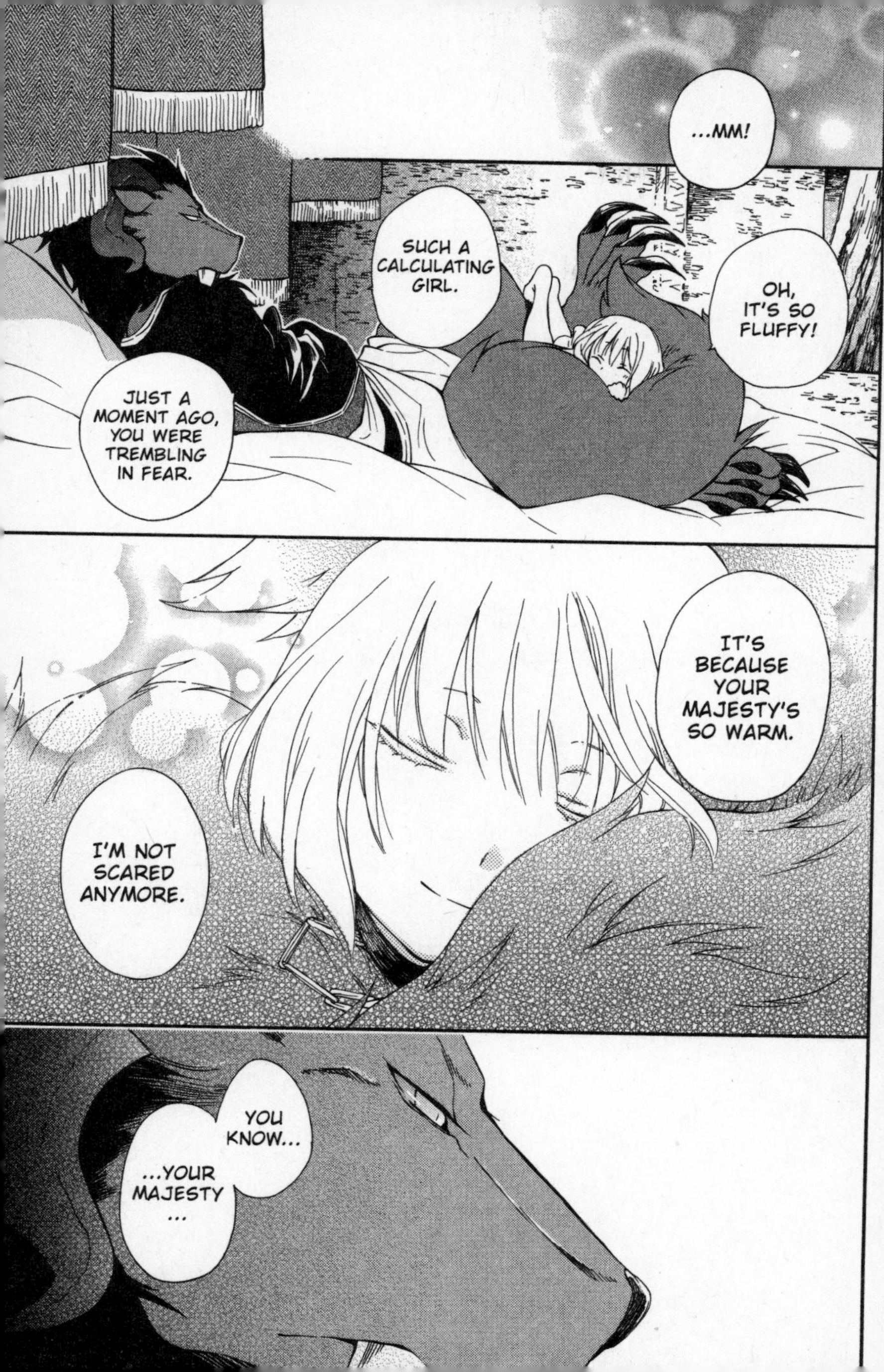

...MM!
OH, IT'S SO FLUFFY!
SUCH A CALCULATING GIRL.
JUST A MOMENT AGO, YOU WERE TREMBLING IN FEAR.
IT'S BECAUSE YOUR MAJESTY'S SO WARM.
I'M NOT SCARED ANYMORE.
YOU KNOW...
...YOUR MAJESTY ...

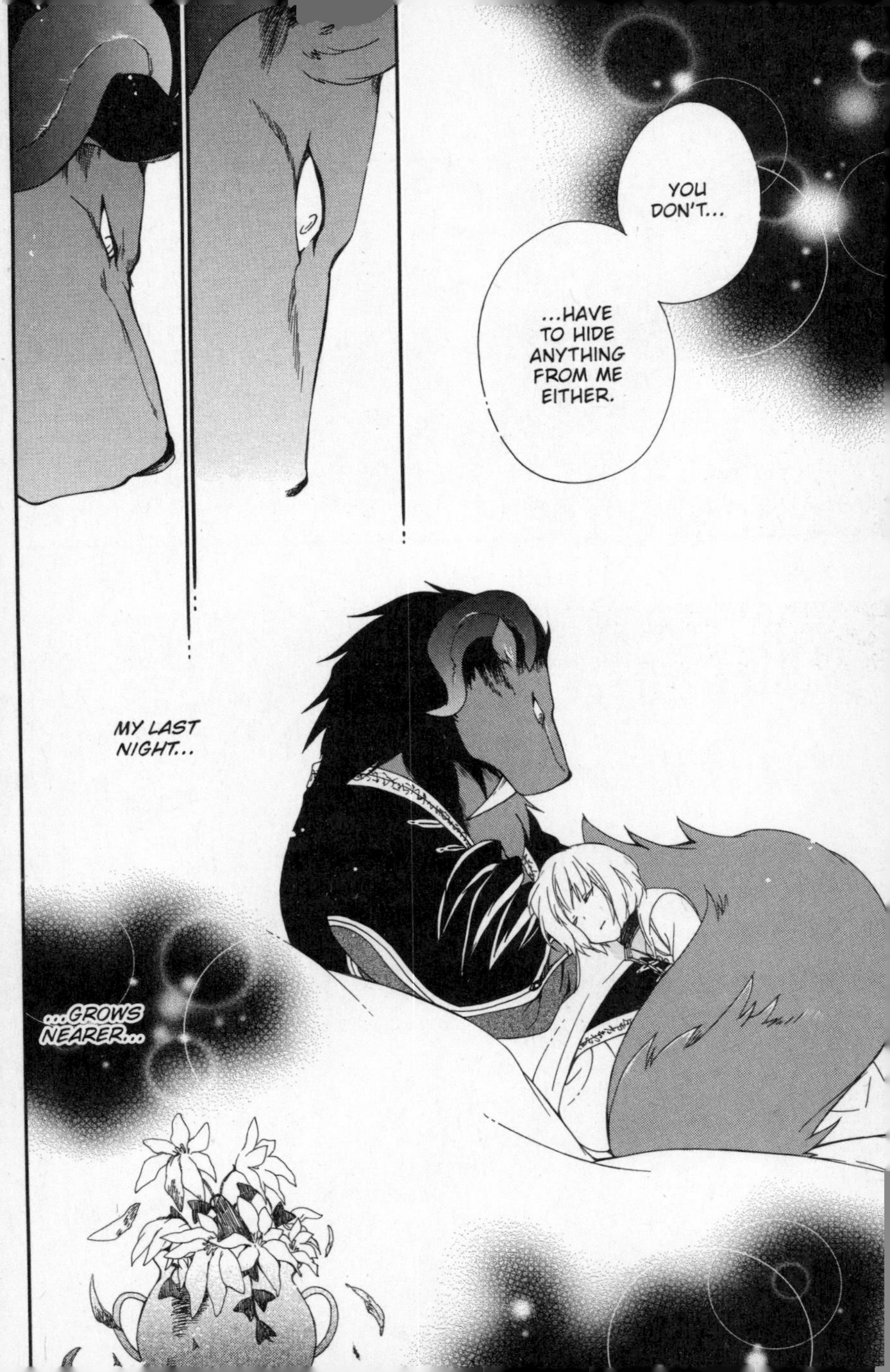
YOU DON'T...
...HAVE TO HIDE ANYTHING FROM ME EITHER.
MY LAST NIGHT...
...GROWS NEARER...

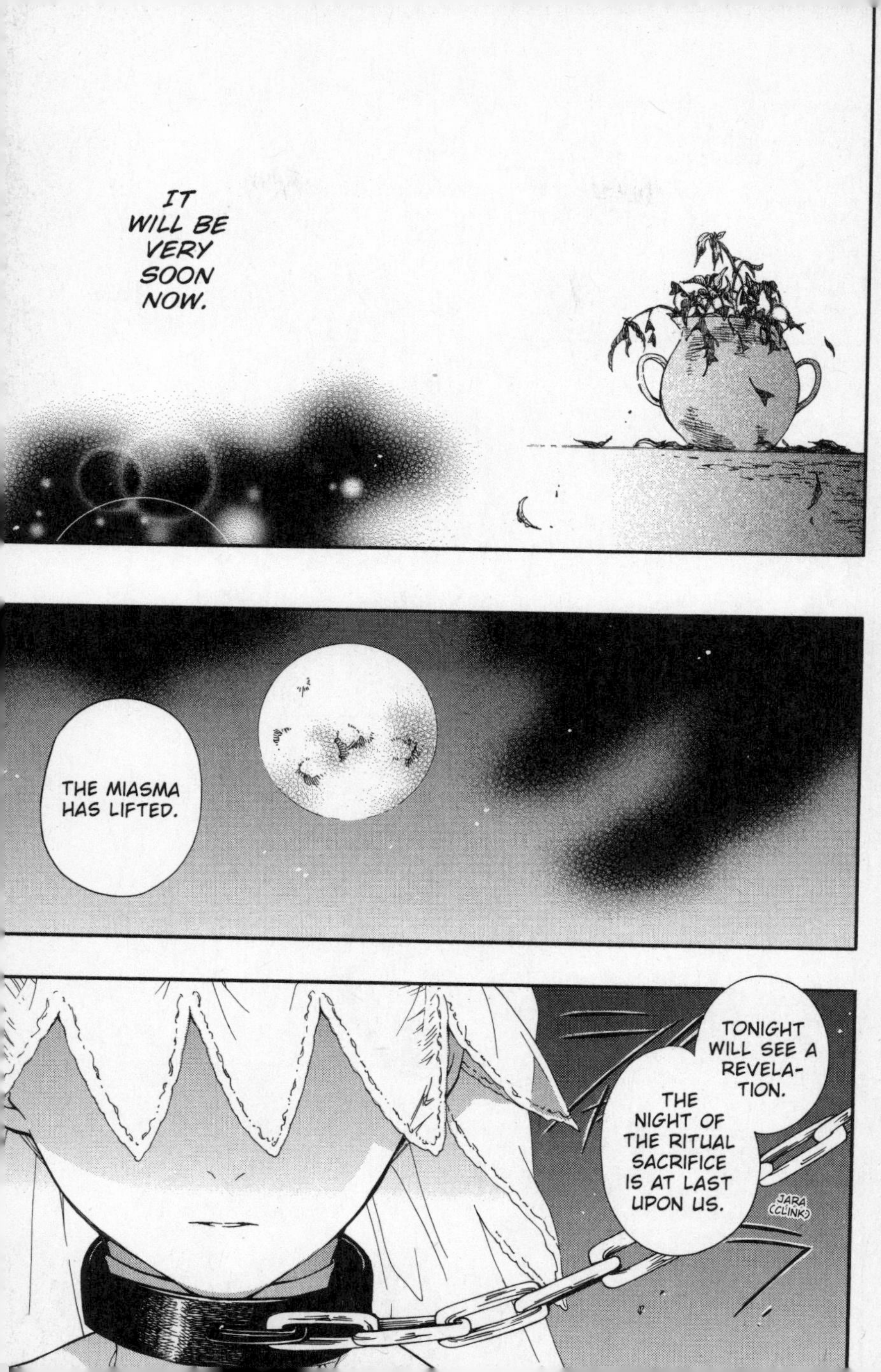
IT WILL BE VERY SOON NOW.
THE MIASMA HAS LIFTED.
TONIGHT WILL SEE A REVELA-TION.
THE NIGHT OF THE RITUAL SACRIFICE IS AT LAST UPON US.
JARA (CLINK)

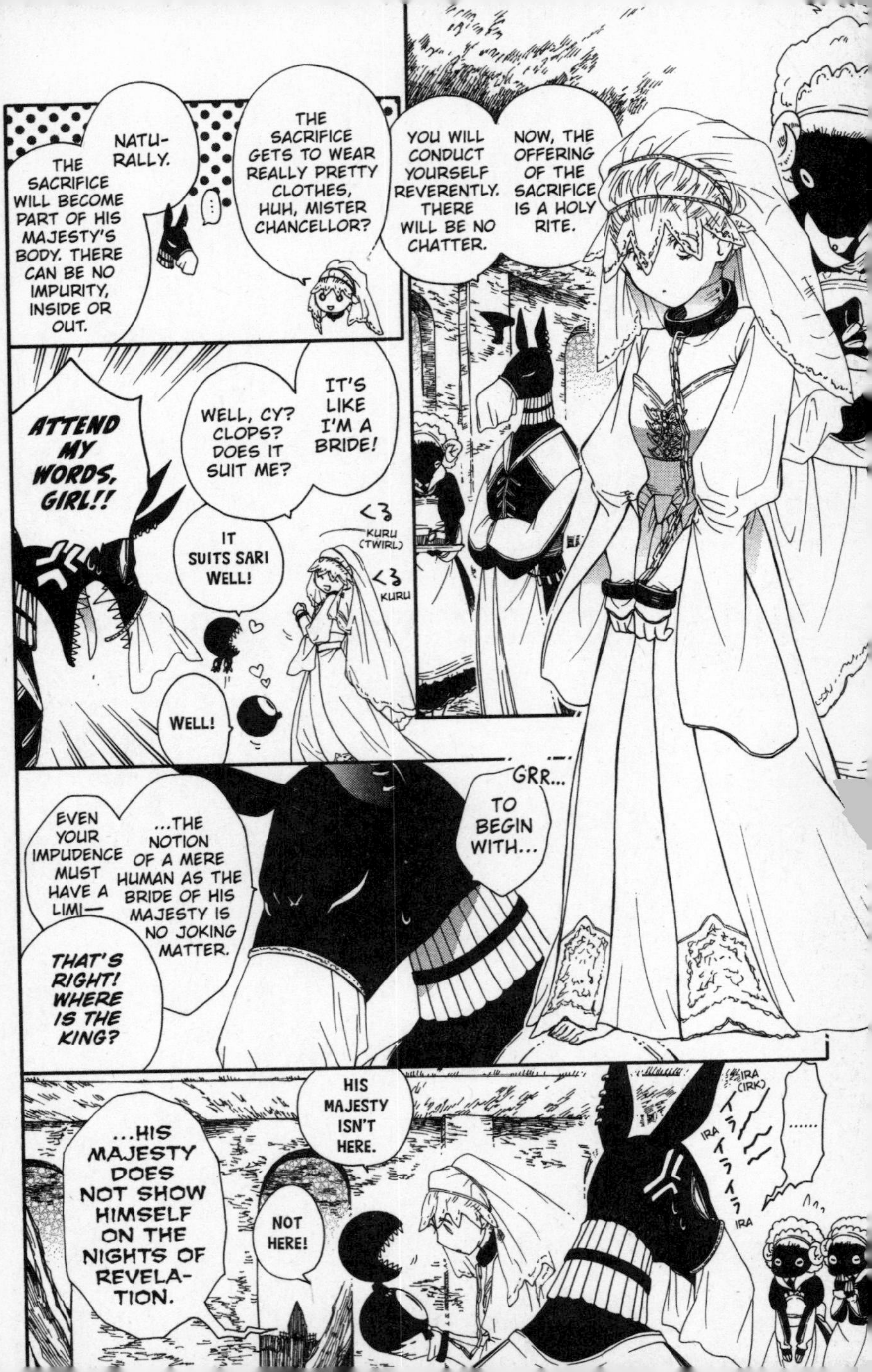
NOW, THE OFFERING OF THE SACRIFICE IS A HOLY RITE.
YOU WILL CONDUCT YOURSELF REVERENTLY. THERE WILL BE NO CHATTER.
THE SACRIFICE GETS TO WEAR REALLY PRETTY CLOTHES, HUH, MISTER CHANCELLOR?
NATU-RALLY.
THE SACRIFICE WILL BECOME PART OF HIS MAJESTY'S BODY. THERE CAN BE NO IMPURITY, INSIDE OR OUT.
…
IT'S LIKE I'M A BRIDE!
WELL, CY? CLOPS? DOES IT SUIT ME?
くる KURU (TWIRL)
くる KURU
IT SUITS SARI WELL!
ATTEND MY WORDS, GIRL!!
WELL!
GRR...
TO BEGIN WITH...
...THE NOTION OF A MERE HUMAN AS THE BRIDE OF HIS MAJESTY IS NO JOKING MATTER.
EVEN YOUR IMPUDENCE MUST HAVE A LIMI—
THAT'S RIGHT! WHERE IS THE KING?
......
IRA (IRK)
IRA
IRA
HIS MAJESTY ISN'T HERE.
NOT HERE!
...HIS MAJESTY DOES NOT SHOW HIMSELF ON THE NIGHTS OF REVELATION.

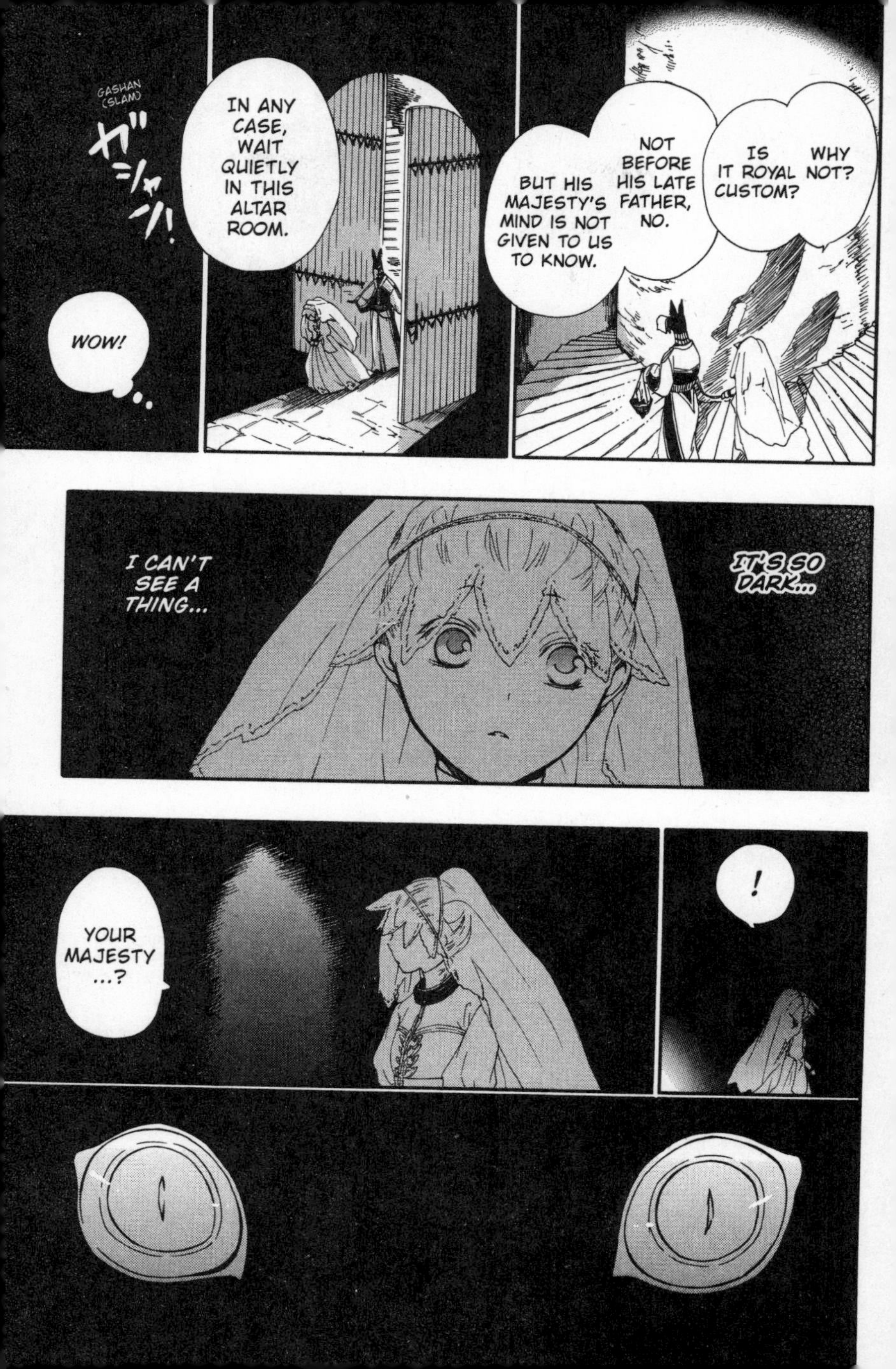
WHY NOT?
IS IT ROYAL CUSTOM?
NOT BEFORE HIS LATE FATHER, NO.
BUT HIS MAJESTY'S MIND IS NOT GIVEN TO US TO KNOW.
IN ANY CASE, WAIT QUIETLY IN THIS ALTAR ROOM.
GASHAN (SLAM)
WOW!
IT'S SO DARK...
I CAN'T SEE A THING...
!
YOUR MAJESTY ...?

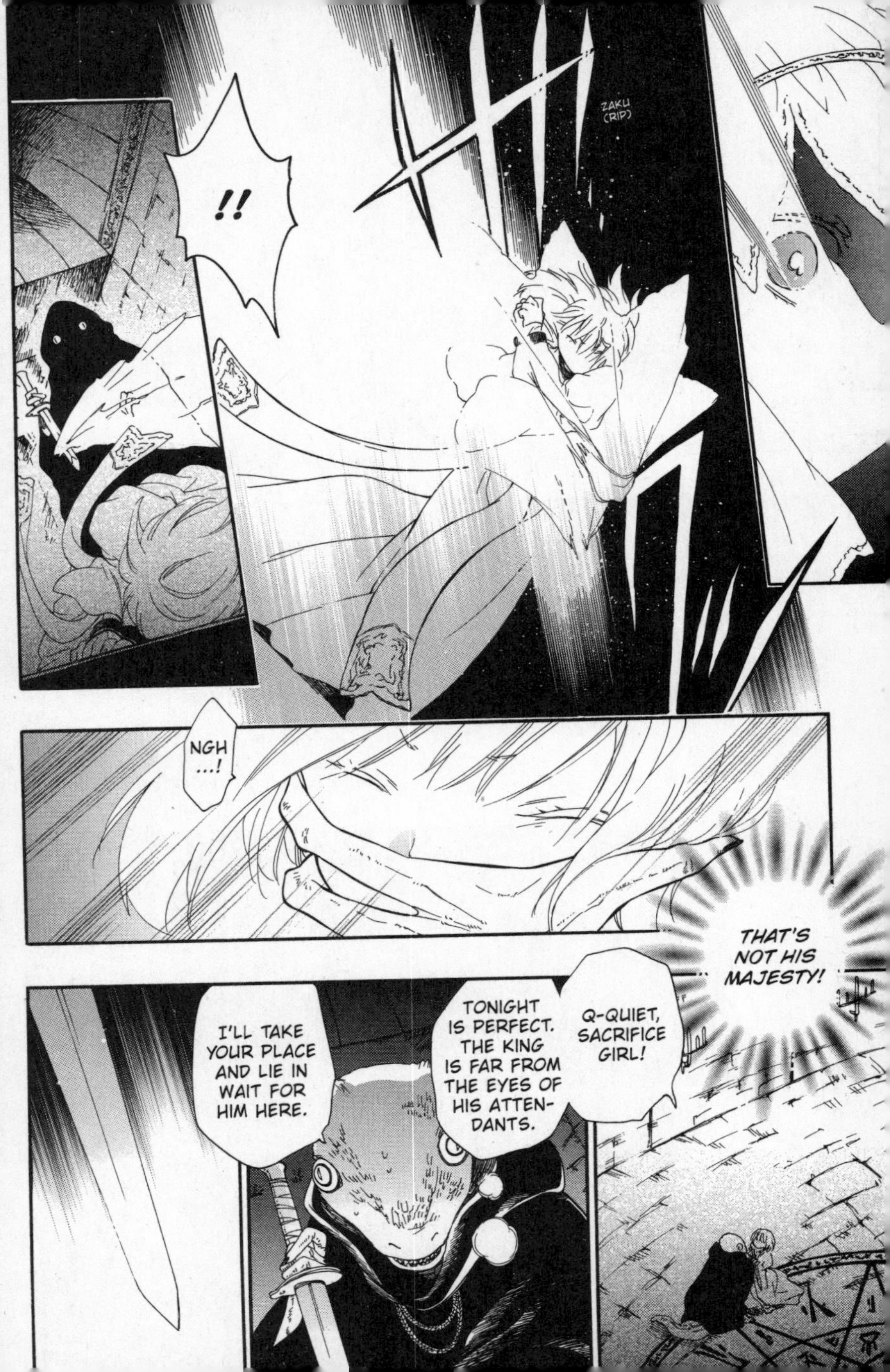
ZAKU (RIP)
!!
NGH ...!
THAT'S NOT HIS MAJESTY!
Q-QUIET, SACRIFICE GIRL!
TONIGHT IS PERFECT. THE KING IS FAR FROM THE EYES OF HIS ATTENDANTS.
I'LL TAKE YOUR PLACE AND LIE IN WAIT FOR HIM HERE.

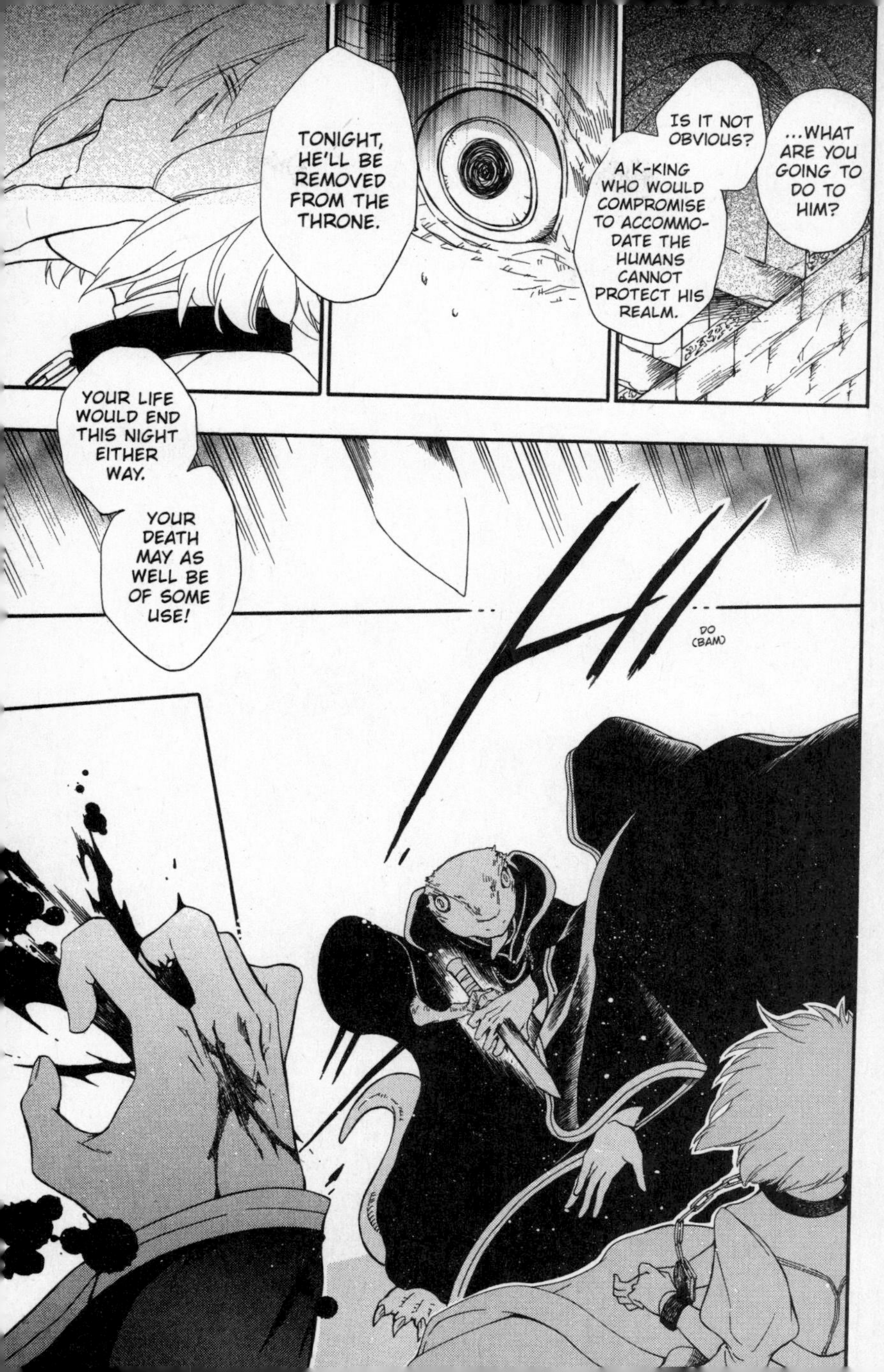
...WHAT ARE YOU GOING TO DO TO HIM?
IS IT NOT OBVIOUS?
A K-KING WHO WOULD COMPROMISE TO ACCOMMODATE THE HUMANS CANNOT PROTECT HIS REALM.
TONIGHT, HE'LL BE REMOVED FROM THE THRONE.
YOUR LIFE WOULD END THIS NIGHT EITHER WAY.
YOUR DEATH MAY AS WELL BE OF SOME USE!
DO (BAM)

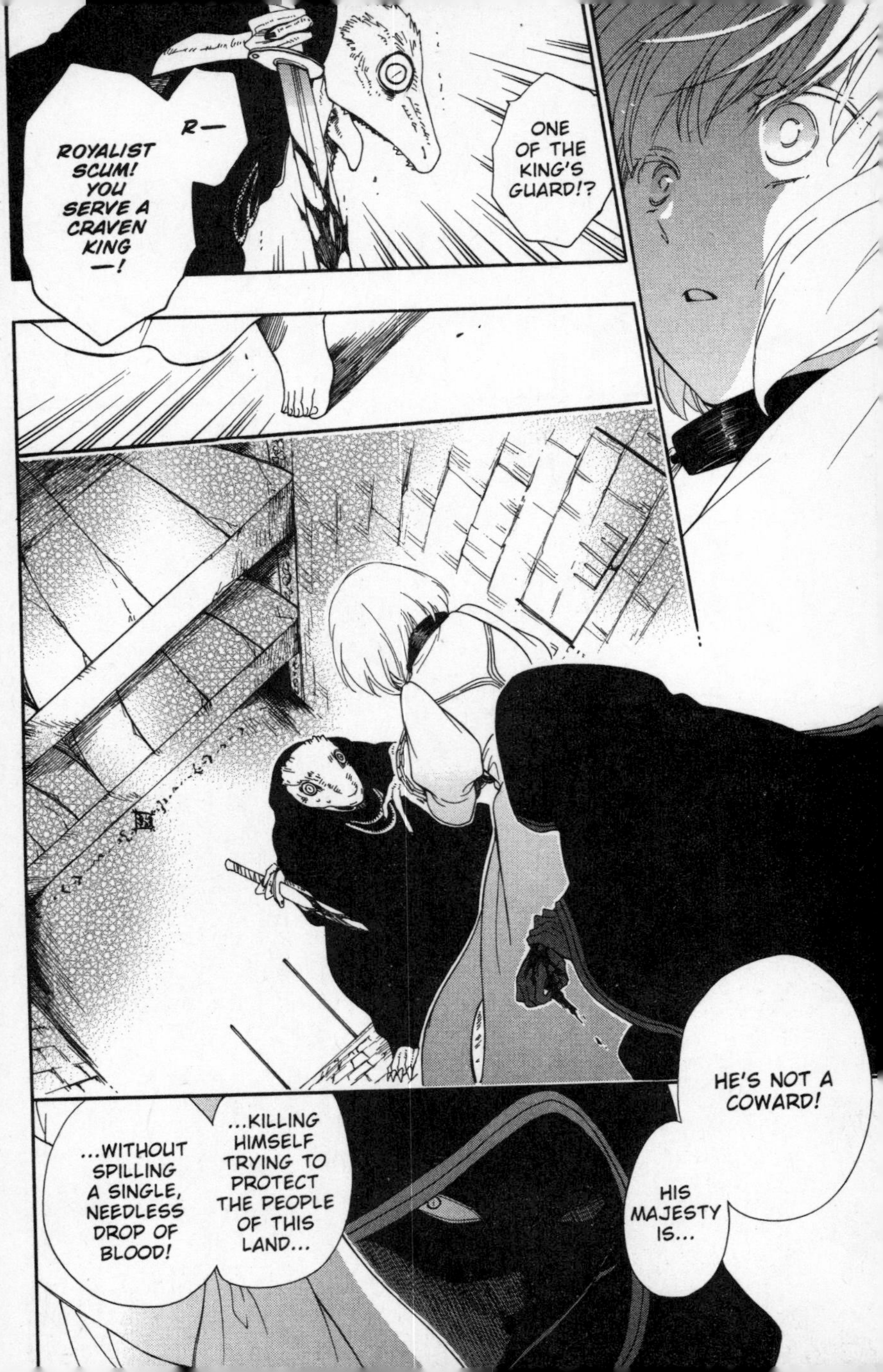
ONE OF THE KING'S GUARD!?
R— ROYALIST SCUM! YOU SERVE A CRAVEN KING —!
HE'S NOT A COWARD!
HIS MAJESTY IS...
...KILLING HIMSELF TRYING TO PROTECT THE PEOPLE OF THIS LAND...
...WITHOUT SPILLING A SINGLE, NEEDLESS DROP OF BLOOD!

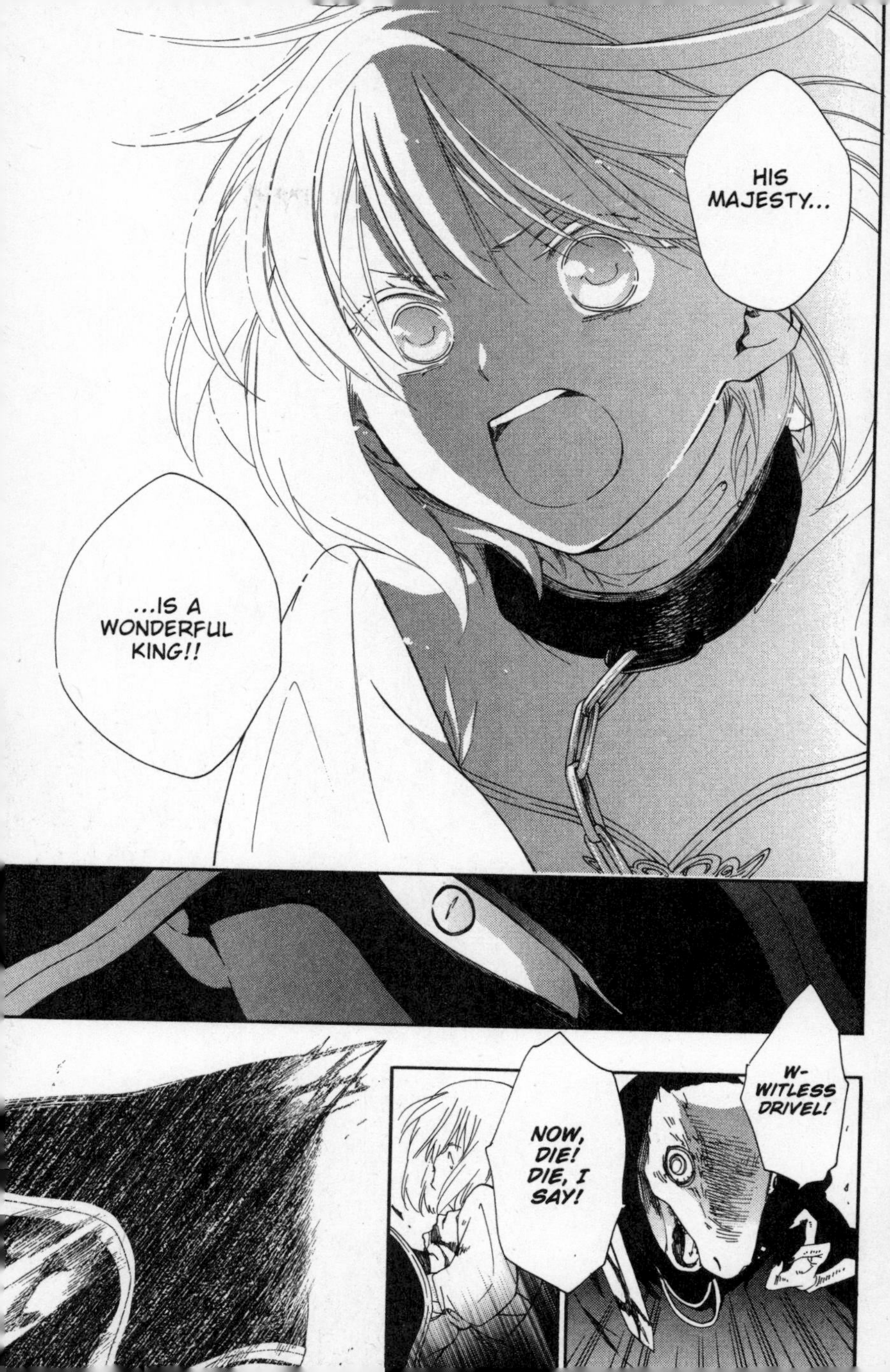
HIS MAJESTY...
...IS A WONDERFUL KING!!
W-WITLESS DRIVEL!
NOW, DIE! DIE, I SAY!

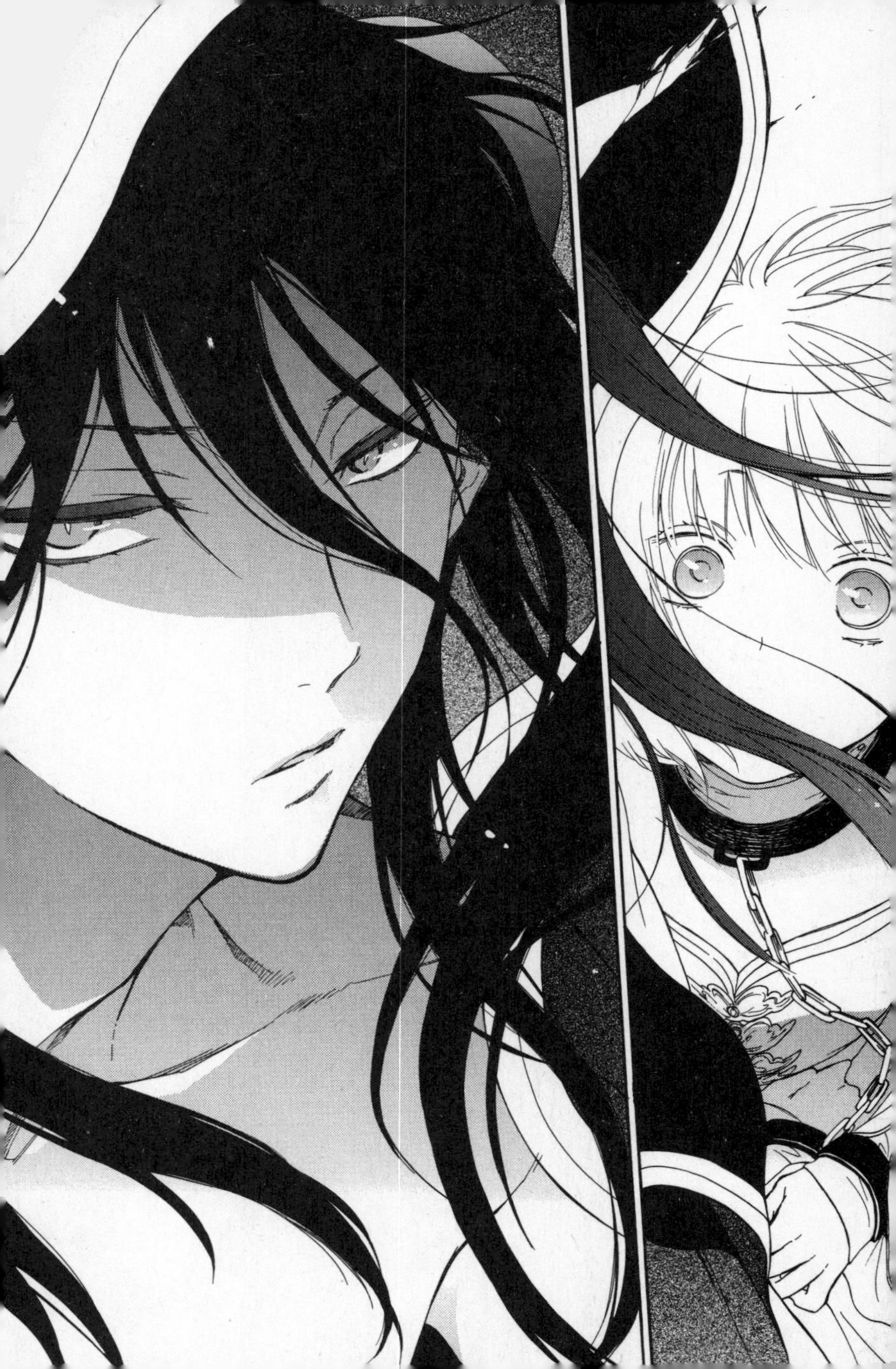

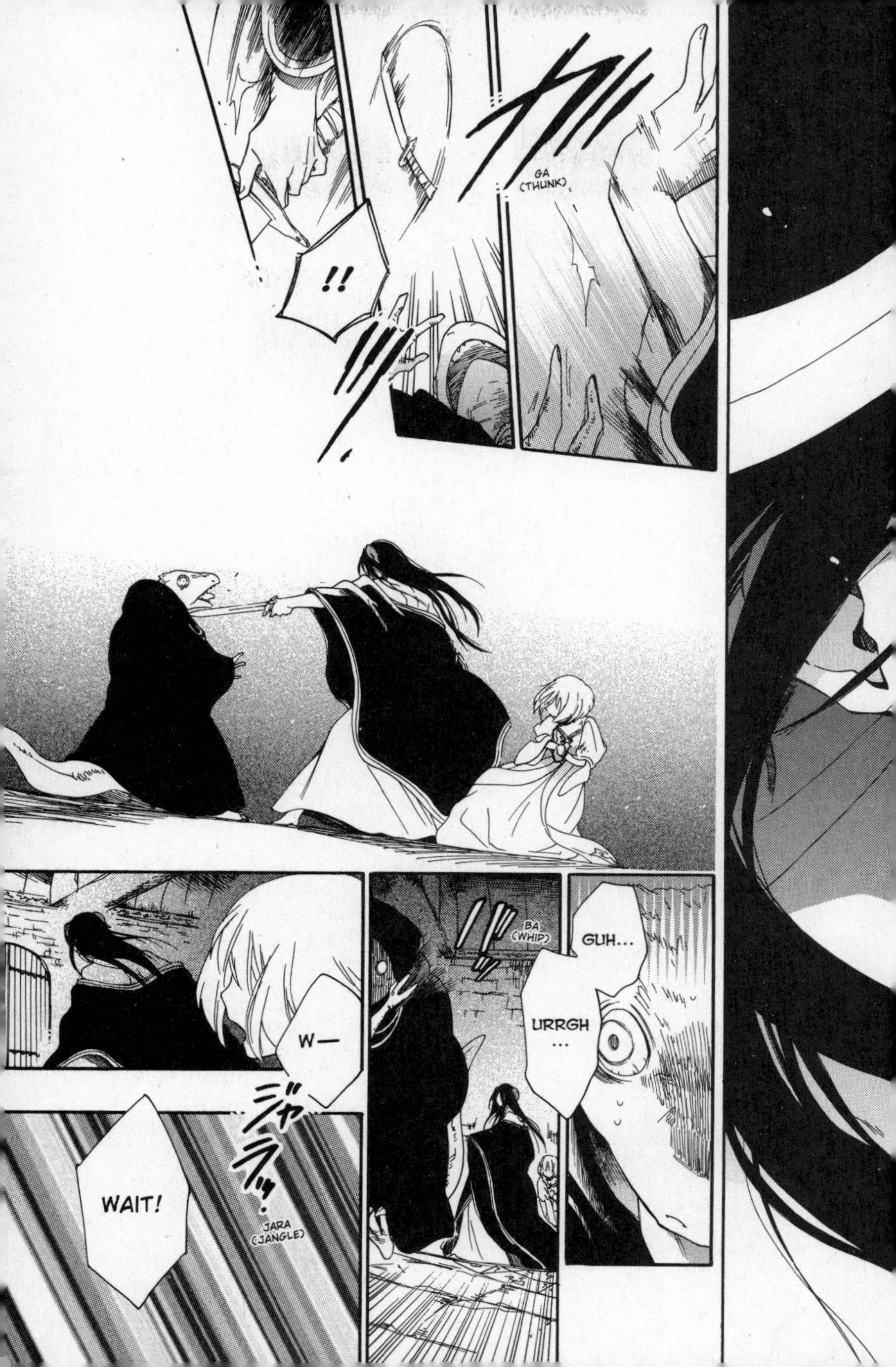
GA
(THUNK)
!!
GUH...
URRGH
...
BA
(WHIP)
W—
ジャラッ
JARA
(JANGLE)
WAIT!

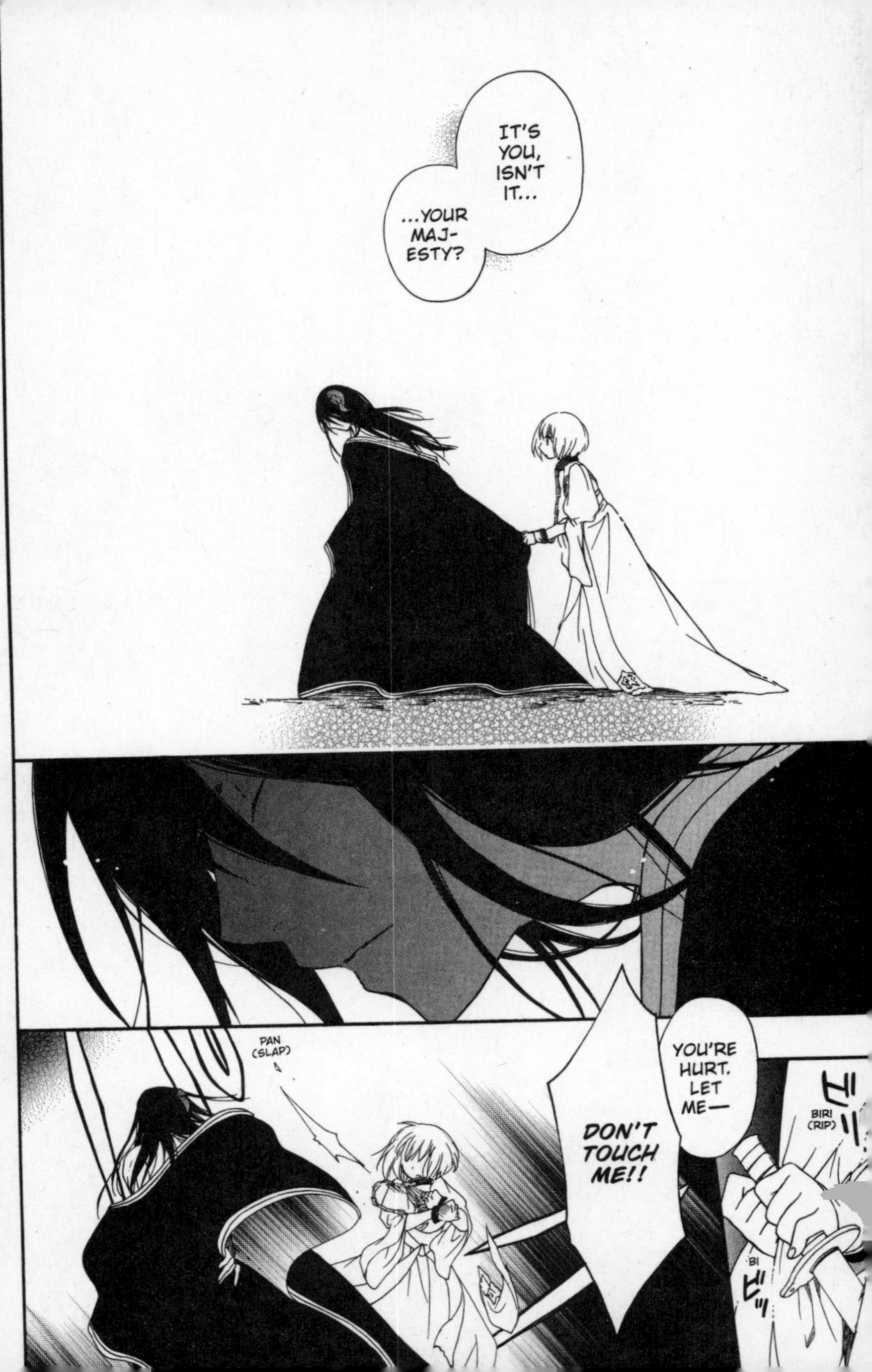
IT'S YOU, ISN'T IT...
...YOUR MAJ-ESTY?
BIRI (RIP)
BI
YOU'RE HURT. LET ME—
DON'T TOUCH ME!!
PAN (SLAP)

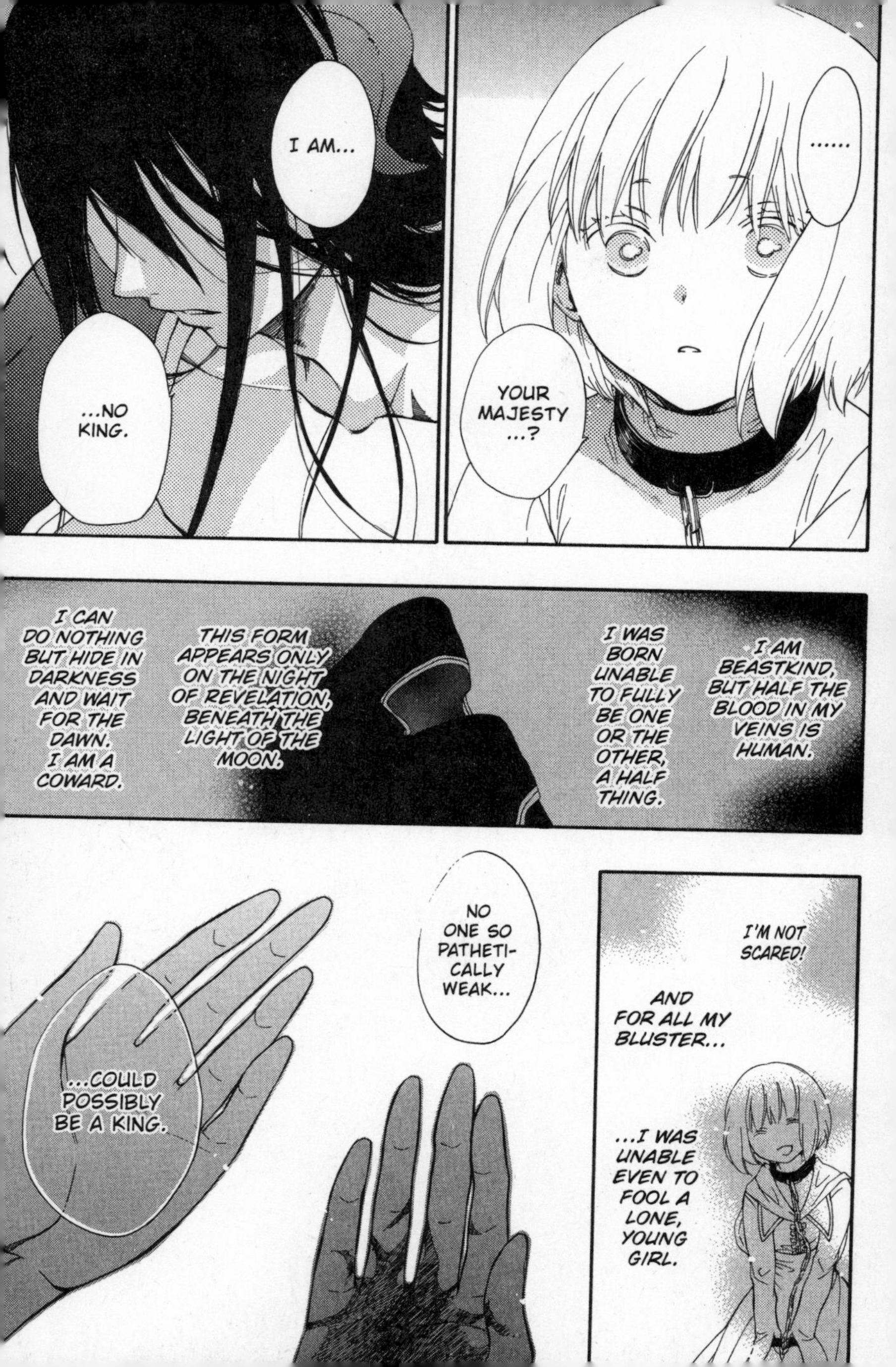
......
YOUR MAJESTY ...?
I AM...
...NO KING.
I AM BEASTKIND, BUT HALF THE BLOOD IN MY VEINS IS HUMAN.
I WAS BORN UNABLE TO FULLY BE ONE OR THE OTHER, A HALF THING.
THIS FORM APPEARS ONLY ON THE NIGHT OF REVELATION, BENEATH THE LIGHT OF THE MOON.
I CAN DO NOTHING BUT HIDE IN DARKNESS AND WAIT FOR THE DAWN. I AM A COWARD.
I'M NOT SCARED!
AND FOR ALL MY BLUSTER...
...I WAS UNABLE EVEN TO FOOL A LONE, YOUNG GIRL.
NO ONE SO PATHETI-CALLY WEAK...
...COULD POSSIBLY BE A KING.

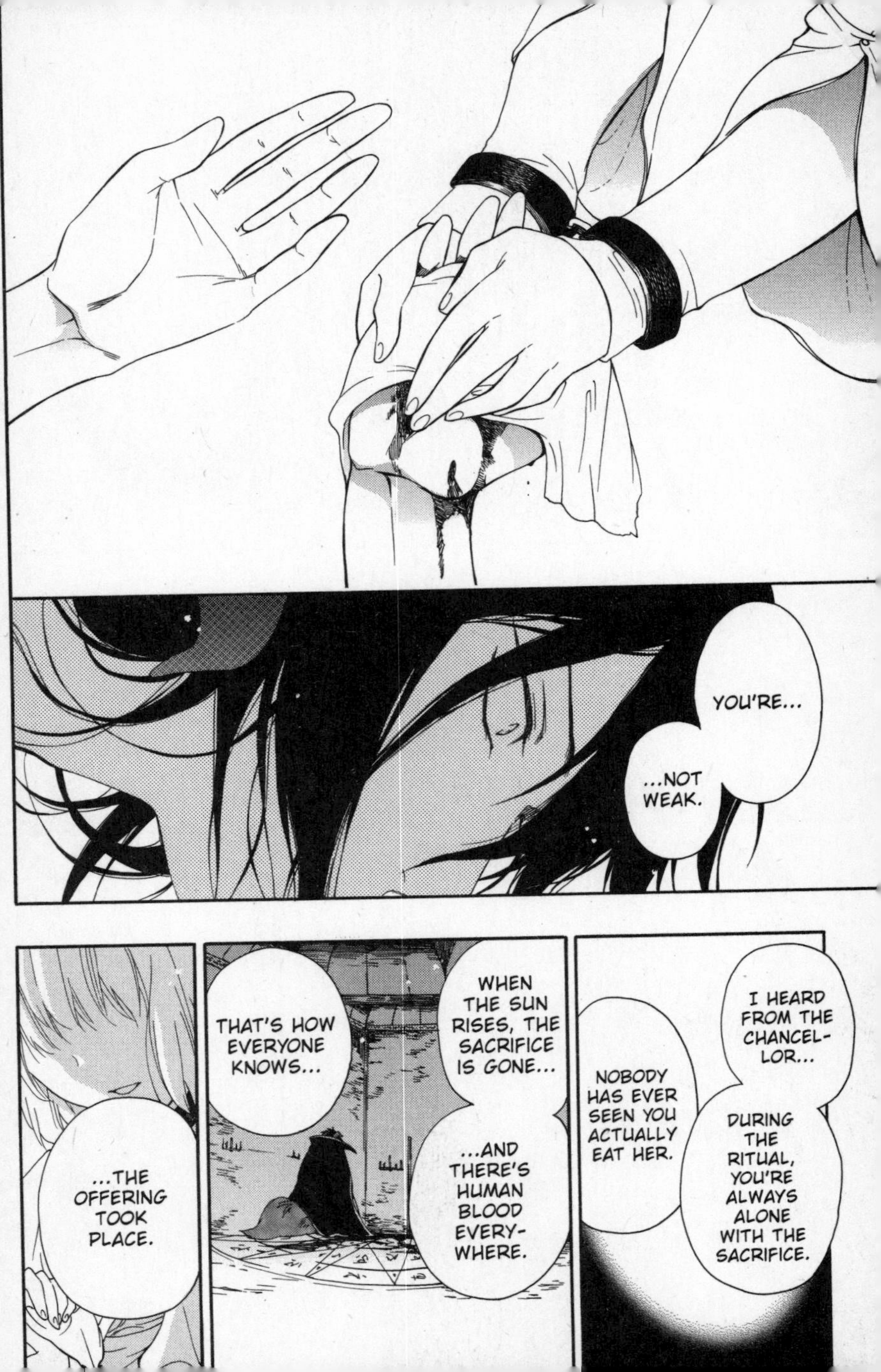
YOU'RE...
...NOT WEAK.
I HEARD FROM THE CHANCEL-LOR...
DURING THE RITUAL, YOU'RE ALWAYS ALONE WITH THE SACRIFICE.
NOBODY HAS EVER SEEN YOU ACTUALLY EAT HER.
WHEN THE SUN RISES, THE SACRIFICE IS GONE...
...AND THERE'S HUMAN BLOOD EVERY-WHERE.
THAT'S HOW EVERYONE KNOWS...
...THE OFFERING TOOK PLACE.

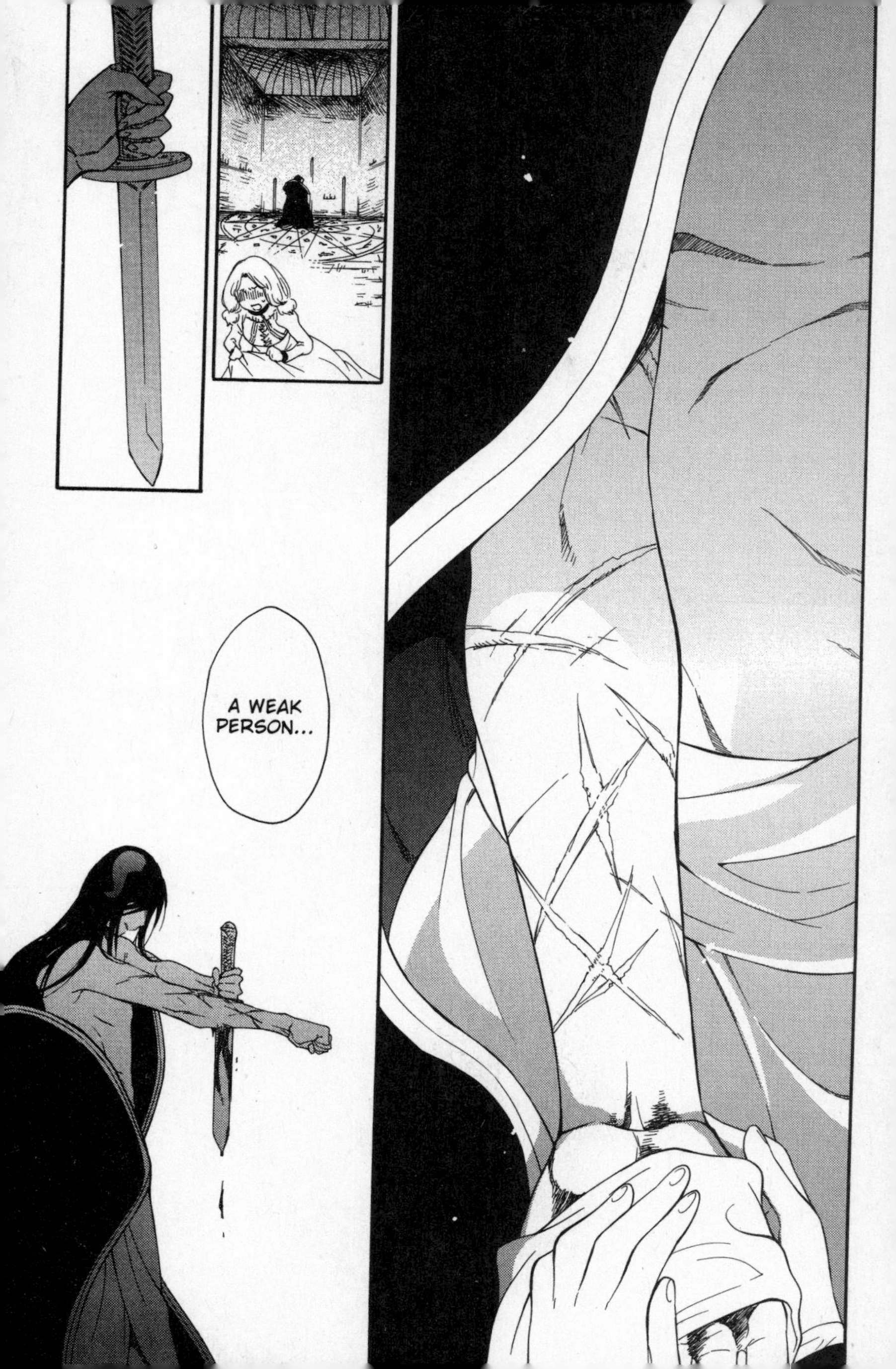
A WEAK PERSON...

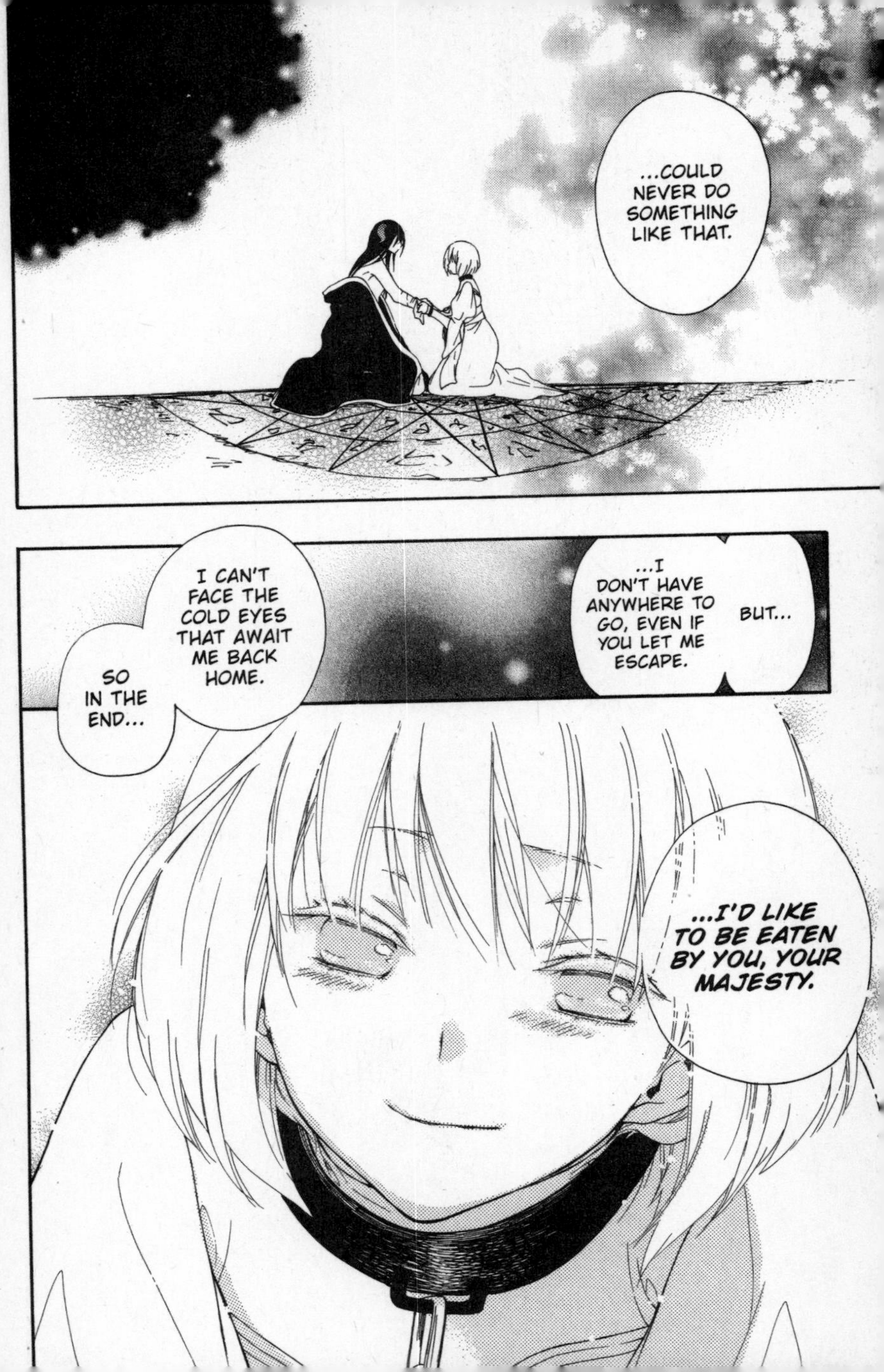
...COULD NEVER DO SOMETHING LIKE THAT.
BUT...
...I DON'T HAVE ANYWHERE TO GO, EVEN IF YOU LET ME ESCAPE.
I CAN'T FACE THE COLD EYES THAT AWAIT ME BACK HOME.
SO IN THE END...
...I'D LIKE TO BE EATEN BY YOU, YOUR MAJESTY.

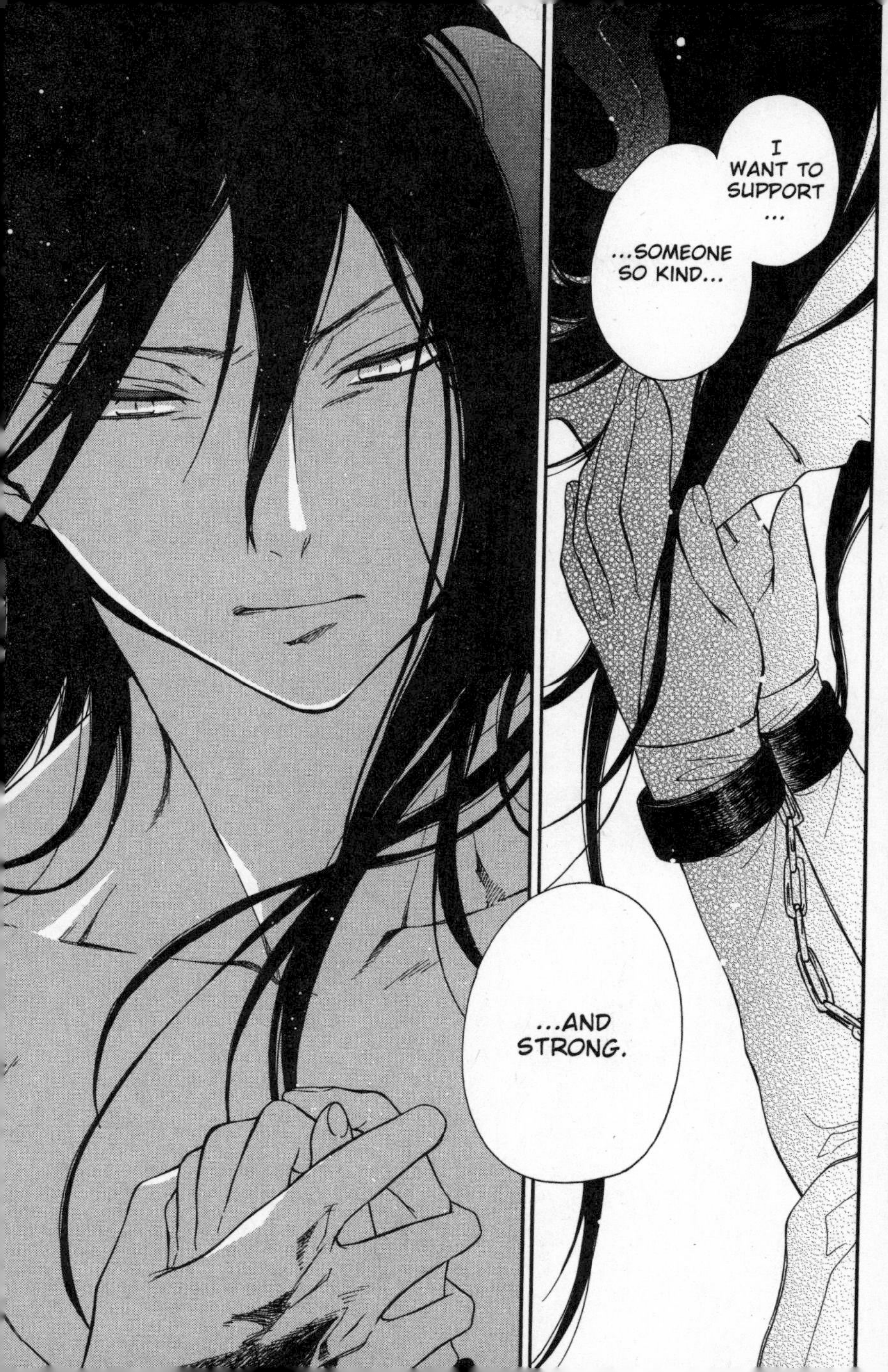
I WANT TO SUPPORT ...
...SOMEONE SO KIND...
...AND STRONG.

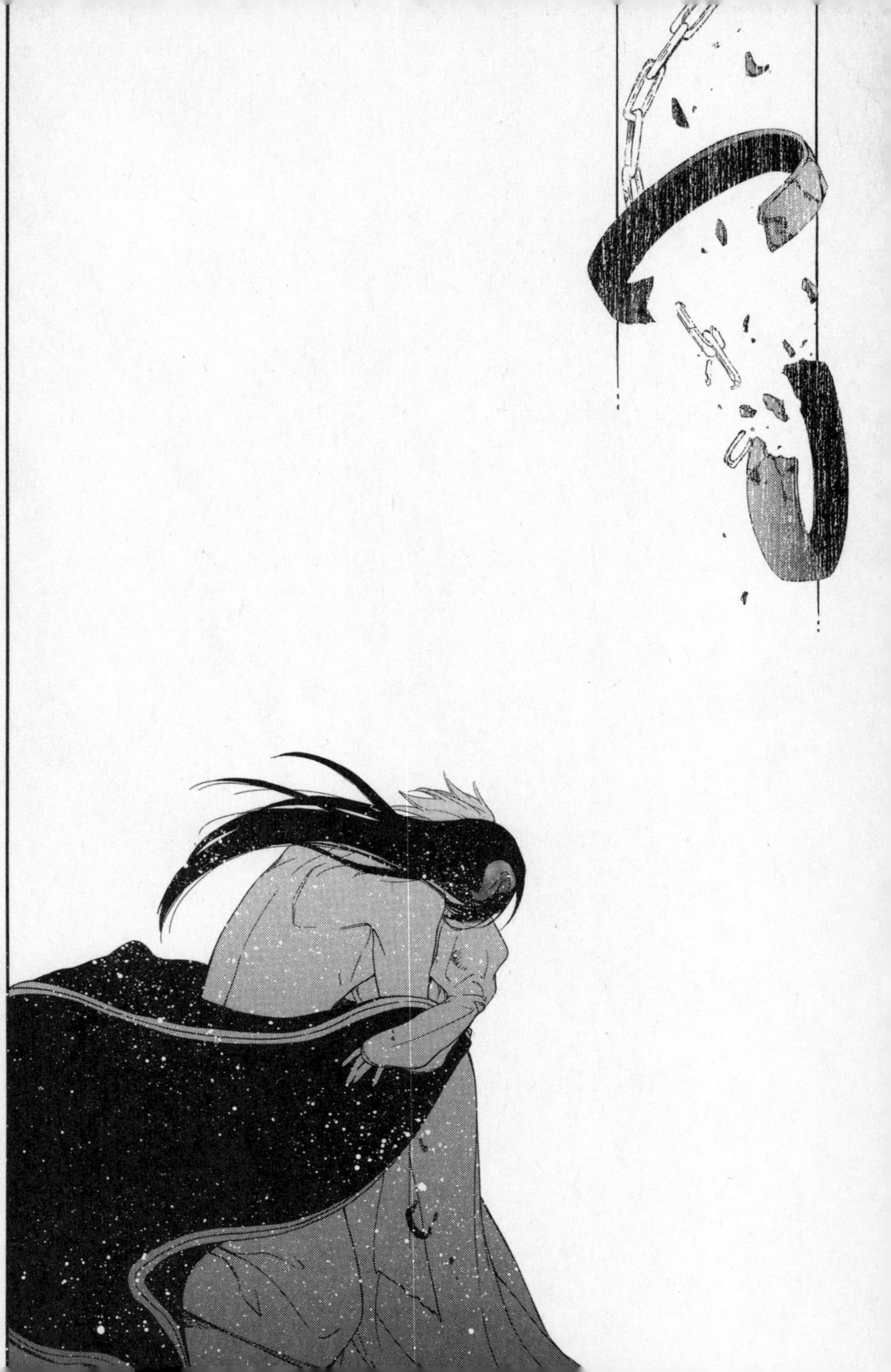

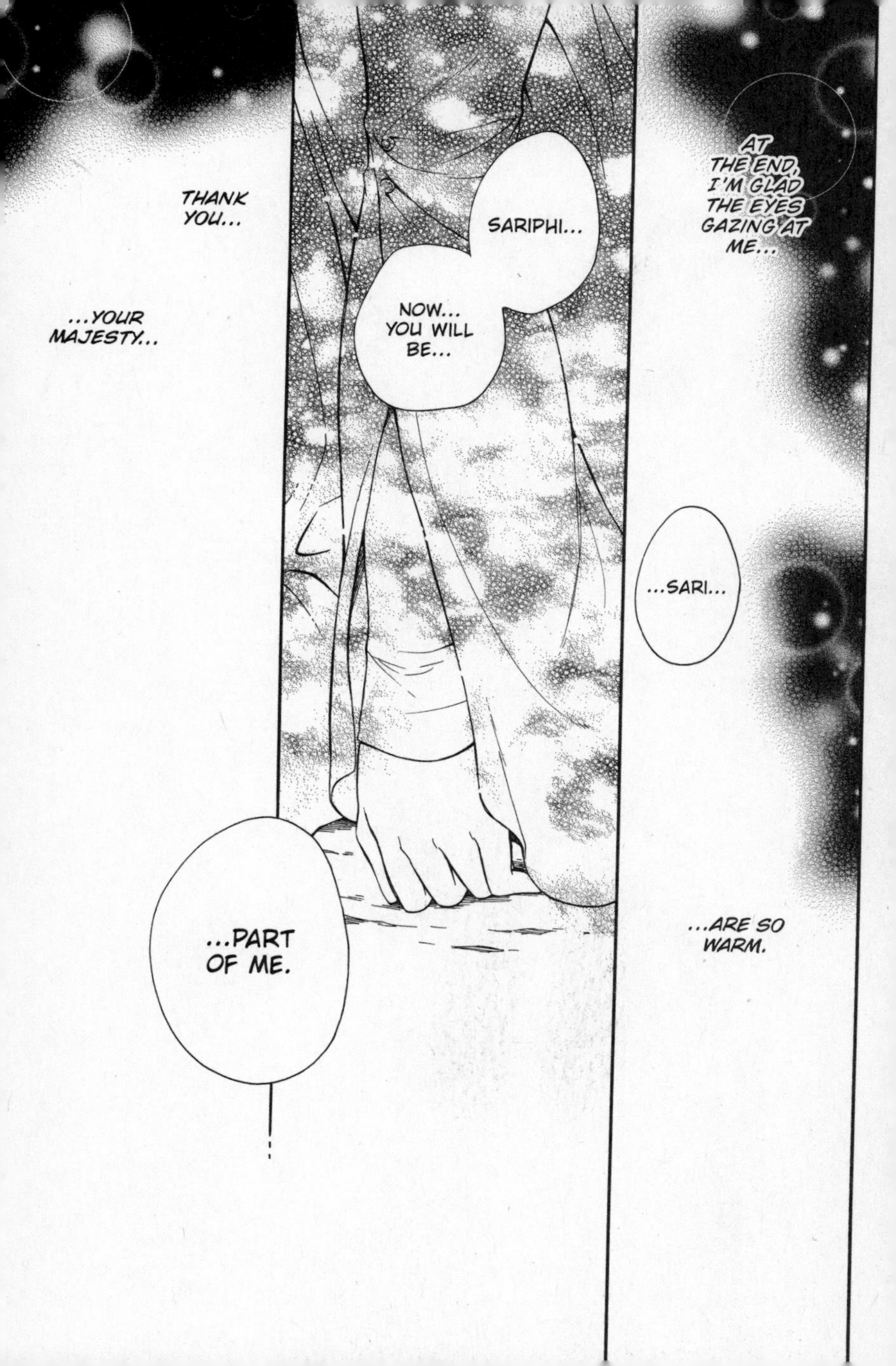
AT THE END, I'M GLAD THE EYES GAZING AT ME...
...SARI...
...ARE SO WARM.
SARIPHI...
NOW... YOU WILL BE...
...PART OF ME.
THANK YOU...
...YOUR MAJESTY...

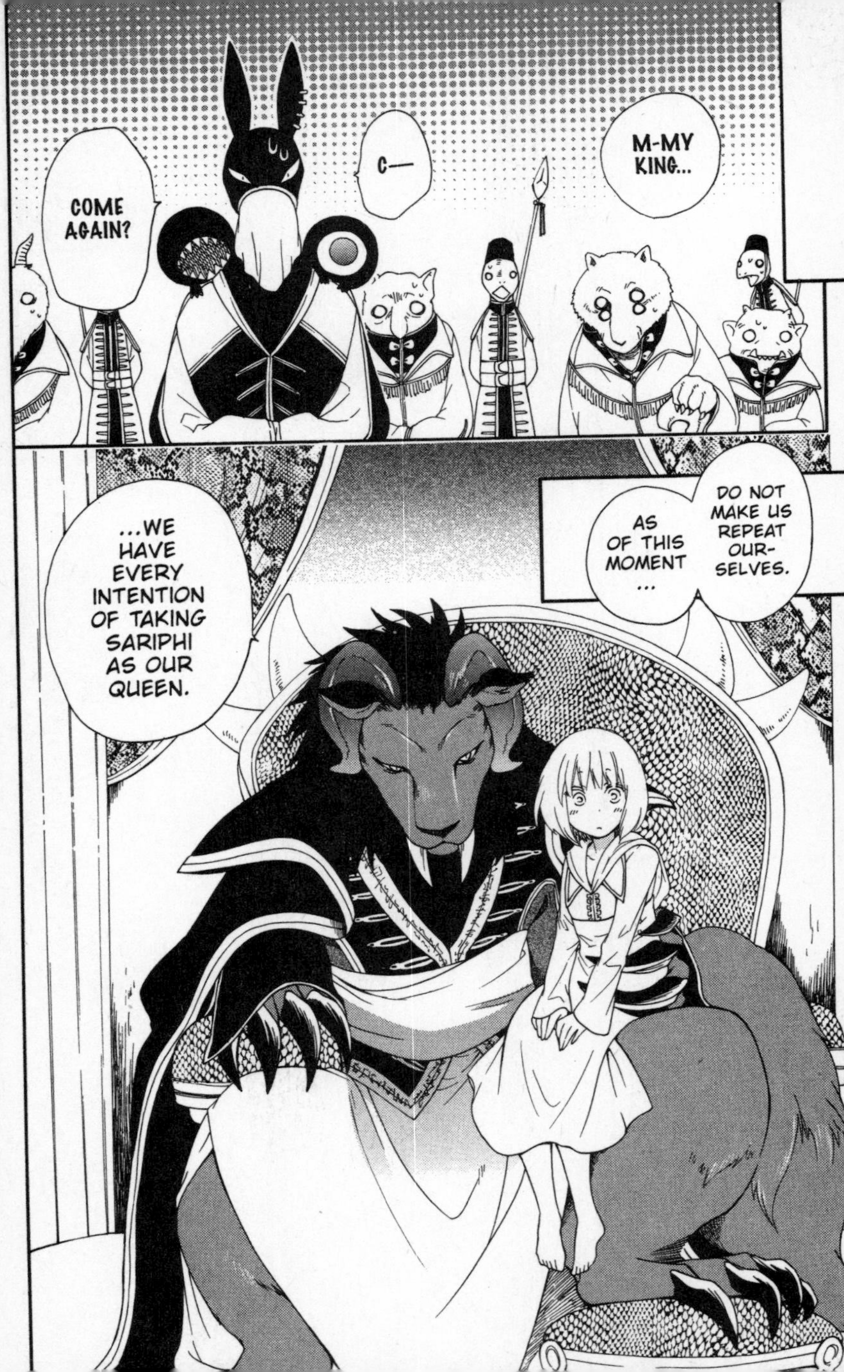
M-MY KING...
C—
COME AGAIN?
DO NOT MAKE US REPEAT OUR-SELVES.
AS OF THIS MOMENT...
...WE HAVE EVERY INTENTION OF TAKING SARIPHI AS OUR QUEEN.

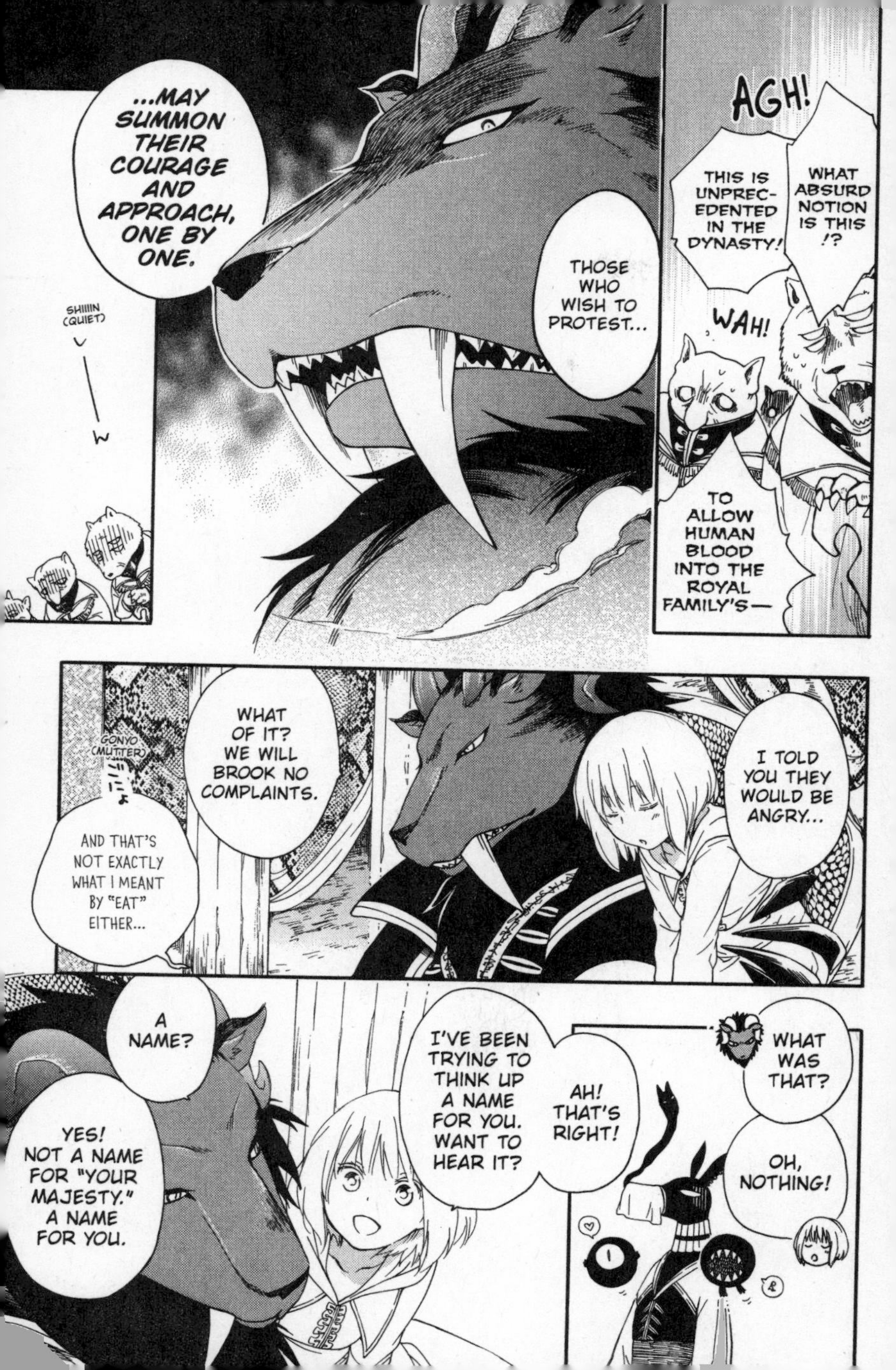
AGH!
WHAT ABSURD NOTION IS THIS!?
THIS IS UNPREC-EDENTED IN THE DYNASTY!
WAH!
TO ALLOW HUMAN BLOOD INTO THE ROYAL FAMILY'S—
THOSE WHO WISH TO PROTEST...
...MAY SUMMON THEIR COURAGE AND APPROACH, ONE BY ONE.
SHIIIN (QUIET)
I TOLD YOU THEY WOULD BE ANGRY...
WHAT OF IT? WE WILL BROOK NO COMPLAINTS.
GONYO (MUTTER)
AND THAT'S NOT EXACTLY WHAT I MEANT BY "EAT" EITHER...
WHAT WAS THAT?
OH, NOTHING!
AH! THAT'S RIGHT!
I'VE BEEN TRYING TO THINK UP A NAME FOR YOU. WANT TO HEAR IT?
A NAME?
YES! NOT A NAME FOR "YOUR MAJESTY." A NAME FOR YOU.

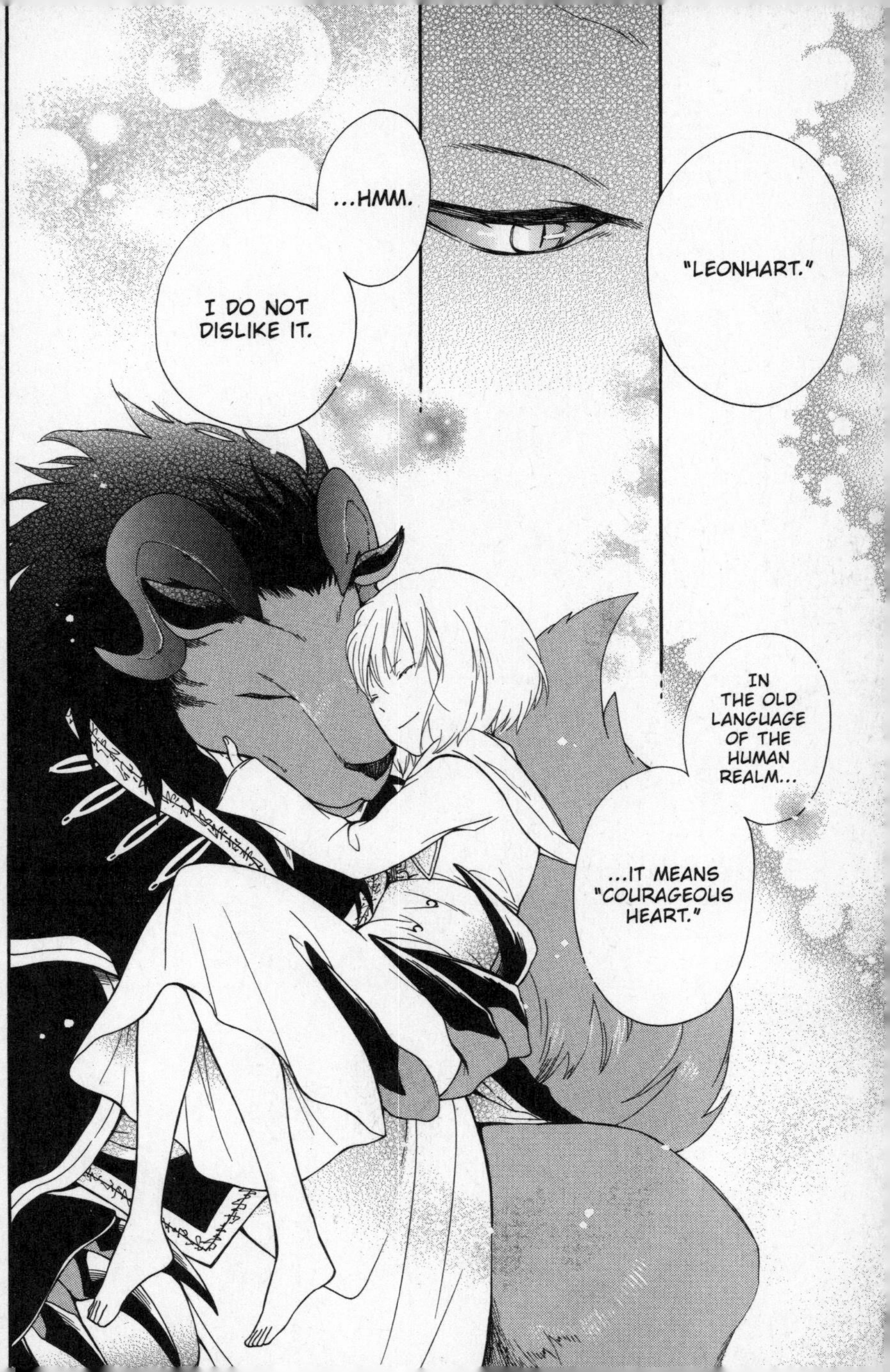
"LEONHART."
IN THE OLD LANGUAGE OF THE HUMAN REALM...
...IT MEANS "COURAGEOUS HEART."
...HMM.
I DO NOT DISLIKE IT.

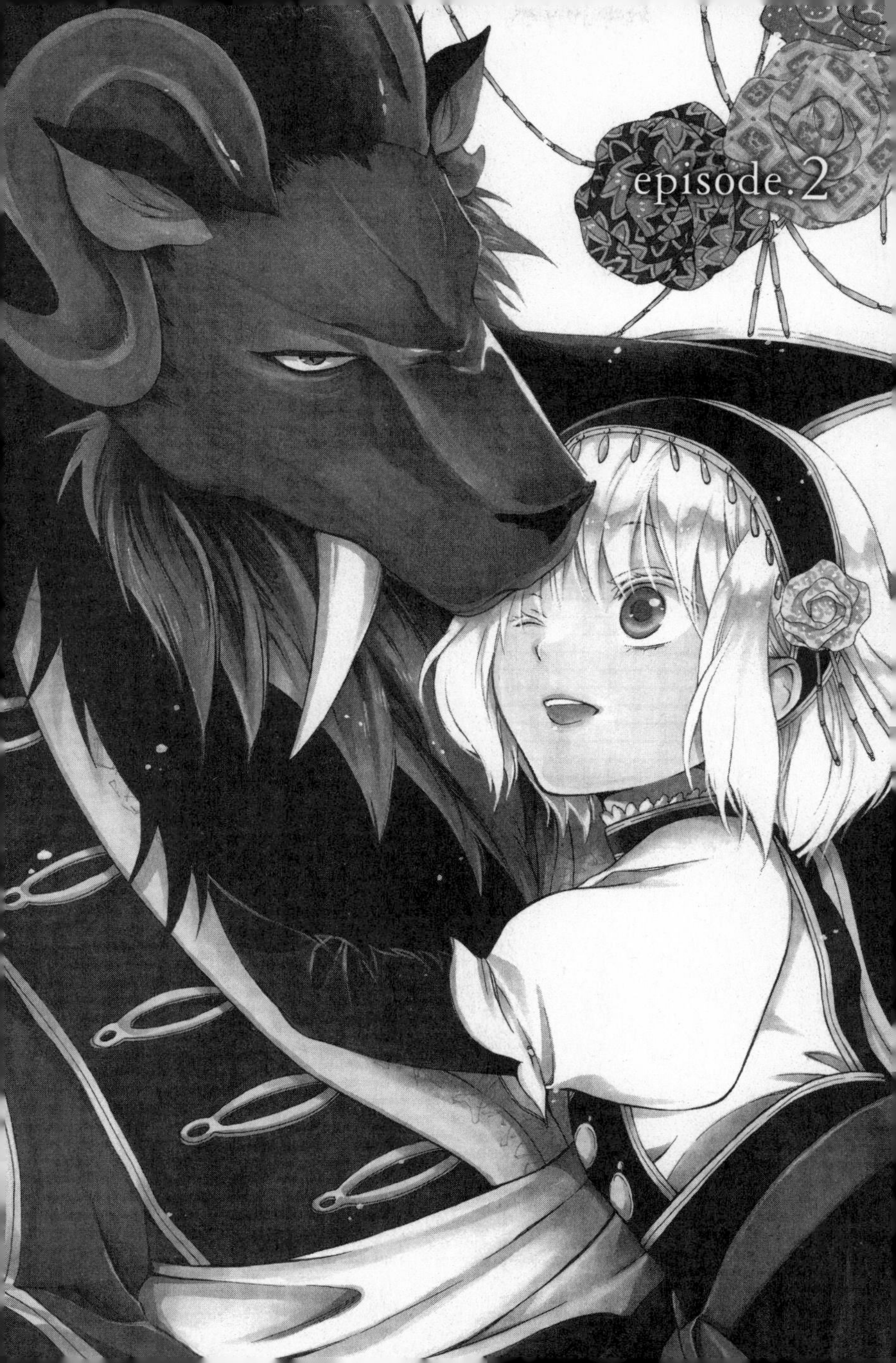
episode.2

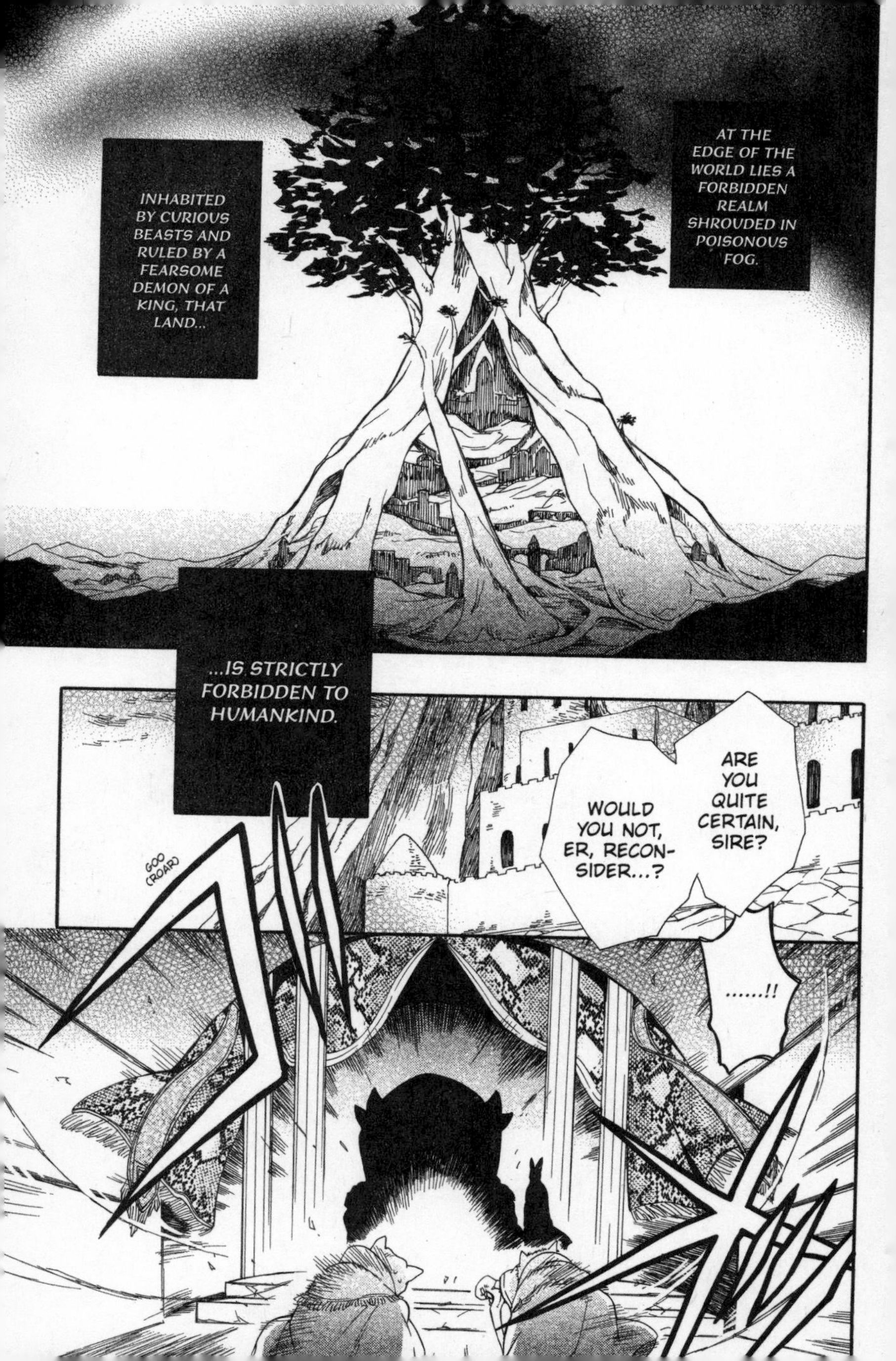

AT THE EDGE OF THE WORLD LIES A FORBIDDEN REALM SHROUDED IN POISONOUS FOG.
INHABITED BY CURIOUS BEASTS AND RULED BY A FEARSOME DEMON OF A KING, THAT LAND...
...IS STRICTLY FORBIDDEN TO HUMANKIND.
ARE YOU QUITE CERTAIN, SIRE?
WOULD YOU NOT, ER, RECON-SIDER...?
GOO (ROAR)
......!!

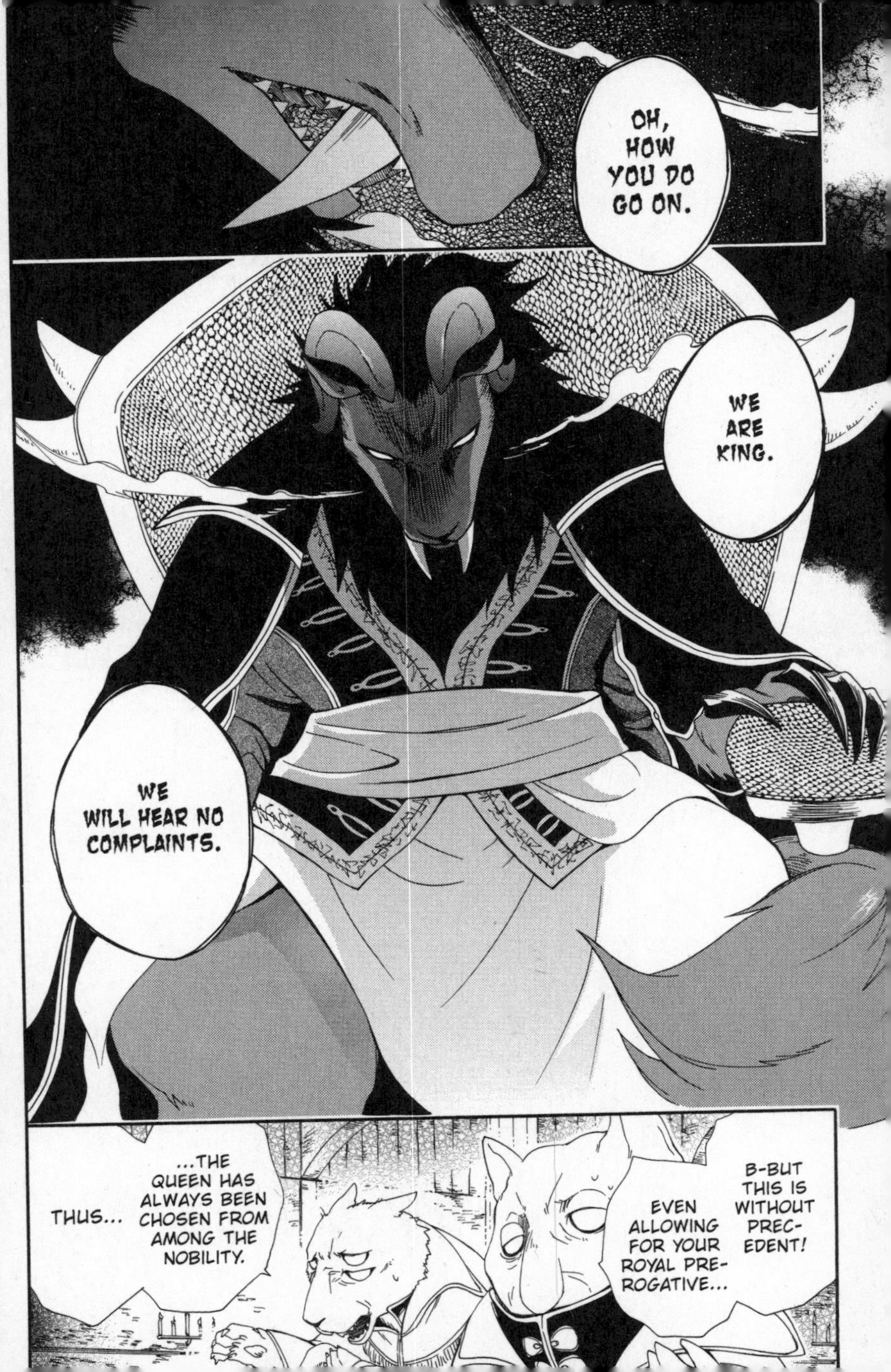
OH, HOW YOU DO GO ON.
WE ARE KING.
WE WILL HEAR NO COMPLAINTS.
B-BUT THIS IS WITHOUT PREC-EDENT!
EVEN ALLOWING FOR YOUR ROYAL PRE-ROGATIVE...
...THE QUEEN HAS ALWAYS BEEN CHOSEN FROM AMONG THE NOBILITY.
THUS...

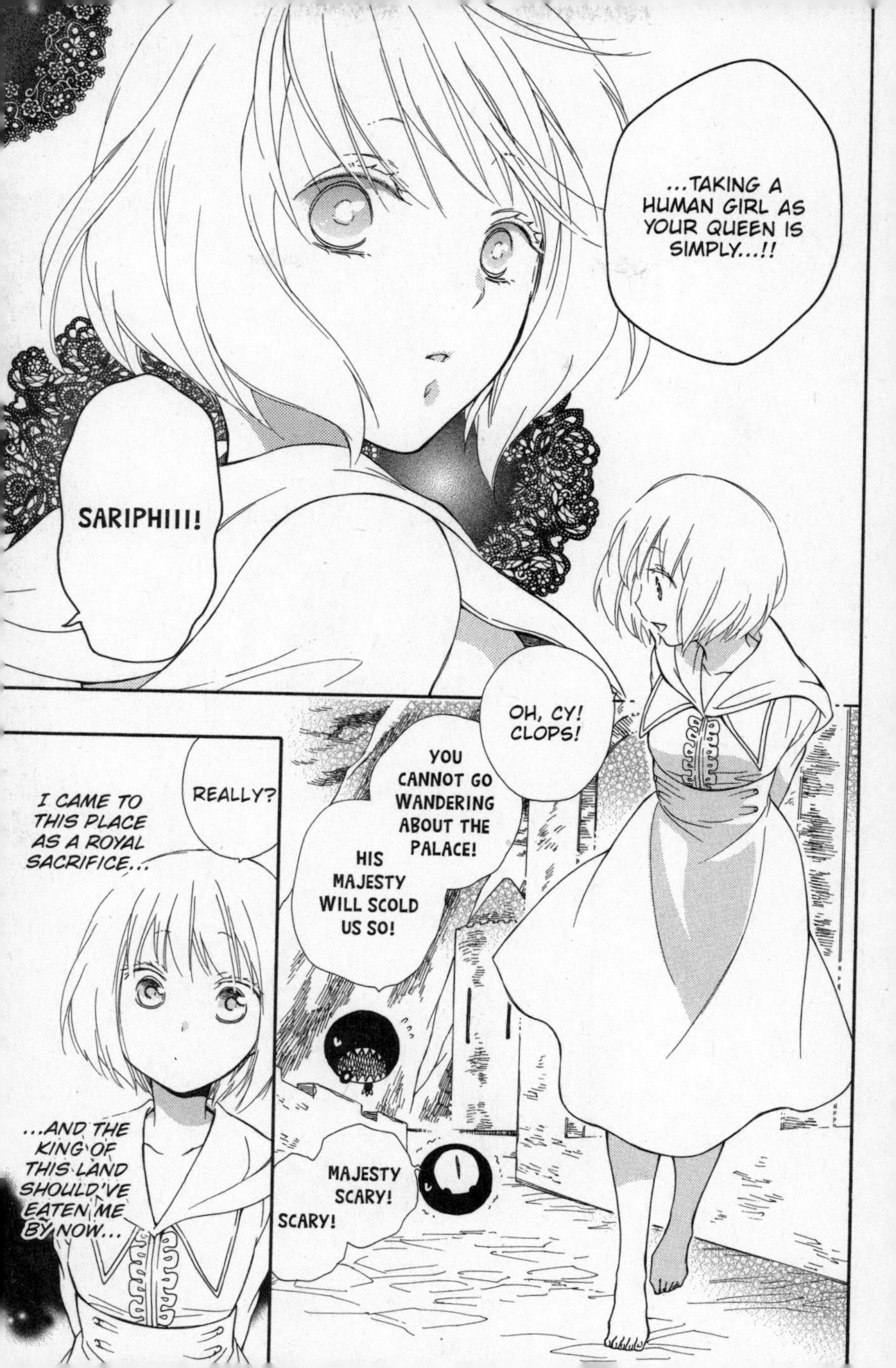
...TAKING A HUMAN GIRL AS YOUR QUEEN IS SIMPLY...!!
SARIPHIIII!
OH, CY! CLOPS!
YOU CANNOT GO WANDERING ABOUT THE PALACE!
HIS MAJESTY WILL SCOLD US SO!
MAJESTY SCARY!
SCARY!
REALLY?
I CAME TO THIS PLACE AS A ROYAL SACRIFICE...
...AND THE KING OF THIS LAND SHOULD'VE EATEN ME BY NOW...

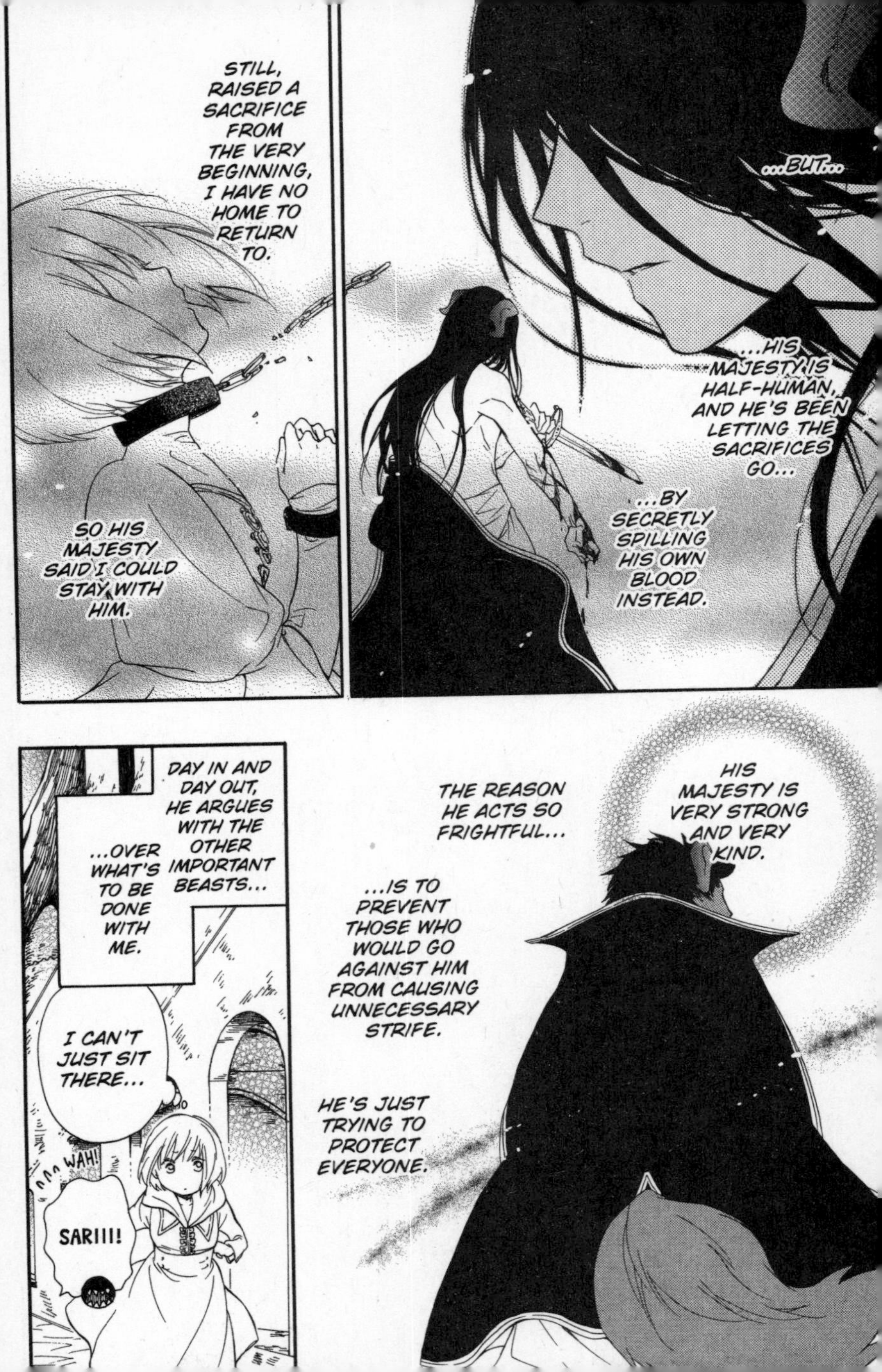
...BUT...
...HIS MAJESTY IS HALF-HUMAN, AND HE'S BEEN LETTING THE SACRIFICES GO...
...BY SECRETLY SPILLING HIS OWN BLOOD INSTEAD.
STILL, RAISED A SACRIFICE FROM THE VERY BEGINNING, I HAVE NO HOME TO RETURN TO.
SO HIS MAJESTY SAID I COULD STAY WITH HIM.
HIS MAJESTY IS VERY STRONG AND VERY KIND.
THE REASON HE ACTS SO FRIGHTFUL...
...IS TO PREVENT THOSE WHO WOULD GO AGAINST HIM FROM CAUSING UNNECESSARY STRIFE.
HE'S JUST TRYING TO PROTECT EVERYONE.
DAY IN AND DAY OUT, HE ARGUES WITH THE OTHER IMPORTANT BEASTS...
...OVER WHAT'S TO BE DONE WITH ME.
I CAN'T JUST SIT THERE...
WAH!
SARIII!

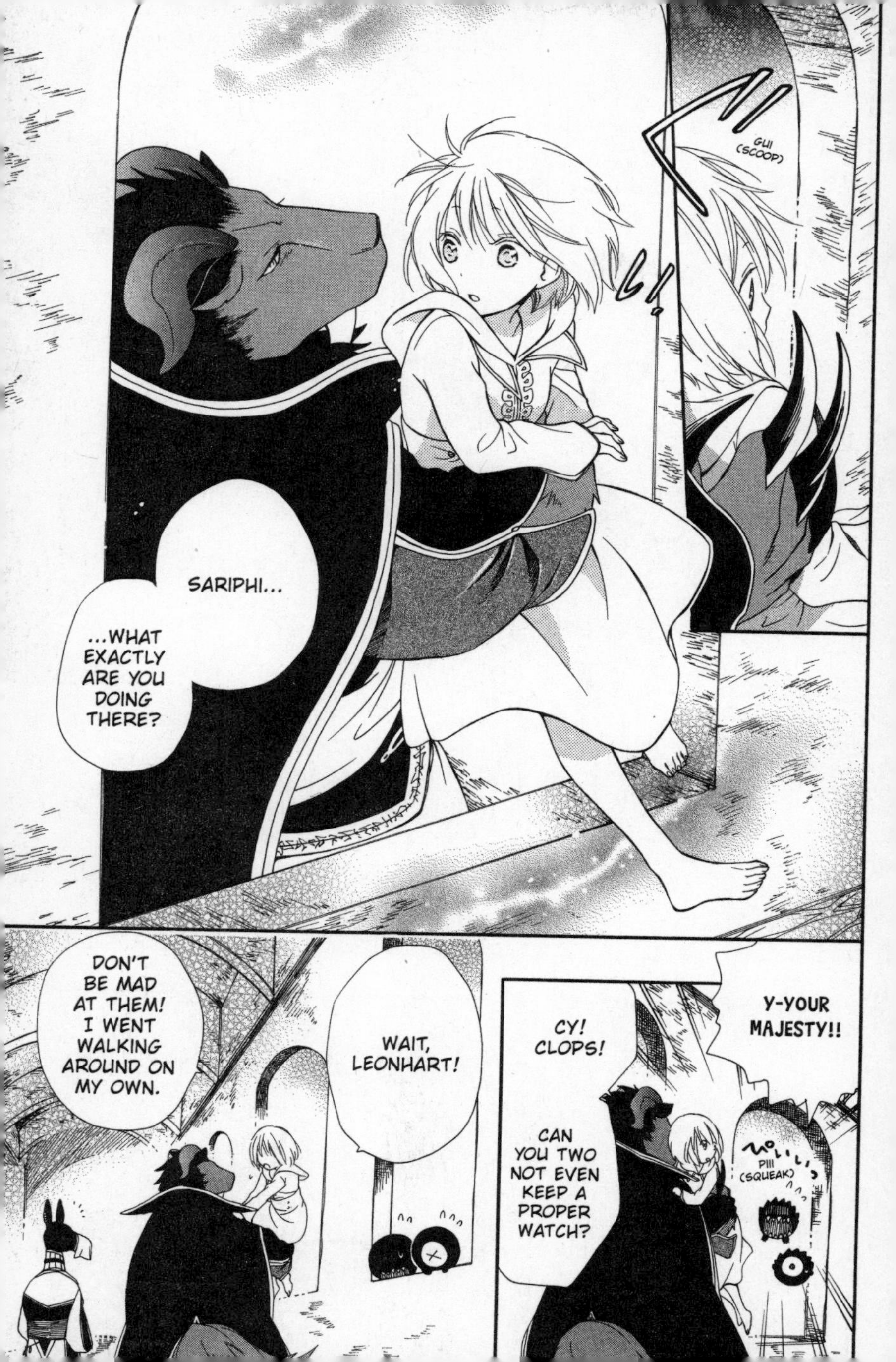
GUI (SCOOP)
SARIPHI...
...WHAT EXACTLY ARE YOU DOING THERE?
Y-YOUR MAJESTY!!
CY! CLOPS!
CAN YOU TWO NOT EVEN KEEP A PROPER WATCH?
PIII (SQUEAK)
WAIT, LEONHART!
DON'T BE MAD AT THEM! I WENT WALKING AROUND ON MY OWN.

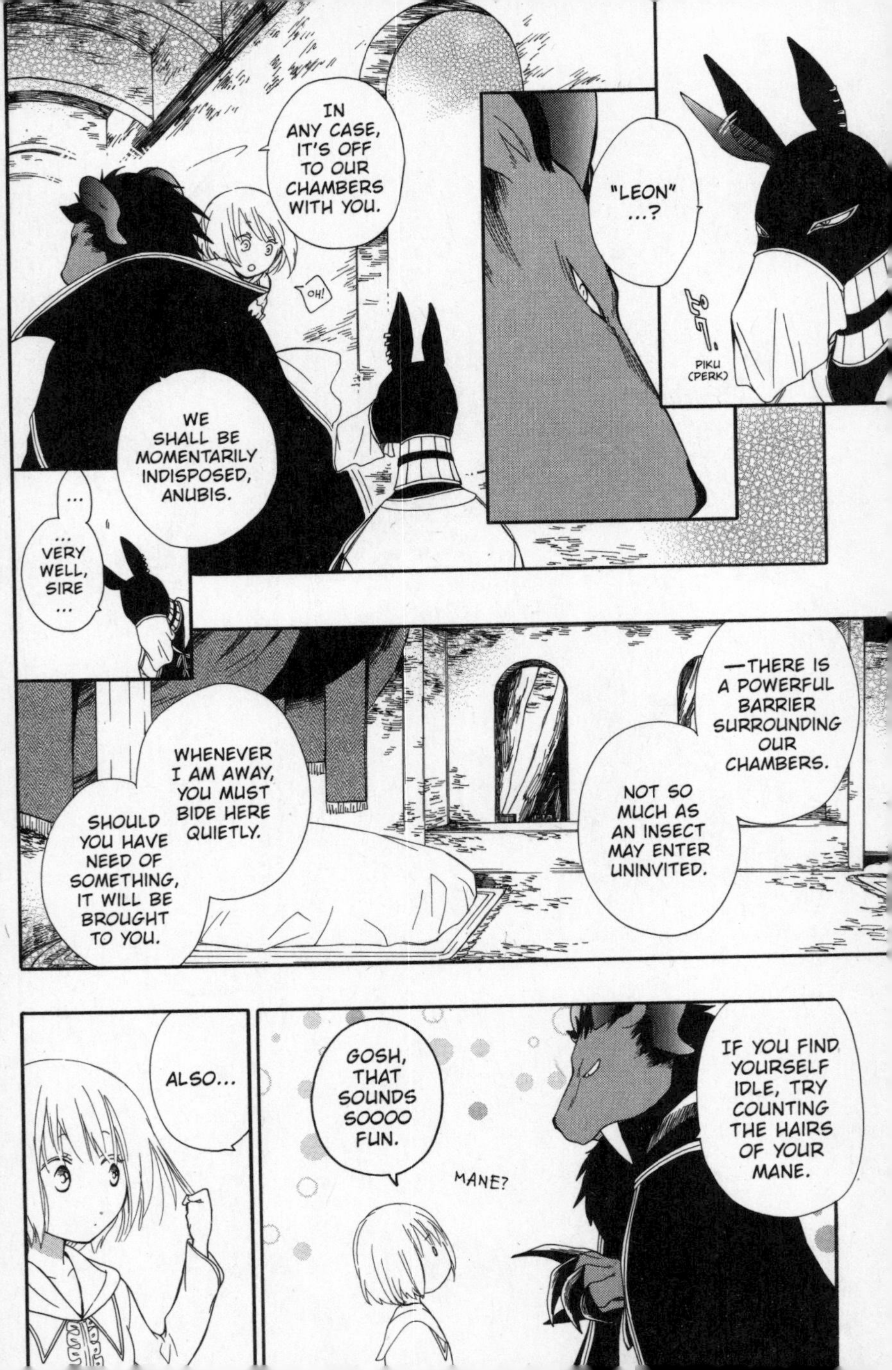
"LEON" ...?
PIKU (PERK)
IN ANY CASE, IT'S OFF TO OUR CHAMBERS WITH YOU.
OH!
WE SHALL BE MOMENTARILY INDISPOSED, ANUBIS.
...
... VERY WELL, SIRE ...
—THERE IS A POWERFUL BARRIER SURROUNDING OUR CHAMBERS.
NOT SO MUCH AS AN INSECT MAY ENTER UNINVITED.
WHENEVER I AM AWAY, YOU MUST BIDE HERE QUIETLY.
SHOULD YOU HAVE NEED OF SOMETHING, IT WILL BE BROUGHT TO YOU.
IF YOU FIND YOURSELF IDLE, TRY COUNTING THE HAIRS OF YOUR MANE.
GOSH, THAT SOUNDS SOOOO FUN.
MANE?
ALSO...

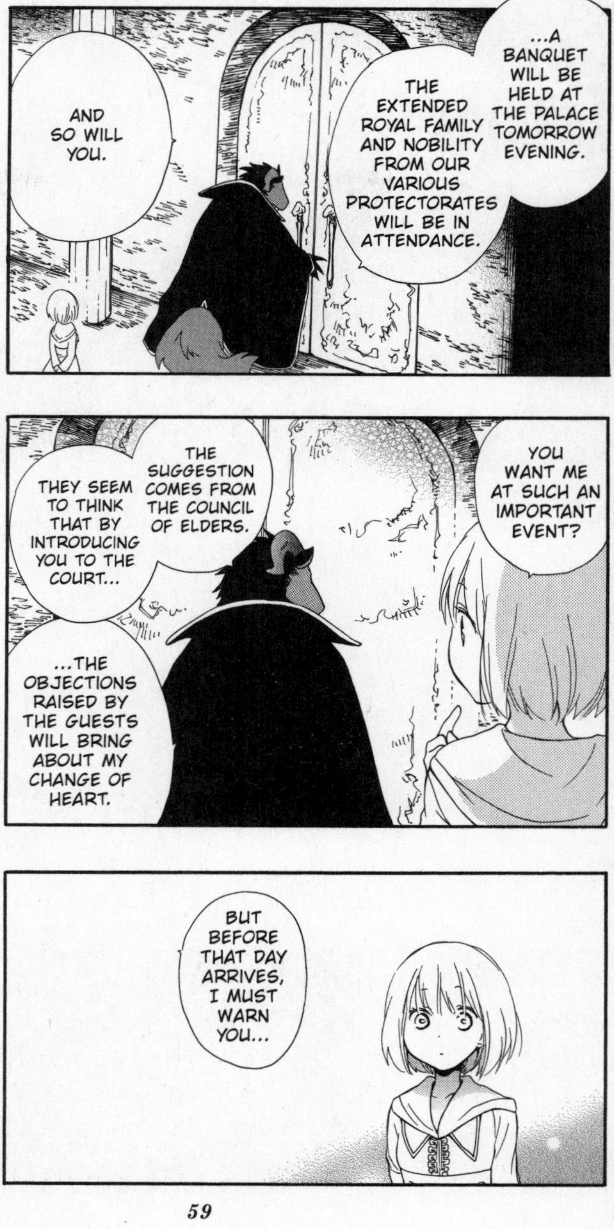
...A BANQUET WILL BE HELD AT THE PALACE TOMORROW EVENING.
THE EXTENDED ROYAL FAMILY AND NOBILITY FROM OUR VARIOUS PROTECTORATES WILL BE IN ATTENDANCE.
AND SO WILL YOU.
YOU WANT ME AT SUCH AN IMPORTANT EVENT?
THE SUGGESTION COMES FROM THE COUNCIL OF ELDERS.
THEY SEEM TO THINK THAT BY INTRODUCING YOU TO THE COURT...
...THE OBJECTIONS RAISED BY THE GUESTS WILL BRING ABOUT MY CHANGE OF HEART.
BUT BEFORE THAT DAY ARRIVES, I MUST WARN YOU...

PROTOTYPE SARIPHI ①

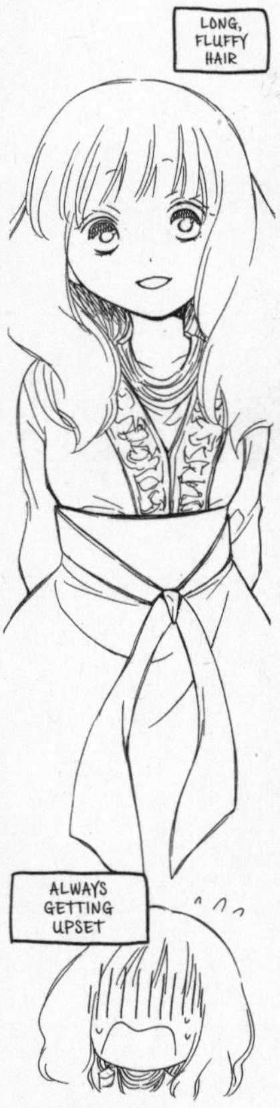
LONG, FLUFFY HAIR
ALWAYS GETTING UPSET

I CAME UP WITH TWO VERSIONS OF SARIPHI: LONG HAIR AND BOB. I QUICKLY SETTLED ON THE BOB. THEIR PERSONALITIES WERE WORLDS APART TOO, AND THE STORY WOULD'VE BEEN VERY DIFFERENT IF I'D GONE WITH THIS SARIPHI.

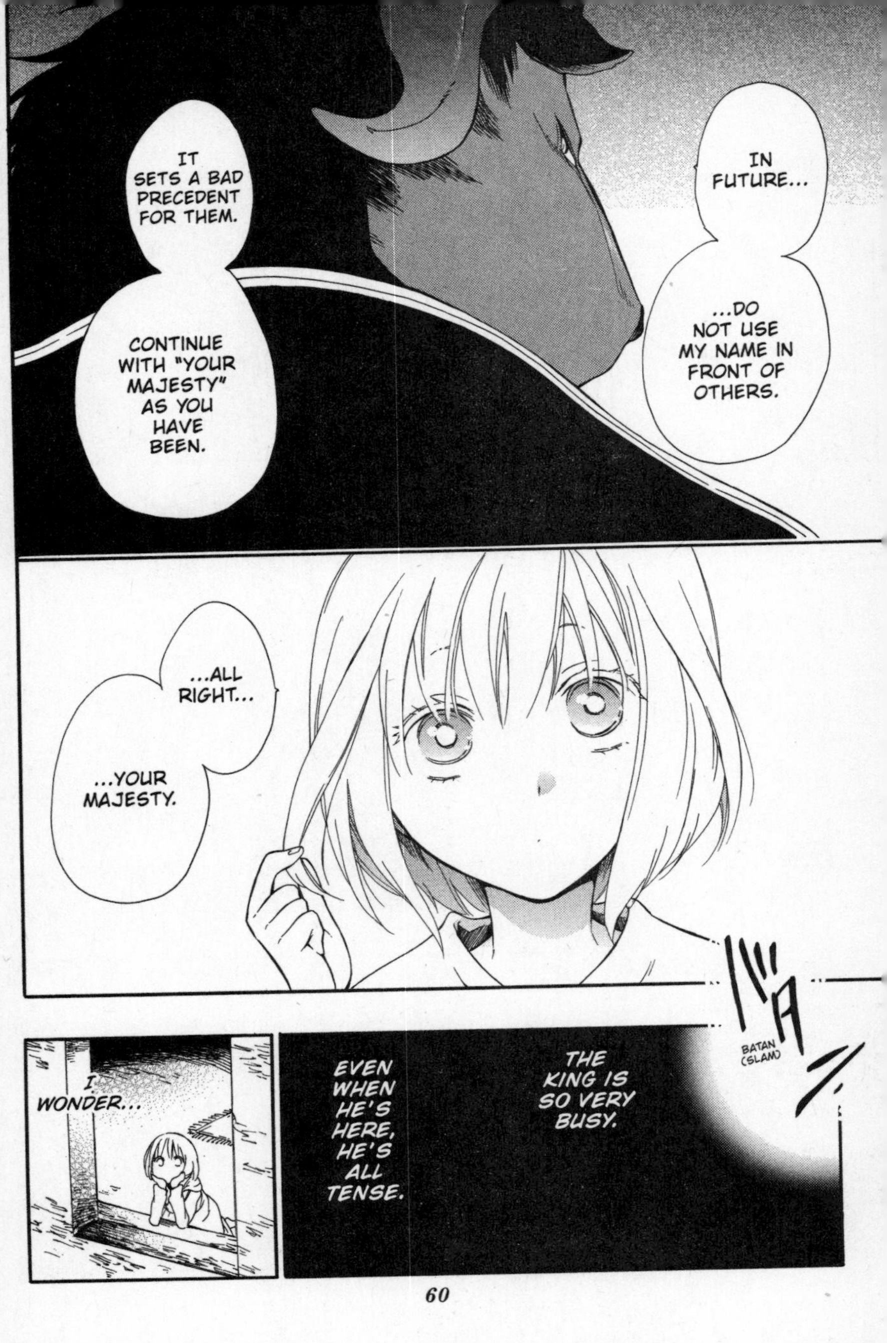
IN FUTURE...
...DO NOT USE MY NAME IN FRONT OF OTHERS.
IT SETS A BAD PRECEDENT FOR THEM.
CONTINUE WITH "YOUR MAJESTY" AS YOU HAVE BEEN.
...ALL RIGHT...
...YOUR MAJESTY.
BATAN (SLAM)
THE KING IS SO VERY BUSY.
EVEN WHEN HE'S HERE, HE'S ALL TENSE.
I WONDER...

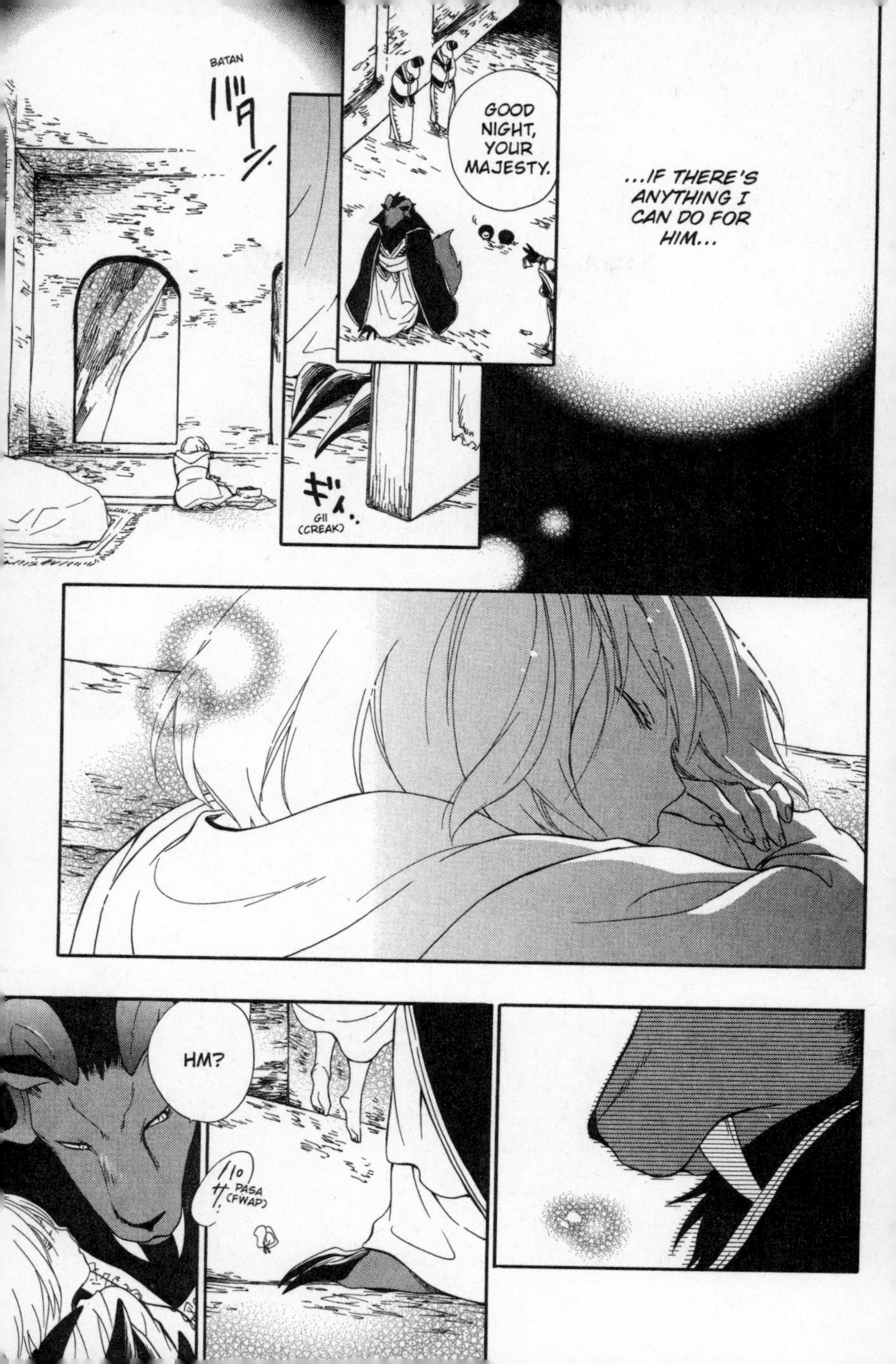
...IF THERE'S ANYTHING I CAN DO FOR HIM...
GOOD NIGHT, YOUR MAJESTY.
GII (CREAK)
BATAN
PASA (FWAP)
HM?

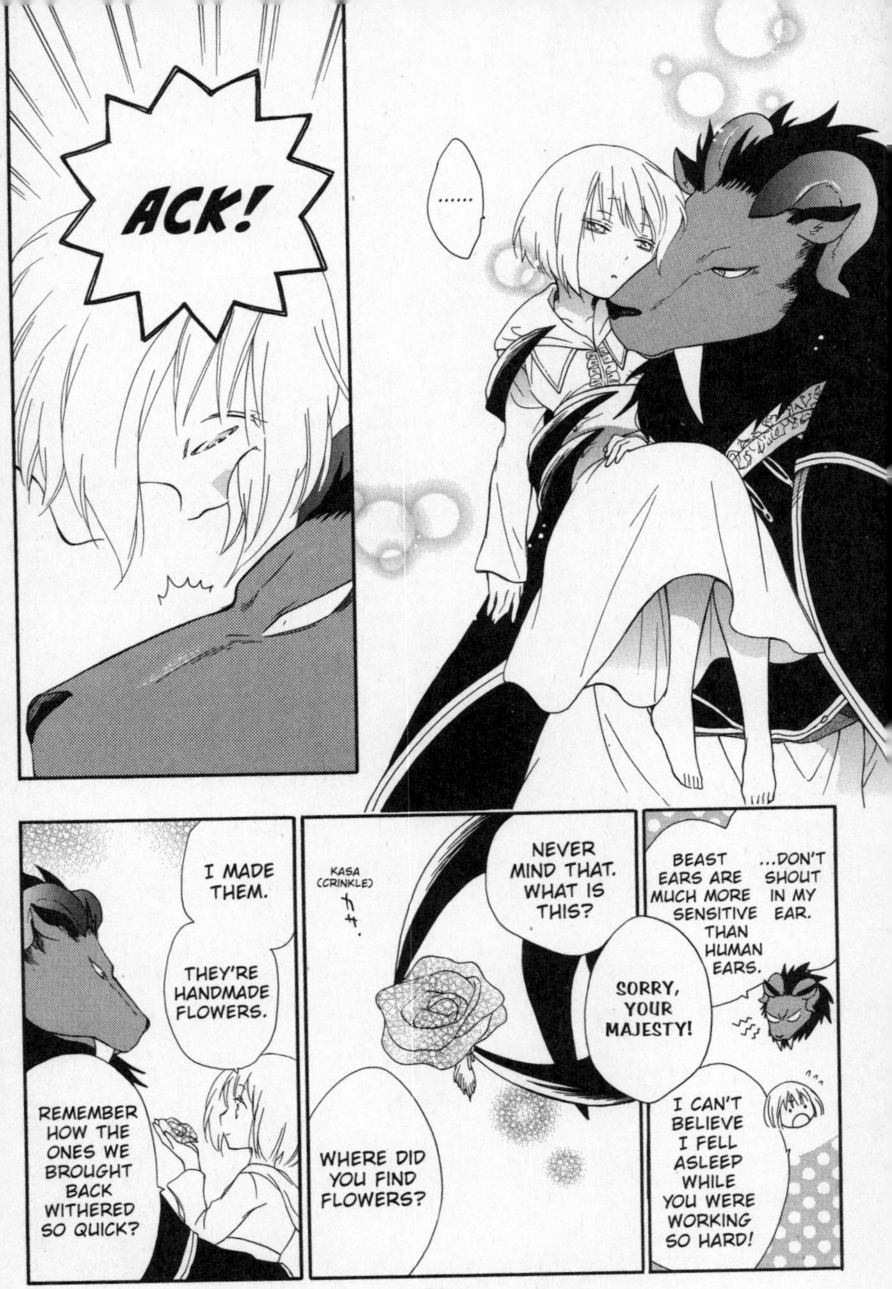

......
ACK!
...DON'T SHOUT IN MY EAR.
BEAST EARS ARE MUCH MORE SENSITIVE THAN HUMAN EARS.
SORRY, YOUR MAJESTY!
I CAN'T BELIEVE I FELL ASLEEP WHILE YOU WERE WORKING SO HARD!
NEVER MIND THAT. WHAT IS THIS?
KASA (CRINKLE)
WHERE DID YOU FIND FLOWERS?
I MADE THEM.
THEY'RE HANDMADE FLOWERS.
REMEMBER HOW THE ONES WE BROUGHT BACK WITHERED SO QUICK?

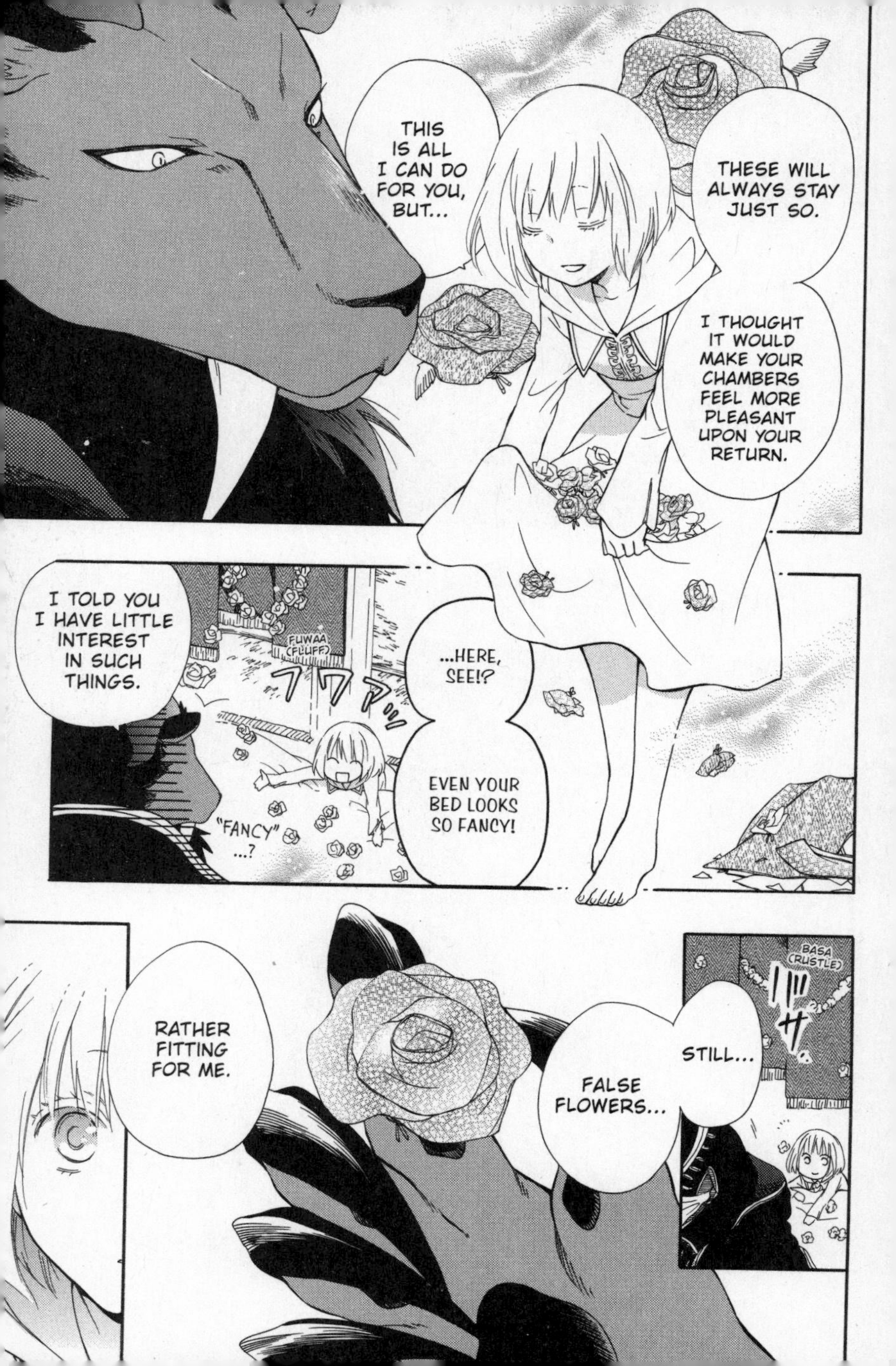
THESE WILL ALWAYS STAY JUST SO.
I THOUGHT IT WOULD MAKE YOUR CHAMBERS FEEL MORE PLEASANT UPON YOUR RETURN.
THIS IS ALL I CAN DO FOR YOU, BUT...
...HERE, SEE!?
FUWAA (FLUFF)
EVEN YOUR BED LOOKS SO FANCY!
I TOLD YOU I HAVE LITTLE INTEREST IN SUCH THINGS.
"FANCY" ...?
BASA (RUSTLE)
STILL...
FALSE FLOWERS...
RATHER FITTING FOR ME.

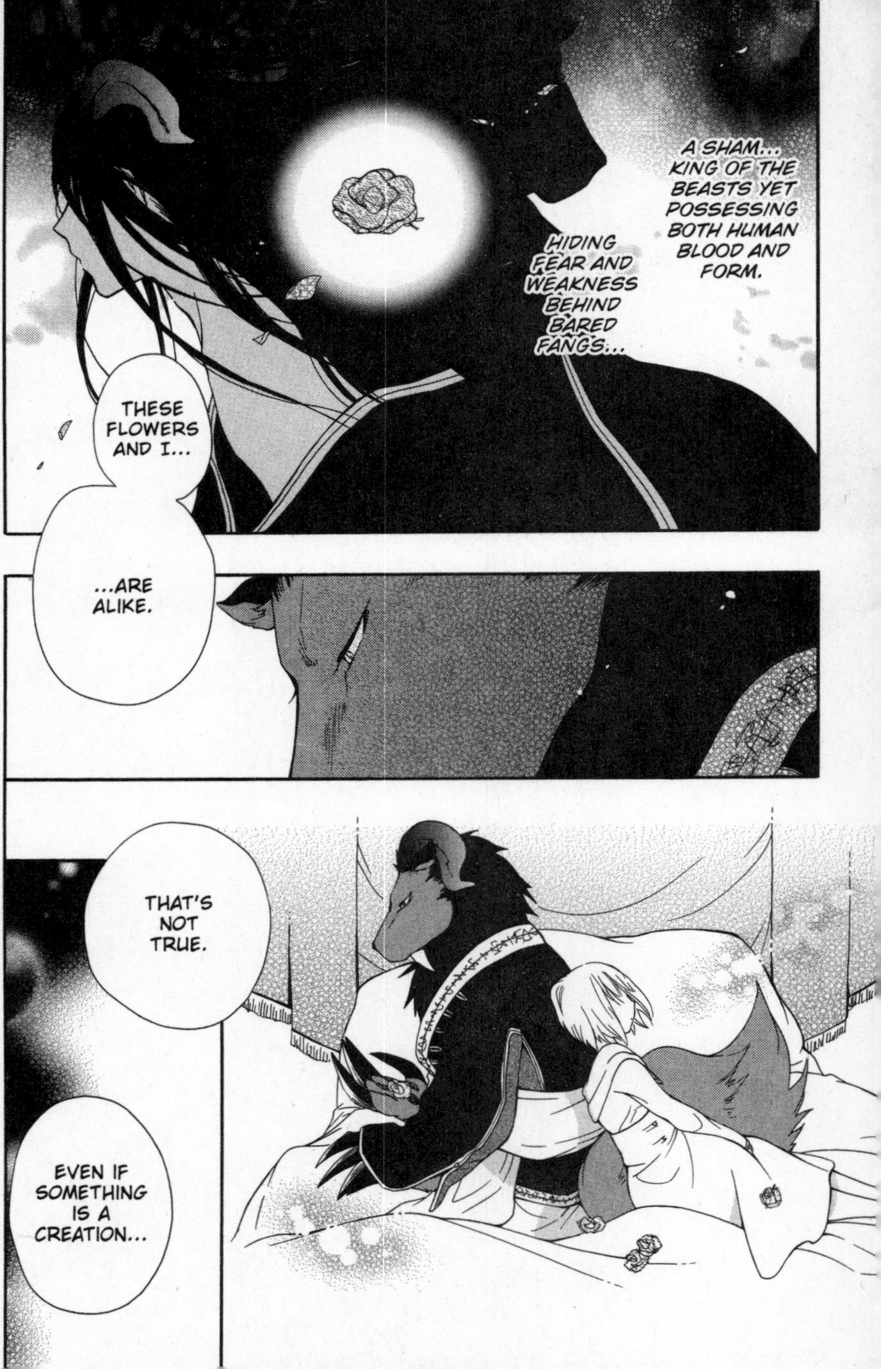
A SHAM... KING OF THE BEASTS YET POSSESSING BOTH HUMAN BLOOD AND FORM.
HIDING FEAR AND WEAKNESS BEHIND BARED FANGS...
THESE FLOWERS AND I...
...ARE ALIKE.
THAT'S NOT TRUE.
EVEN IF SOMETHING IS A CREATION...

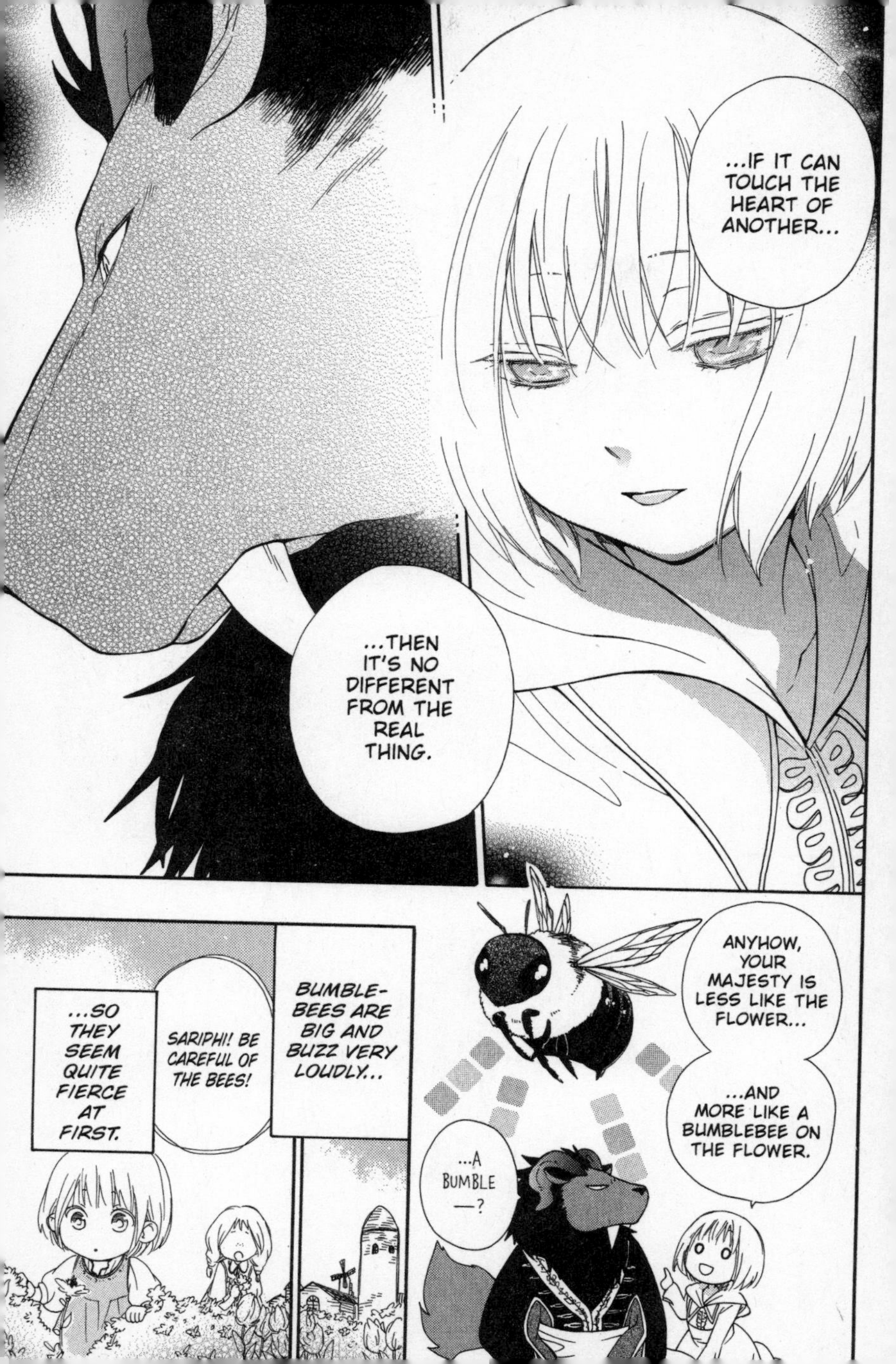
...IF IT CAN TOUCH THE HEART OF ANOTHER...
...THEN IT'S NO DIFFERENT FROM THE REAL THING.
ANYHOW, YOUR MAJESTY IS LESS LIKE THE FLOWER...
...AND MORE LIKE A BUMBLEBEE ON THE FLOWER.
...A BUMBLE—?
BUMBLE-BEES ARE BIG AND BUZZ VERY LOUDLY...
SARIPHI! BE CAREFUL OF THE BEES!
...SO THEY SEEM QUITE FIERCE AT FIRST.

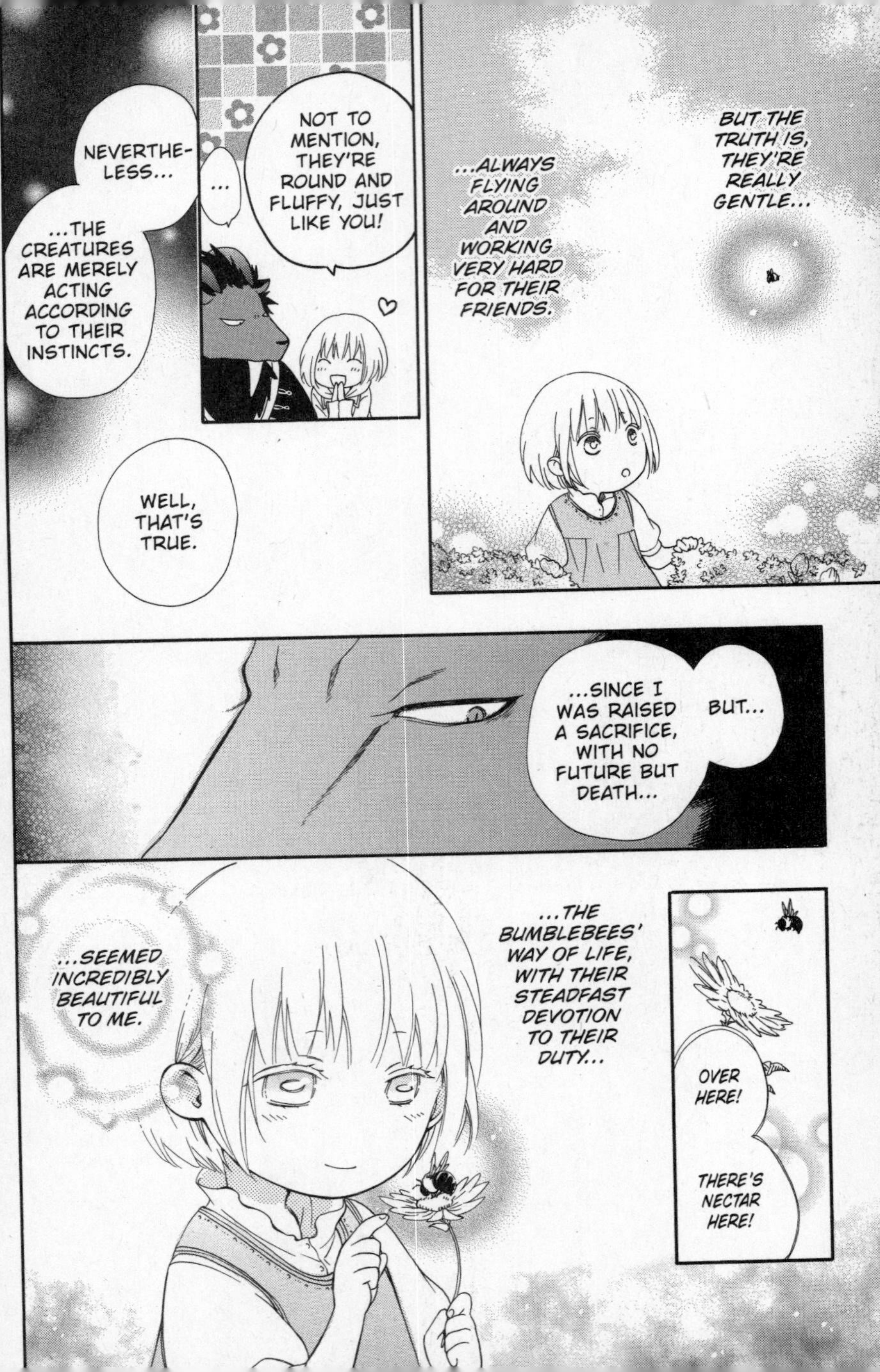

BUT THE TRUTH IS, THEY'RE REALLY GENTLE...
...ALWAYS FLYING AROUND AND WORKING VERY HARD FOR THEIR FRIENDS.
NOT TO MENTION, THEY'RE ROUND AND FLUFFY, JUST LIKE YOU!
...
NEVERTHE-LESS...
...THE CREATURES ARE MERELY ACTING ACCORDING TO THEIR INSTINCTS.
WELL, THAT'S TRUE.
BUT...
...SINCE I WAS RAISED A SACRIFICE, WITH NO FUTURE BUT DEATH...
OVER HERE!
THERE'S NECTAR HERE!
...THE BUMBLEBEES' WAY OF LIFE, WITH THEIR STEADFAST DEVOTION TO THEIR DUTY...
...SEEMED INCREDIBLY BEAUTIFUL TO ME.

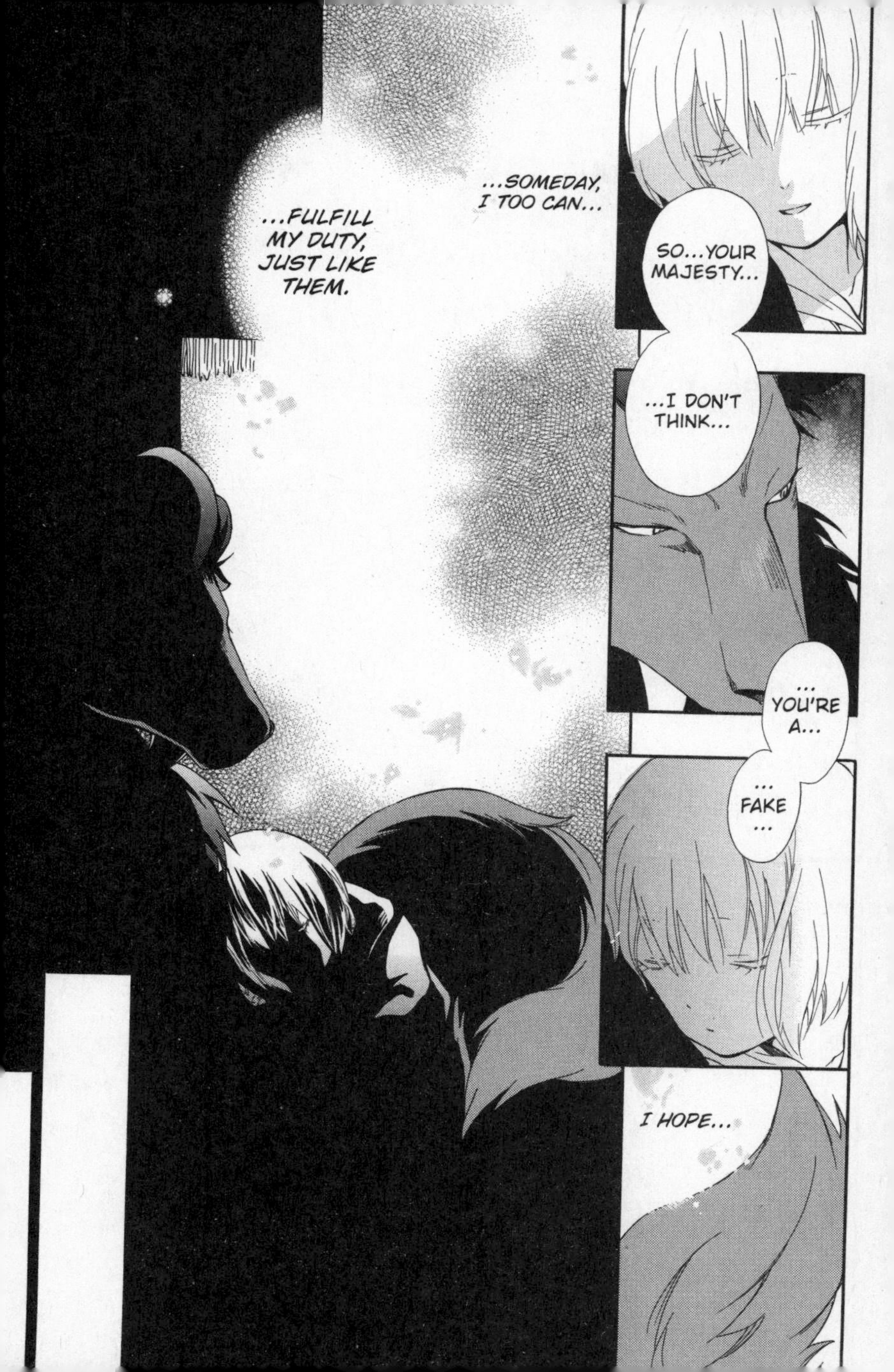
SO...YOUR MAJESTY...
...I DON'T THINK...
...YOU'RE A...
...FAKE...
I HOPE...
...SOMEDAY, I TOO CAN...
...FULFILL MY DUTY, JUST LIKE THEM.

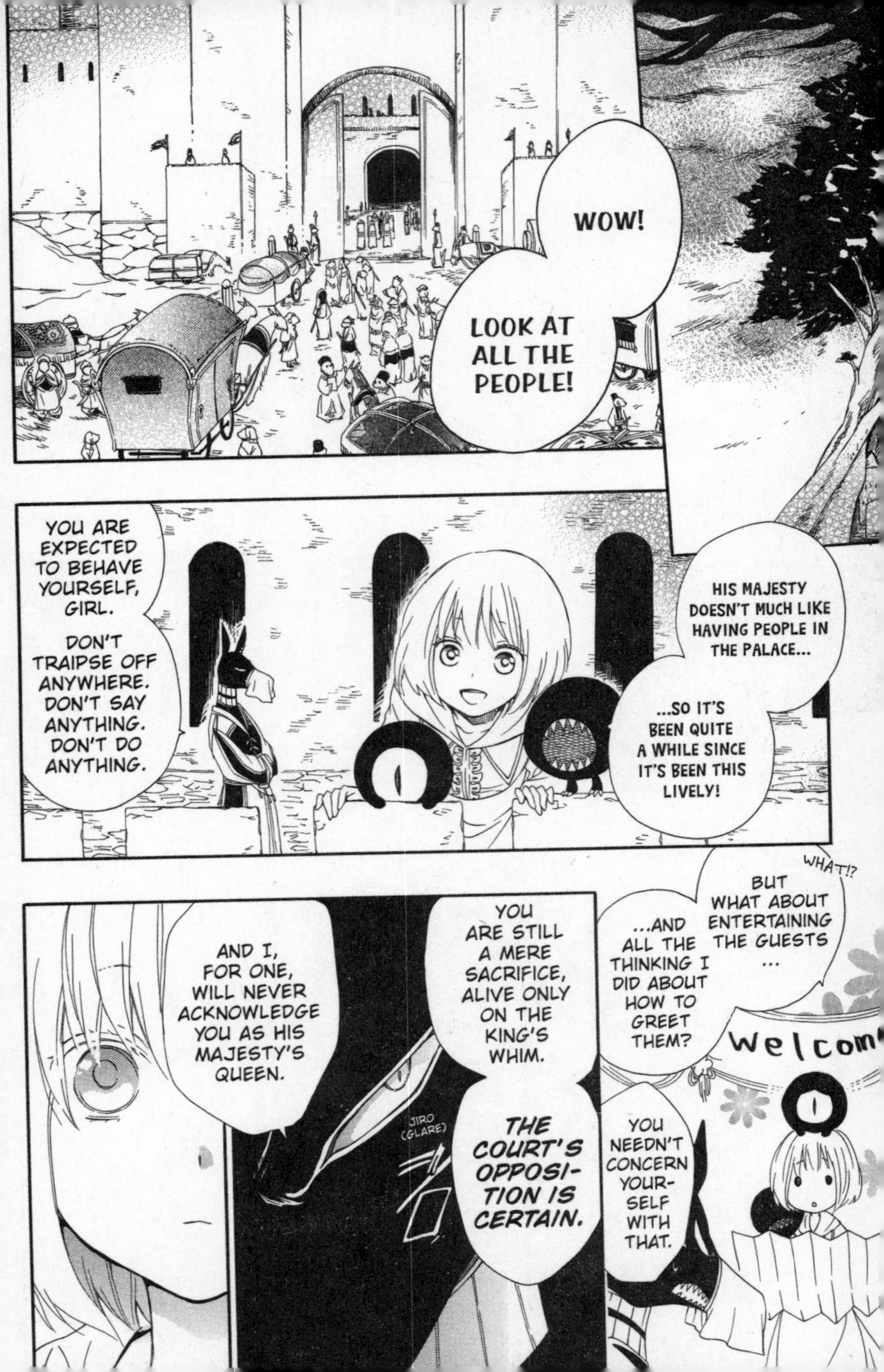
WOW!
LOOK AT ALL THE PEOPLE!
HIS MAJESTY DOESN'T MUCH LIKE HAVING PEOPLE IN THE PALACE...
...SO IT'S BEEN QUITE A WHILE SINCE IT'S BEEN THIS LIVELY!
YOU ARE EXPECTED TO BEHAVE YOURSELF, GIRL.
DON'T TRAIPSE OFF ANYWHERE. DON'T SAY ANYTHING. DON'T DO ANYTHING.
WHAT!?
BUT WHAT ABOUT ENTERTAINING THE GUESTS...
...AND ALL THE THINKING I DID ABOUT HOW TO GREET THEM?
Welcom
YOU NEEDN'T CONCERN YOURSELF WITH THAT.
YOU ARE STILL A MERE SACRIFICE, ALIVE ONLY ON THE KING'S WHIM.
JIRO (GLARE)
THE COURT'S OPPOSITION IS CERTAIN.
AND I, FOR ONE, WILL NEVER ACKNOWLEDGE YOU AS HIS MAJESTY'S QUEEN.

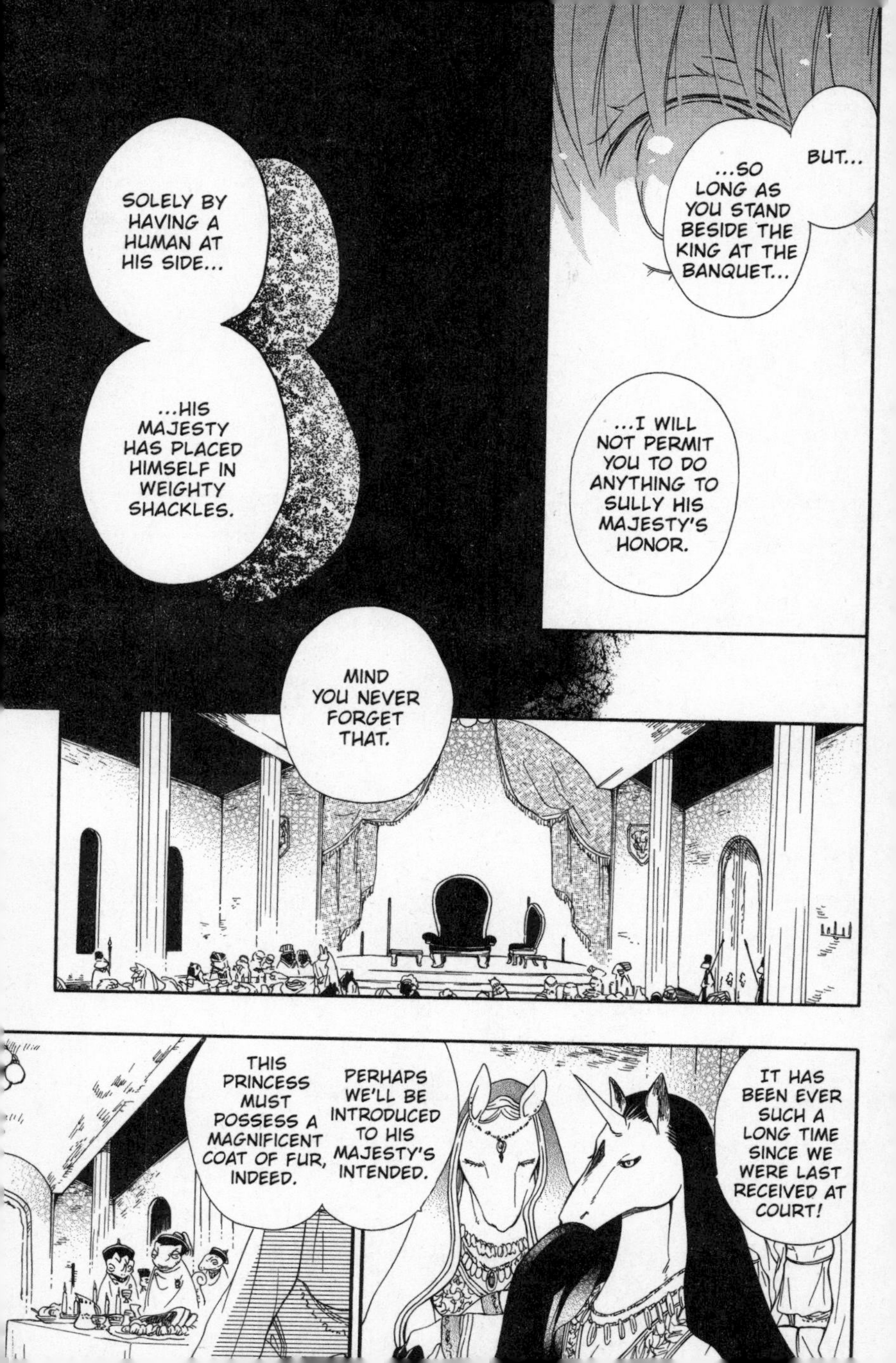
BUT...
...SO LONG AS YOU STAND BESIDE THE KING AT THE BANQUET...
...I WILL NOT PERMIT YOU TO DO ANYTHING TO SULLY HIS MAJESTY'S HONOR.
SOLELY BY HAVING A HUMAN AT HIS SIDE...
...HIS MAJESTY HAS PLACED HIMSELF IN WEIGHTY SHACKLES.
MIND YOU NEVER FORGET THAT.
IT HAS BEEN EVER SUCH A LONG TIME SINCE WE WERE LAST RECEIVED AT COURT!
PERHAPS WE'LL BE INTRODUCED TO HIS MAJESTY'S INTENDED.
THIS PRINCESS MUST POSSESS A MAGNIFICENT COAT OF FUR, INDEED.

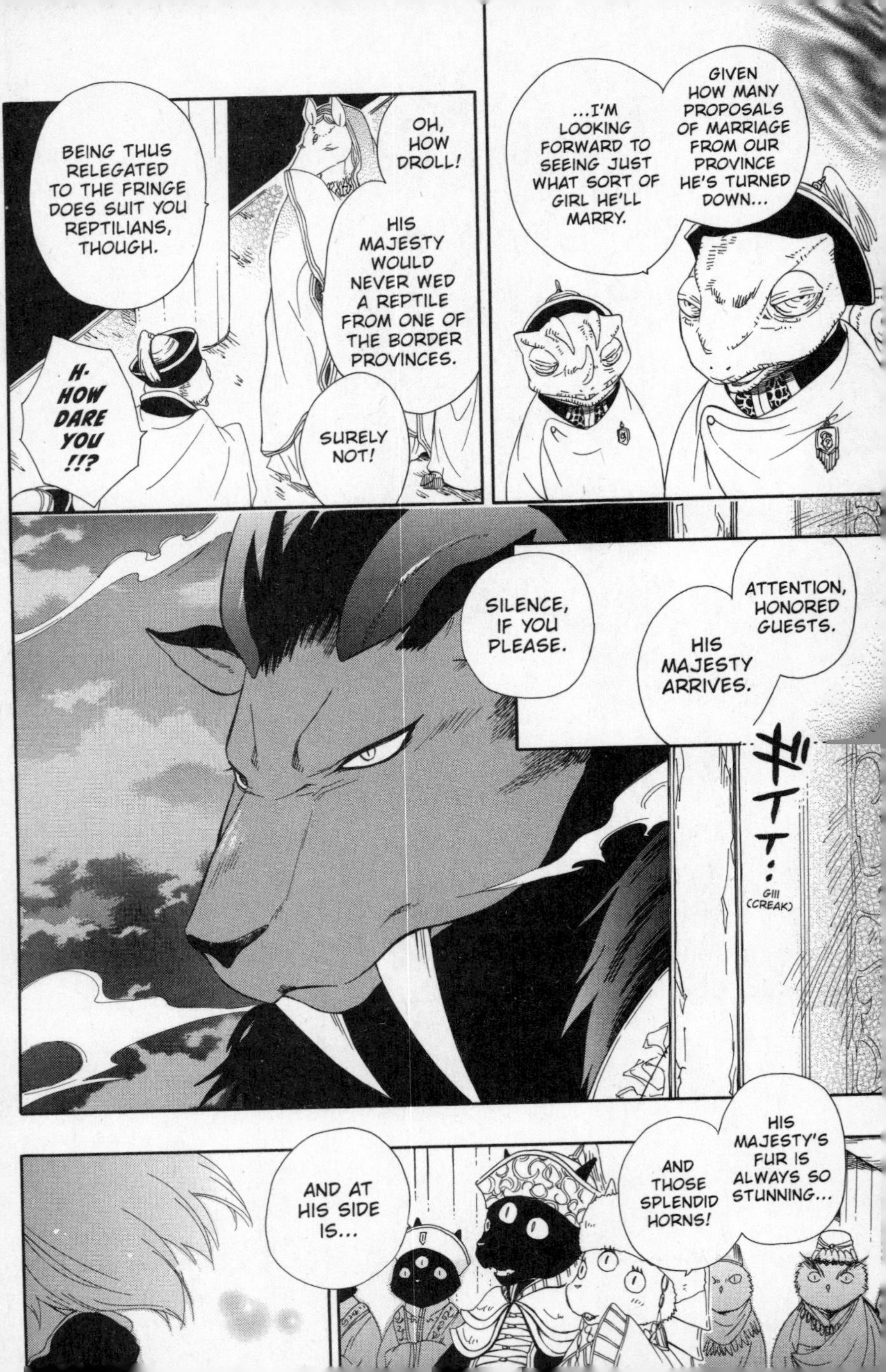
GIVEN HOW MANY PROPOSALS OF MARRIAGE FROM OUR PROVINCE HE'S TURNED DOWN...
...I'M LOOKING FORWARD TO SEEING JUST WHAT SORT OF GIRL HE'LL MARRY.
OH, HOW DROLL!
HIS MAJESTY WOULD NEVER WED A REPTILE FROM ONE OF THE BORDER PROVINCES.
SURELY NOT!
BEING THUS RELEGATED TO THE FRINGE DOES SUIT YOU REPTILIANS, THOUGH.
H-HOW DARE YOU!!?
ATTENTION, HONORED GUESTS.
HIS MAJESTY ARRIVES.
SILENCE, IF YOU PLEASE.
GIII (CREAK)
HIS MAJESTY'S FUR IS ALWAYS SO STUNNING...
AND THOSE SPLENDID HORNS!
AND AT HIS SIDE IS...

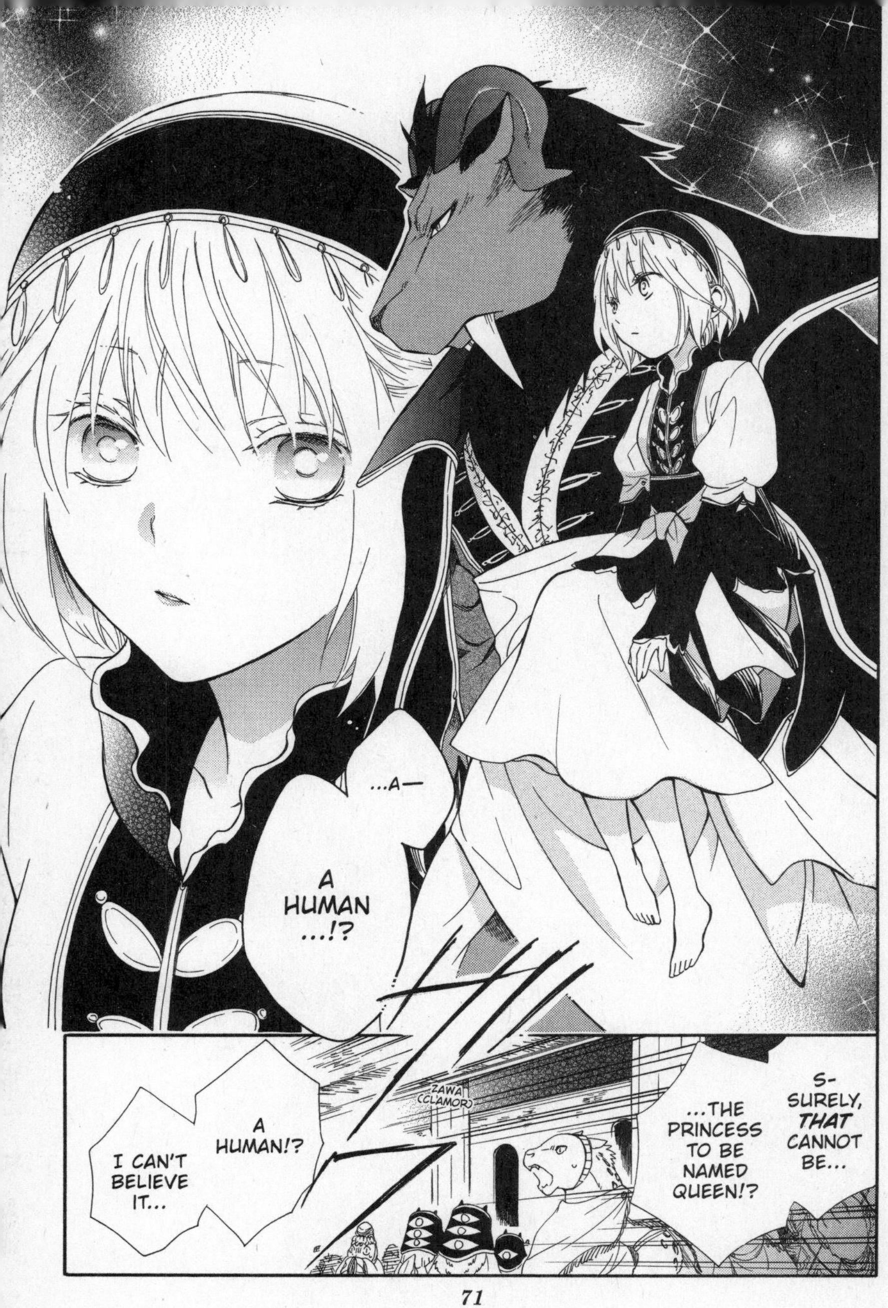
...A—
A HUMAN ...!?
S-SURELY, *THAT* CANNOT BE...
...THE PRINCESS TO BE NAMED QUEEN!?
ZAWA (CLAMOR)
A HUMAN!?
I CAN'T BELIEVE IT...

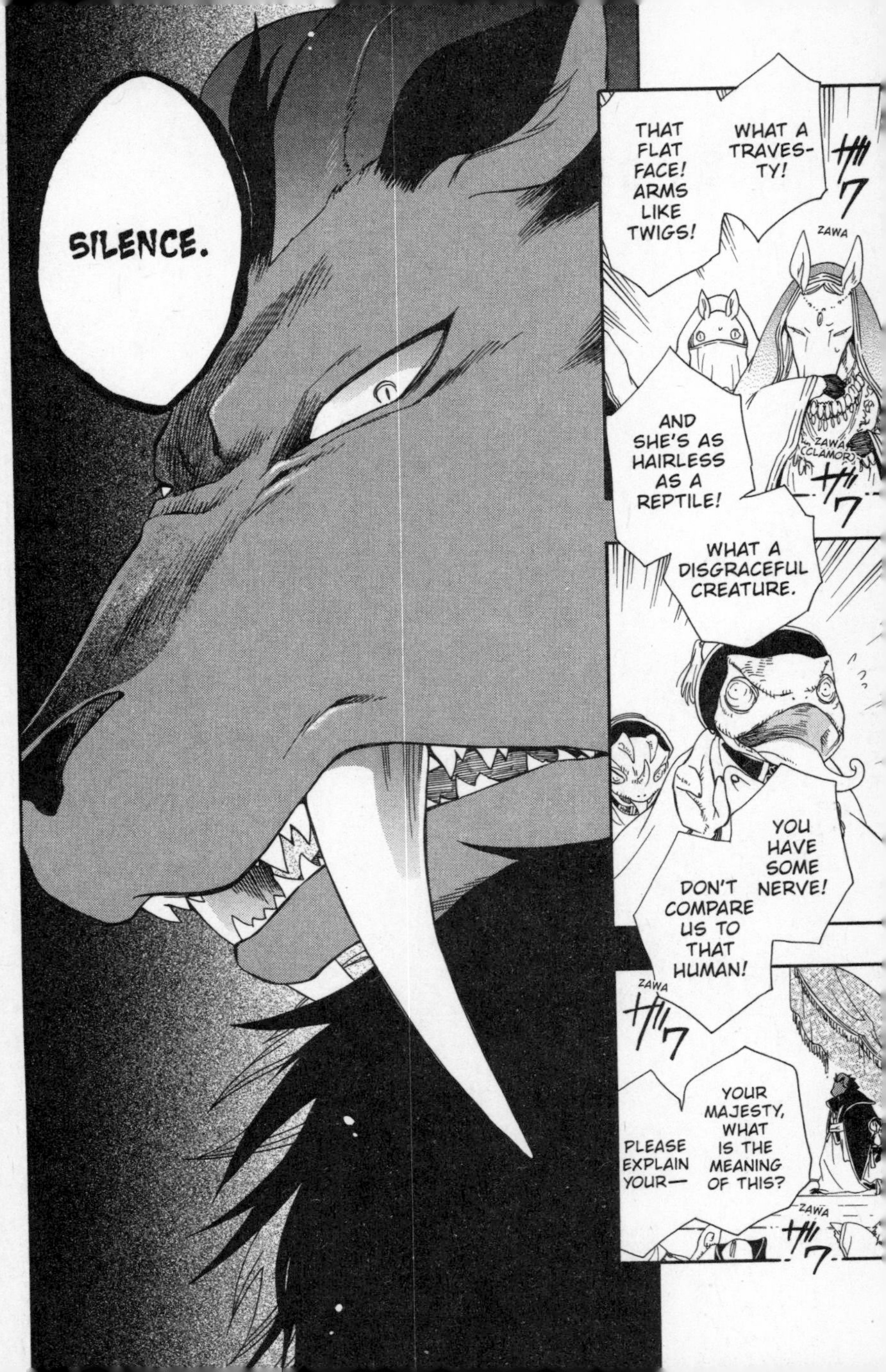
WHAT A TRAVES-TY!
THAT FLAT FACE! ARMS LIKE TWIGS!
ZAWA
AND SHE'S AS HAIRLESS AS A REPTILE!
ZAWA (CLAMOR)
WHAT A DISGRACEFUL CREATURE.
YOU HAVE SOME NERVE!
DON'T COMPARE US TO THAT HUMAN!
ZAWA
YOUR MAJESTY, WHAT IS THE MEANING OF THIS?
PLEASE EXPLAIN YOUR—
ZAWA
SILENCE.

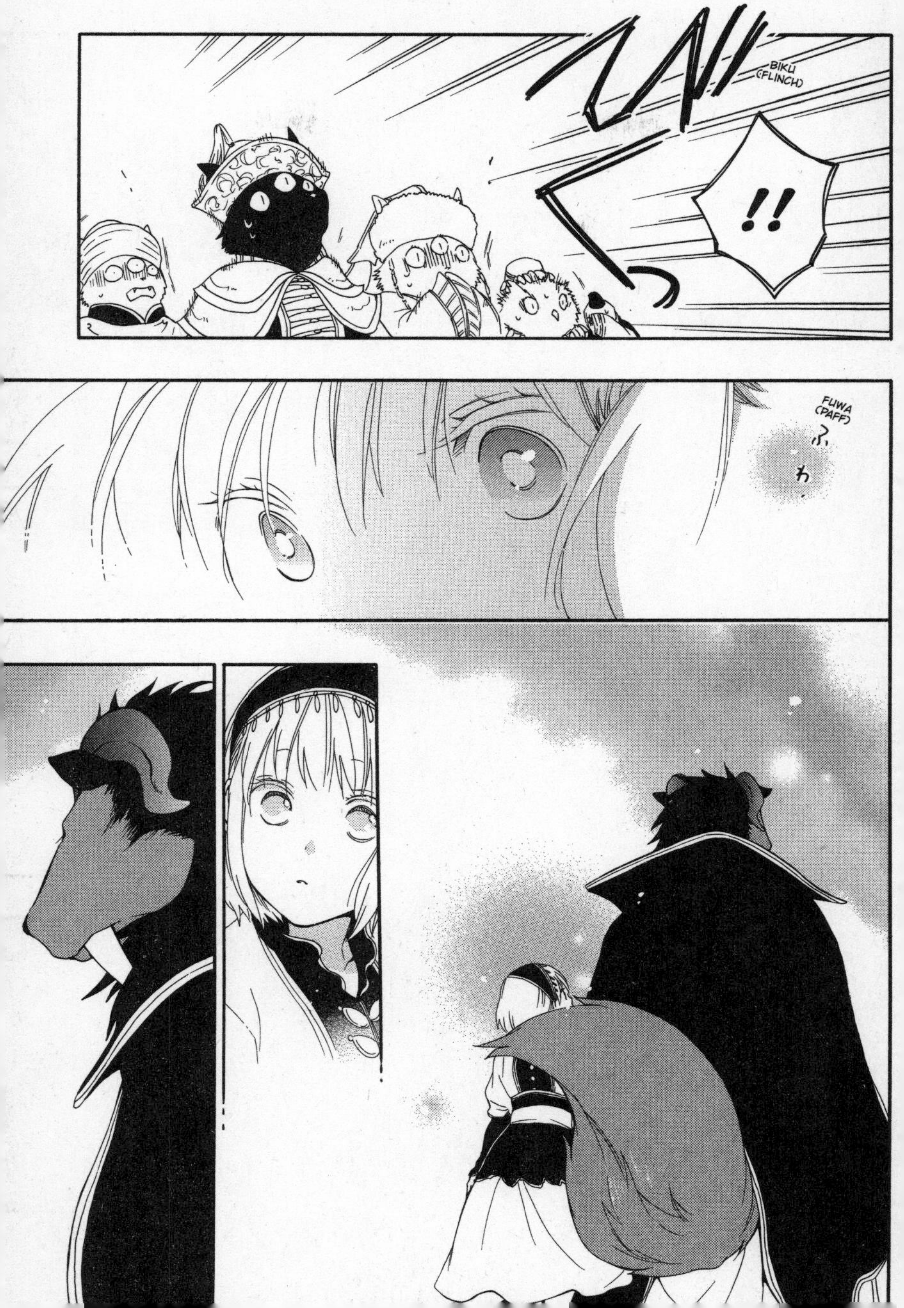

BIKU (FLINCH)
!!
FUWA (PAFF)
ふわ

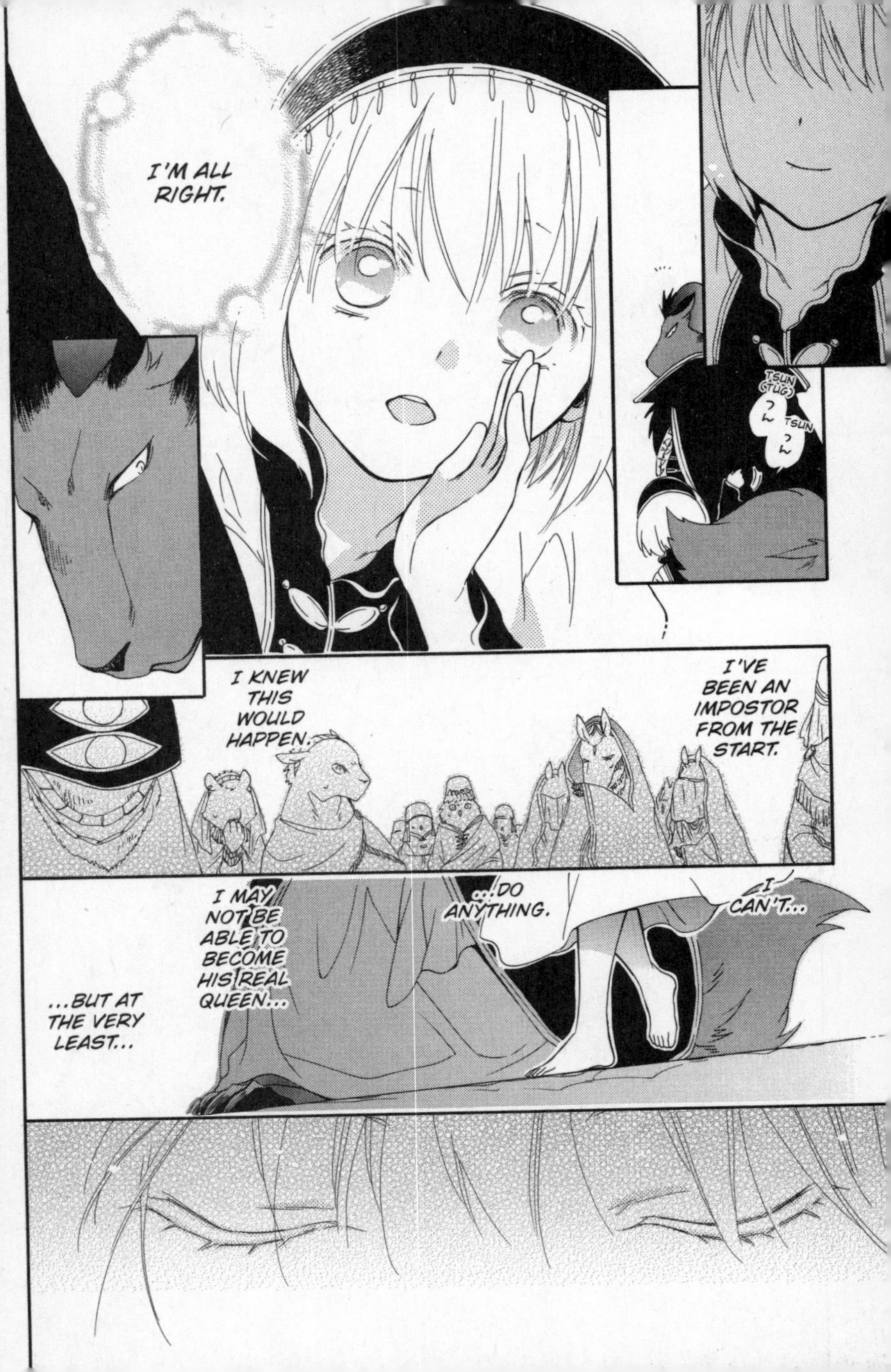
TSUN (TUG)
TSUN
I'M ALL RIGHT.
I'VE BEEN AN IMPOSTOR FROM THE START.
I KNEW THIS WOULD HAPPEN.
I CAN'T...
...DO ANYTHING.
I MAY NOT BE ABLE TO BECOME HIS REAL QUEEN...
...BUT AT THE VERY LEAST...

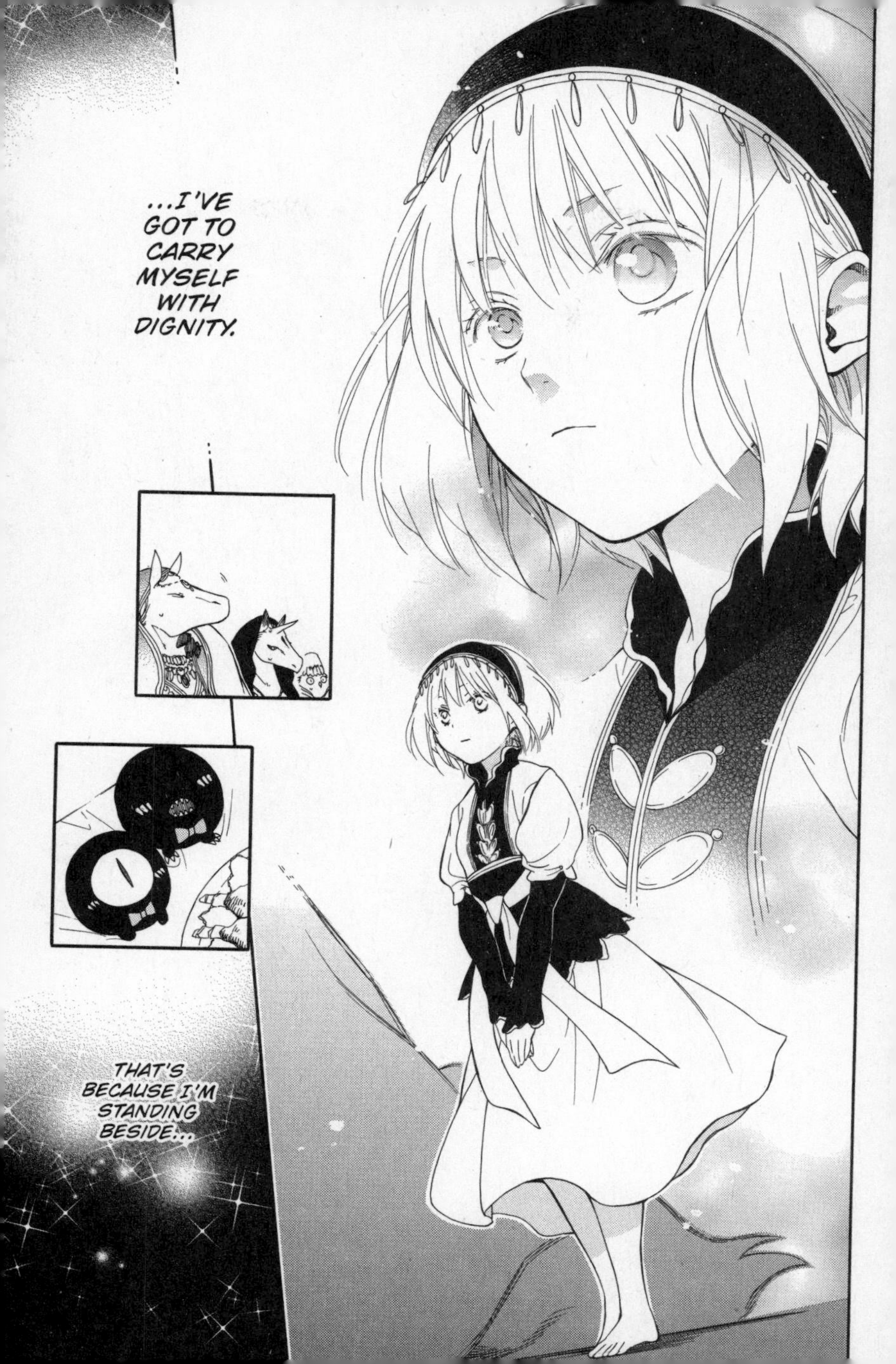
...I'VE GOT TO CARRY MYSELF WITH DIGNITY.
THAT'S BECAUSE I'M STANDING BESIDE...

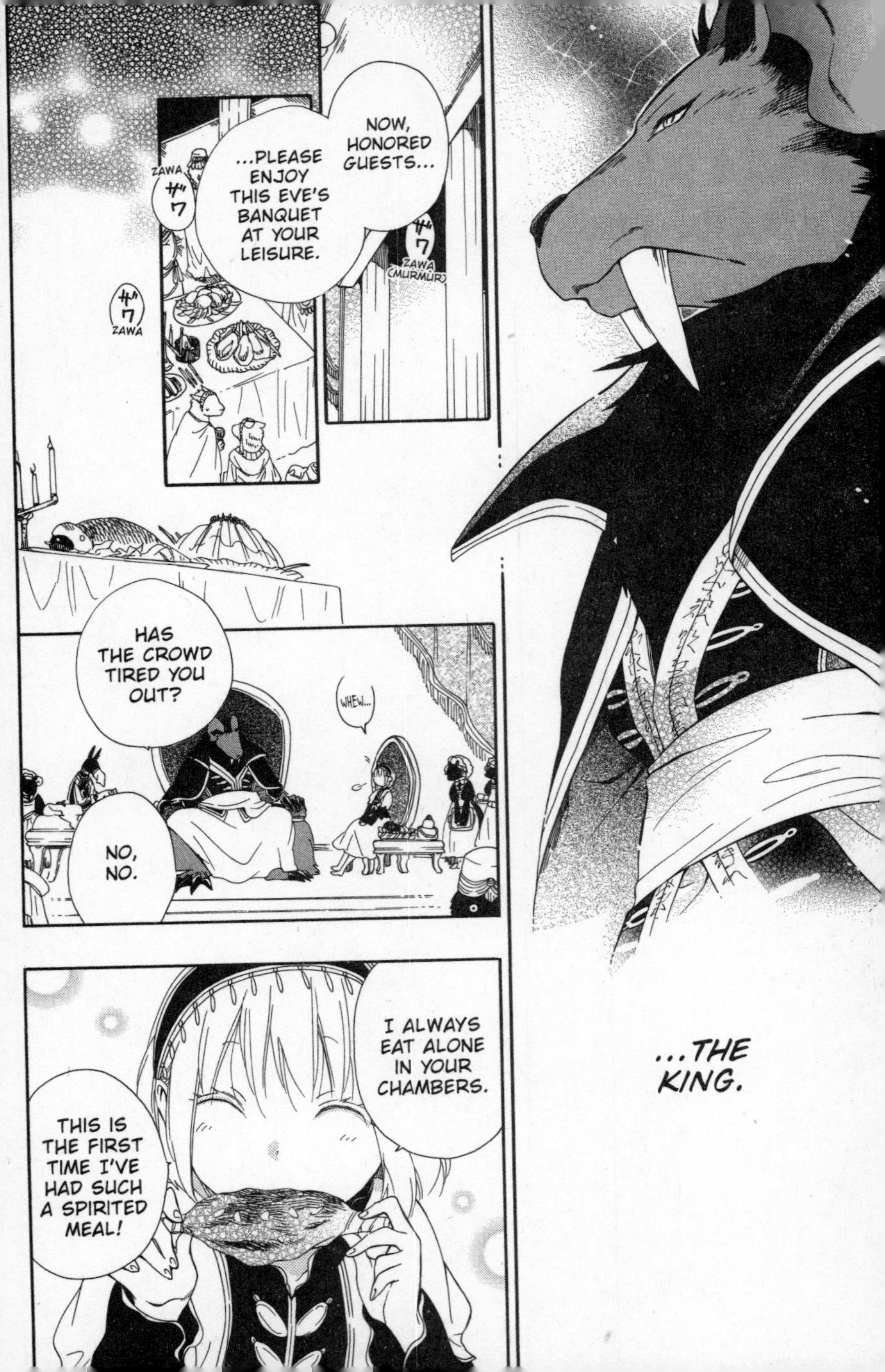
...THE KING.
NOW, HONORED GUESTS...
...PLEASE ENJOY THIS EVE'S BANQUET AT YOUR LEISURE.
ザワ ZAWA (MURMUR)
ザワ ZAWA
ザワ ZAWA
HAS THE CROWD TIRED YOU OUT?
WHEW...
NO, NO.
I ALWAYS EAT ALONE IN YOUR CHAMBERS.
THIS IS THE FIRST TIME I'VE HAD SUCH A SPIRITED MEAL!

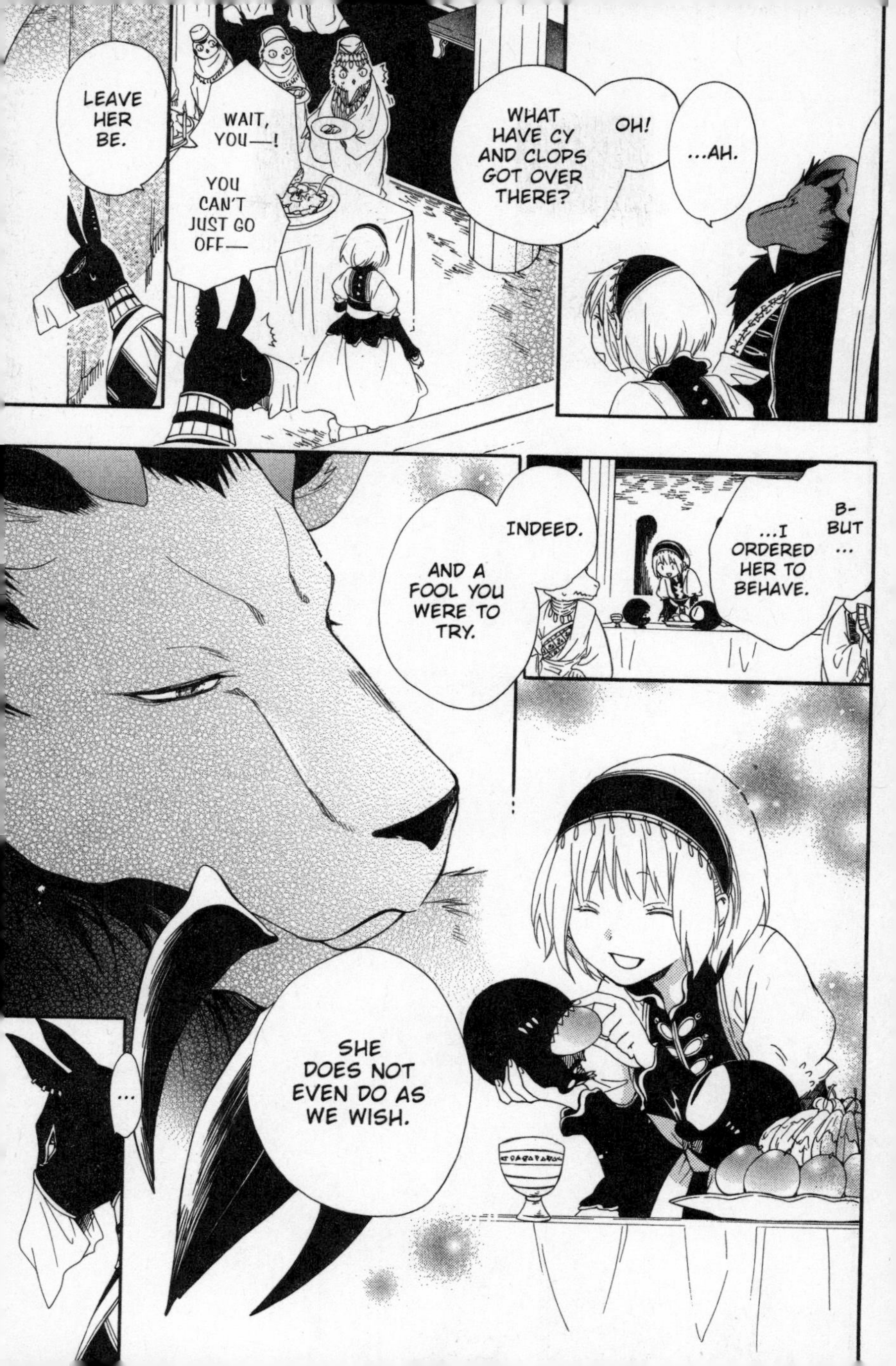
...AH.
OH!
WHAT HAVE CY AND CLOPS GOT OVER THERE?
WAIT, YOU—!
YOU CAN'T JUST GO OFF—
LEAVE HER BE.
B-BUT...
...I ORDERED HER TO BEHAVE.
INDEED.
AND A FOOL YOU WERE TO TRY.
SHE DOES NOT EVEN DO AS WE WISH.
...

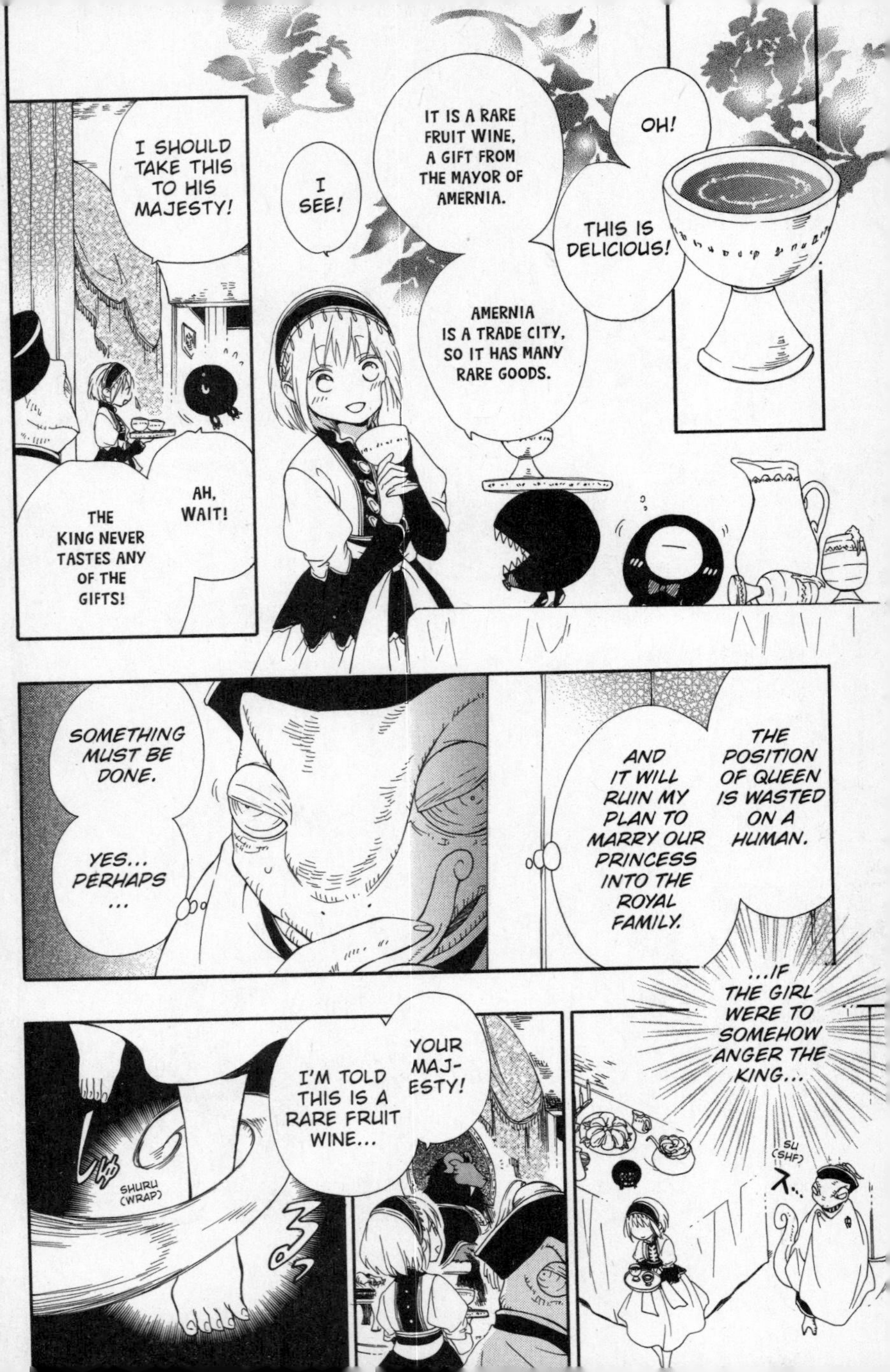
OH!
THIS IS DELICIOUS!
IT IS A RARE FRUIT WINE, A GIFT FROM THE MAYOR OF AMERNIA.
I SEE!
AMERNIA IS A TRADE CITY, SO IT HAS MANY RARE GOODS.
I SHOULD TAKE THIS TO HIS MAJESTY!
AH, WAIT!
THE KING NEVER TASTES ANY OF THE GIFTS!
THE POSITION OF QUEEN IS WASTED ON A HUMAN.
AND IT WILL RUIN MY PLAN TO MARRY OUR PRINCESS INTO THE ROYAL FAMILY.
SOMETHING MUST BE DONE.
YES... PERHAPS ...
...IF THE GIRL WERE TO SOMEHOW ANGER THE KING...
SU (SHF)
YOUR MAJ-ESTY!
I'M TOLD THIS IS A RARE FRUIT WINE...
SHURU (WRAP)

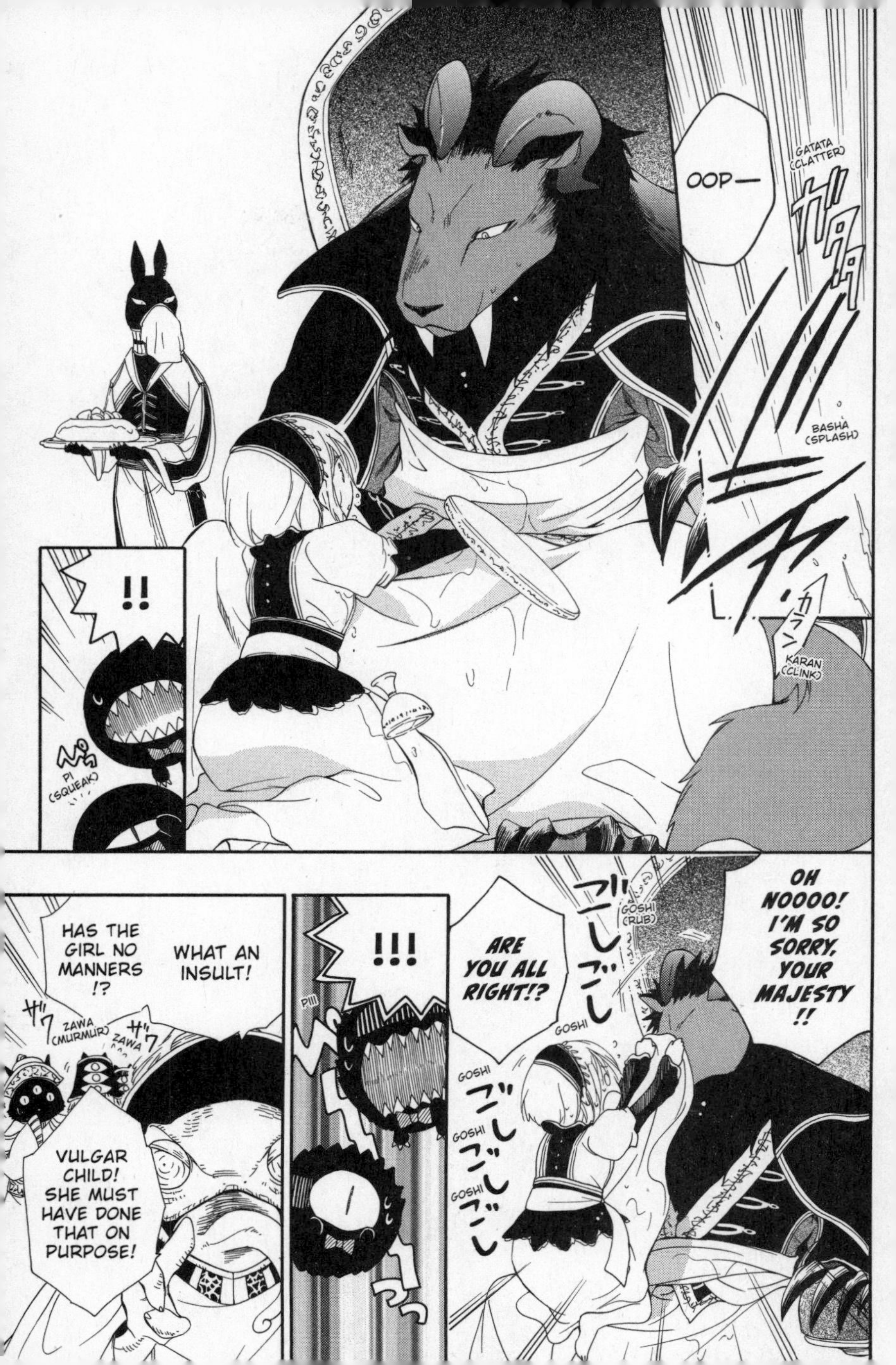
OOP—
GATATA (CLATTER)
BASHA (SPLASH)
KARAN (CLINK)
!!
PI (SQUEAK)
OH NOOOO! I'M SO SORRY, YOUR MAJESTY!!
ARE YOU ALL RIGHT!?
GOSHI (RUB)
GOSHI
GOSHI
GOSHI
GOSHI
!!!
PIII
WHAT AN INSULT!
HAS THE GIRL NO MANNERS!?
ZAWA (MURMUR)
ZAWA
VULGAR CHILD! SHE MUST HAVE DONE THAT ON PURPOSE!

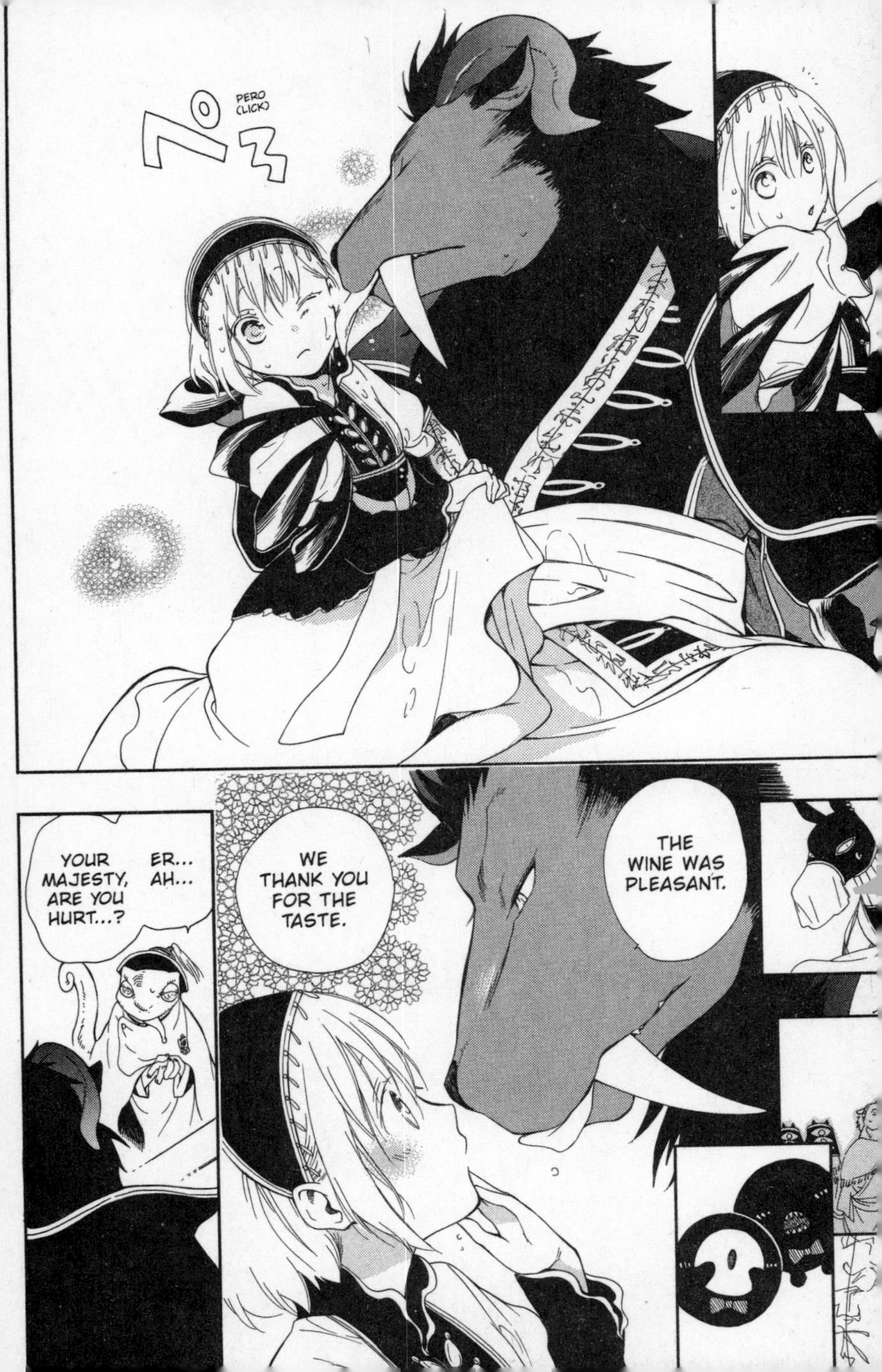
ペロ
PERO (LICK)
THE WINE WAS PLEASANT.
WE THANK YOU FOR THE TASTE.
ER... AH...
YOUR MAJESTY, ARE YOU HURT...?

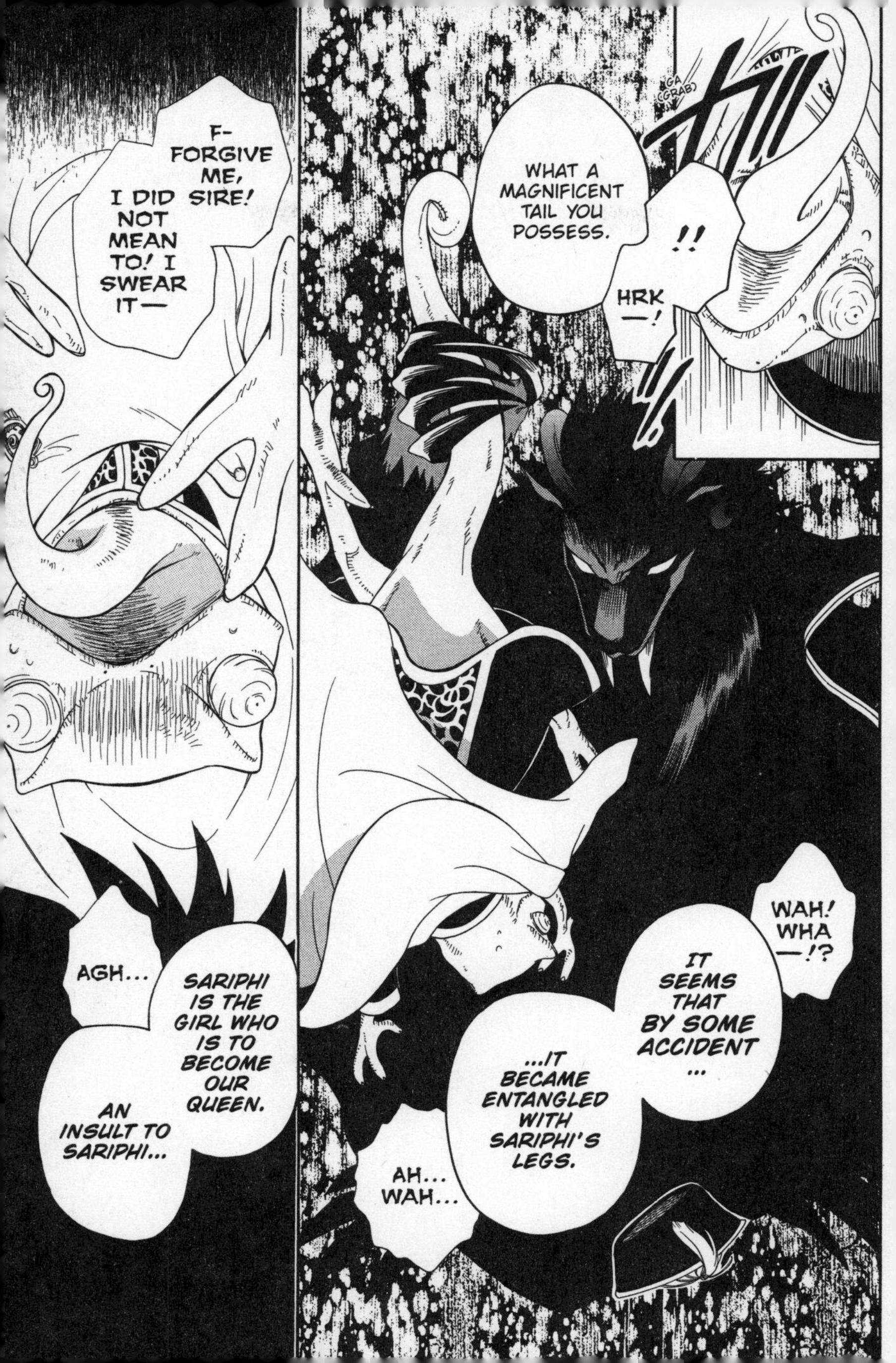
GA (GRAB)
!!
HRK —!
WHAT A MAGNIFICENT TAIL YOU POSSESS.
WAH! WHA—!?
IT SEEMS THAT BY SOME ACCIDENT ...
...IT BECAME ENTANGLED WITH SARIPHI'S LEGS.
AH... WAH...
F-FORGIVE ME, SIRE! I DID NOT MEAN TO! I SWEAR IT—
SARIPHI IS THE GIRL WHO IS TO BECOME OUR QUEEN.
AGH...
AN INSULT TO SARIPHI...

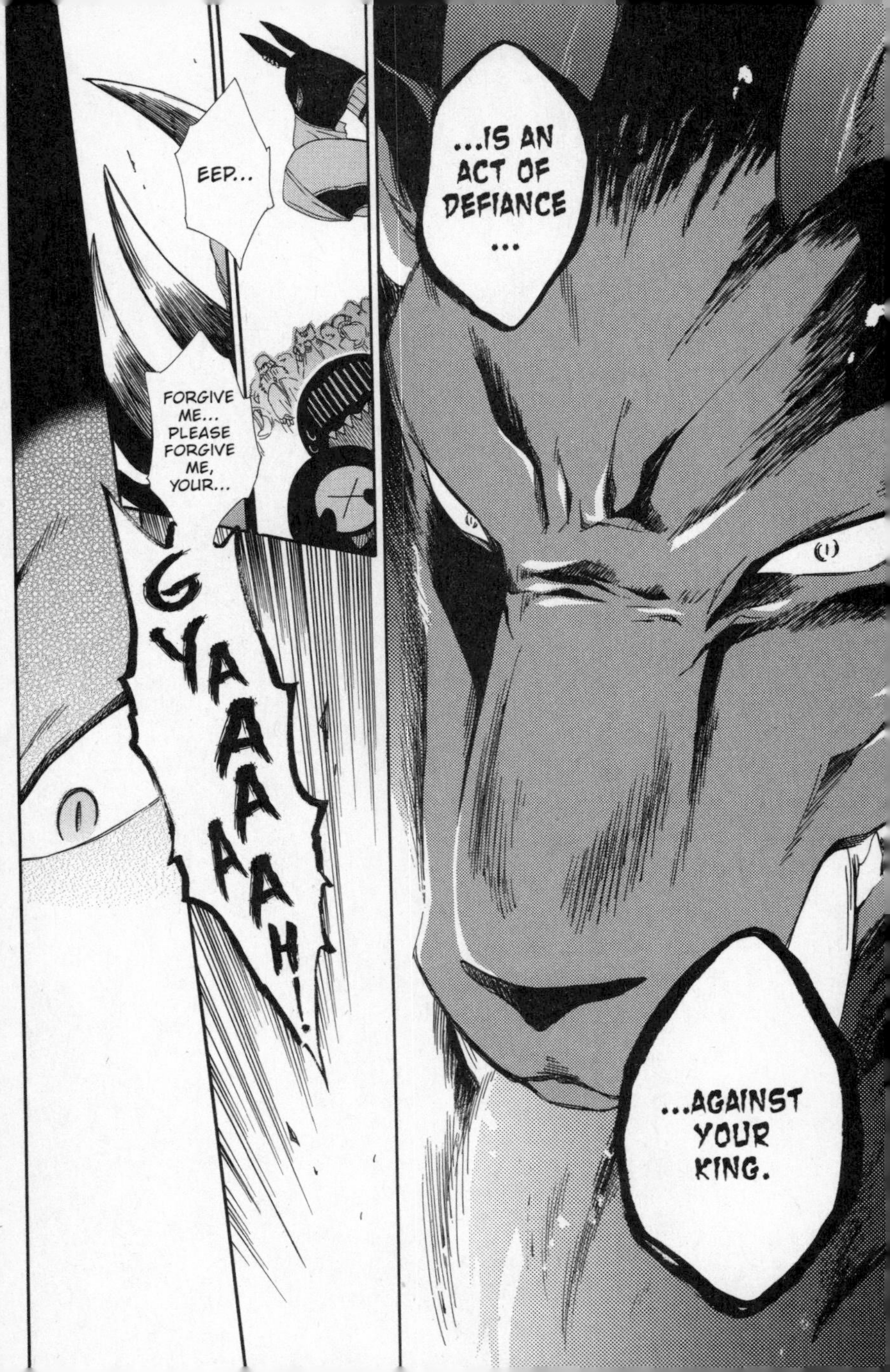
...IS AN ACT OF DEFIANCE...
...AGAINST YOUR KING.
EEP...
FORGIVE ME... PLEASE FORGIVE ME, YOUR...
GYAAAAAH!

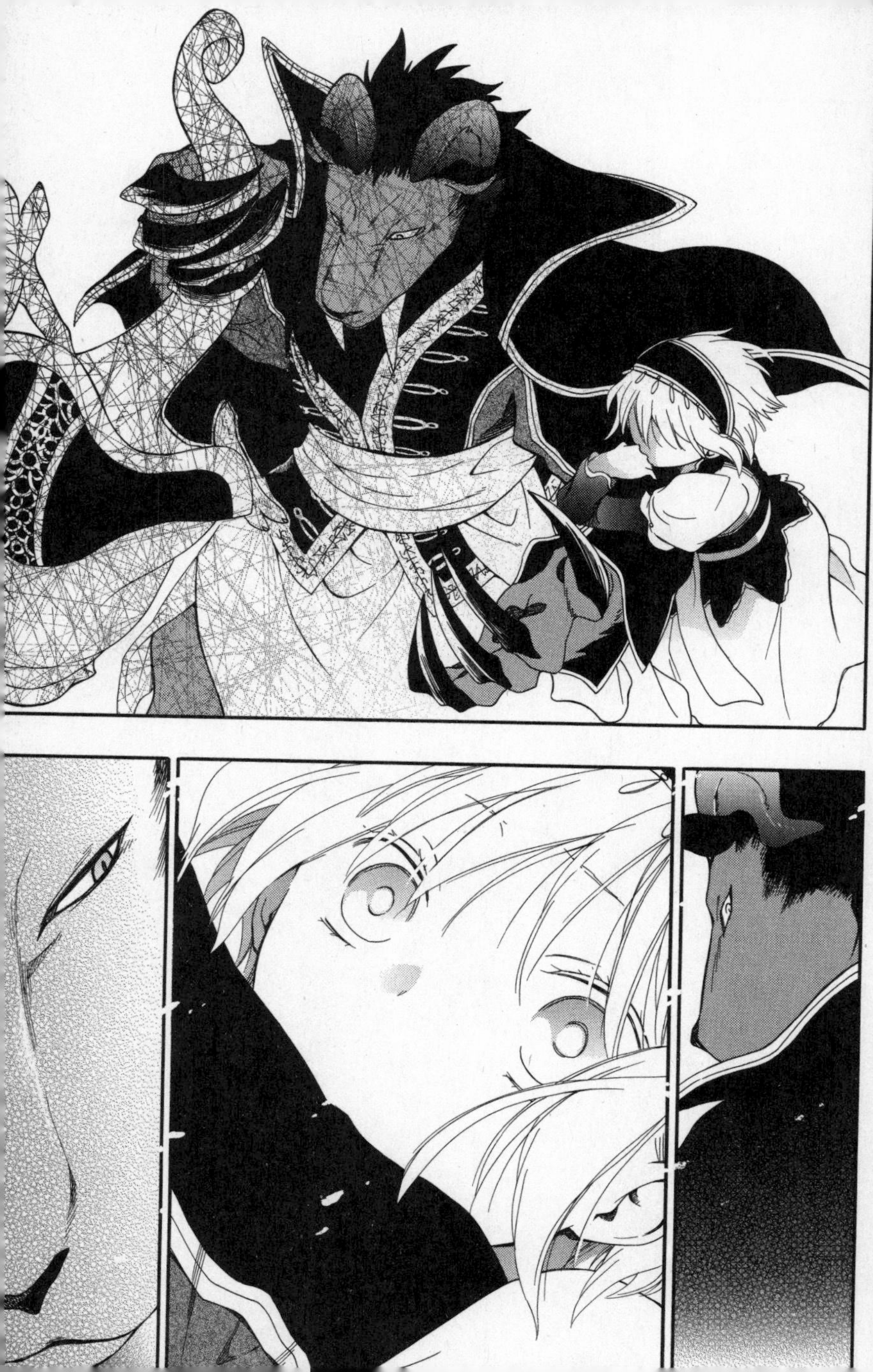

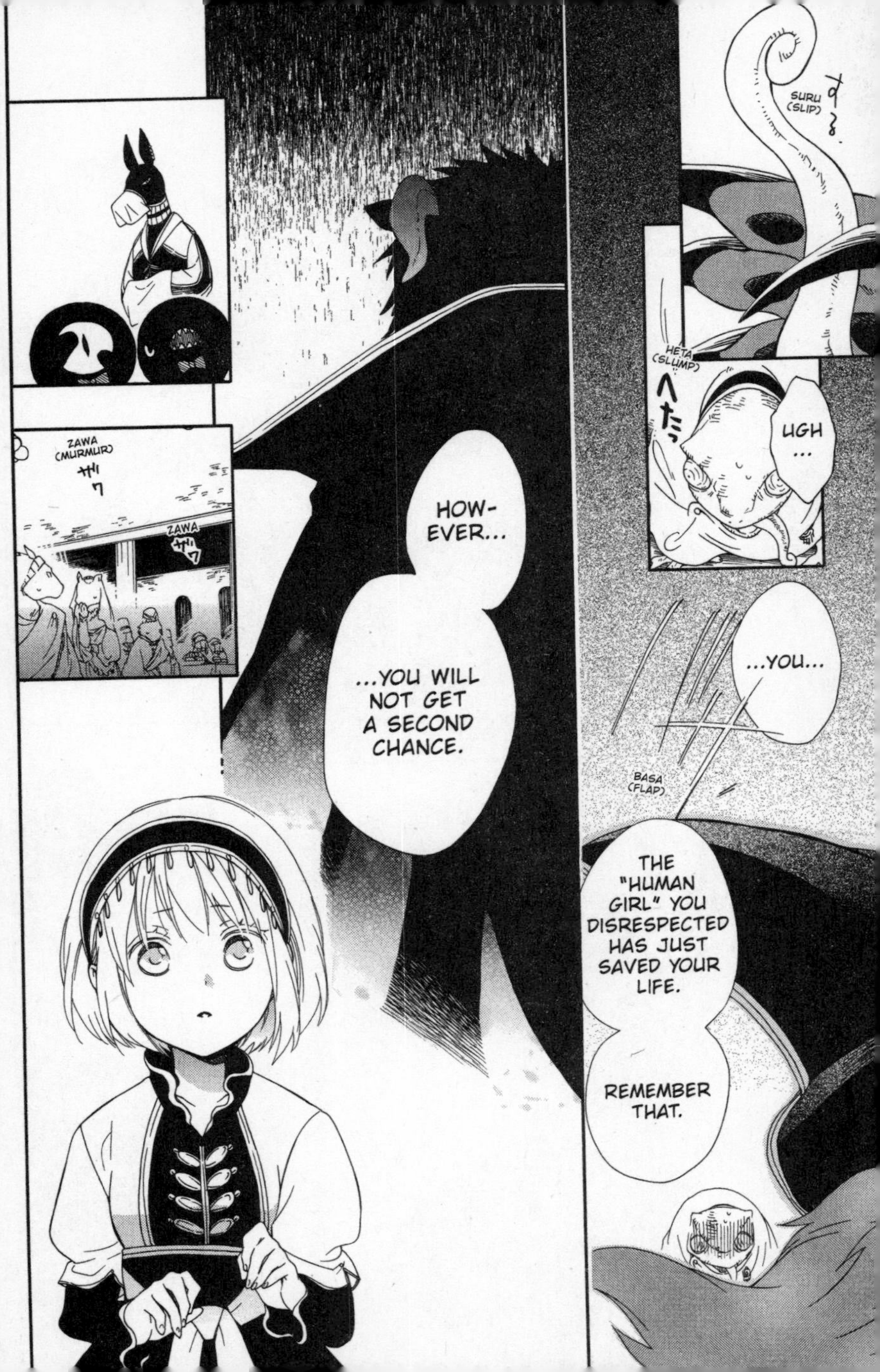
SURU (SLIP)
する.
HETA (SLUMP)
へたっ
UGH ...
...YOU...
BASA (FLAP)
THE "HUMAN GIRL" YOU DISRESPECTED HAS JUST SAVED YOUR LIFE.
REMEMBER THAT.
HOW-EVER...
...YOU WILL NOT GET A SECOND CHANCE.
ZAWA (MURMUR)
ザワ
ZAWA
ザワ

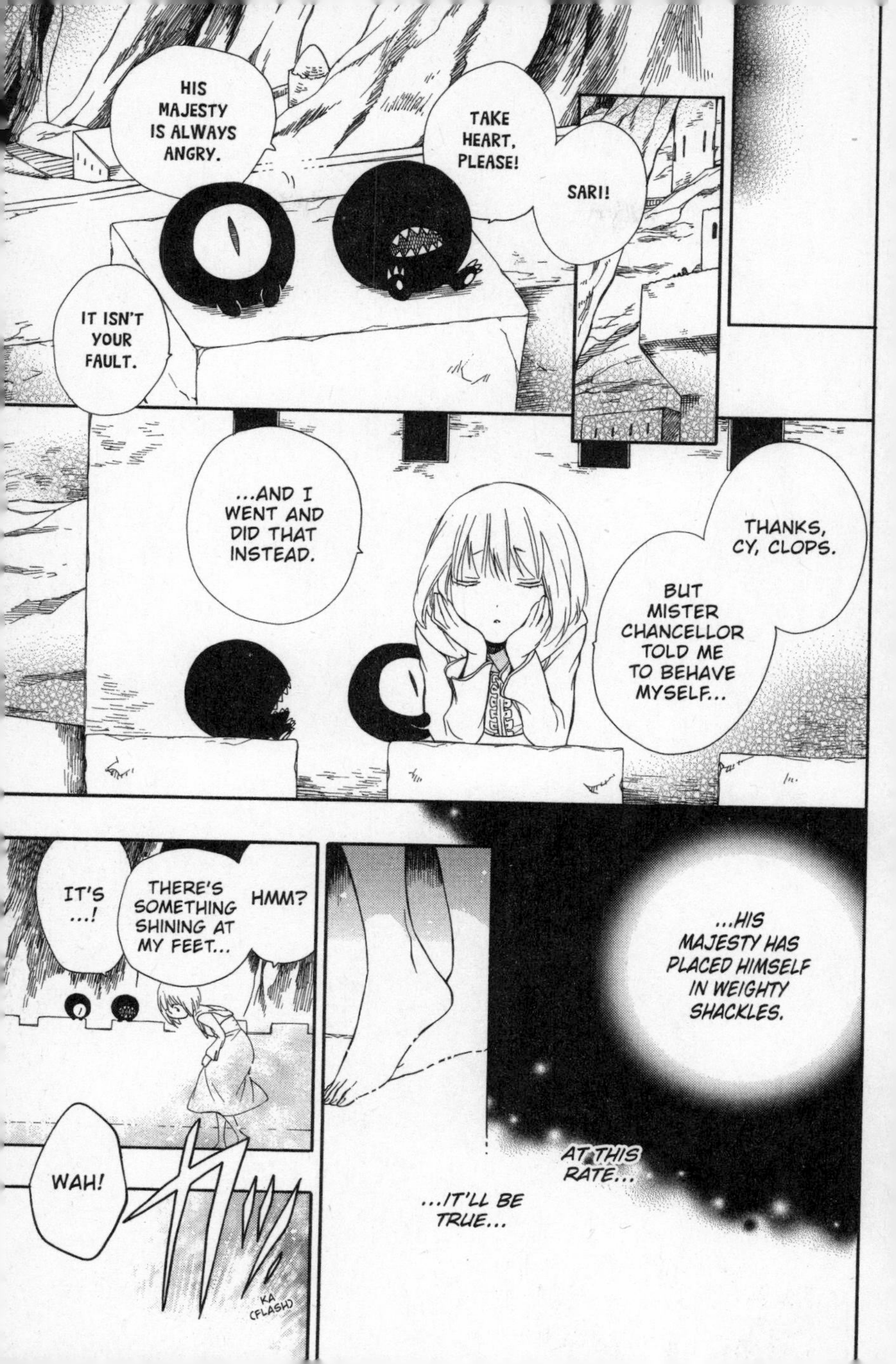
SARI!
TAKE HEART, PLEASE!
HIS MAJESTY IS ALWAYS ANGRY.
IT ISN'T YOUR FAULT.
THANKS, CY, CLOPS.
BUT MISTER CHANCELLOR TOLD ME TO BEHAVE MYSELF...
...AND I WENT AND DID THAT INSTEAD.
...HIS MAJESTY HAS PLACED HIMSELF IN WEIGHTY SHACKLES.
AT THIS RATE...
...IT'LL BE TRUE...
HMM?
THERE'S SOMETHING SHINING AT MY FEET...
IT'S ...!
WAH!
KA (FLASH)

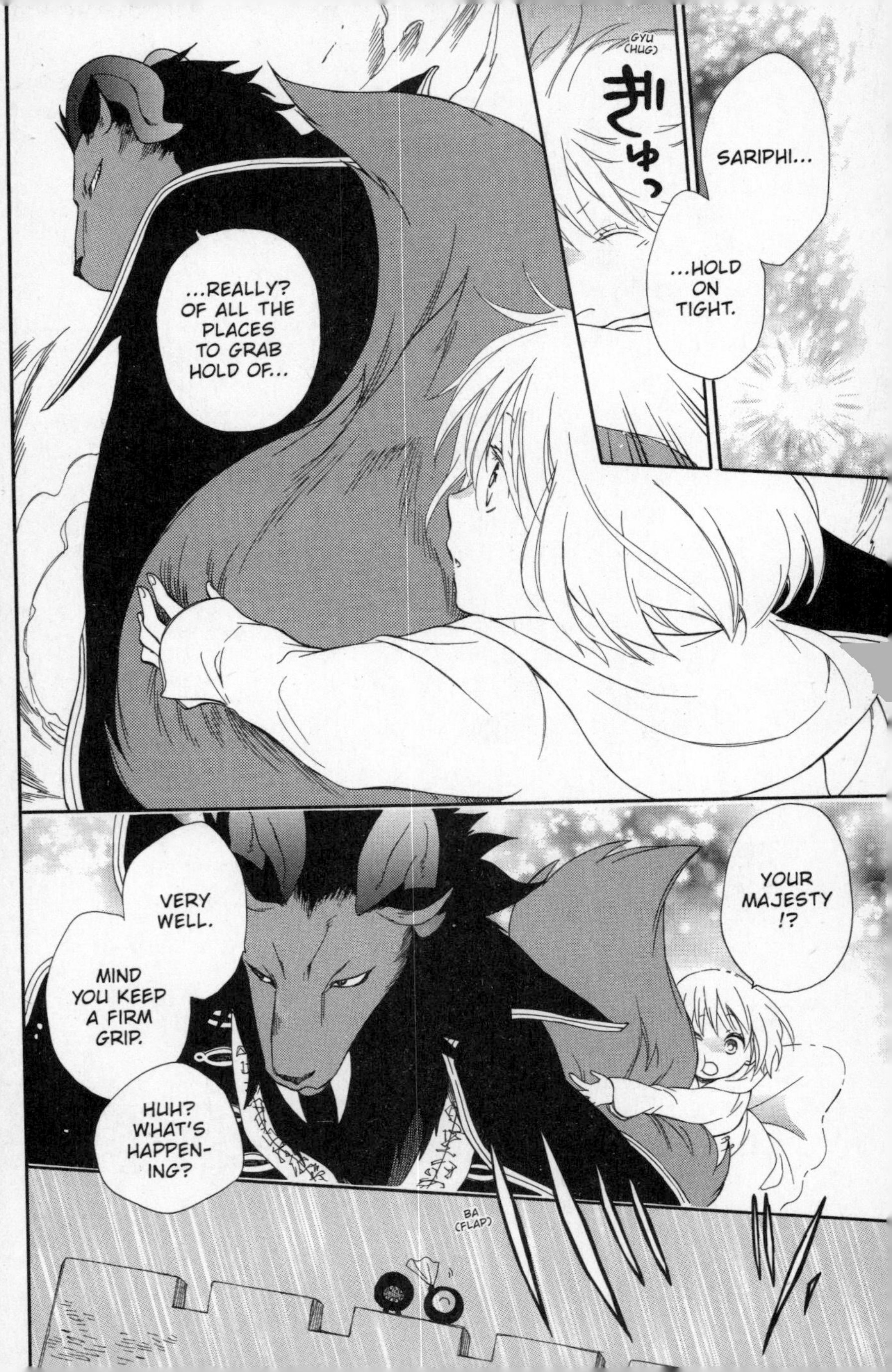
GYU (HUG)
ぎゅっ
SARIPHI...
...HOLD ON TIGHT.
...REALLY? OF ALL THE PLACES TO GRAB HOLD OF...
YOUR MAJESTY !?
VERY WELL.
MIND YOU KEEP A FIRM GRIP.
HUH? WHAT'S HAPPEN- ING?
BA (FLAP)

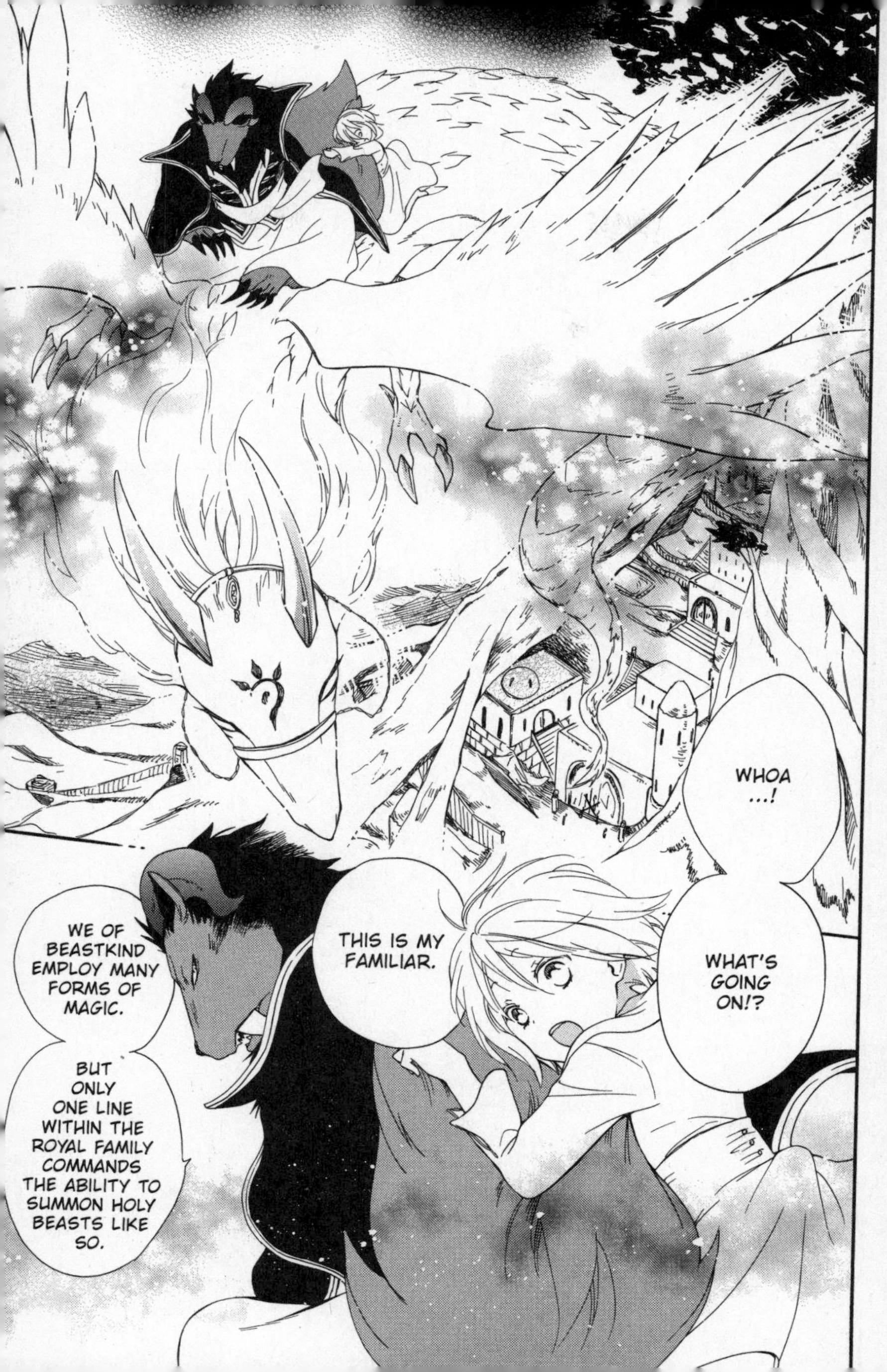
WHOA ...!
WHAT'S GOING ON!?
THIS IS MY FAMILIAR.
WE OF BEASTKIND EMPLOY MANY FORMS OF MAGIC.
BUT ONLY ONE LINE WITHIN THE ROYAL FAMILY COMMANDS THE ABILITY TO SUMMON HOLY BEASTS LIKE SO.

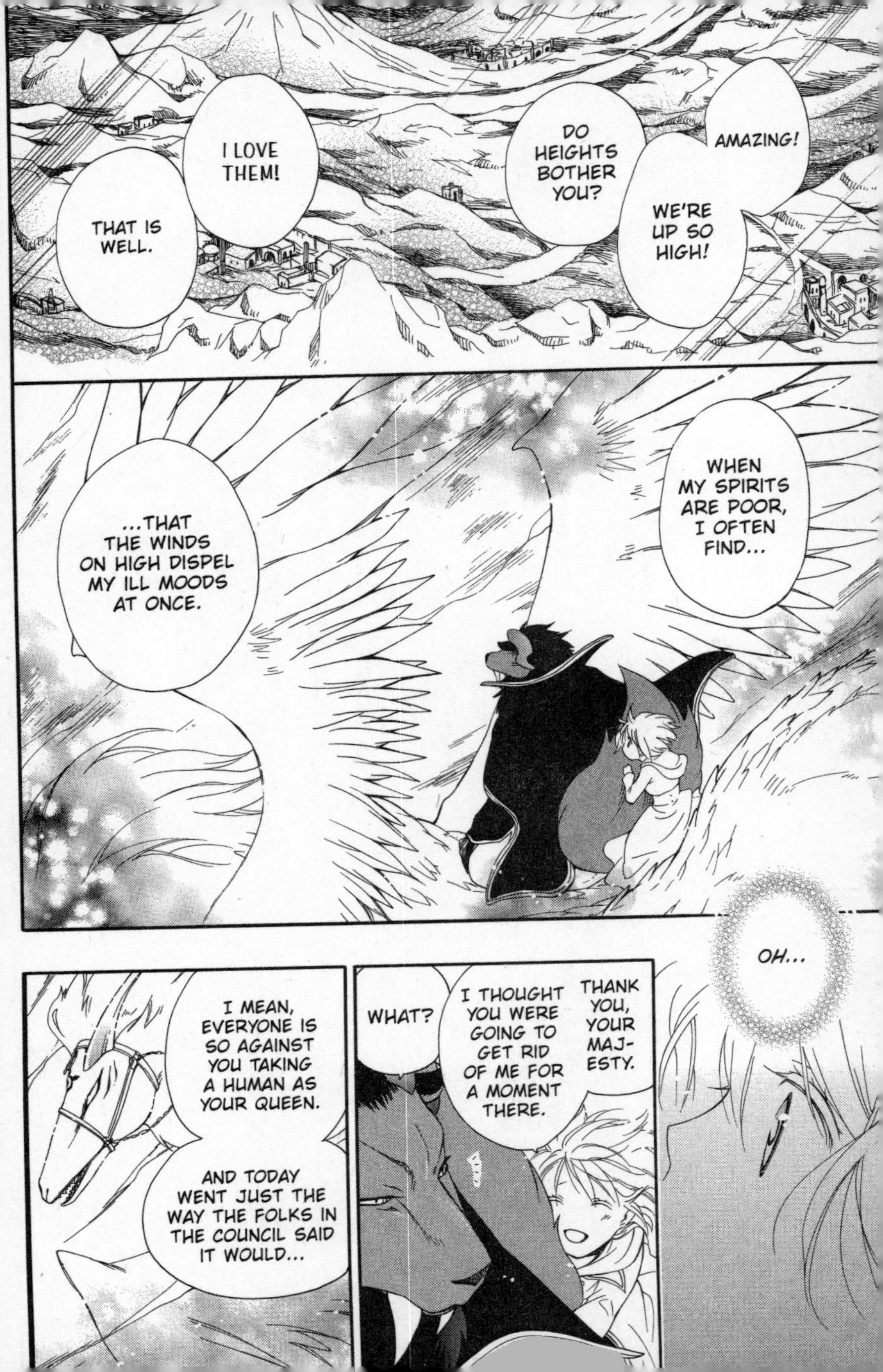
AMAZING!
WE'RE UP SO HIGH!
DO HEIGHTS BOTHER YOU?
I LOVE THEM!
THAT IS WELL.
WHEN MY SPIRITS ARE POOR, I OFTEN FIND...
...THAT THE WINDS ON HIGH DISPEL MY ILL MOODS AT ONCE.
OH...
THANK YOU, YOUR MAJ-ESTY.
I THOUGHT YOU WERE GOING TO GET RID OF ME FOR A MOMENT THERE.
WHAT?
I MEAN, EVERYONE IS SO AGAINST YOU TAKING A HUMAN AS YOUR QUEEN.
AND TODAY WENT JUST THE WAY THE FOLKS IN THE COUNCIL SAID IT WOULD...

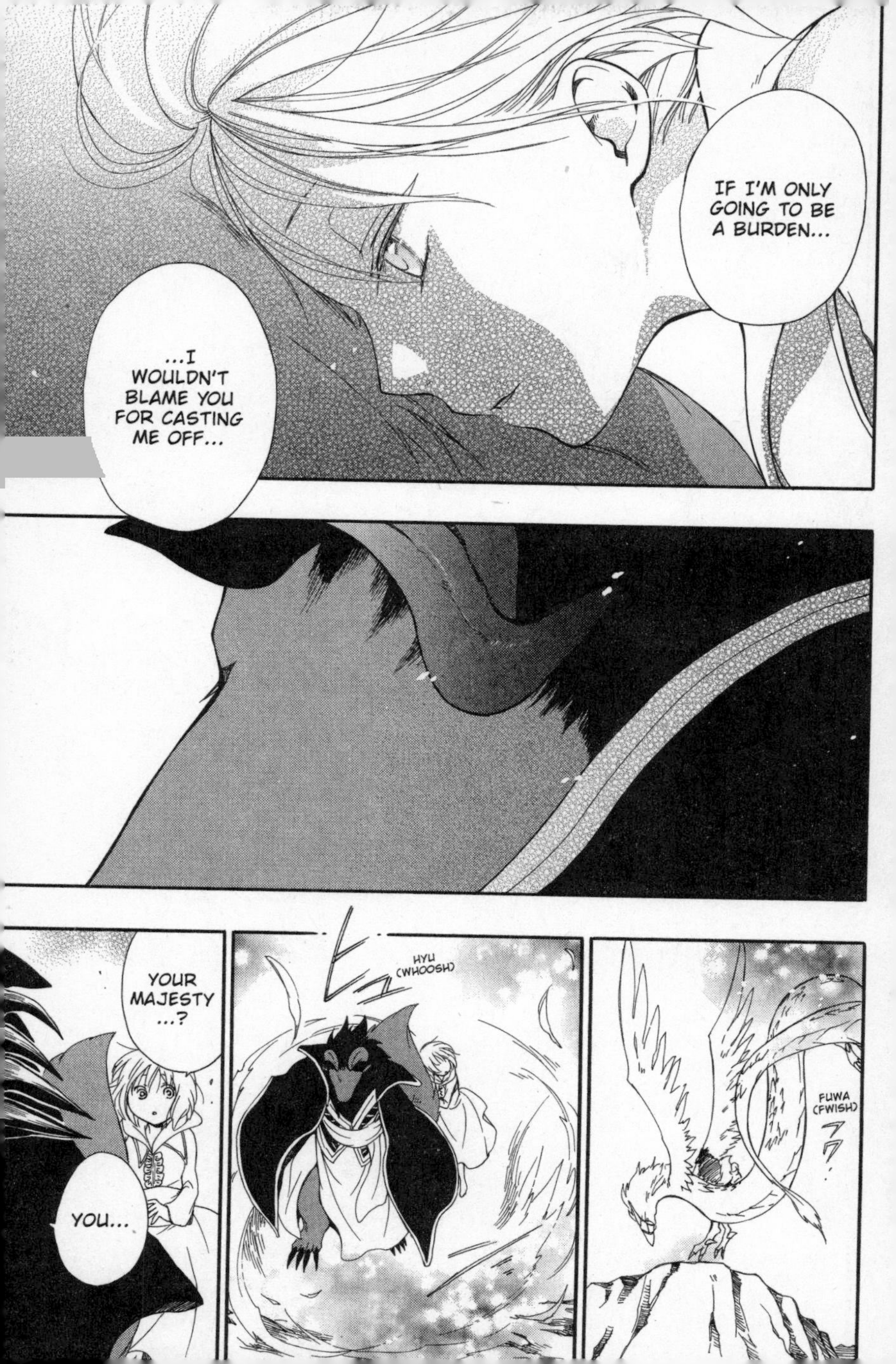
IF I'M ONLY GOING TO BE A BURDEN...
...I WOULDN'T BLAME YOU FOR CASTING ME OFF...
FUWA (FWISH)
HYU (WHOOSH)
YOUR MAJESTY ...?
YOU...

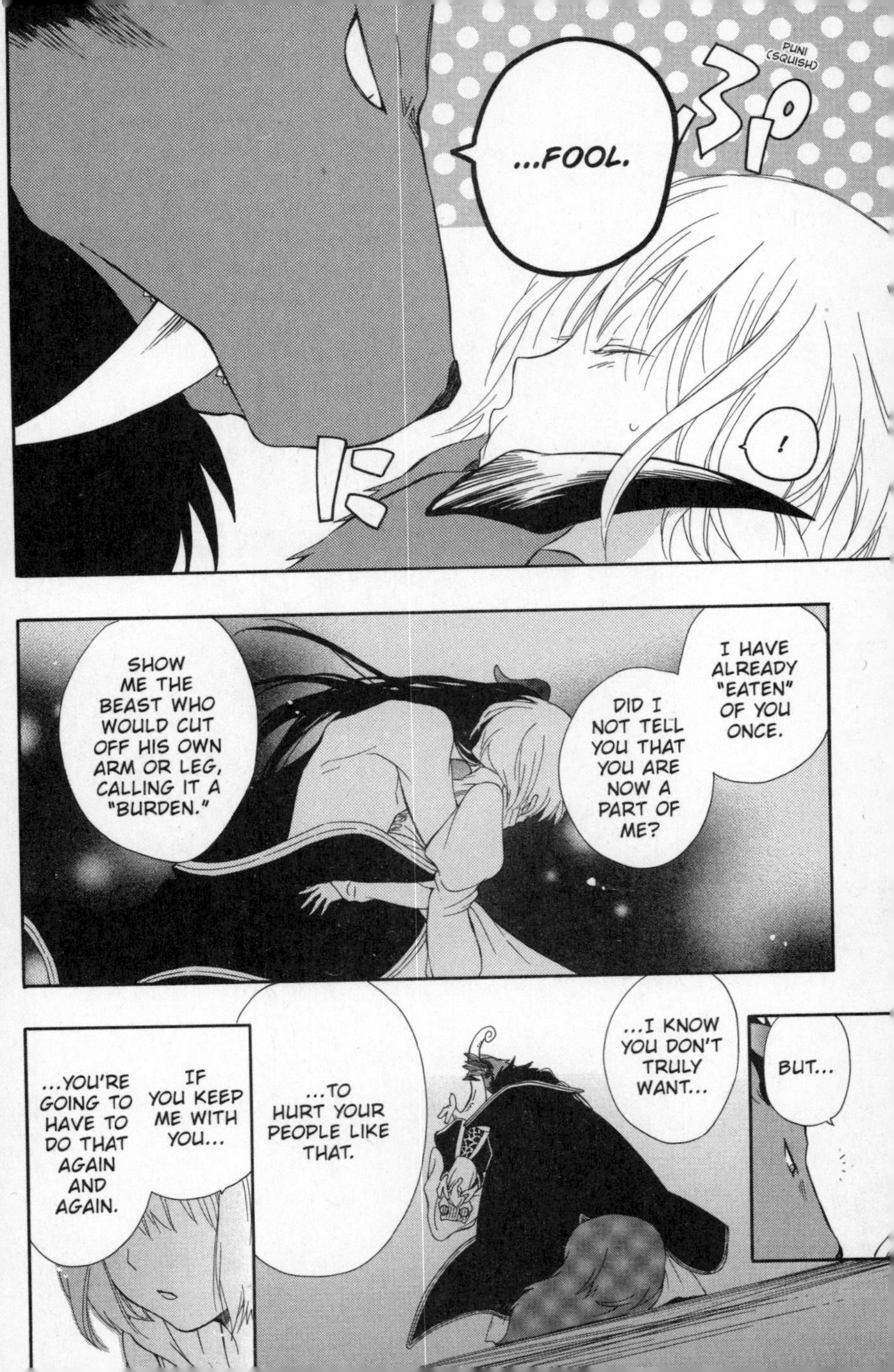
PUNI (SQUISH)
...FOOL.
!
I HAVE ALREADY "EATEN" OF YOU ONCE.
DID I NOT TELL YOU THAT YOU ARE NOW A PART OF ME?
SHOW ME THE BEAST WHO WOULD CUT OFF HIS OWN ARM OR LEG, CALLING IT A "BURDEN."
BUT...
...I KNOW YOU DON'T TRULY WANT...
...TO HURT YOUR PEOPLE LIKE THAT.
IF YOU KEEP ME WITH YOU...
...YOU'RE GOING TO HAVE TO DO THAT AGAIN AND AGAIN.

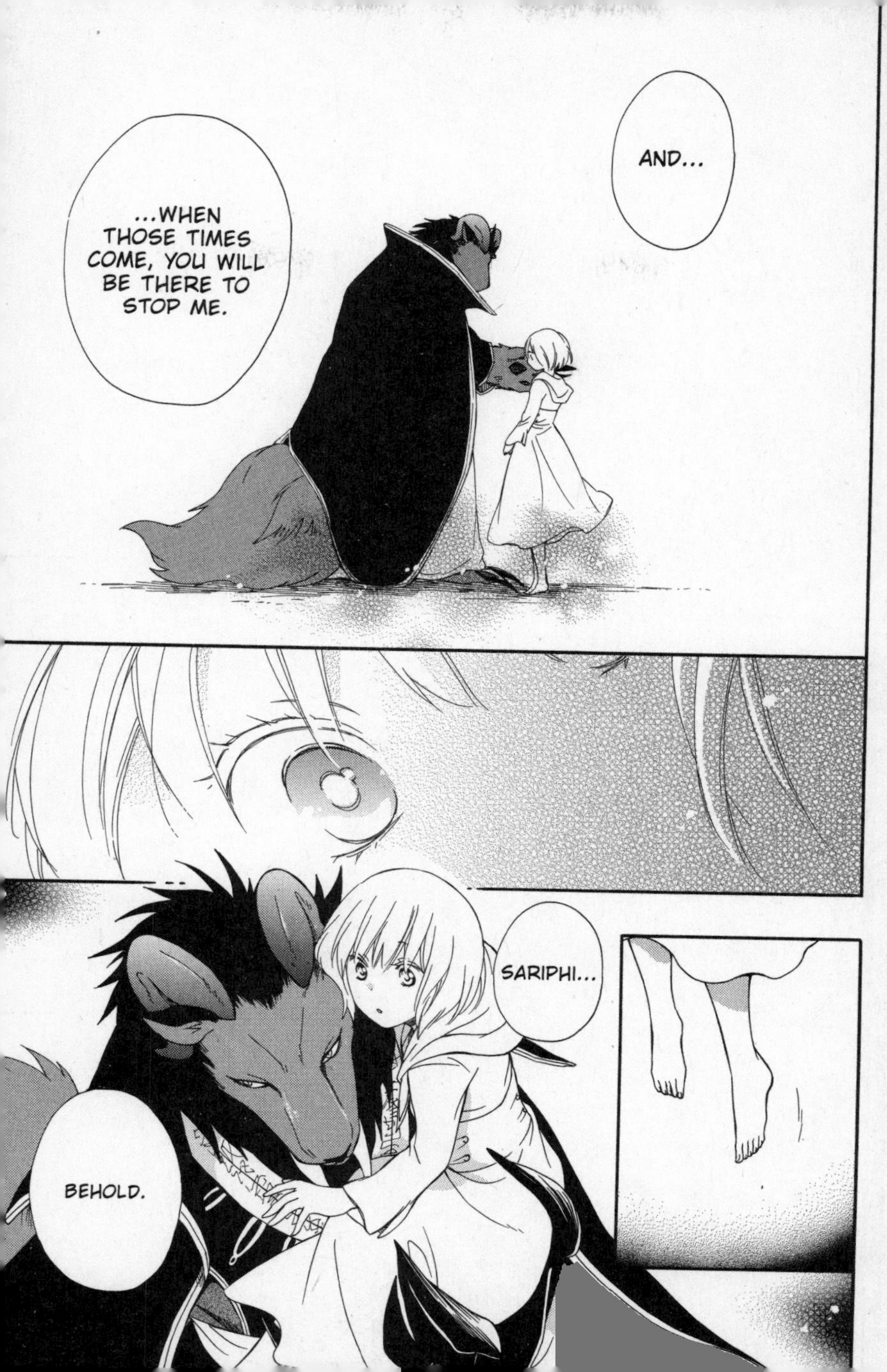
AND...
...WHEN THOSE TIMES COME, YOU WILL BE THERE TO STOP ME.
SARIPHI...
BEHOLD.

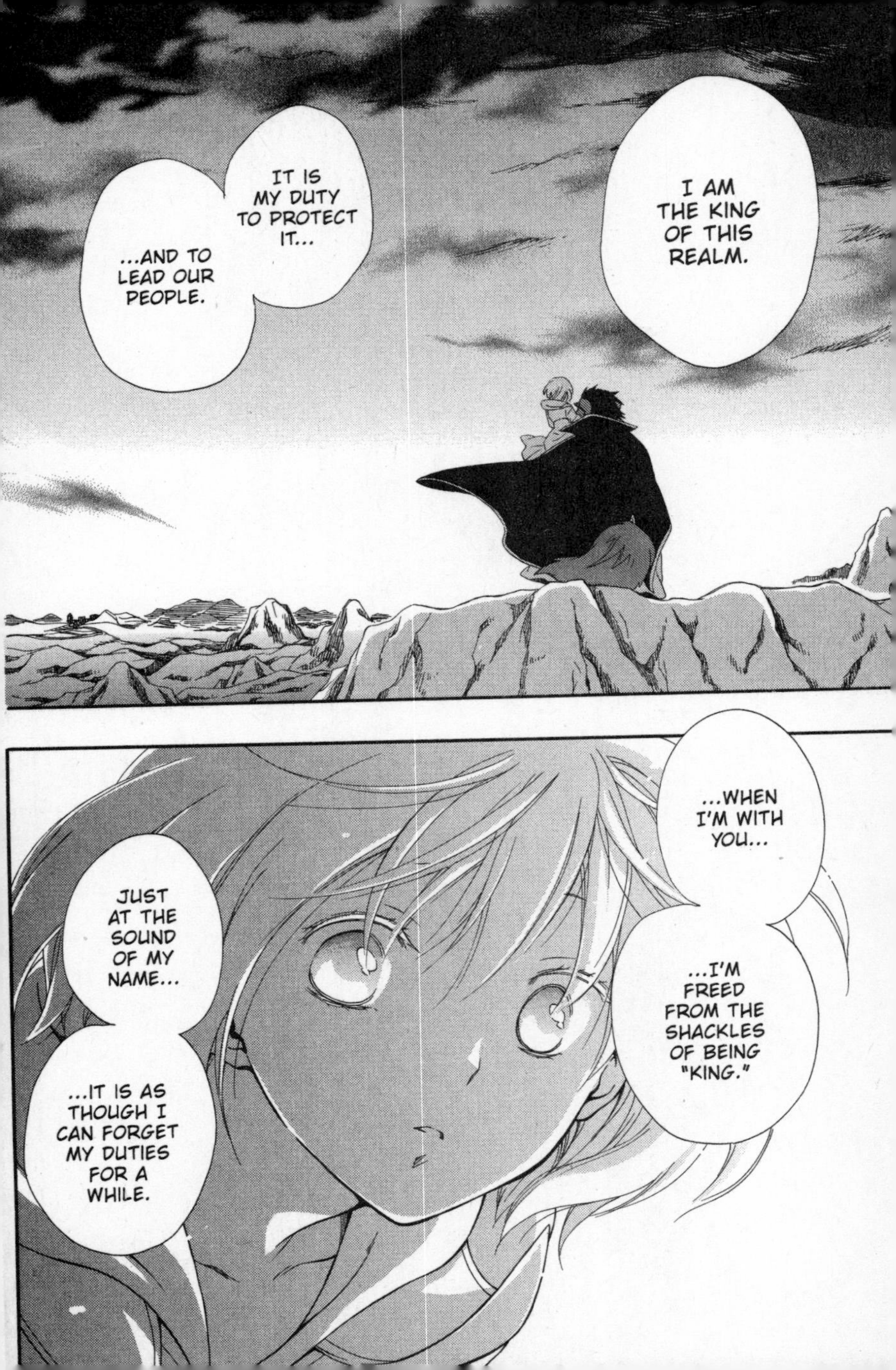
I AM THE KING OF THIS REALM.
IT IS MY DUTY TO PROTECT IT...
...AND TO LEAD OUR PEOPLE.
...WHEN I'M WITH YOU...
...I'M FREED FROM THE SHACKLES OF BEING "KING."
JUST AT THE SOUND OF MY NAME...
...IT IS AS THOUGH I CAN FORGET MY DUTIES FOR A WHILE.

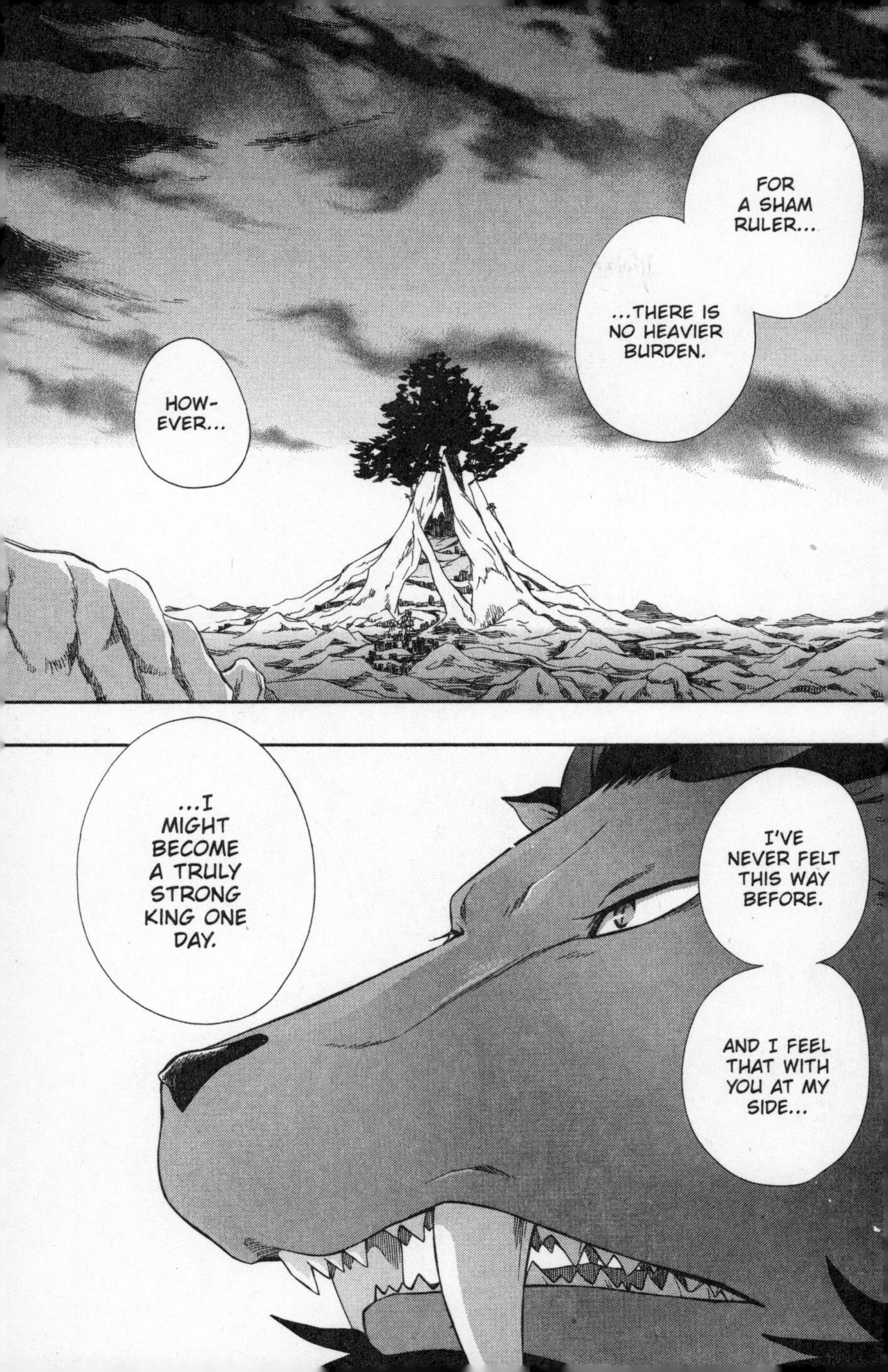
FOR A SHAM RULER...
...THERE IS NO HEAVIER BURDEN.
HOW-EVER...
I'VE NEVER FELT THIS WAY BEFORE.
AND I FEEL THAT WITH YOU AT MY SIDE...
...I MIGHT BECOME A TRULY STRONG KING ONE DAY.

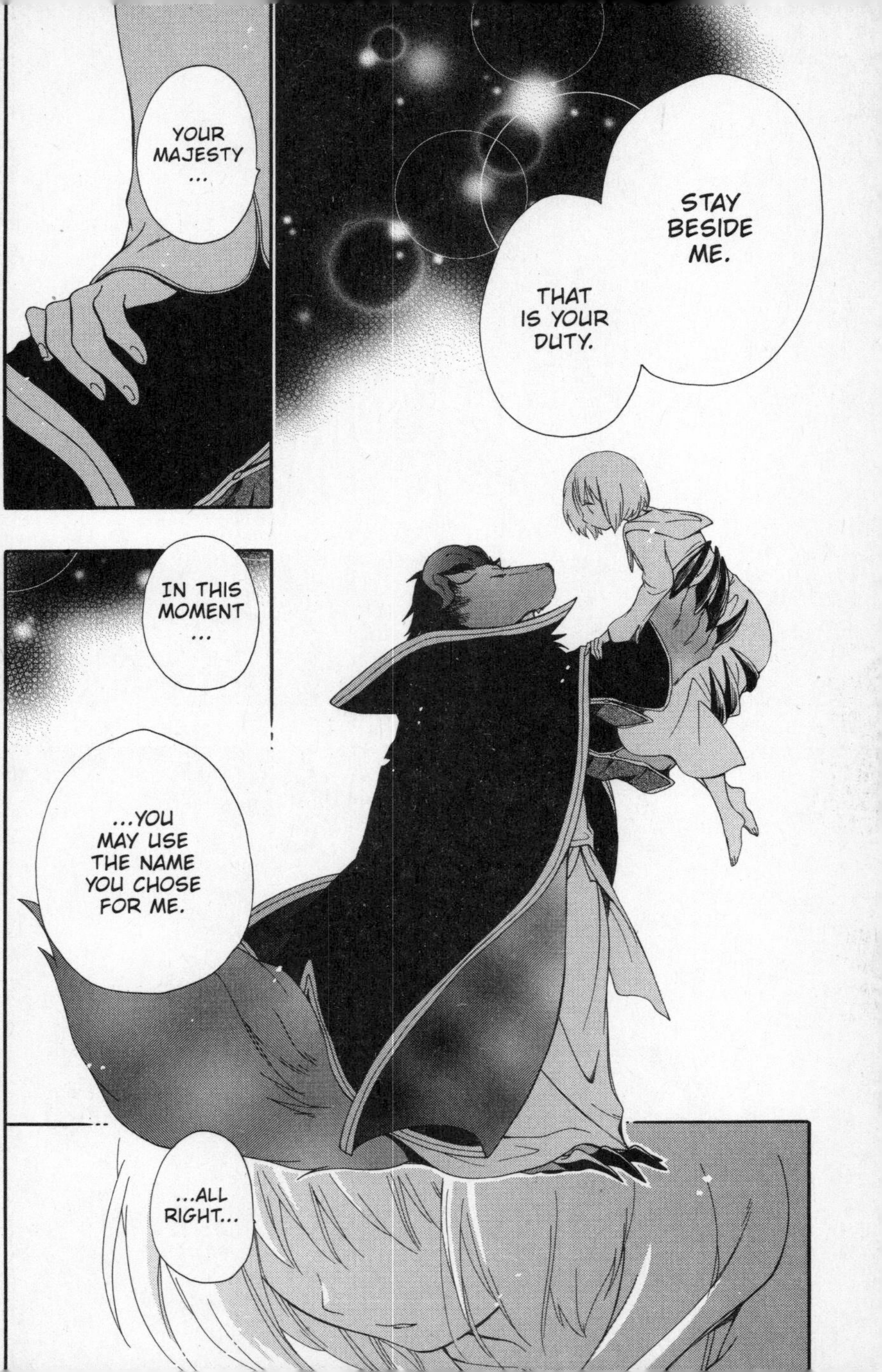
STAY BESIDE ME.
THAT IS YOUR DUTY.
YOUR MAJESTY...
IN THIS MOMENT...
...YOU MAY USE THE NAME YOU CHOSE FOR ME.
...ALL RIGHT...

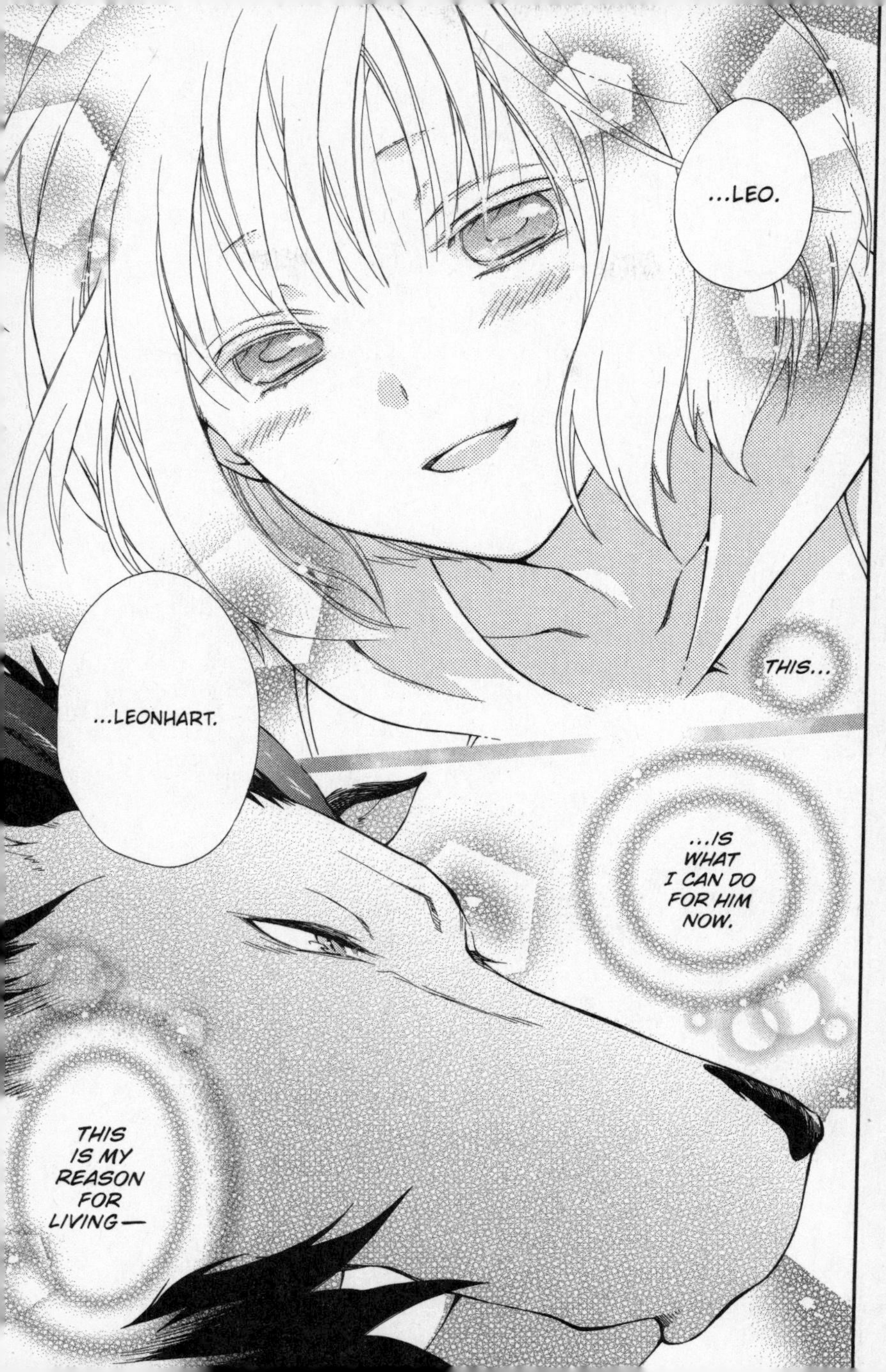
...LEO.
...LEONHART.
THIS...
...IS WHAT I CAN DO FOR HIM NOW.
THIS IS MY REASON FOR LIVING—

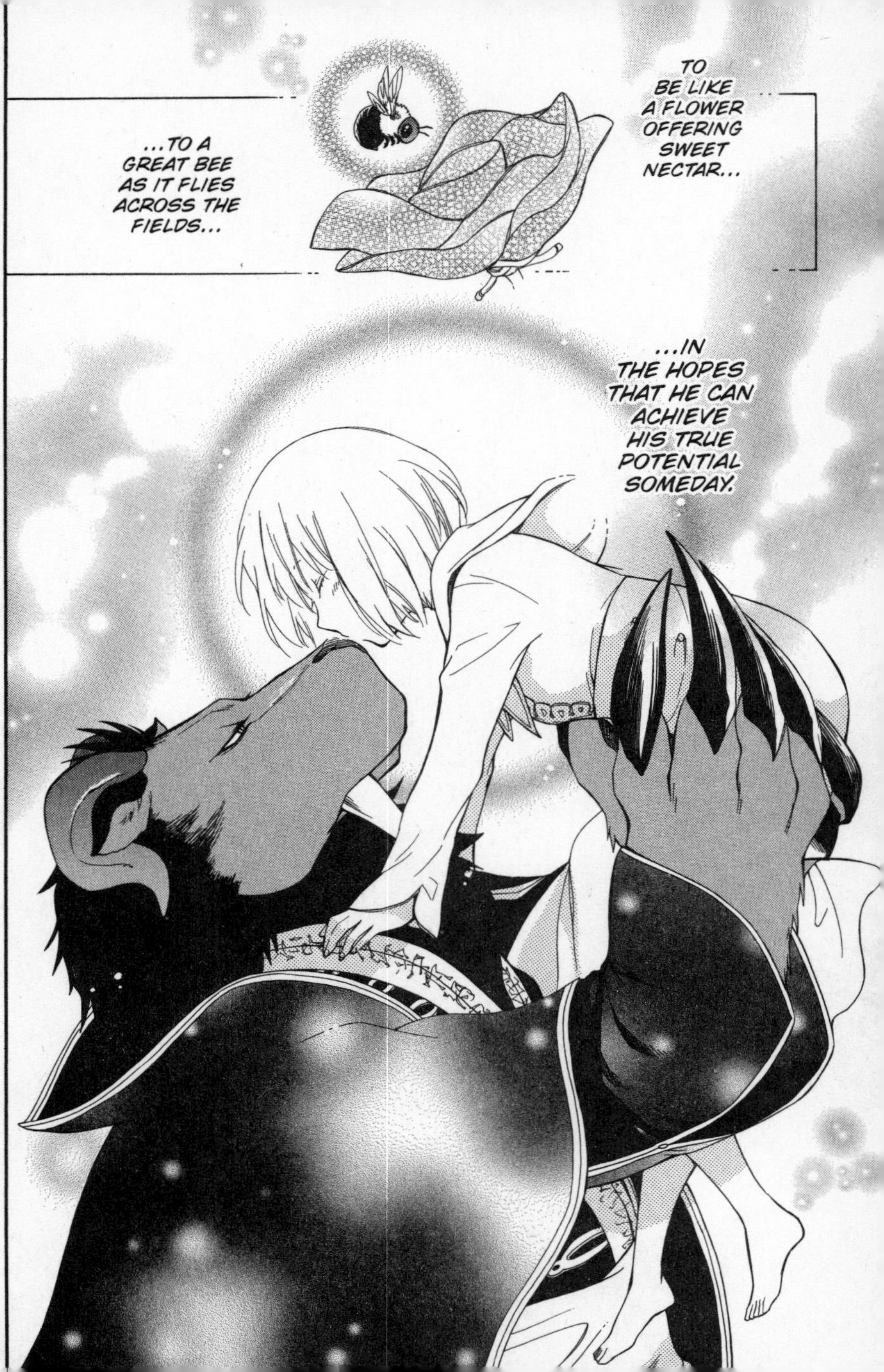
TO BE LIKE A FLOWER OFFERING SWEET NECTAR...
...TO A GREAT BEE AS IT FLIES ACROSS THE FIELDS...
...IN THE HOPES THAT HE CAN ACHIEVE HIS TRUE POTENTIAL SOMEDAY.

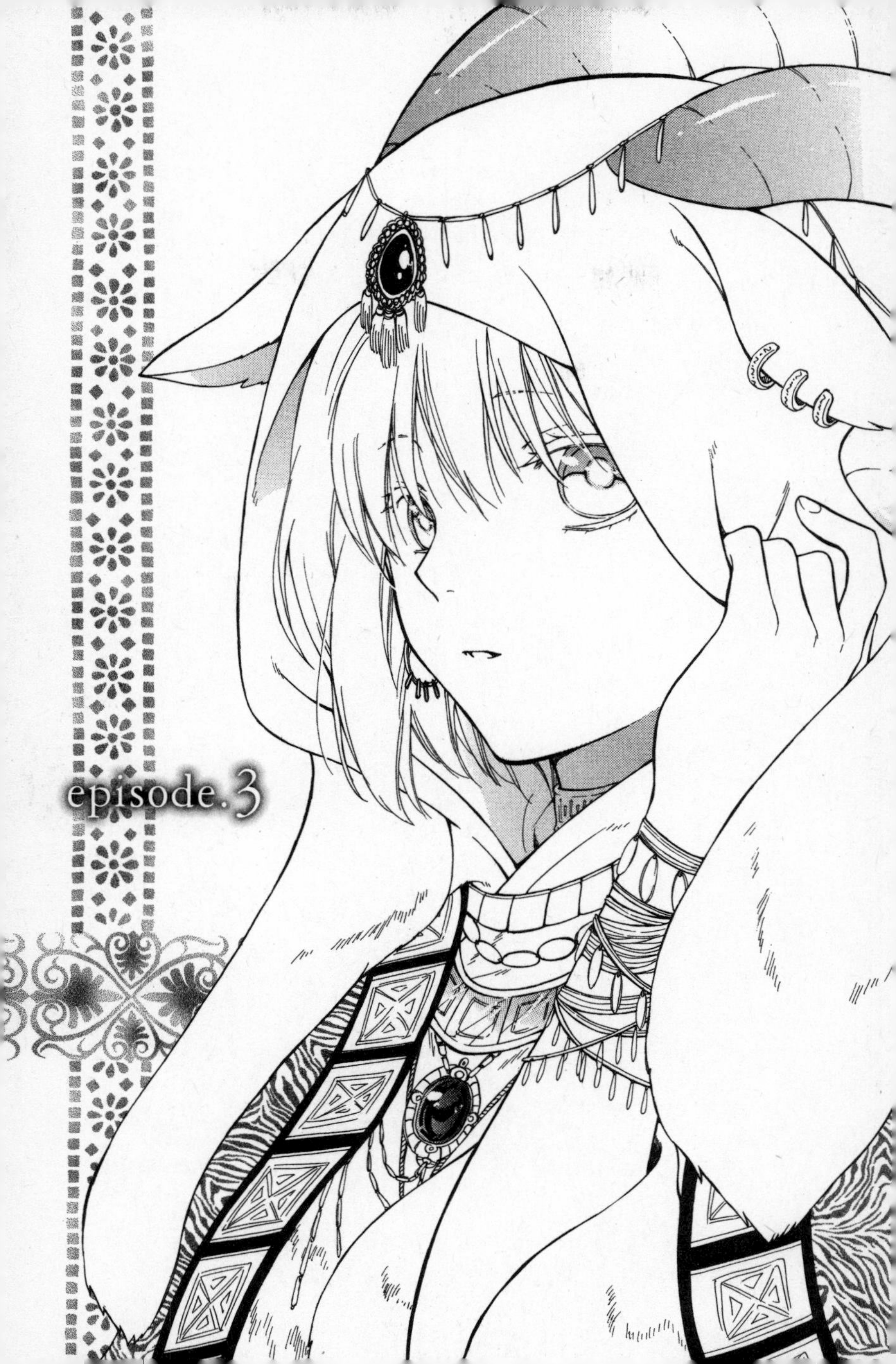
episode. 3

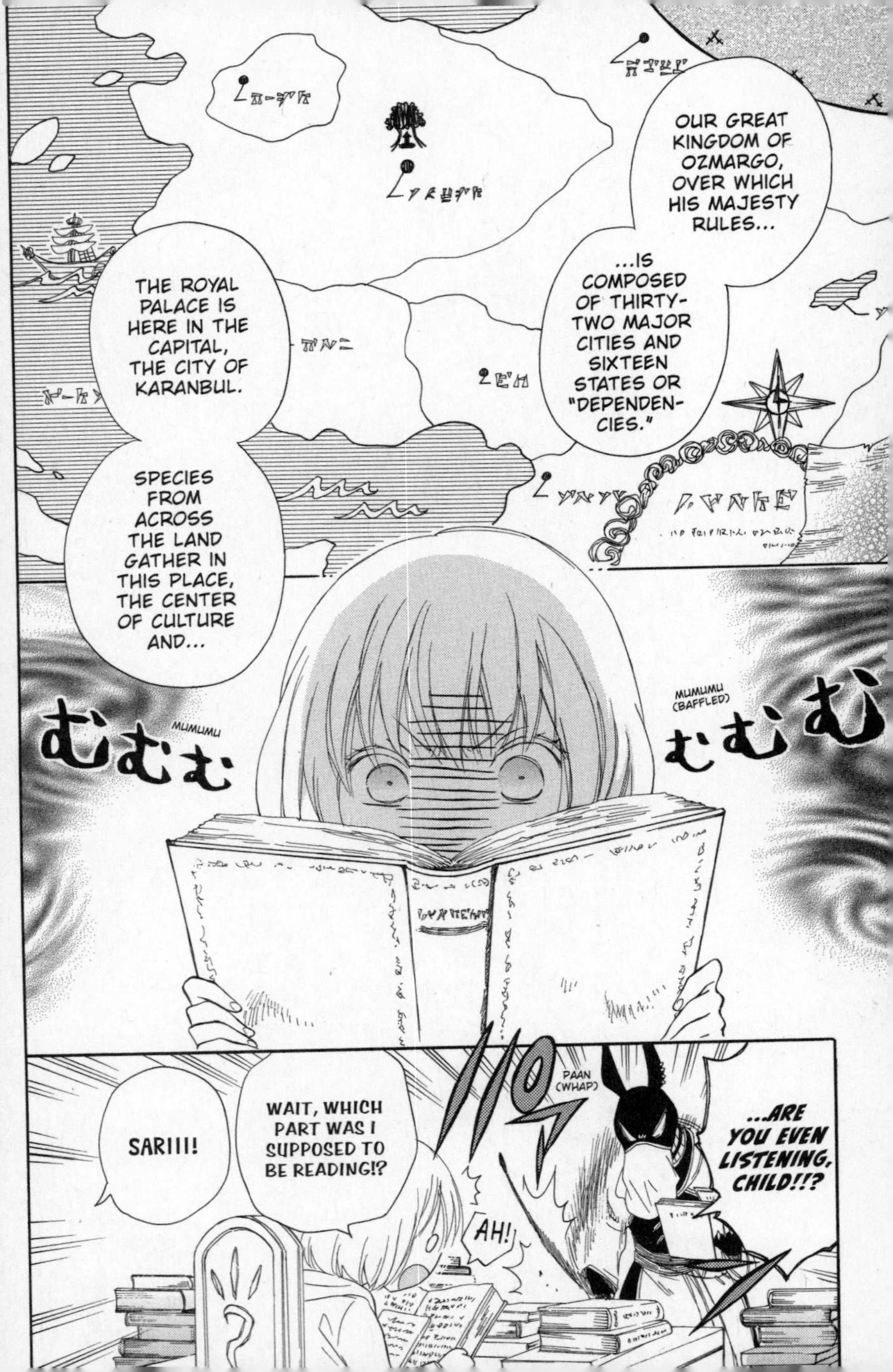
OUR GREAT KINGDOM OF OZMARGO, OVER WHICH HIS MAJESTY RULES...
...IS COMPOSED OF THIRTY-TWO MAJOR CITIES AND SIXTEEN STATES OR "DEPENDENCIES."
THE ROYAL PALACE IS HERE IN THE CAPITAL, THE CITY OF KARANBUL.
SPECIES FROM ACROSS THE LAND GATHER IN THIS PLACE, THE CENTER OF CULTURE AND...
むむむ
MUMUMU (BAFFLED)
むむむ
MUMUMU
...ARE YOU EVEN LISTENING, CHILD!!?
PAAN (WHAP)
AH!
WAIT, WHICH PART WAS I SUPPOSED TO BE READING!?
SARIII!

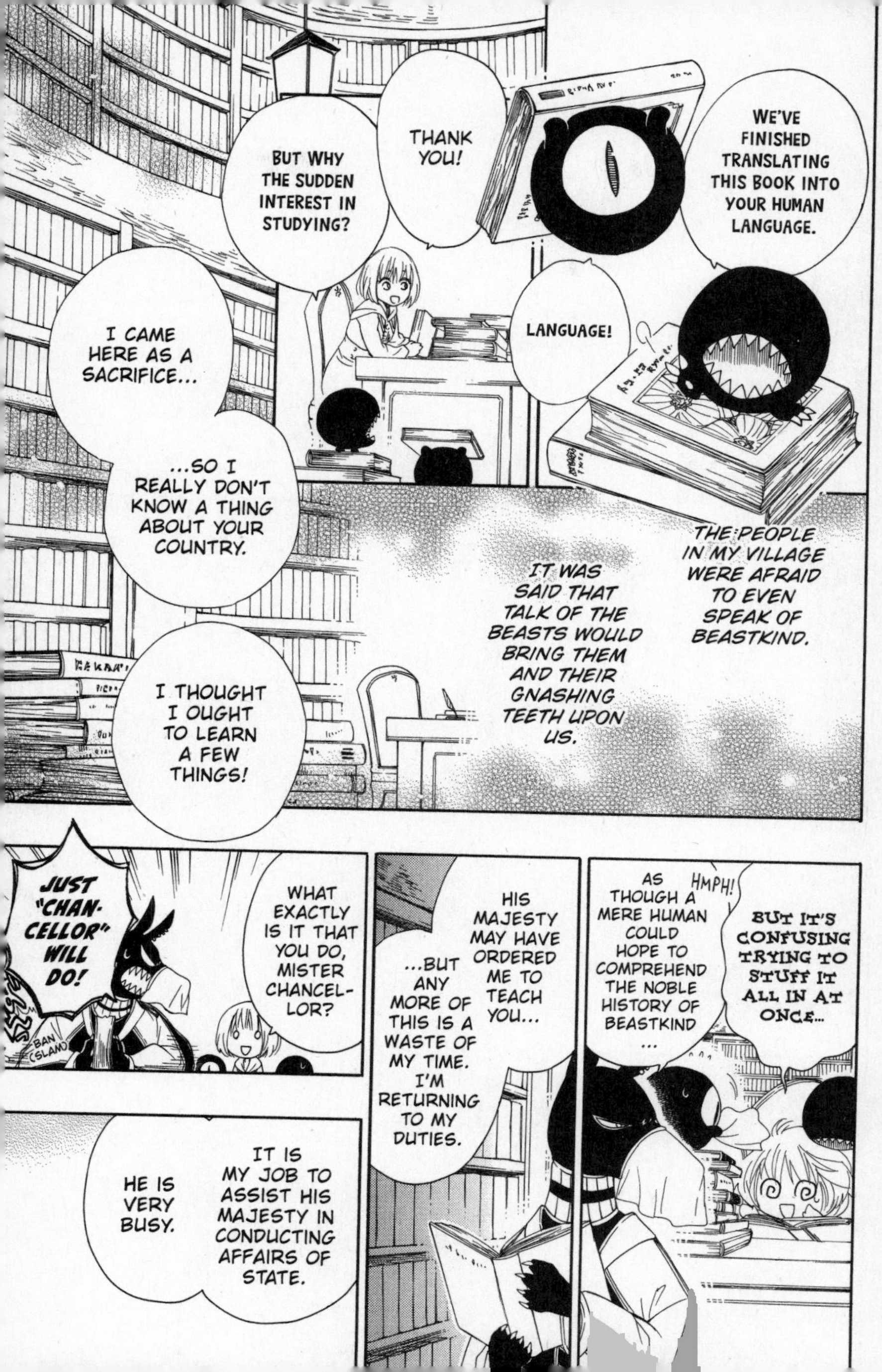
WE'VE FINISHED TRANSLATING THIS BOOK INTO YOUR HUMAN LANGUAGE.
LANGUAGE!
THANK YOU!
BUT WHY THE SUDDEN INTEREST IN STUDYING?
I CAME HERE AS A SACRIFICE...
...SO I REALLY DON'T KNOW A THING ABOUT YOUR COUNTRY.
THE PEOPLE IN MY VILLAGE WERE AFRAID TO EVEN SPEAK OF BEASTKIND.
IT WAS SAID THAT TALK OF THE BEASTS WOULD BRING THEM AND THEIR GNASHING TEETH UPON US.
I THOUGHT I OUGHT TO LEARN A FEW THINGS!
BUT IT'S CONFUSING TRYING TO STUFF IT ALL IN AT ONCE...
HMPH!
AS THOUGH A MERE HUMAN COULD HOPE TO COMPREHEND THE NOBLE HISTORY OF BEASTKIND...
HIS MAJESTY MAY HAVE ORDERED ME TO TEACH YOU...
...BUT ANY MORE OF THIS IS A WASTE OF MY TIME. I'M RETURNING TO MY DUTIES.
WHAT EXACTLY IS IT THAT YOU DO, MISTER CHANCELLOR?
JUST "CHANCELLOR" WILL DO!
BAN (SLAM)
IT IS MY JOB TO ASSIST HIS MAJESTY IN CONDUCTING AFFAIRS OF STATE.
HE IS VERY BUSY.

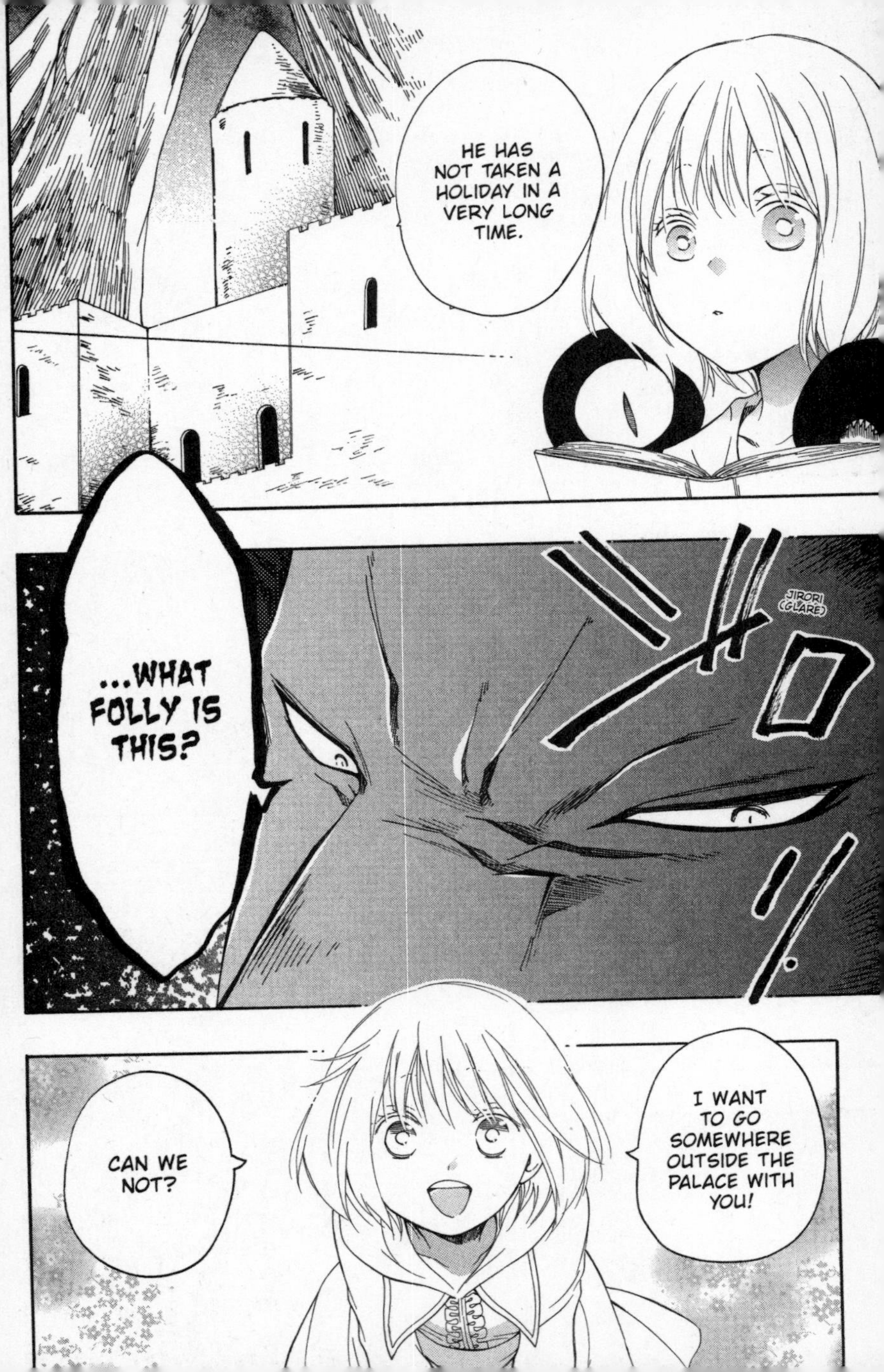
HE HAS NOT TAKEN A HOLIDAY IN A VERY LONG TIME.
JIRORI (GLARE)
...WHAT FOLLY IS THIS?
I WANT TO GO SOMEWHERE OUTSIDE THE PALACE WITH YOU!
CAN WE NOT?

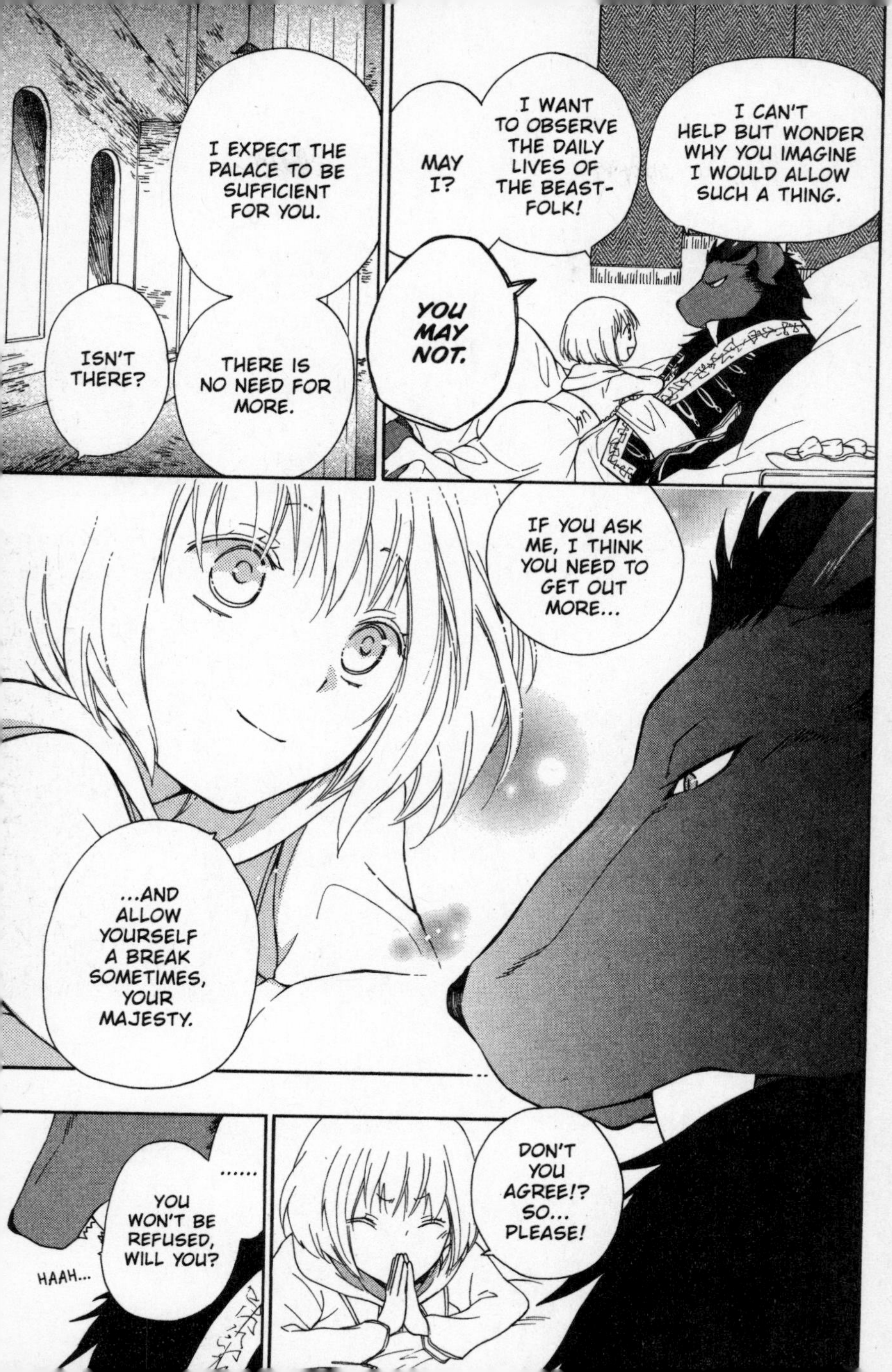
I CAN'T HELP BUT WONDER WHY YOU IMAGINE I WOULD ALLOW SUCH A THING.
I WANT TO OBSERVE THE DAILY LIVES OF THE BEAST-FOLK!
MAY I?
YOU MAY NOT.
I EXPECT THE PALACE TO BE SUFFICIENT FOR YOU.
THERE IS NO NEED FOR MORE.
ISN'T THERE?
IF YOU ASK ME, I THINK YOU NEED TO GET OUT MORE...
...AND ALLOW YOURSELF A BREAK SOMETIMES, YOUR MAJESTY.
DON'T YOU AGREE!? SO... PLEASE!
......
YOU WON'T BE REFUSED, WILL YOU?
HAAH...

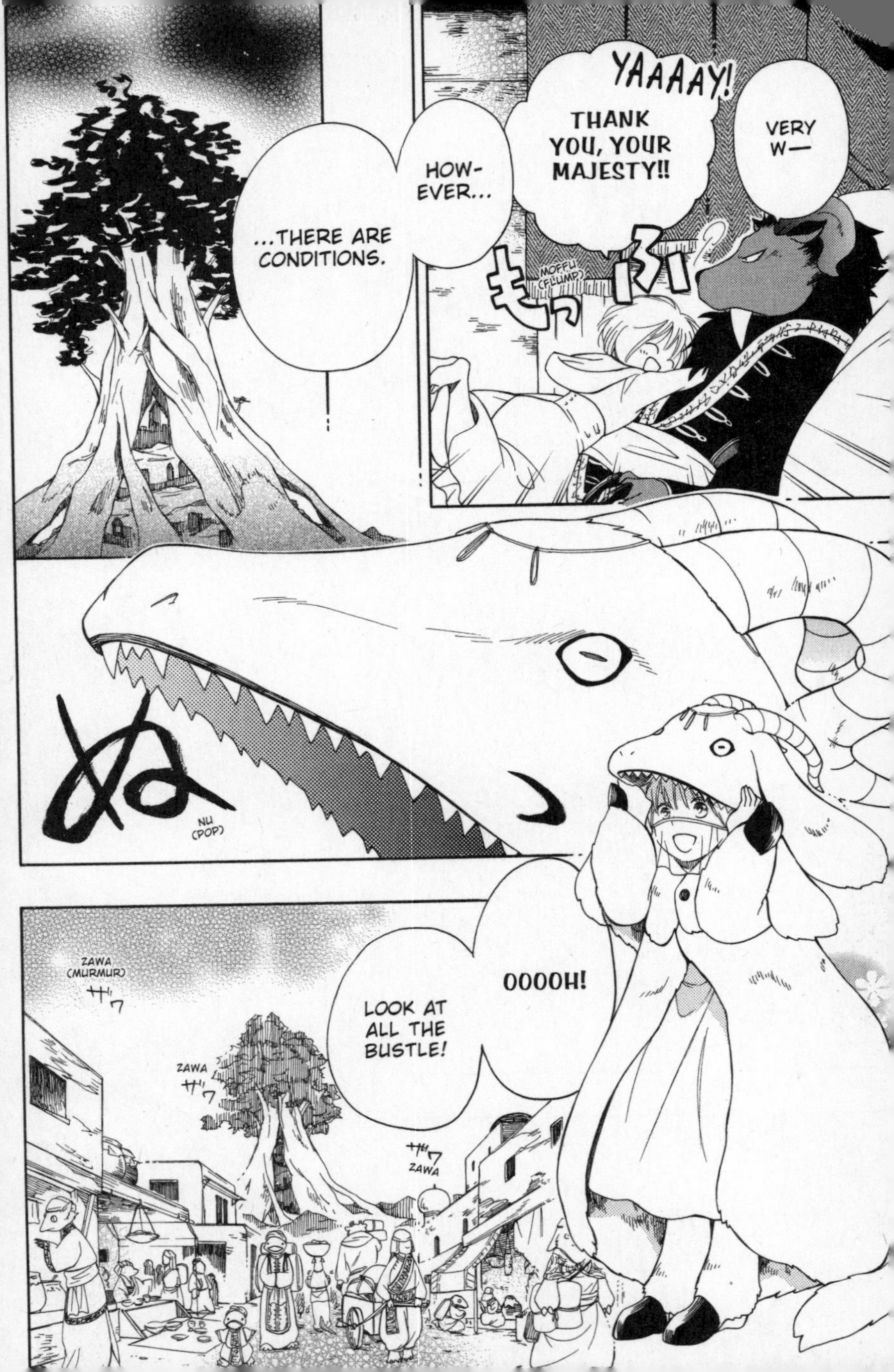
VERY W—
YAAAAY!
THANK YOU, YOUR MAJESTY!!
MOFU (FLUMP)
HOW-EVER...
...THERE ARE CONDITIONS.
NU (POP)
OOOOH!
LOOK AT ALL THE BUSTLE!
ZAWA
ZAWA (MURMUR)
ZAWA

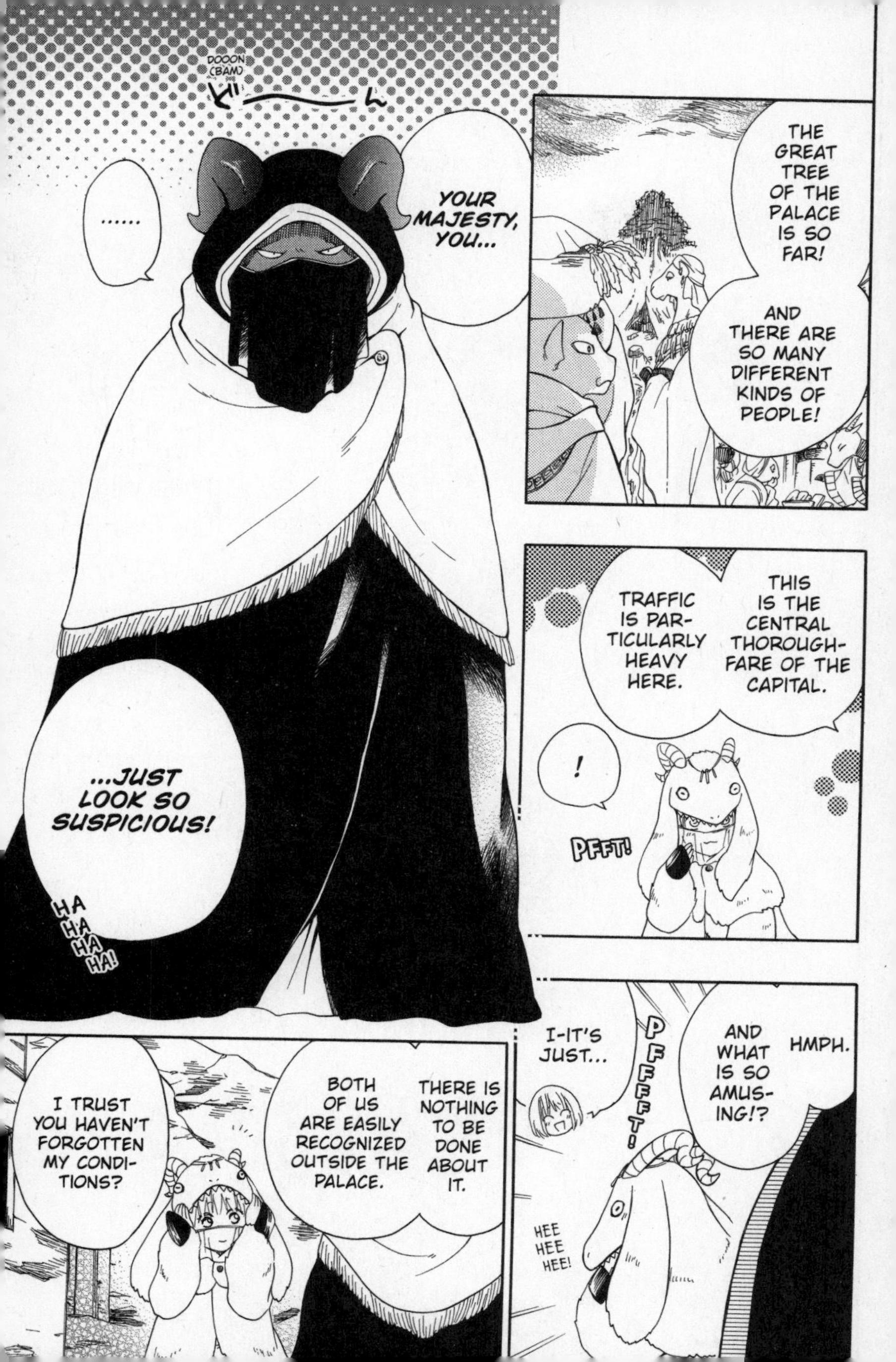
THE GREAT TREE OF THE PALACE IS SO FAR!
AND THERE ARE SO MANY DIFFERENT KINDS OF PEOPLE!
THIS IS THE CENTRAL THOROUGHFARE OF THE CAPITAL.
TRAFFIC IS PARTICULARLY HEAVY HERE.
!
PFFT!
DOOON (BAM)
......
YOUR MAJESTY, YOU...
...JUST LOOK SO SUSPICIOUS!
HA HA HA HA!
HMPH.
AND WHAT IS SO AMUSING!?
PFFFFT!
I-IT'S JUST...
HEE HEE HEE!
THERE IS NOTHING TO BE DONE ABOUT IT.
BOTH OF US ARE EASILY RECOGNIZED OUTSIDE THE PALACE.
I TRUST YOU HAVEN'T FORGOTTEN MY CONDITIONS?

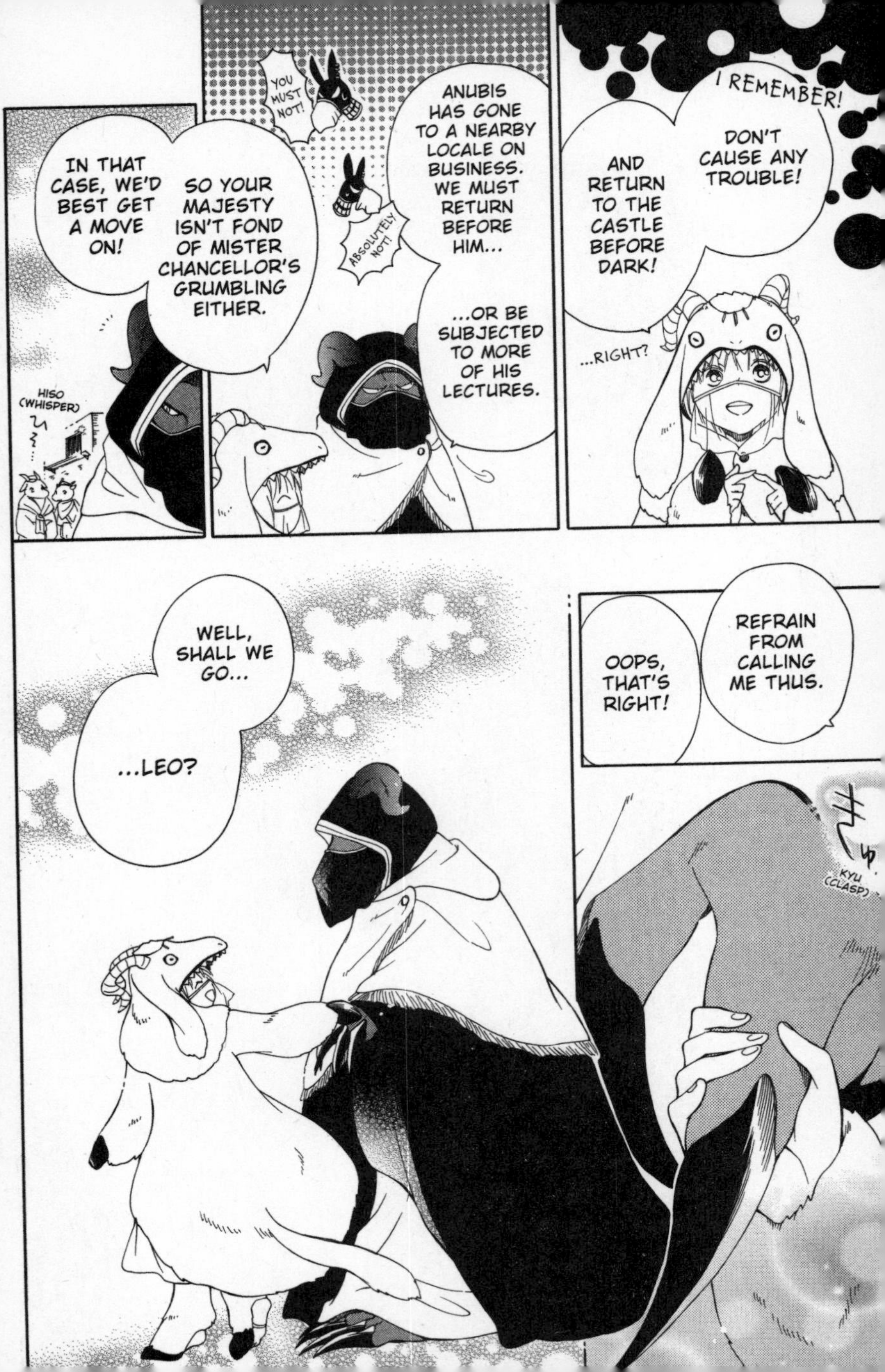
I REMEMBER!
DON'T CAUSE ANY TROUBLE!
AND RETURN TO THE CASTLE BEFORE DARK!
...RIGHT?
ANUBIS HAS GONE TO A NEARBY LOCALE ON BUSINESS. WE MUST RETURN BEFORE HIM...
YOU MUST NOT!
ABSOLUTELY NOT!
...OR BE SUBJECTED TO MORE OF HIS LECTURES.
SO YOUR MAJESTY ISN'T FOND OF MISTER CHANCELLOR'S GRUMBLING EITHER.
IN THAT CASE, WE'D BEST GET A MOVE ON!
HISO (WHISPER)
REFRAIN FROM CALLING ME THUS.
OOPS, THAT'S RIGHT!
KYU (CLASP)
WELL, SHALL WE GO...
...LEO?

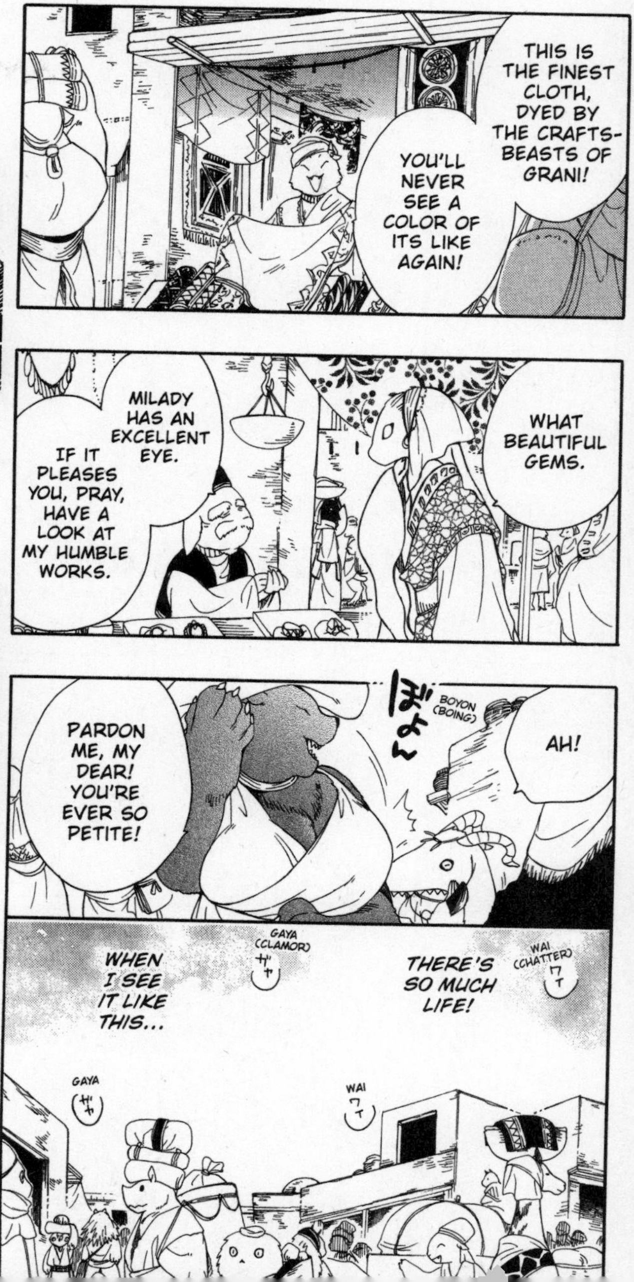
THIS IS THE FINEST CLOTH, DYED BY THE CRAFTS-BEASTS OF GRANI!
YOU'LL NEVER SEE A COLOR OF ITS LIKE AGAIN!
WHAT BEAUTIFUL GEMS.
MILADY HAS AN EXCELLENT EYE.
IF IT PLEASES YOU, PRAY, HAVE A LOOK AT MY HUMBLE WORKS.
AH!
ぼよん
BOYON (BOING)
PARDON ME, MY DEAR! YOU'RE EVER SO PETITE!
WAI (CHATTER)
ワイ
THERE'S SO MUCH LIFE!
GAYA (CLAMOR)
ガヤ
WHEN I SEE IT LIKE THIS...
WAI
ワイ
GAYA
ガヤ

PROTOTYPE ② KING

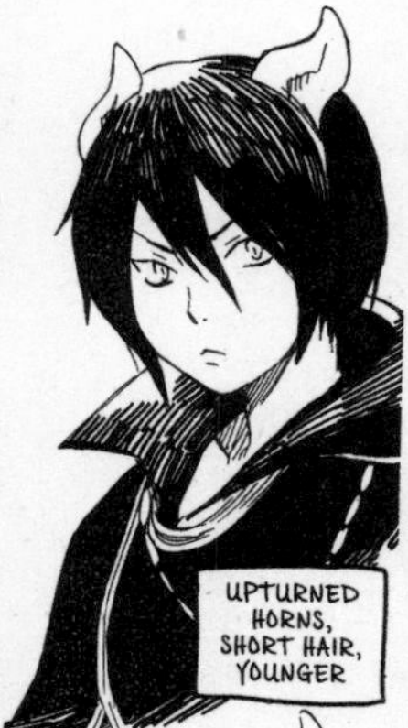
UPTURNED HORNS, SHORT HAIR, YOUNGER

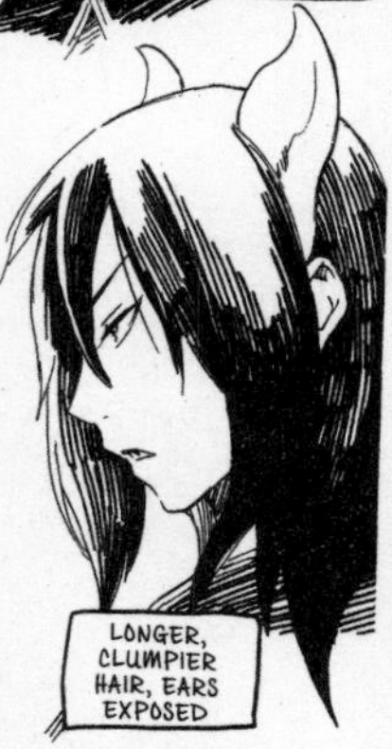
LONGER, CLUMPIER HAIR, EARS EXPOSED

I EXPERIMENTED WITH A BUNCH OF DIFFERENT APPROACHES FOR THE KING: UPTURNED HORNS, DOWN-TURNED HORNS, SHORT HAIR, LONG HAIR...IN THE END, I WENT WITH A SHIRTLESS, LONG-HAIRED VERSION—THE SHIRTLESS-NESS WAS MY EDITOR'S IDEA! I TEND TO PREFER NICE FITTED OUTFITS MYSELF...

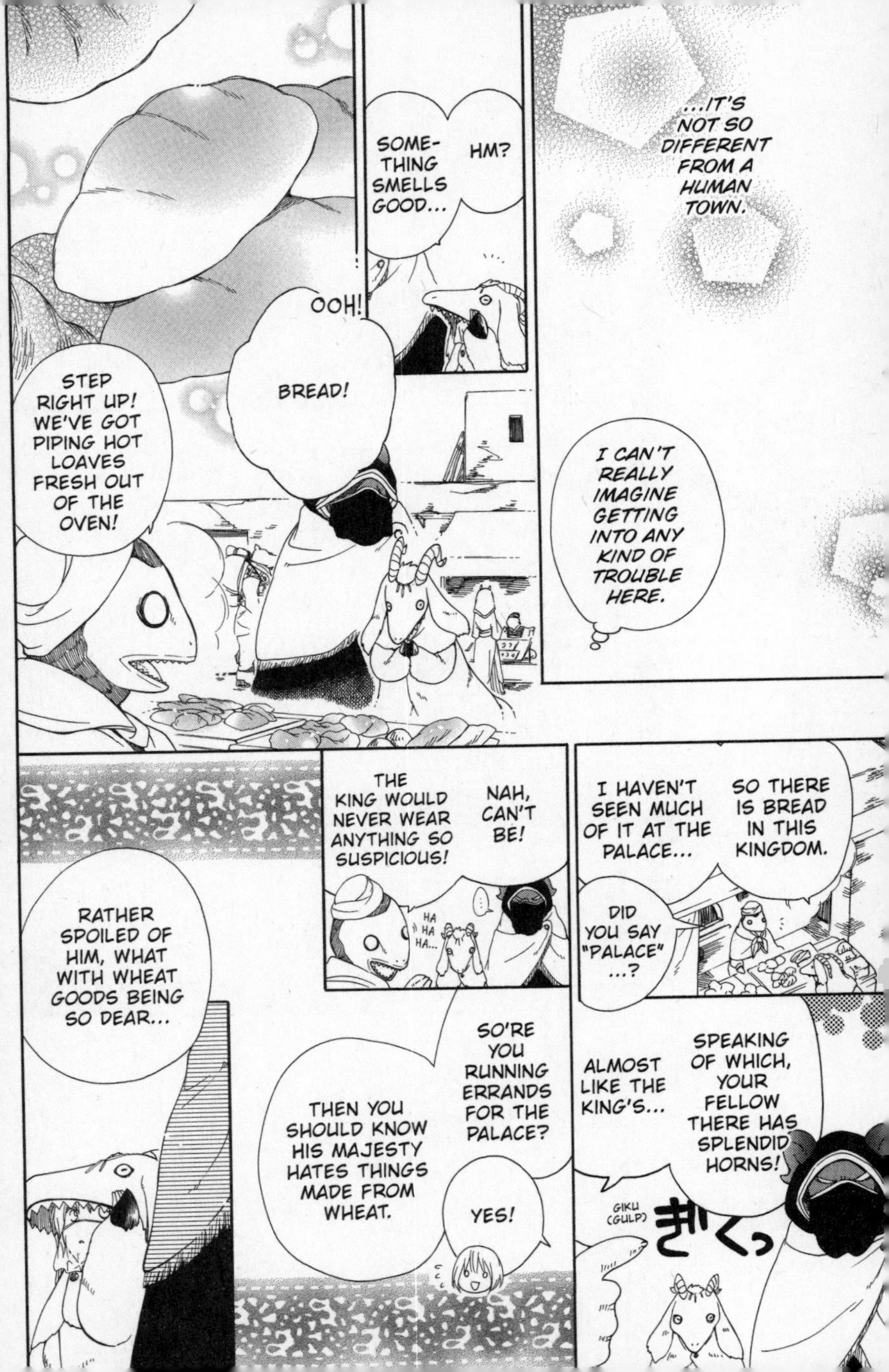
...IT'S NOT SO DIFFERENT FROM A HUMAN TOWN.
I CAN'T REALLY IMAGINE GETTING INTO ANY KIND OF TROUBLE HERE.
HM?
SOME-THING SMELLS GOOD...
OOH!
BREAD!
STEP RIGHT UP! WE'VE GOT PIPING HOT LOAVES FRESH OUT OF THE OVEN!
SO THERE IS BREAD IN THIS KINGDOM.
I HAVEN'T SEEN MUCH OF IT AT THE PALACE...
DID YOU SAY "PALACE" ...?
SPEAKING OF WHICH, YOUR FELLOW THERE HAS SPLENDID HORNS!
ALMOST LIKE THE KING'S...
GIKU (GULP)
ぎくっ
NAH, CAN'T BE!
THE KING WOULD NEVER WEAR ANYTHING SO SUSPICIOUS!
HA HA HA...
SO'RE YOU RUNNING ERRANDS FOR THE PALACE?
YES!
THEN YOU SHOULD KNOW HIS MAJESTY HATES THINGS MADE FROM WHEAT.
RATHER SPOILED OF HIM, WHAT WITH WHEAT GOODS BEING SO DEAR...

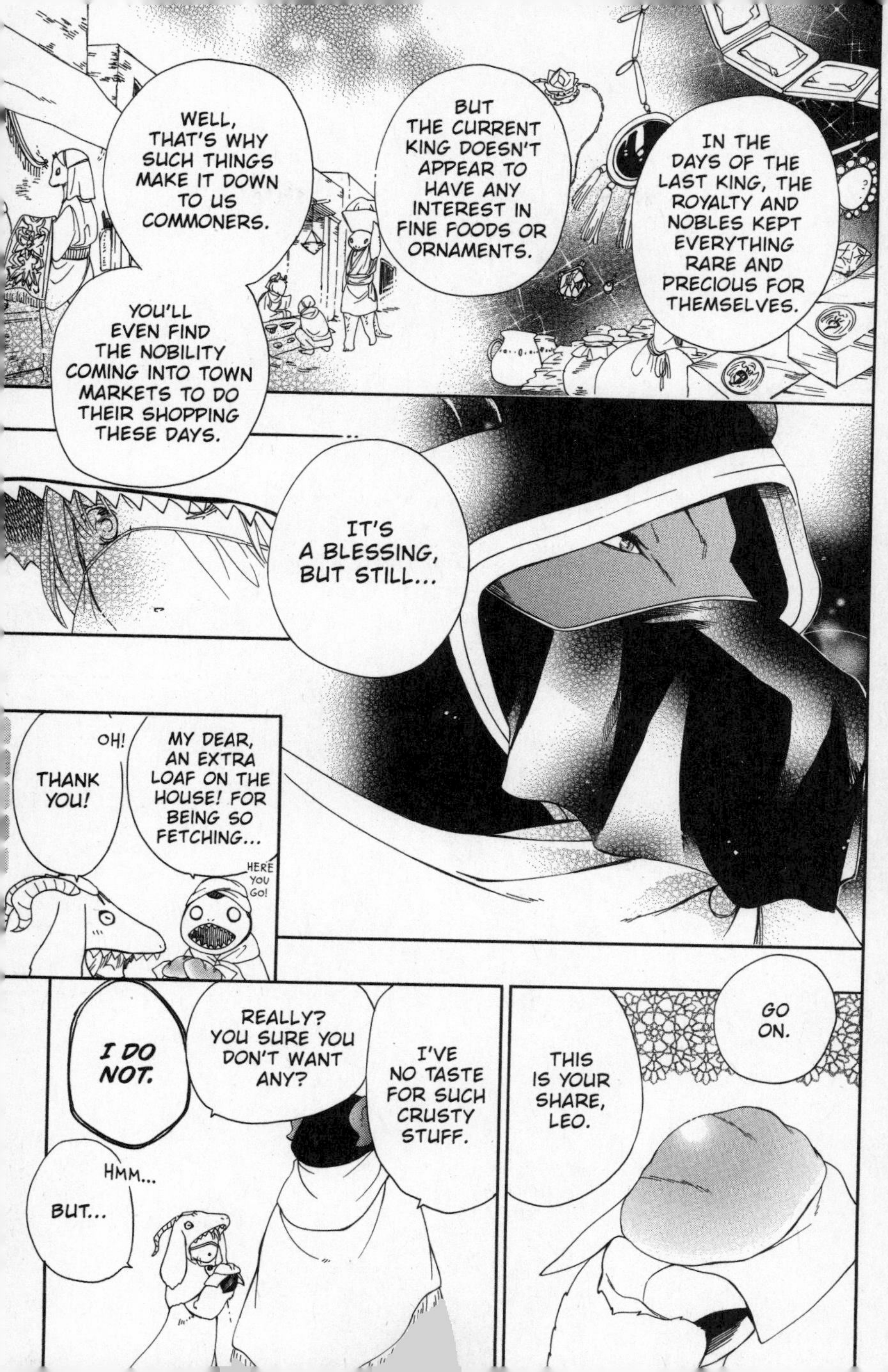
IN THE DAYS OF THE LAST KING, THE ROYALTY AND NOBLES KEPT EVERYTHING RARE AND PRECIOUS FOR THEMSELVES.
BUT THE CURRENT KING DOESN'T APPEAR TO HAVE ANY INTEREST IN FINE FOODS OR ORNAMENTS.
WELL, THAT'S WHY SUCH THINGS MAKE IT DOWN TO US COMMONERS.
YOU'LL EVEN FIND THE NOBILITY COMING INTO TOWN MARKETS TO DO THEIR SHOPPING THESE DAYS.
IT'S A BLESSING, BUT STILL...
MY DEAR, AN EXTRA LOAF ON THE HOUSE! FOR BEING SO FETCHING...
OH!
THANK YOU!
HERE YOU GO!
GO ON.
THIS IS YOUR SHARE, LEO.
I'VE NO TASTE FOR SUCH CRUSTY STUFF.
REALLY? YOU SURE YOU DON'T WANT ANY?
I DO NOT.
HMM...
BUT...

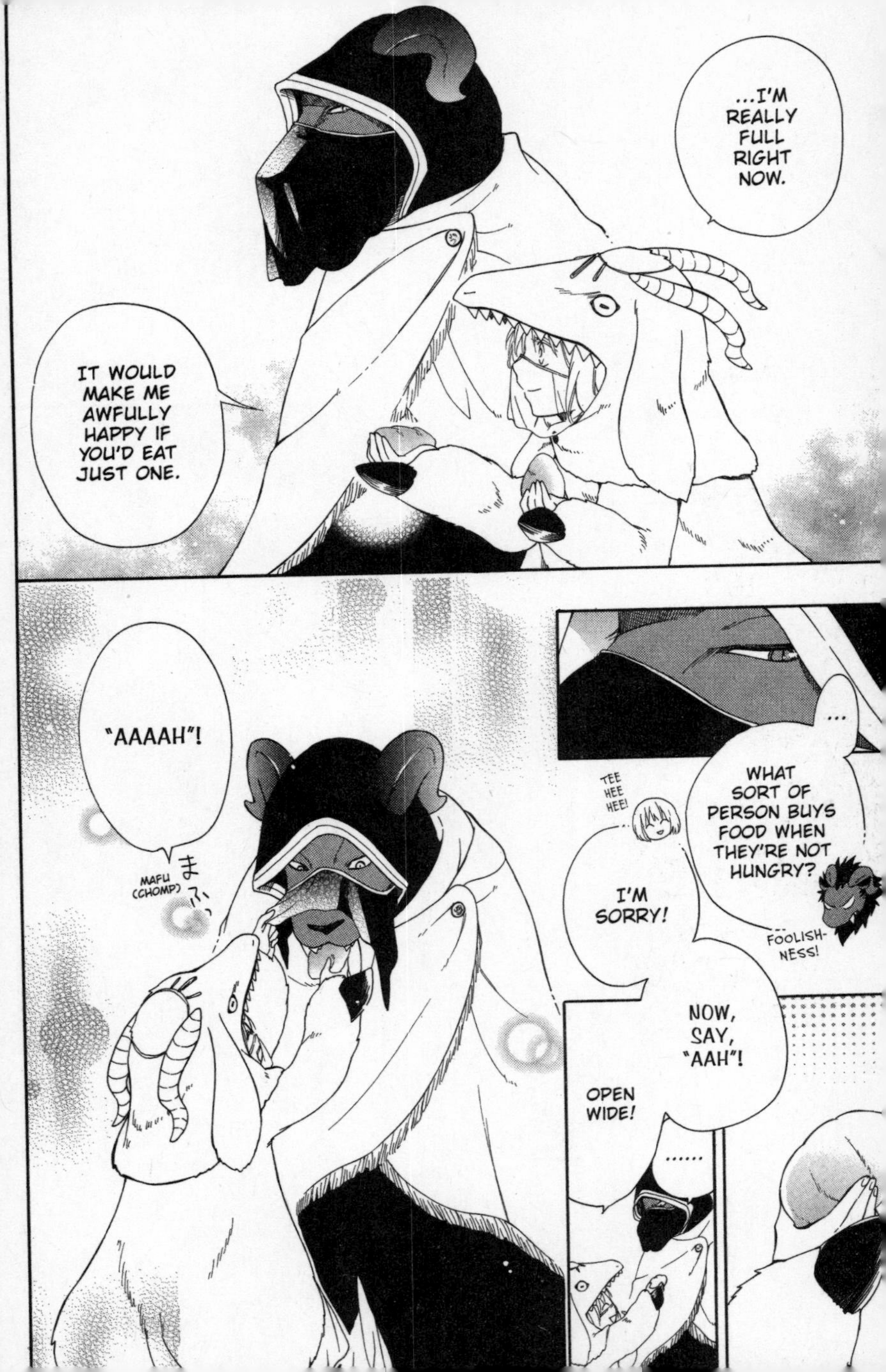
...I'M REALLY FULL RIGHT NOW.
IT WOULD MAKE ME AWFULLY HAPPY IF YOU'D EAT JUST ONE.
...
WHAT SORT OF PERSON BUYS FOOD WHEN THEY'RE NOT HUNGRY?
FOOLISH-NESS!
TEE HEE HEE!
I'M SORRY!
NOW, SAY, "AAH"!
OPEN WIDE!
......
"AAAAH"!
まふっ
MAFU (CHOMP)

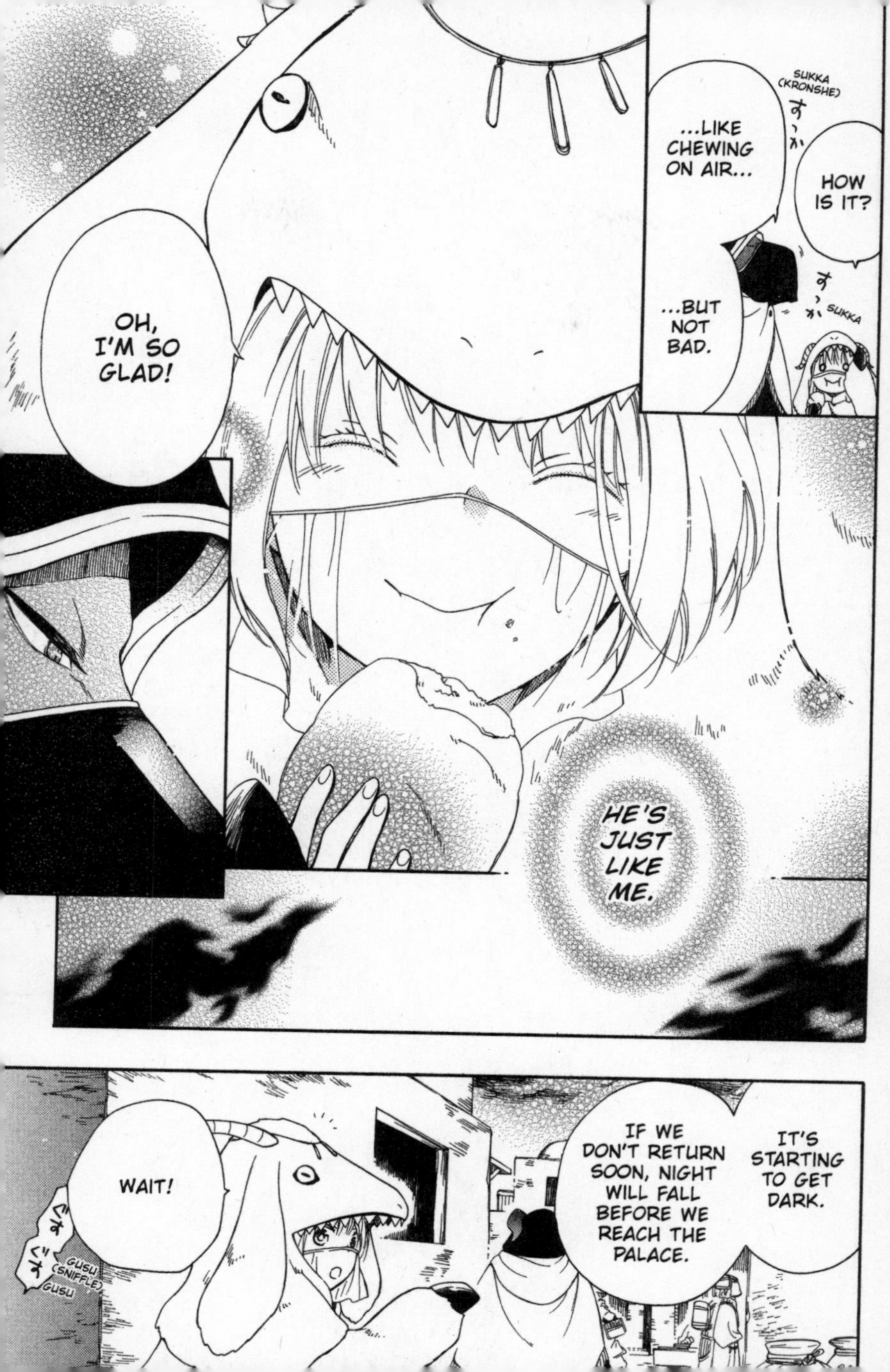
HOW IS IT?
すっか
SUKKA (KRONSHE)
...LIKE CHEWING ON AIR...
...BUT NOT BAD.
すっか
SUKKA
OH, I'M SO GLAD!
HE'S JUST LIKE ME.
IT'S STARTING TO GET DARK.
IF WE DON'T RETURN SOON, NIGHT WILL FALL BEFORE WE REACH THE PALACE.
WAIT!
ぐすぐす
GUSU (SNIFFLE) GUSU

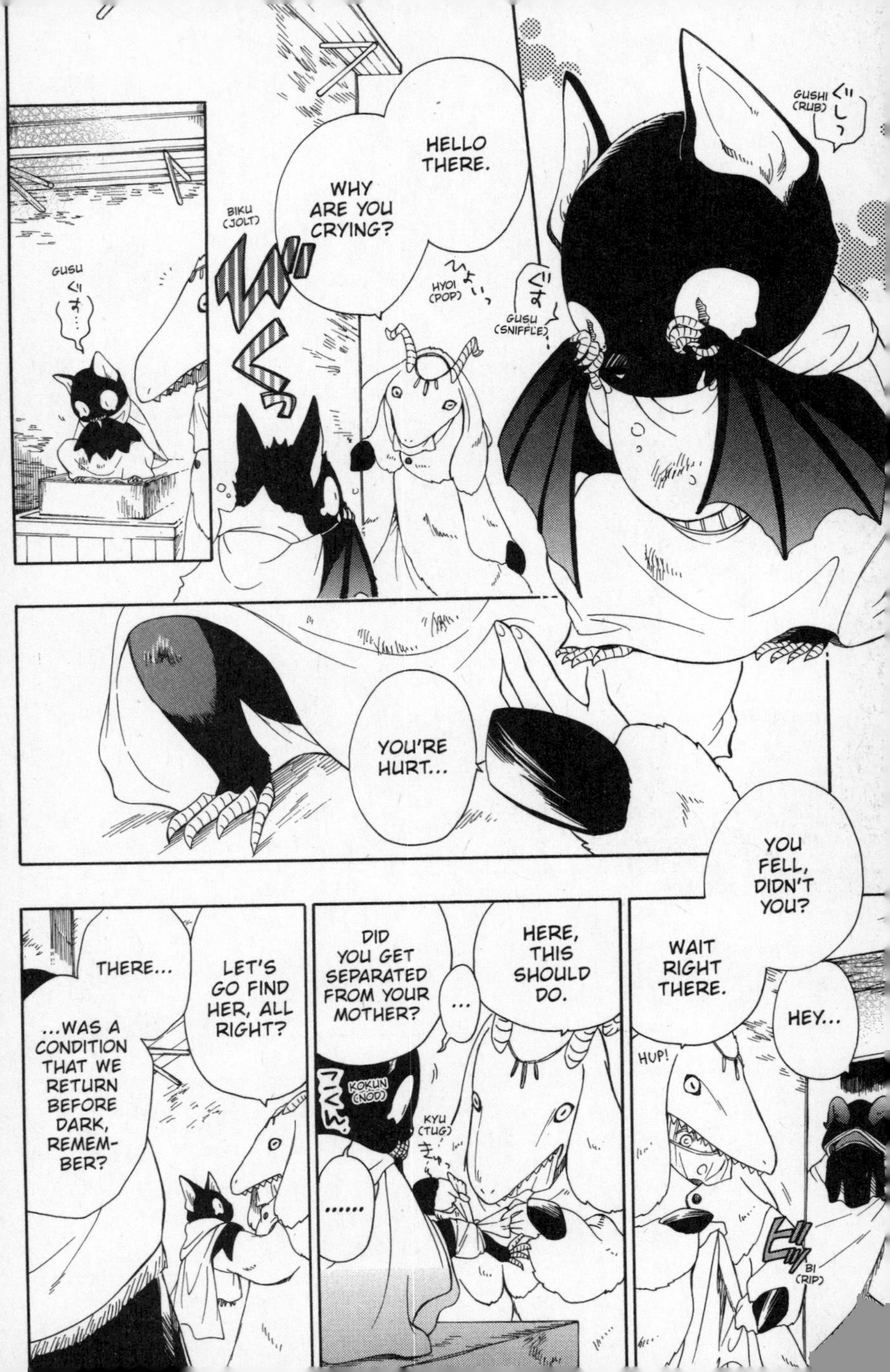

GUSHI (RUB)
ぐしっ
GUSU (SNIFFLE)
ぐす
HELLO THERE.
WHY ARE YOU CRYING?
HYOI (POP)
ひょいっ
BIKU (JOLT)
GUSU
ぐす…
YOU'RE HURT...
YOU FELL, DIDN'T YOU?
HEY...
WAIT RIGHT THERE.
HUP!
BI (RIP)
HERE, THIS SHOULD DO.
...
DID YOU GET SEPARATED FROM YOUR MOTHER?
KYU (TUG)
KOKUN (NOD)
......
LET'S GO FIND HER, ALL RIGHT?
THERE...
...WAS A CONDITION THAT WE RETURN BEFORE DARK, REMEMBER?

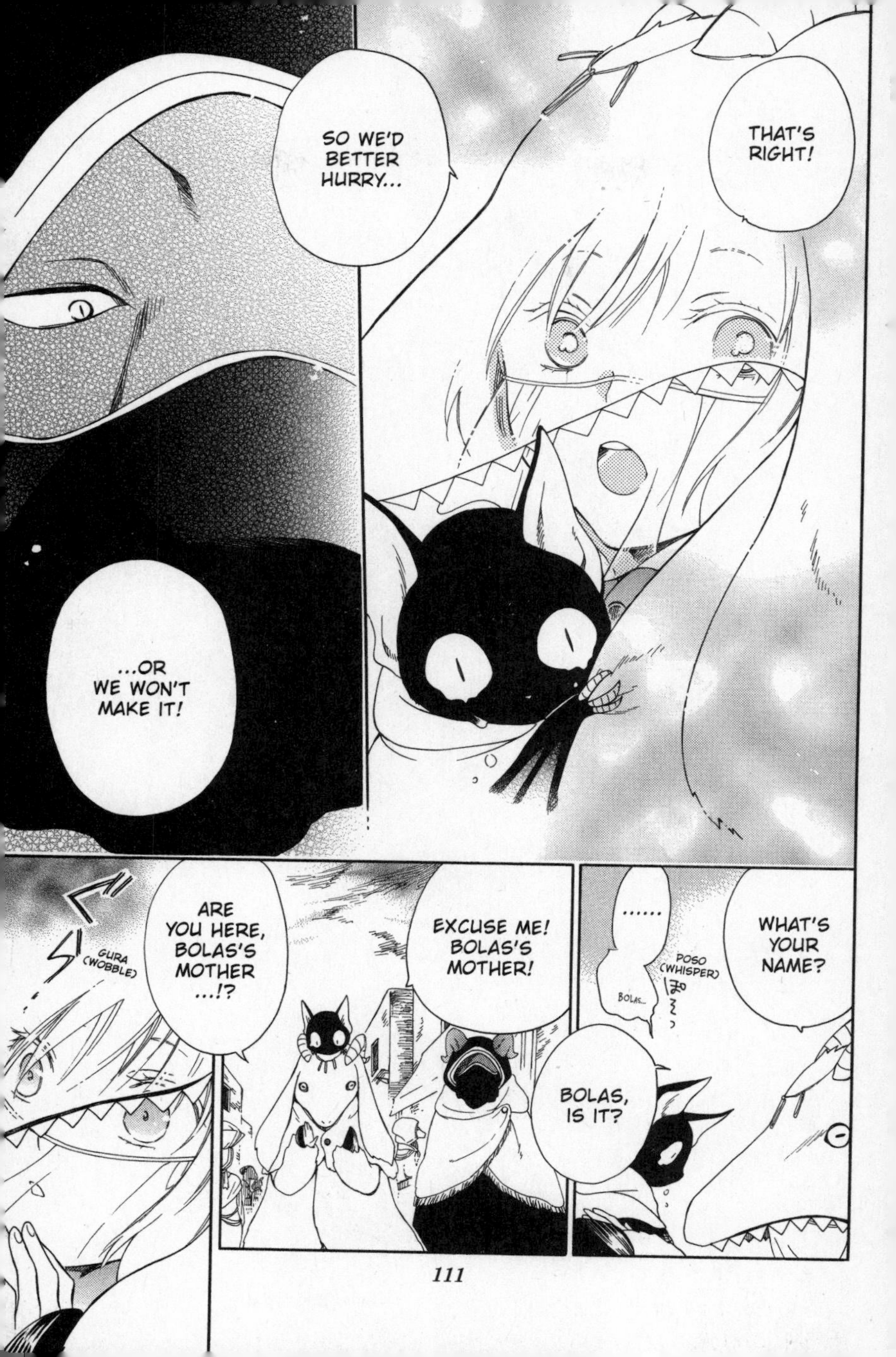
THAT'S RIGHT!
SO WE'D BETTER HURRY...
...OR WE WON'T MAKE IT!
WHAT'S YOUR NAME?
......
POSO (WHISPER)
BOLAS...
BOLAS, IS IT?
EXCUSE ME! BOLAS'S MOTHER!
ARE YOU HERE, BOLAS'S MOTHER ...!?
GURA (WOBBLE)

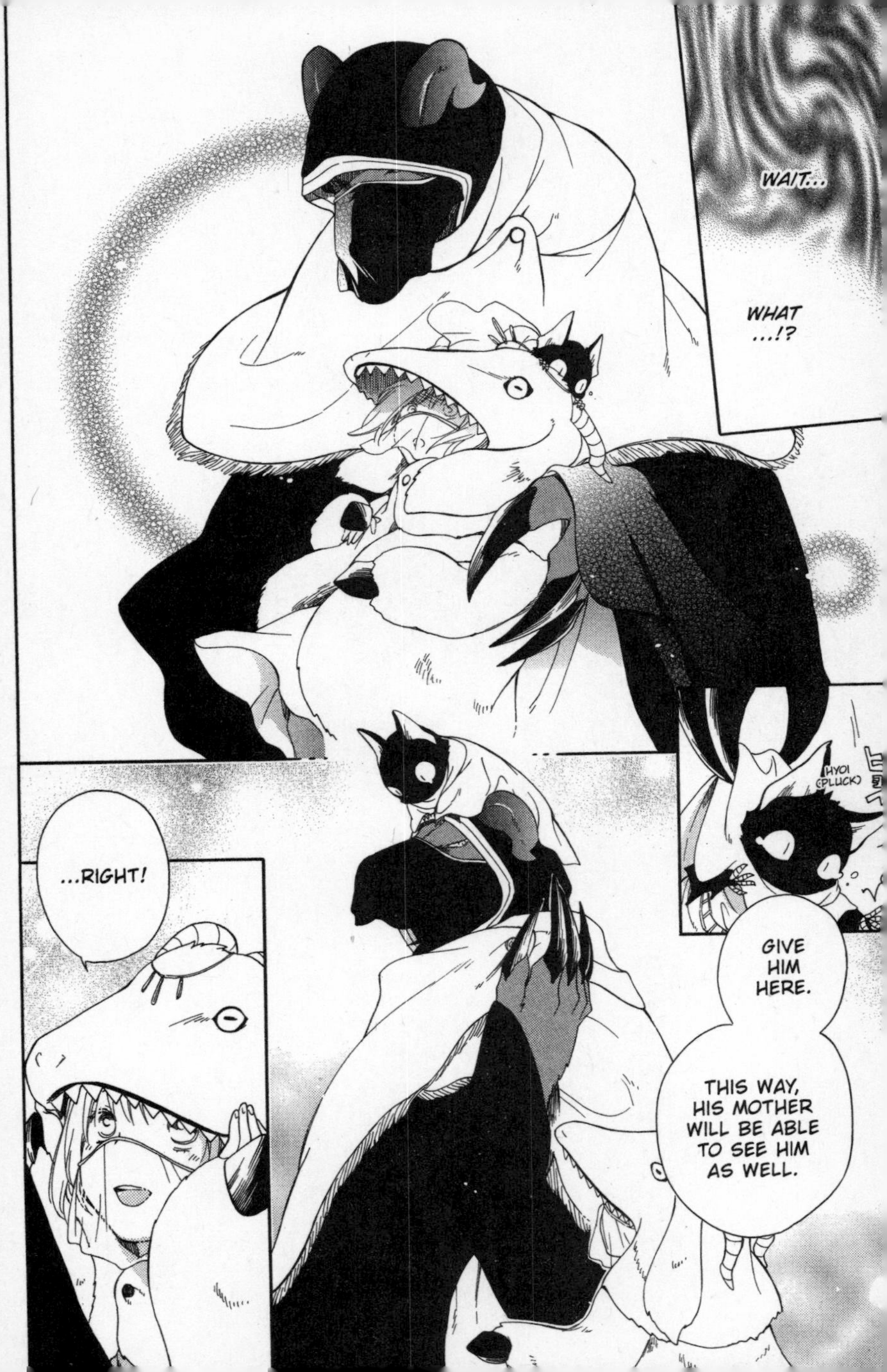
WAIT...
WHAT ...!?
HYOI (PLUCK)
GIVE HIM HERE.
THIS WAY, HIS MOTHER WILL BE ABLE TO SEE HIM AS WELL.
...RIGHT!

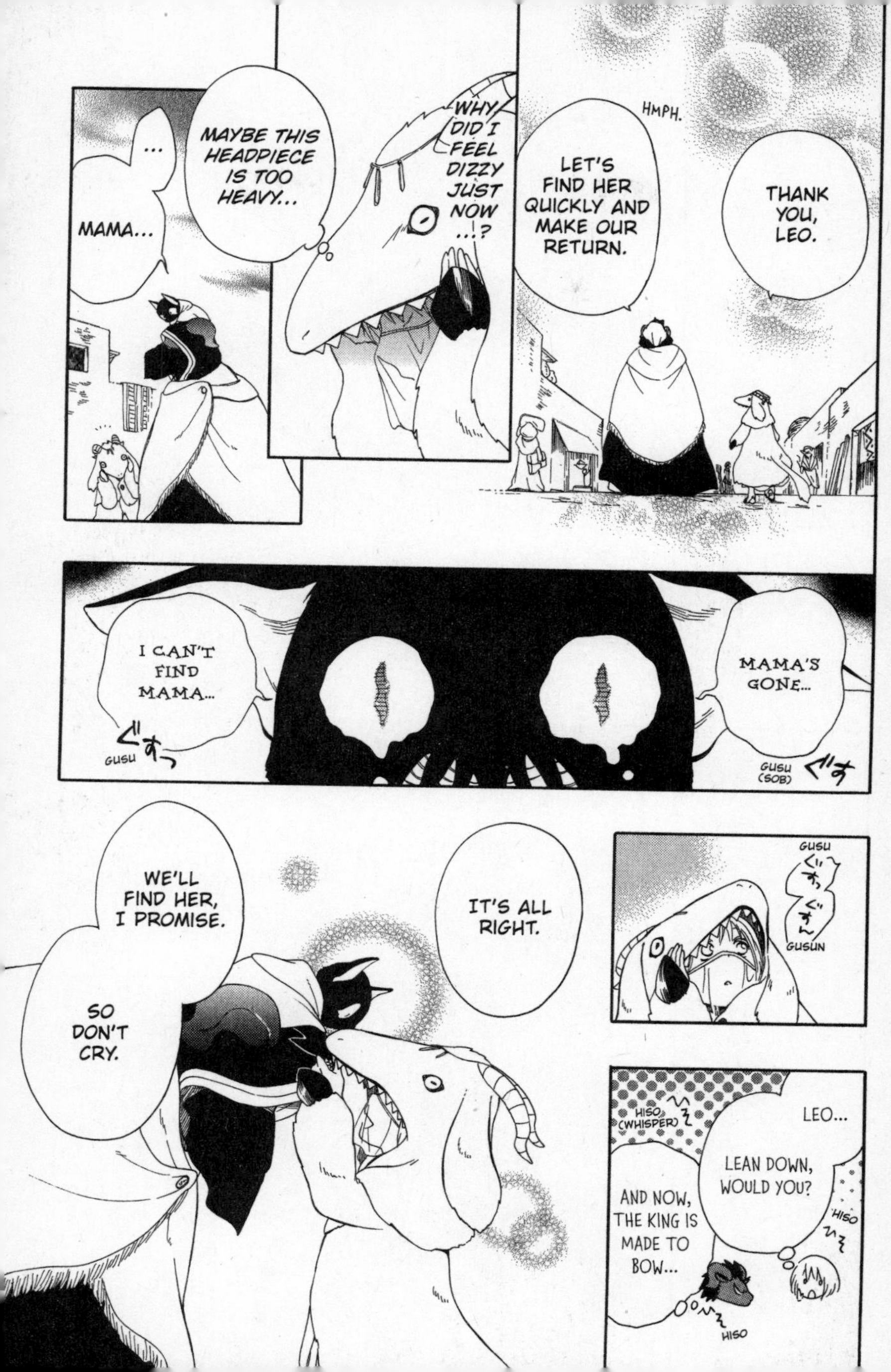
THANK YOU, LEO.
HMPH.
LET'S FIND HER QUICKLY AND MAKE OUR RETURN.
WHY DID I FEEL DIZZY JUST NOW ...!?
MAYBE THIS HEADPIECE IS TOO HEAVY...
...
MAMA...
MAMA'S GONE...
ぐす
GUSU (SOB)
I CAN'T FIND MAMA...
ぐすっ
GUSU
GUSU
ぐすっ
ぐすん
GUSUN
LEO...
LEAN DOWN, WOULD YOU?
HISO (WHISPER)
HISO
AND NOW, THE KING IS MADE TO BOW...
HISO
IT'S ALL RIGHT.
WE'LL FIND HER, I PROMISE.
SO DON'T CRY.

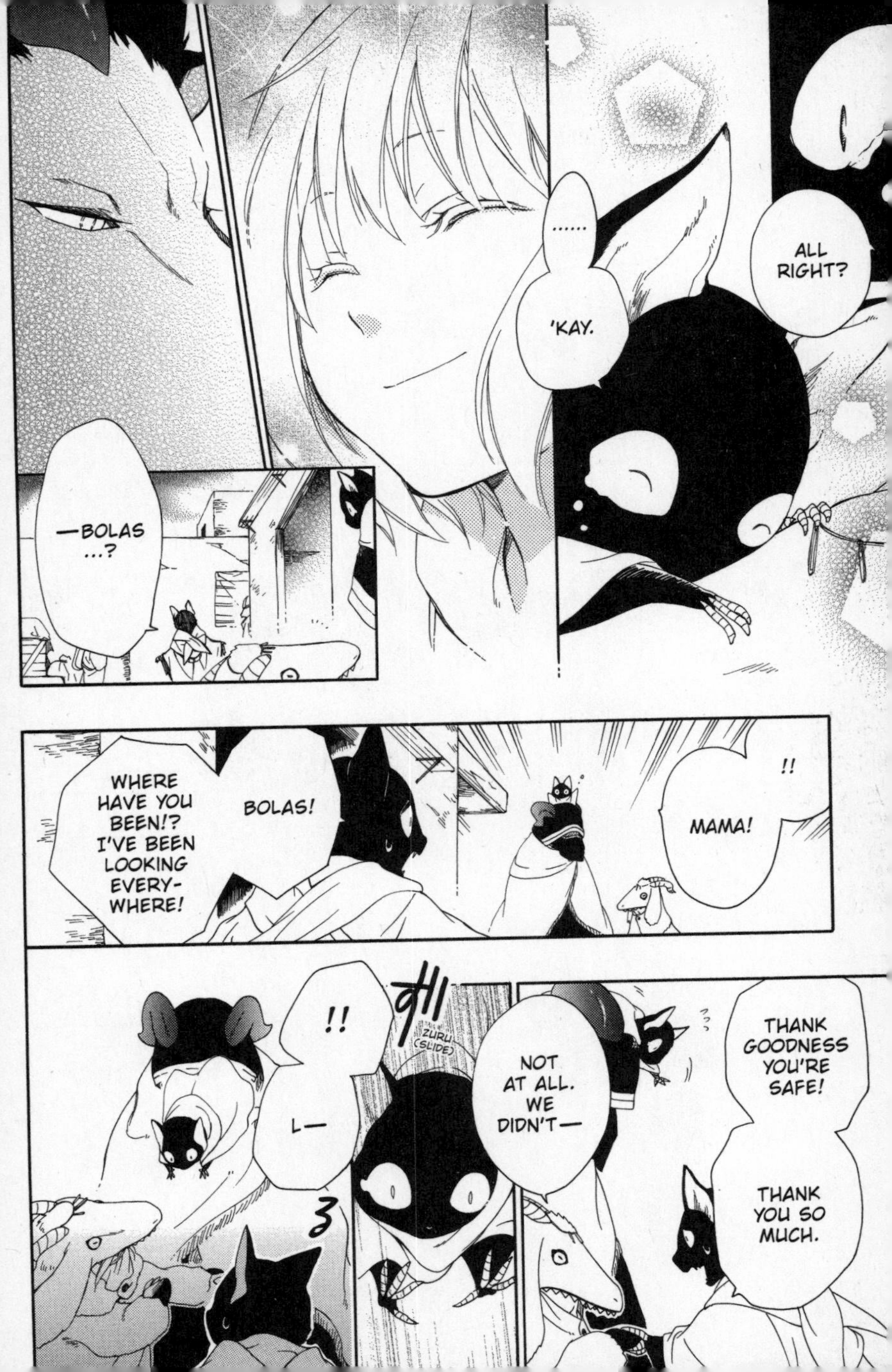
ALL RIGHT?
......
'KAY.
—BOLAS ...?
!!
MAMA!
BOLAS!
WHERE HAVE YOU BEEN!? I'VE BEEN LOOKING EVERY-WHERE!
THANK GOODNESS YOU'RE SAFE!
THANK YOU SO MUCH.
NOT AT ALL. WE DIDN'T—
ZURU (SLIDE)
!!
L—

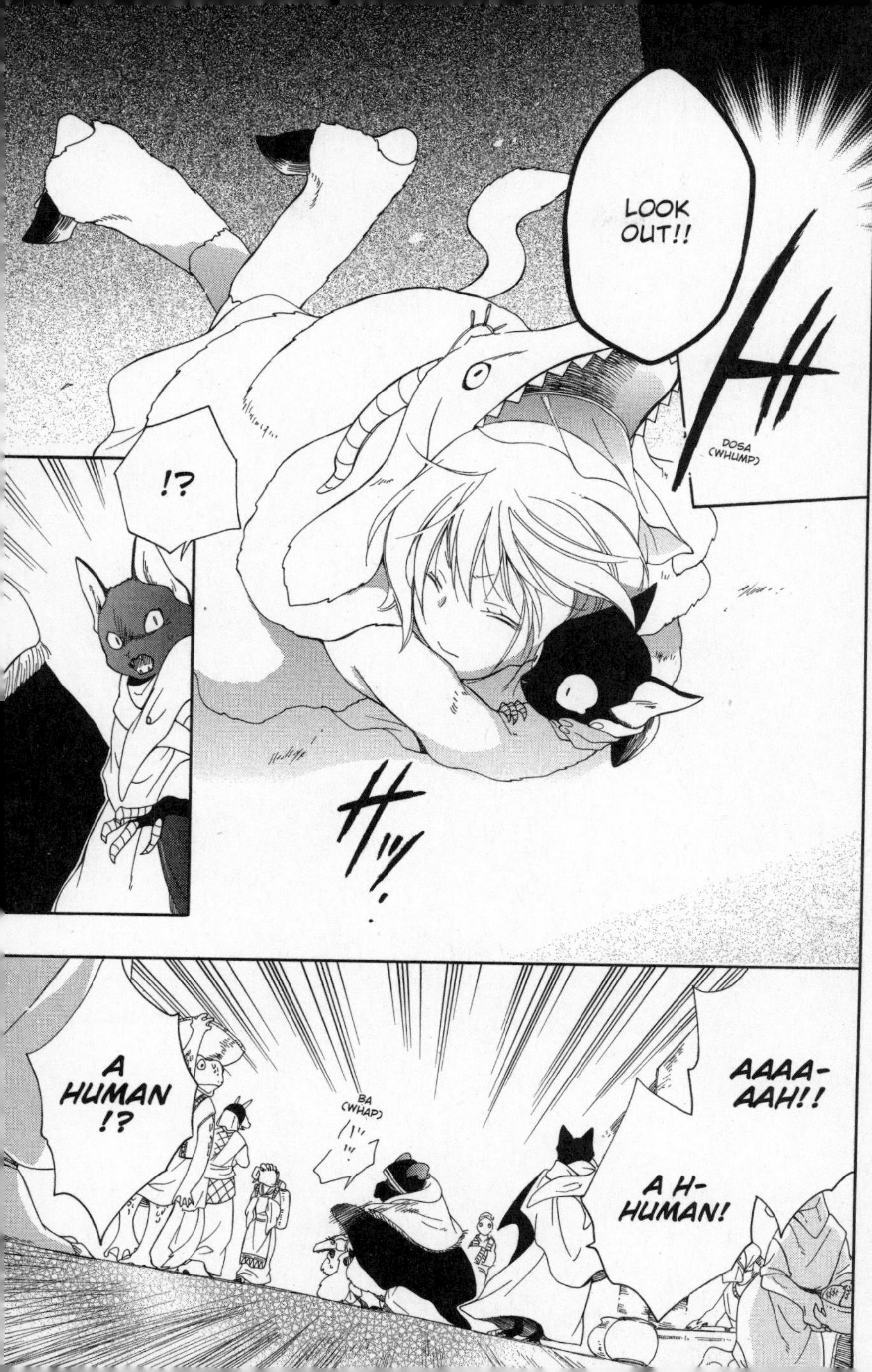
LOOK OUT!!
DOSA (WHUMP)
!?
ハッ
AAAA-AAH!!
A H-HUMAN!
BA (WHAP)
A HUMAN !?

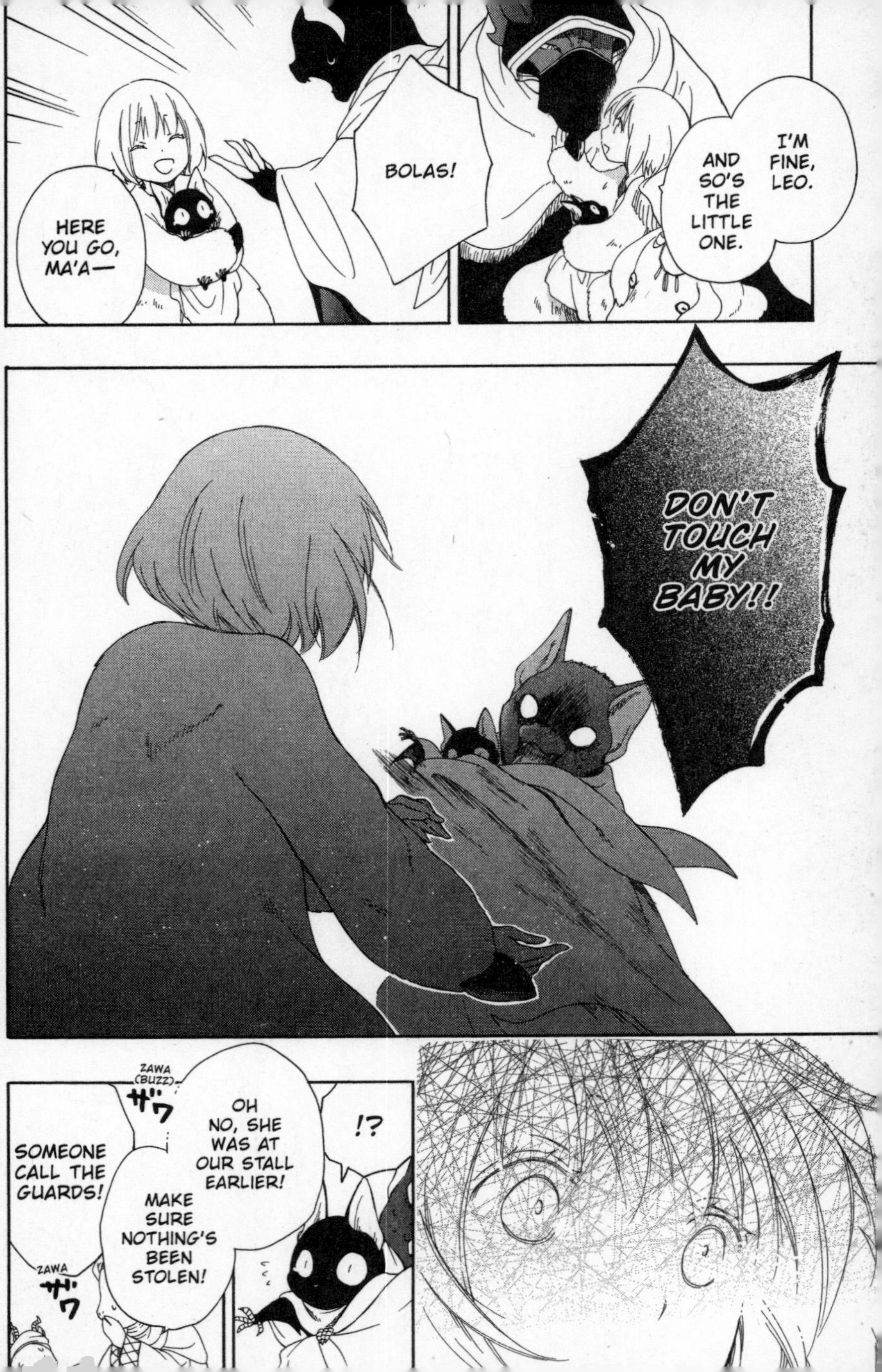
I'M FINE, LEO.
AND SO'S THE LITTLE ONE.
BOLAS!
HERE YOU GO, MA'A—
DON'T TOUCH MY BABY!!
!?
OH NO, SHE WAS AT OUR STALL EARLIER!
ZAWA (BUZZ) ザワ
SOMEONE CALL THE GUARDS!
MAKE SURE NOTHING'S BEEN STOLEN!
ZAWA ザワ

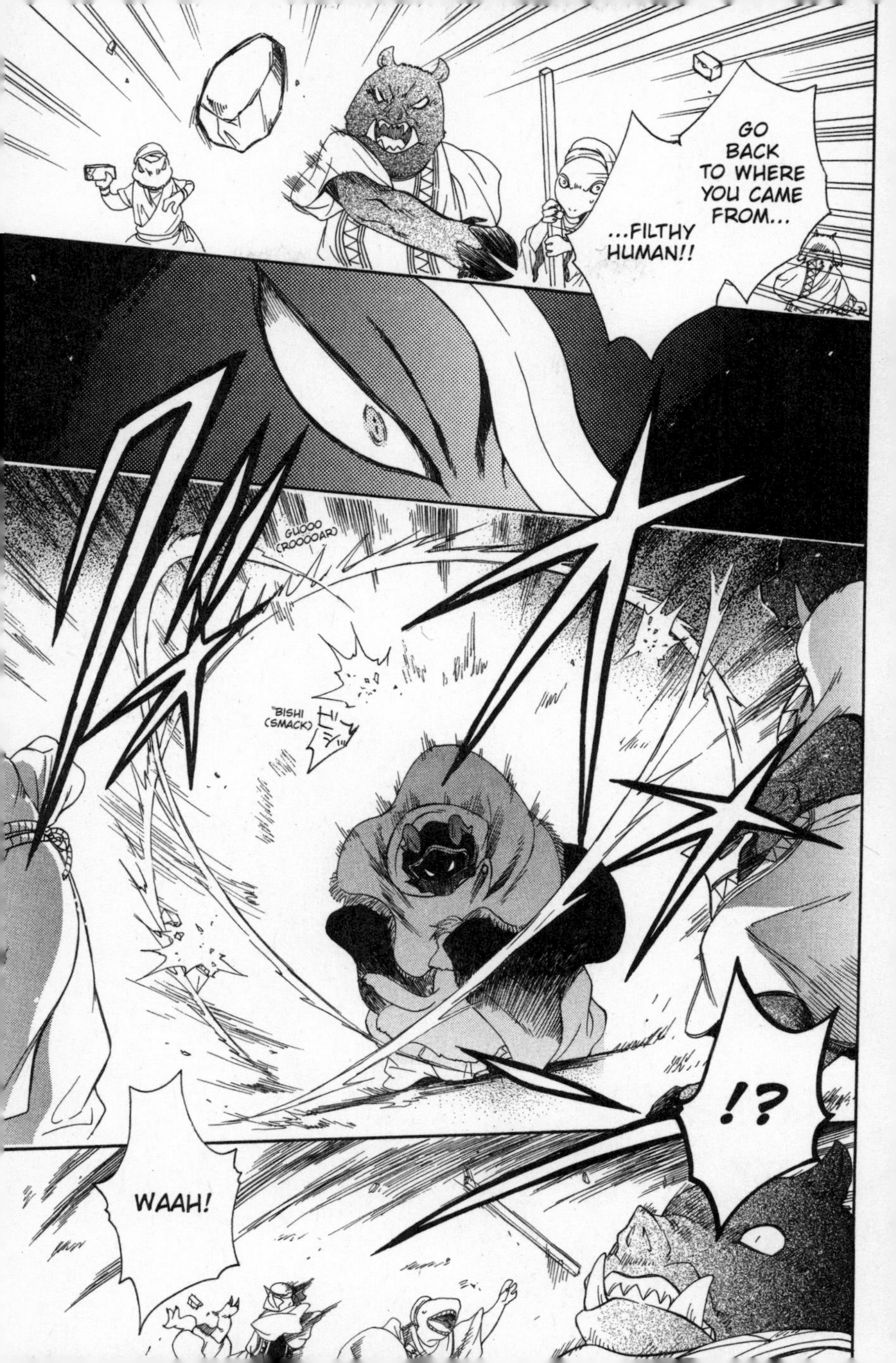
GO BACK TO WHERE YOU CAME FROM...
...FILTHY HUMAN!!
GUOOO (ROOOOAR)
BISHI (SMACK)
!?
WAAH!

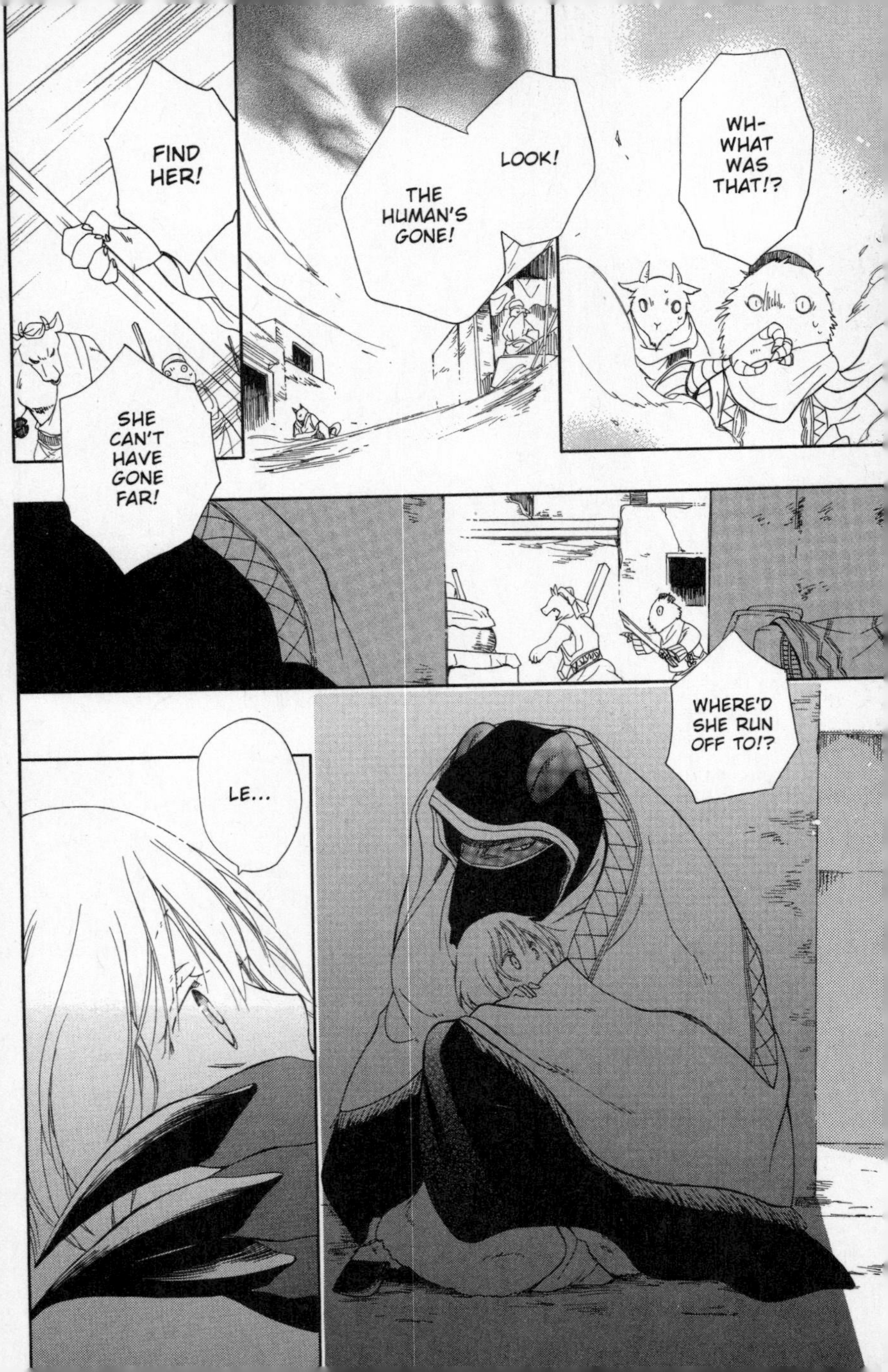
WH- WHAT WAS THAT!?
LOOK!
THE HUMAN'S GONE!
FIND HER!
SHE CAN'T HAVE GONE FAR!
WHERE'D SHE RUN OFF TO!?
LE...

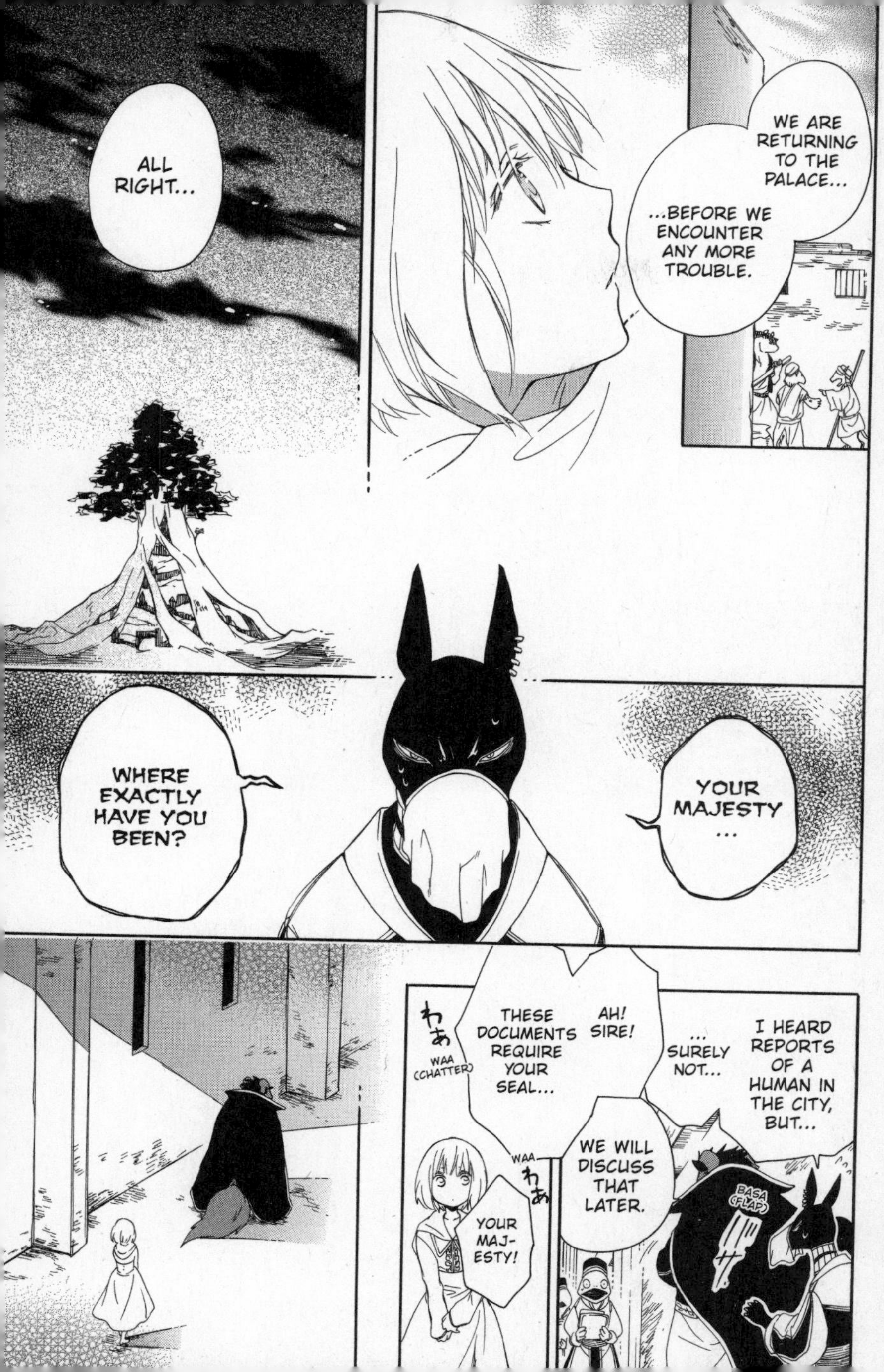
WE ARE RETURNING TO THE PALACE...
...BEFORE WE ENCOUNTER ANY MORE TROUBLE.
ALL RIGHT...
YOUR MAJESTY...
WHERE EXACTLY HAVE YOU BEEN?
I HEARD REPORTS OF A HUMAN IN THE CITY, BUT...
...SURELY NOT...
AH! SIRE!
THESE DOCUMENTS REQUIRE YOUR SEAL...
わあ WAA (CHATTER)
BASA (FLAP)
WE WILL DISCUSS THAT LATER.
わあ WAA
YOUR MAJ-ESTY!

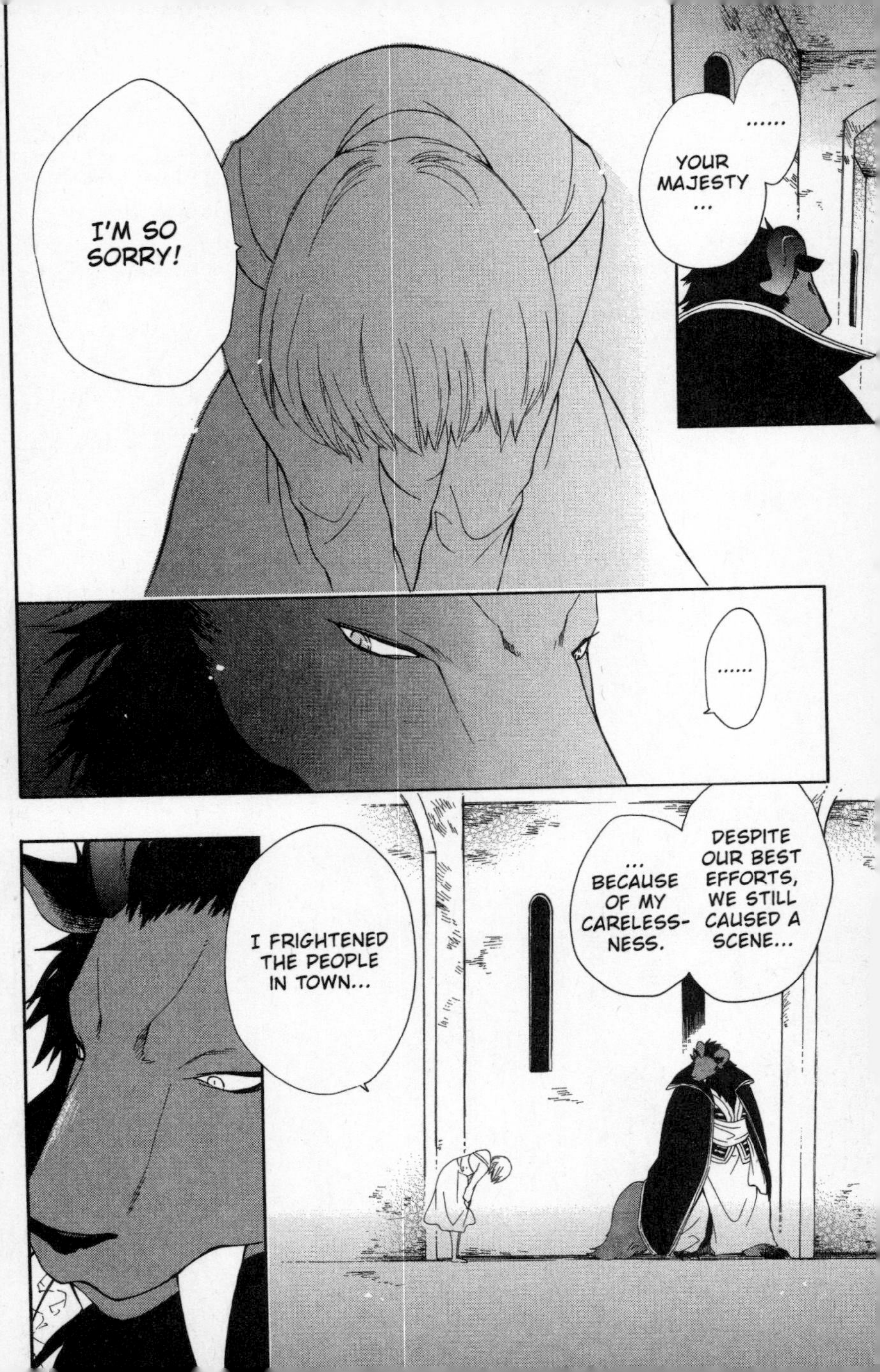
......
YOUR MAJESTY ...
I'M SO SORRY!
......
DESPITE OUR BEST EFFORTS, WE STILL CAUSED A SCENE...
...BECAUSE OF MY CARELESS-NESS.
I FRIGHTENED THE PEOPLE IN TOWN...

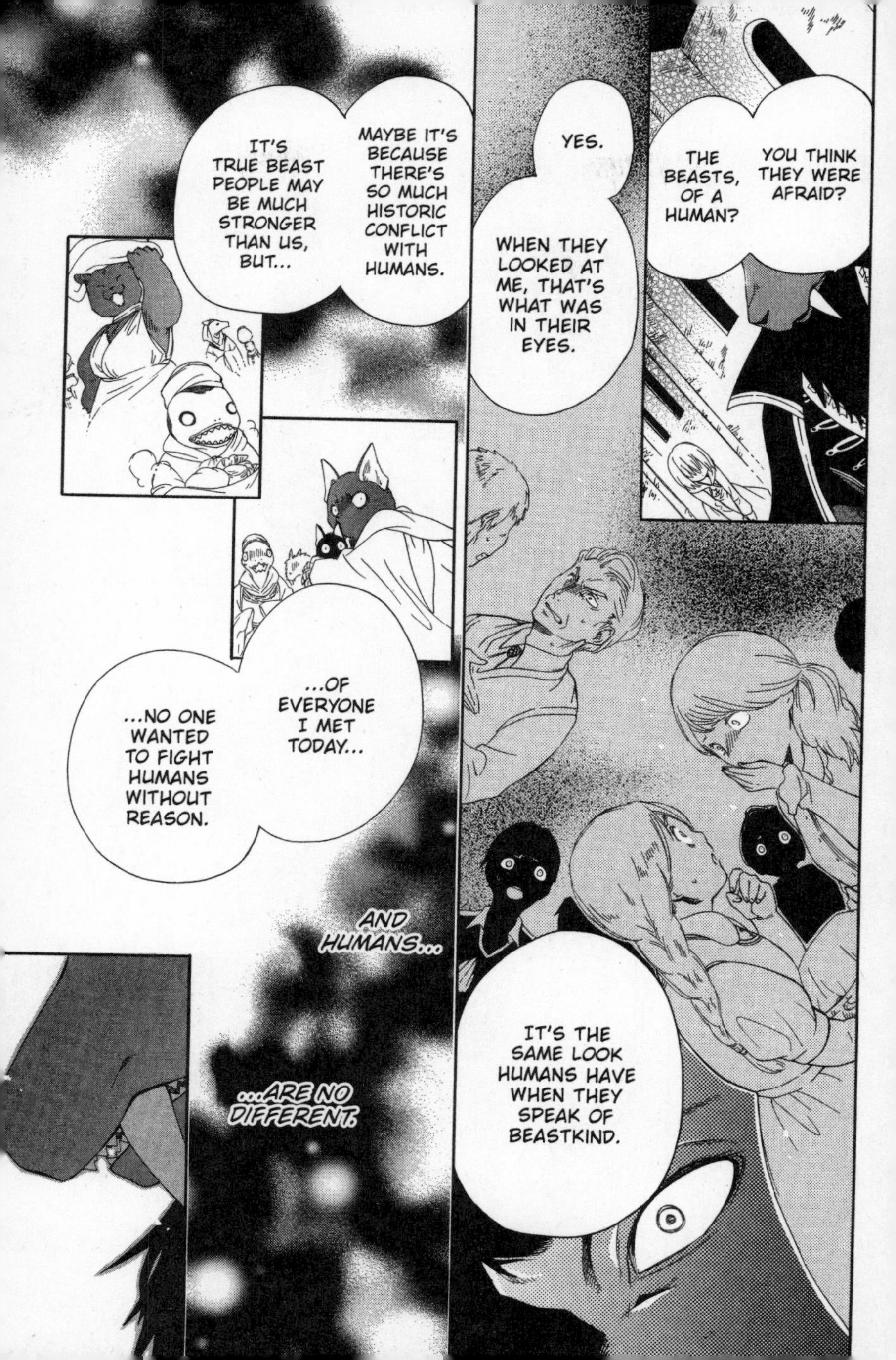
YOU THINK THEY WERE AFRAID?
THE BEASTS, OF A HUMAN?
YES.
WHEN THEY LOOKED AT ME, THAT'S WHAT WAS IN THEIR EYES.
IT'S THE SAME LOOK HUMANS HAVE WHEN THEY SPEAK OF BEASTKIND.
MAYBE IT'S BECAUSE THERE'S SO MUCH HISTORIC CONFLICT WITH HUMANS.
IT'S TRUE BEAST PEOPLE MAY BE MUCH STRONGER THAN US, BUT...
...OF EVERYONE I MET TODAY...
...NO ONE WANTED TO FIGHT HUMANS WITHOUT REASON.
AND HUMANS...
...ARE NO DIFFERENT.

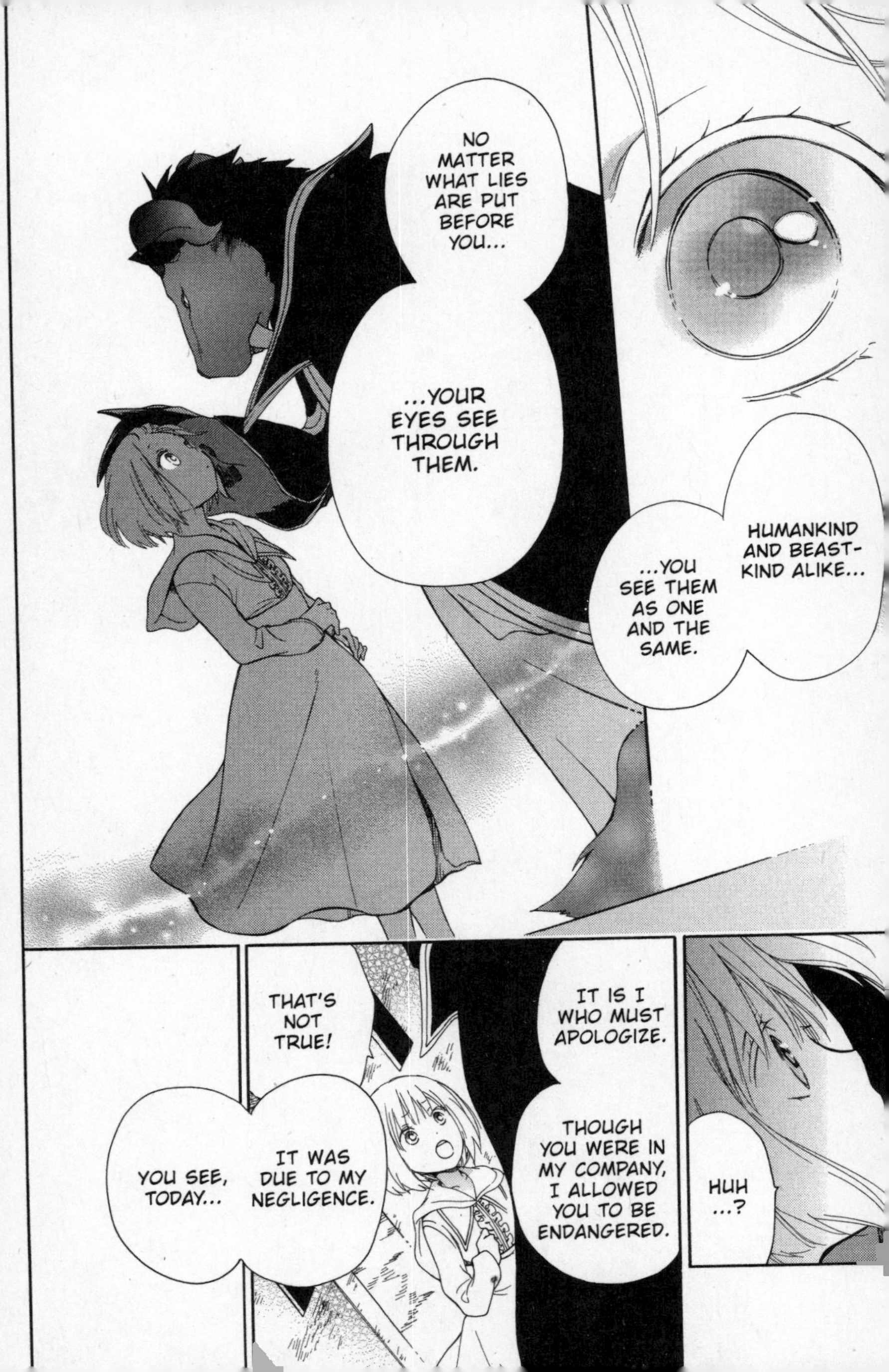
NO MATTER WHAT LIES ARE PUT BEFORE YOU...
...YOUR EYES SEE THROUGH THEM.
HUMANKIND AND BEAST-KIND ALIKE...
...YOU SEE THEM AS ONE AND THE SAME.
HUH ...?
IT IS I WHO MUST APOLOGIZE.
THOUGH YOU WERE IN MY COMPANY, I ALLOWED YOU TO BE ENDANGERED.
THAT'S NOT TRUE!
IT WAS DUE TO MY NEGLIGENCE.
YOU SEE, TODAY...

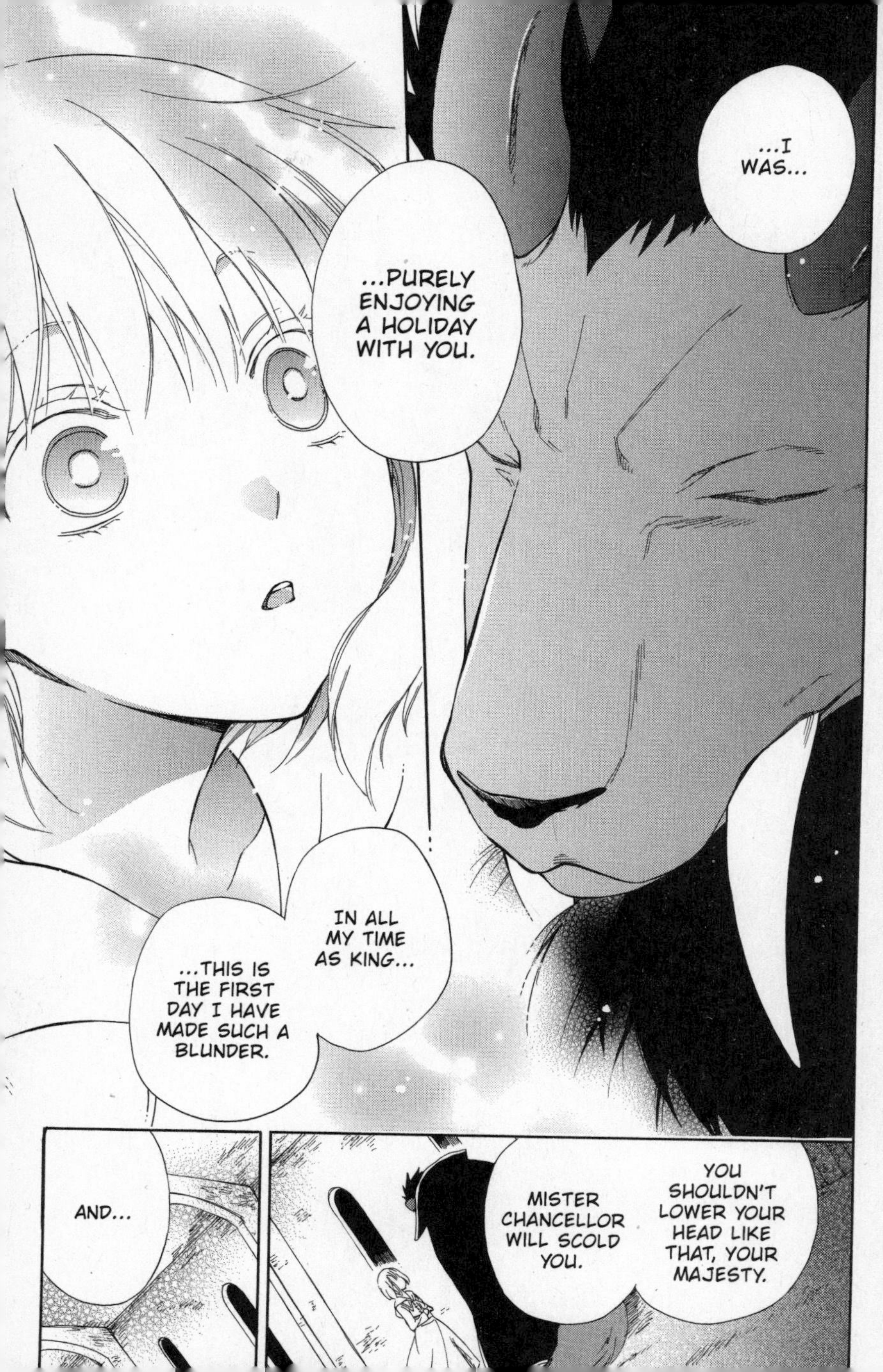
...I WAS...
...PURELY ENJOYING A HOLIDAY WITH YOU.
IN ALL MY TIME AS KING...
...THIS IS THE FIRST DAY I HAVE MADE SUCH A BLUNDER.
YOU SHOULDN'T LOWER YOUR HEAD LIKE THAT, YOUR MAJESTY.
MISTER CHANCELLOR WILL SCOLD YOU.
AND...

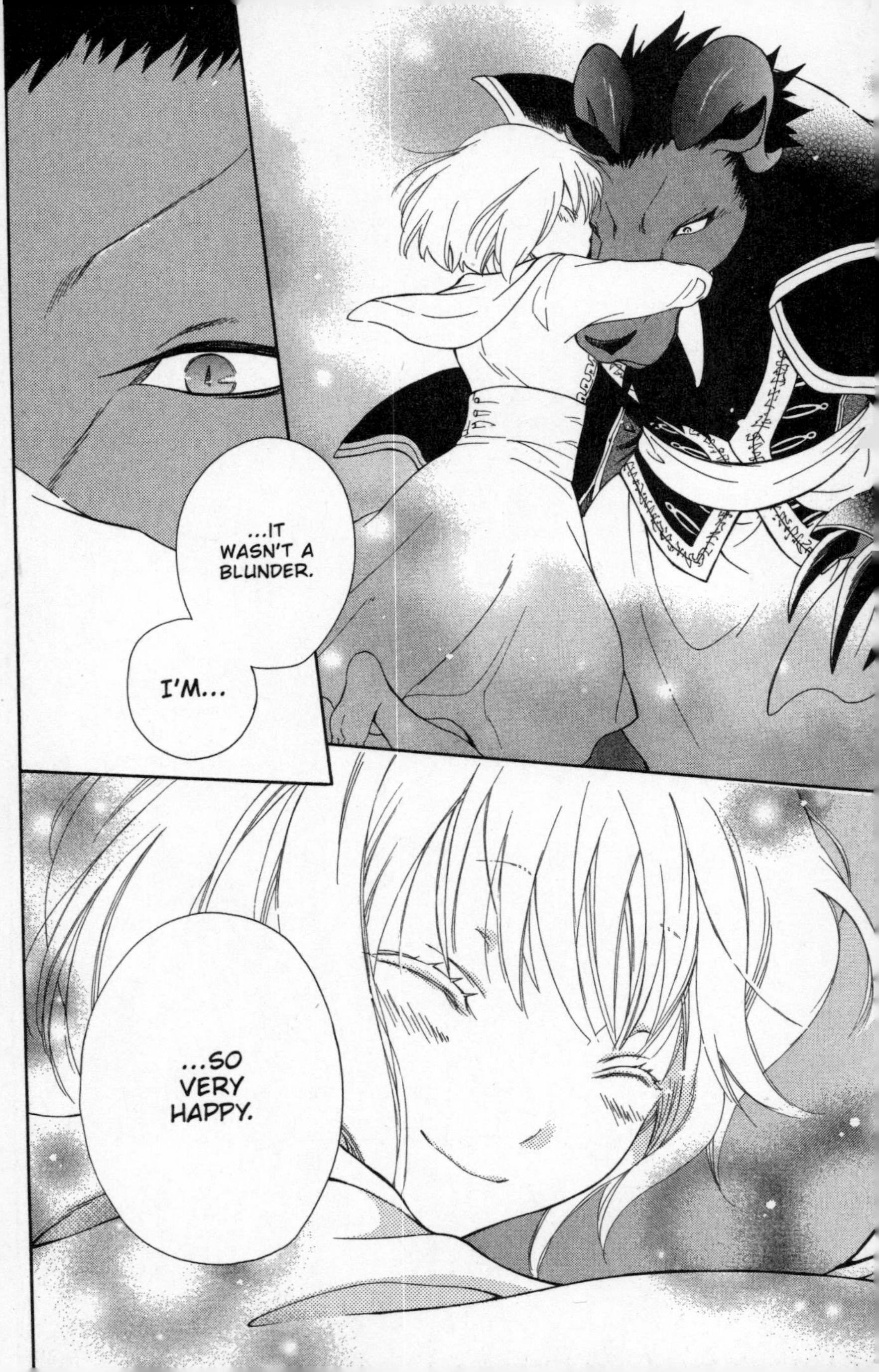
...IT WASN'T A BLUNDER.
I'M...
...SO VERY HAPPY.

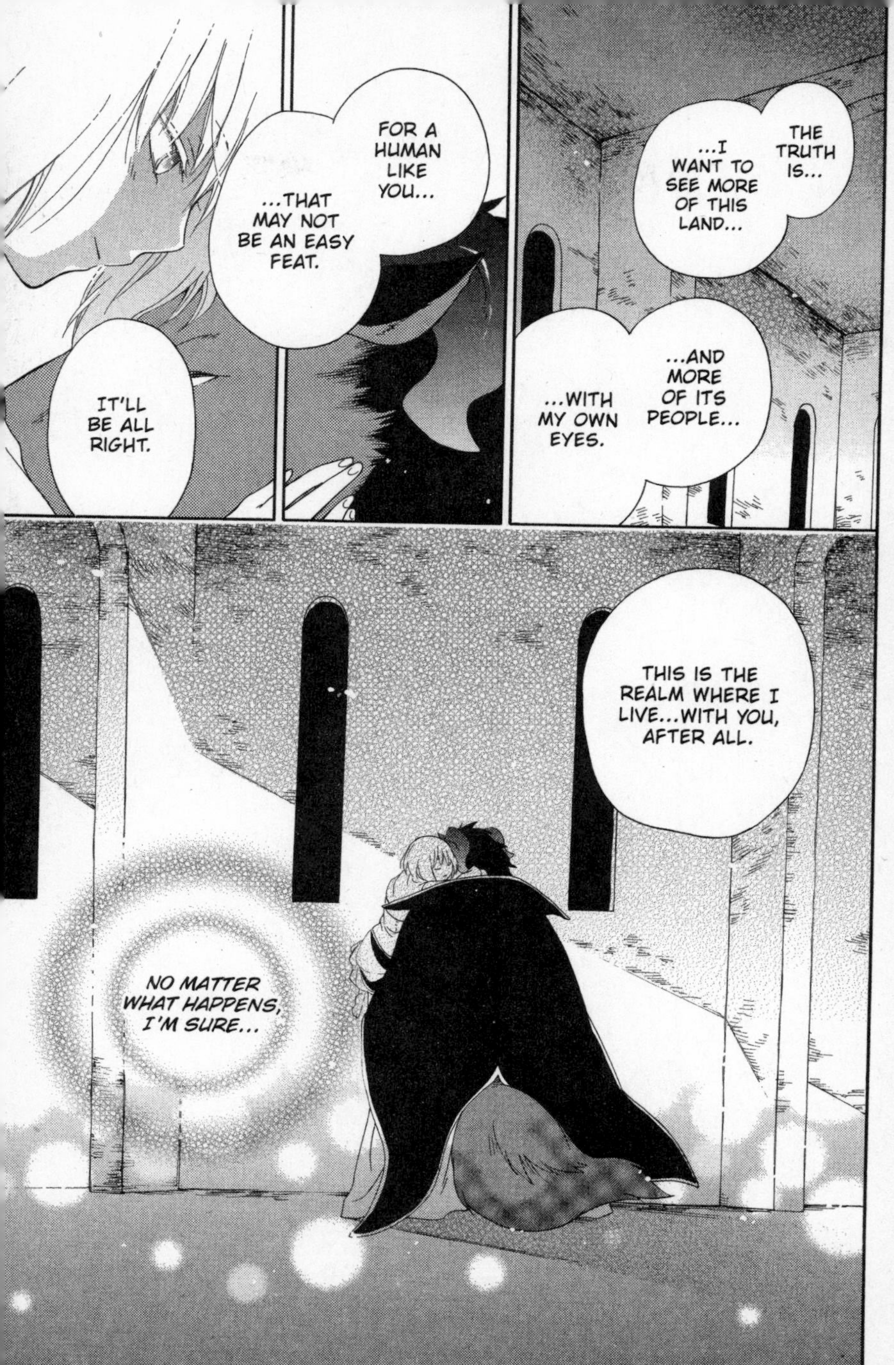
THE TRUTH IS...
...I WANT TO SEE MORE OF THIS LAND...
...AND MORE OF ITS PEOPLE...
...WITH MY OWN EYES.
FOR A HUMAN LIKE YOU...
...THAT MAY NOT BE AN EASY FEAT.
IT'LL BE ALL RIGHT.
THIS IS THE REALM WHERE I LIVE...WITH YOU, AFTER ALL.
NO MATTER WHAT HAPPENS, I'M SURE...

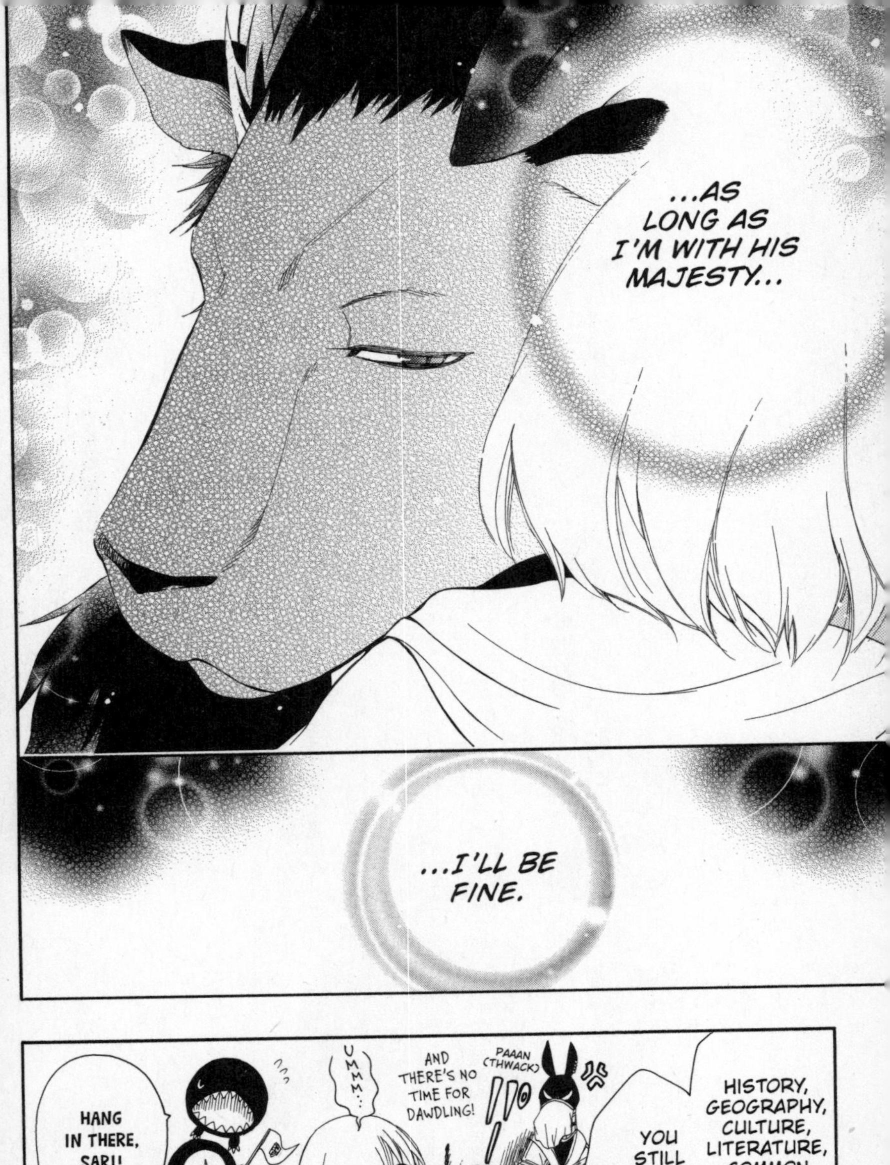
...AS LONG AS I'M WITH HIS MAJESTY...
...I'LL BE FINE.
HISTORY, GEOGRAPHY, CULTURE, LITERATURE, COMMON SENSE—
YOU STILL HAVE MUCH TO LEARN!
PAAAN (THWACK)
AND THERE'S NO TIME FOR DAWDLING!
UMMM...
HANG IN THERE, SARI!

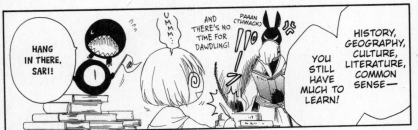

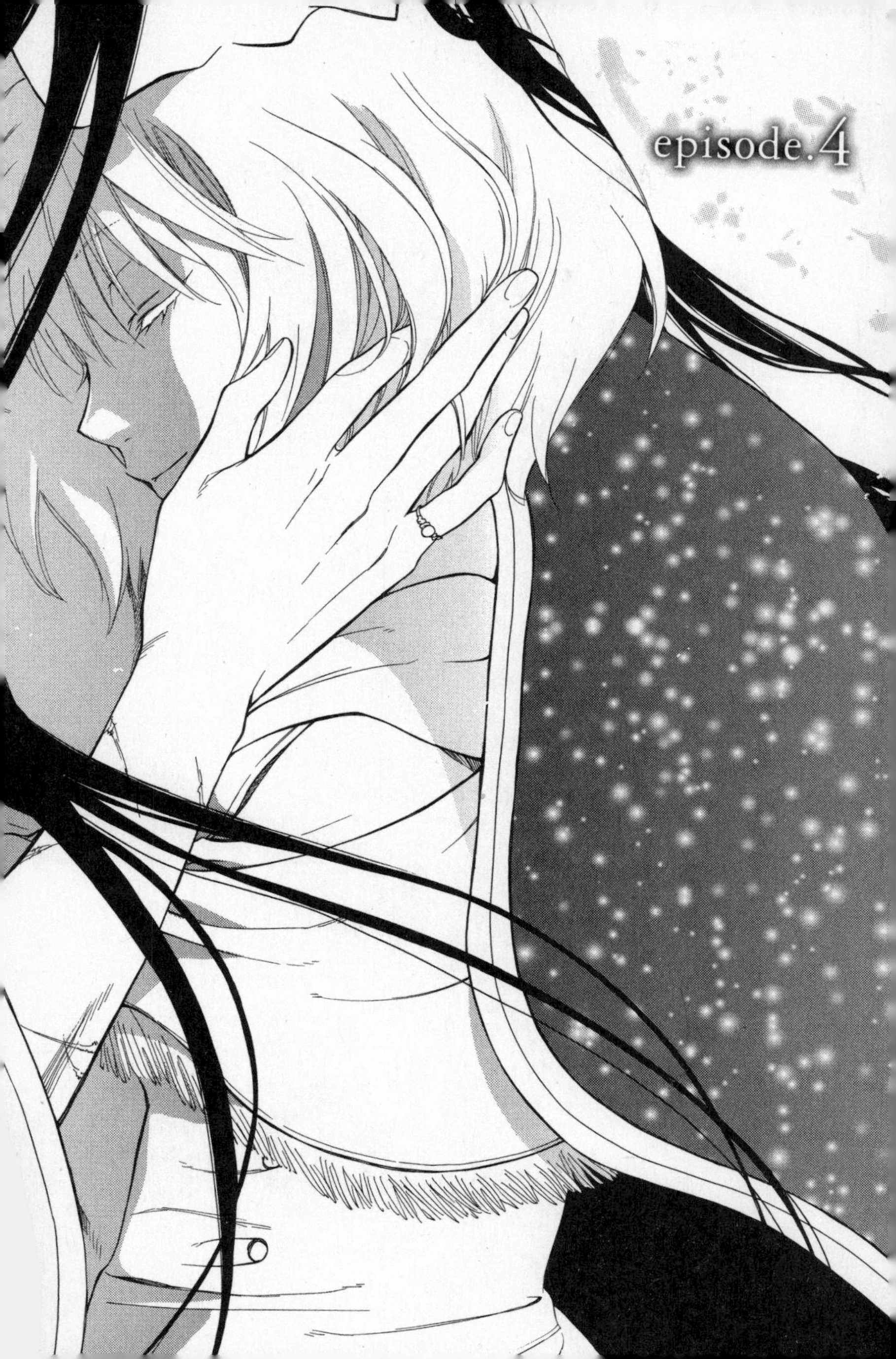
episode.4

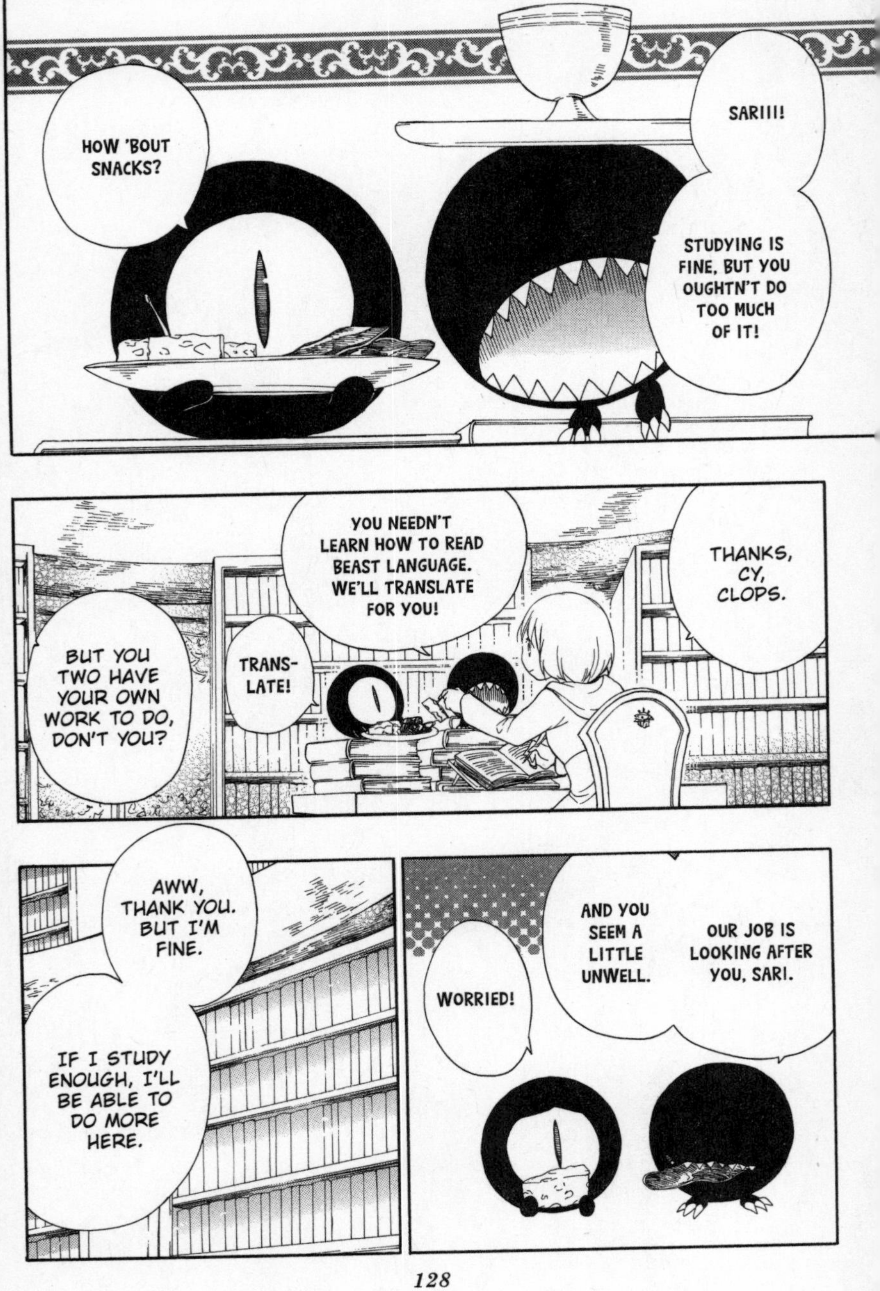
SARIII!
STUDYING IS FINE, BUT YOU OUGHTN'T DO TOO MUCH OF IT!
HOW 'BOUT SNACKS?
THANKS, CY, CLOPS.
YOU NEEDN'T LEARN HOW TO READ BEAST LANGUAGE. WE'LL TRANSLATE FOR YOU!
TRANS-LATE!
BUT YOU TWO HAVE YOUR OWN WORK TO DO, DON'T YOU?
OUR JOB IS LOOKING AFTER YOU, SARI.
AND YOU SEEM A LITTLE UNWELL.
WORRIED!
AWW, THANK YOU. BUT I'M FINE.
IF I STUDY ENOUGH, I'LL BE ABLE TO DO MORE HERE.

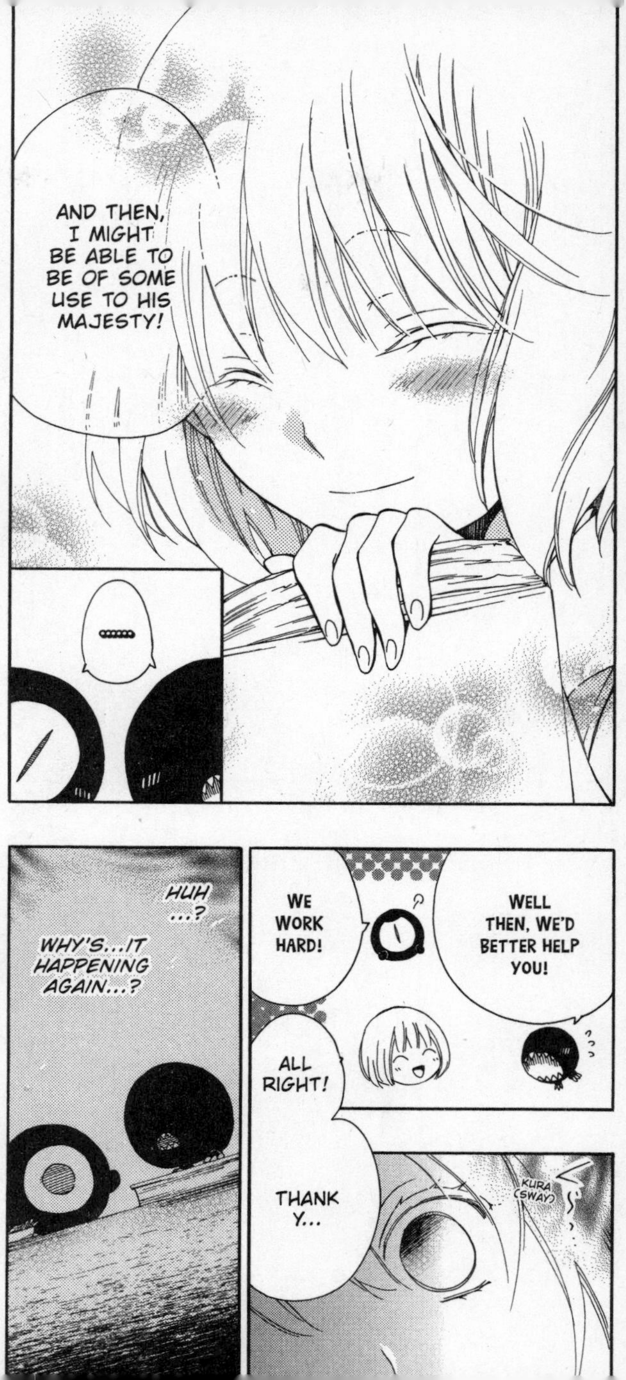
AND THEN, I MIGHT BE ABLE TO BE OF SOME USE TO HIS MAJESTY!
WELL THEN, WE'D BETTER HELP YOU!
WE WORK HARD!
ALL RIGHT!
THANK Y...
KURA (SWAY)
HUH ...?
WHY'S...IT HAPPENING AGAIN...?

③

ANUBIS

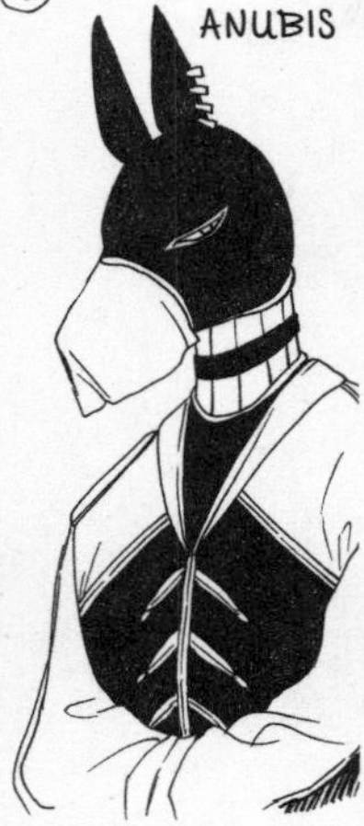

HE'S DRAWN EXACTLY IN THE IMAGE HIS NAME CALLS TO MIND. I WAS PLANNING ON MAKING HIM A LOOKER, BUT MY EDITOR JUST LAUGHED AT ME WHEN I SAID SO BECAUSE ANUBIS'S PERSONALITY IS SO OLD-MAIDISH.

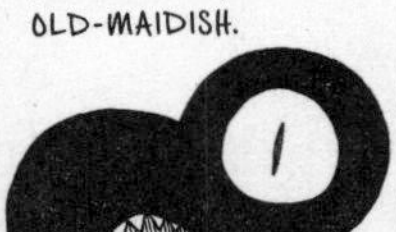

↑ THIS IS CLOPS.

THIS IS CY. ↑

THERE'S LOTS OF STUFF ABOUT "BEASTKIND" IN THESE BOOKS, BUT MOST OF THE BEAST CHARACTERS ARE ANTHROPOMORPHIC ANIMALS. THESE TWO ARE THE MOST MONSTER-Y BEASTS OF THEM ALL.

CONTINUED TO ④ →

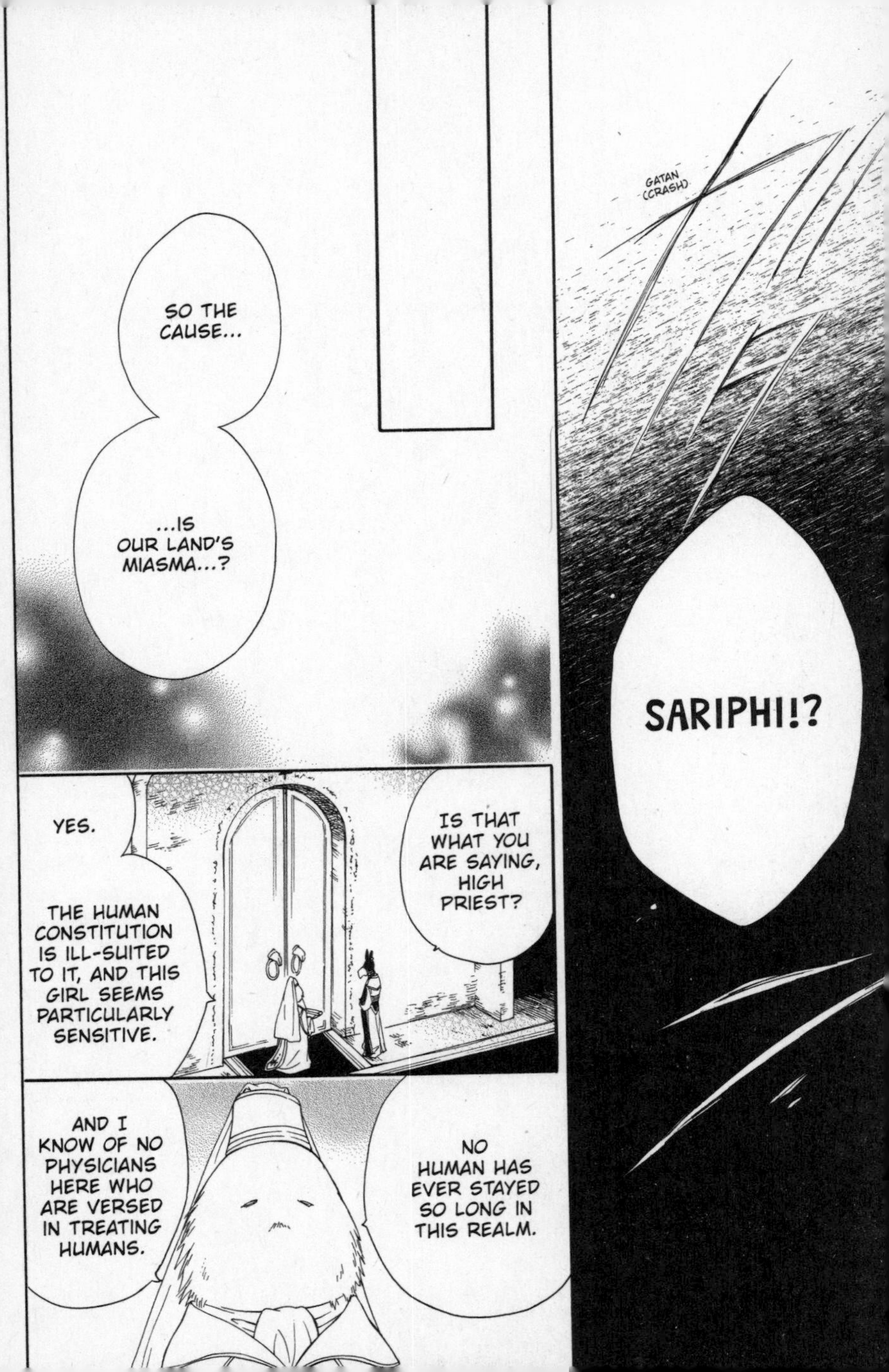
GATAN (CRASH)
SARIPHI!?
SO THE CAUSE...
...IS OUR LAND'S MIASMA...?
IS THAT WHAT YOU ARE SAYING, HIGH PRIEST?
YES.
THE HUMAN CONSTITUTION IS ILL-SUITED TO IT, AND THIS GIRL SEEMS PARTICULARLY SENSITIVE.
NO HUMAN HAS EVER STAYED SO LONG IN THIS REALM.
AND I KNOW OF NO PHYSICIANS HERE WHO ARE VERSED IN TREATING HUMANS.

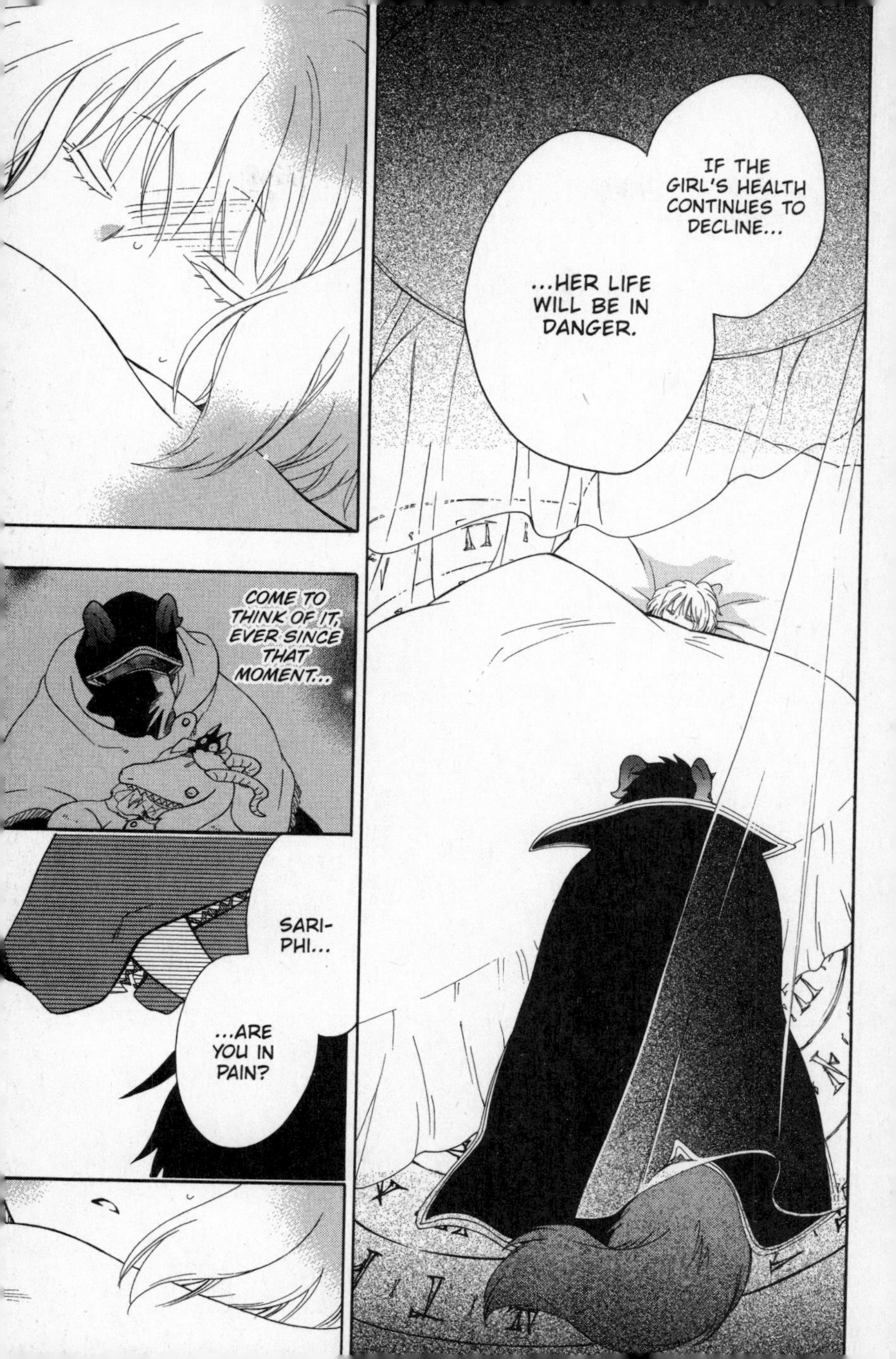

IF THE GIRL'S HEALTH CONTINUES TO DECLINE...
...HER LIFE WILL BE IN DANGER.
COME TO THINK OF IT, EVER SINCE THAT MOMENT...
SARI-PHI...
...ARE YOU IN PAIN?

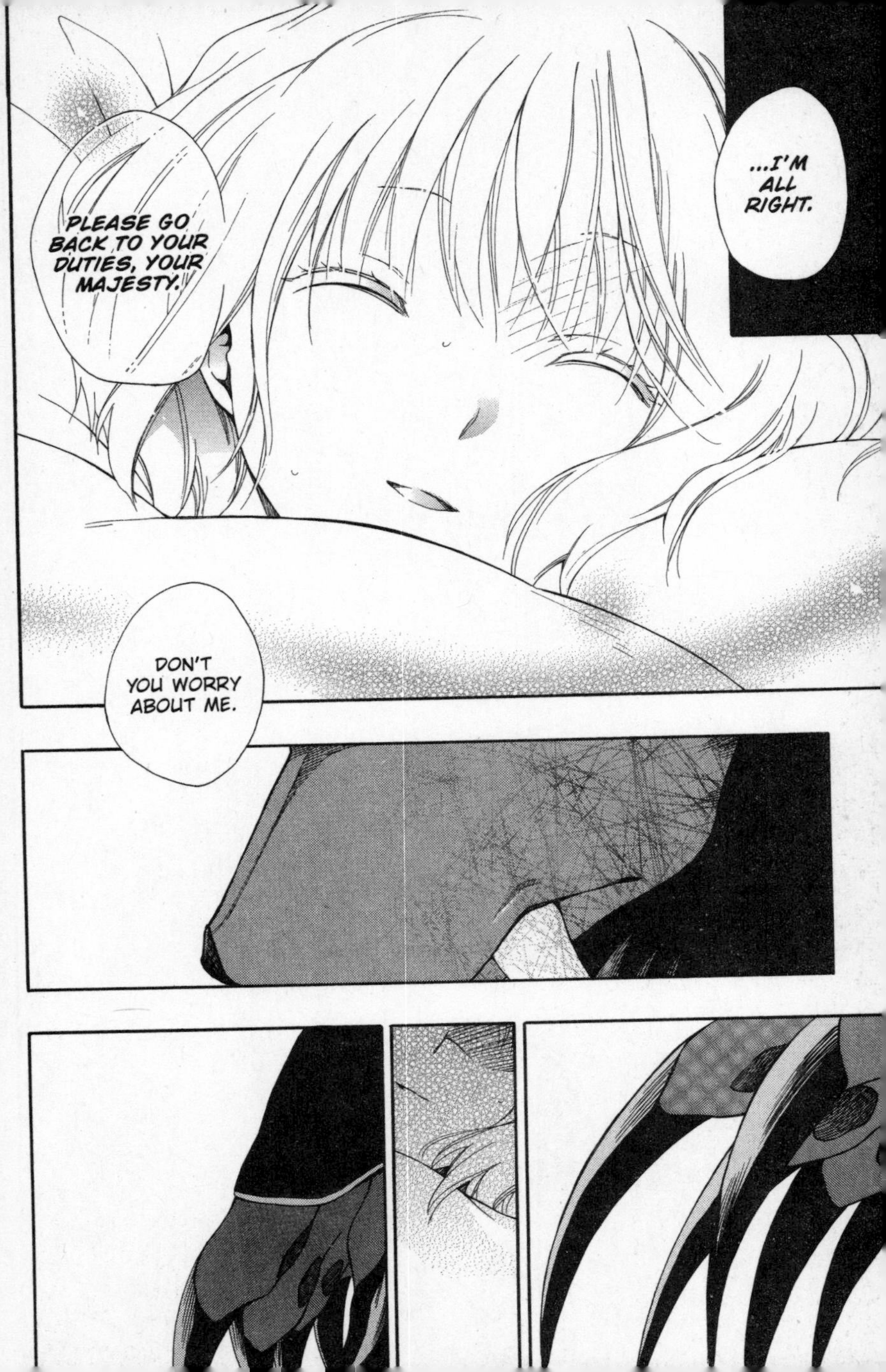
...I'M ALL RIGHT.
PLEASE GO BACK TO YOUR DUTIES, YOUR MAJESTY.
DON'T YOU WORRY ABOUT ME.

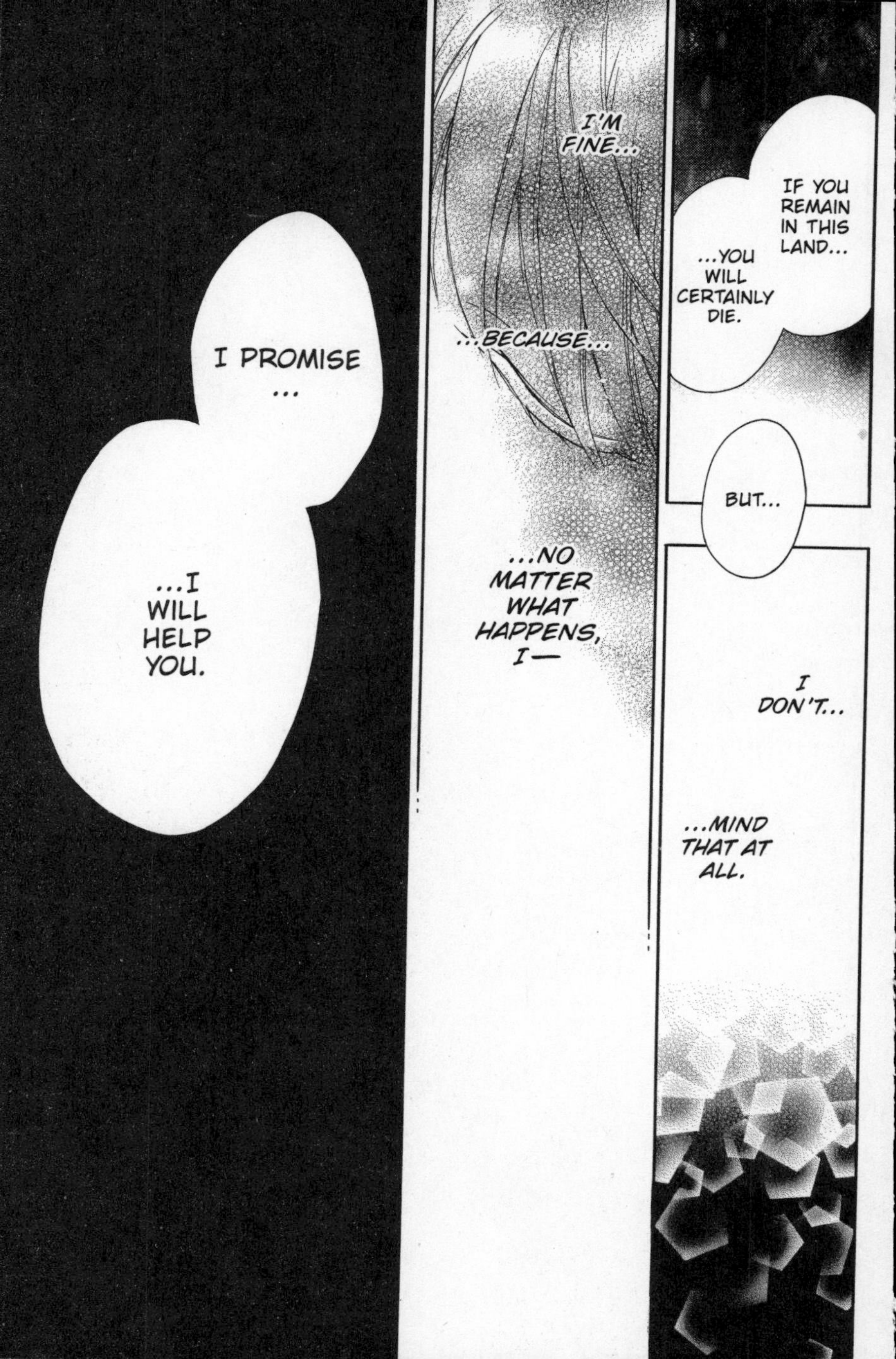
IF YOU REMAIN IN THIS LAND...
...YOU WILL CERTAINLY DIE.
BUT...
I DON'T...
...MIND THAT AT ALL.
I'M FINE...
...BECAUSE...
...NO MATTER WHAT HAPPENS, I—
I PROMISE ...
...I WILL HELP YOU.

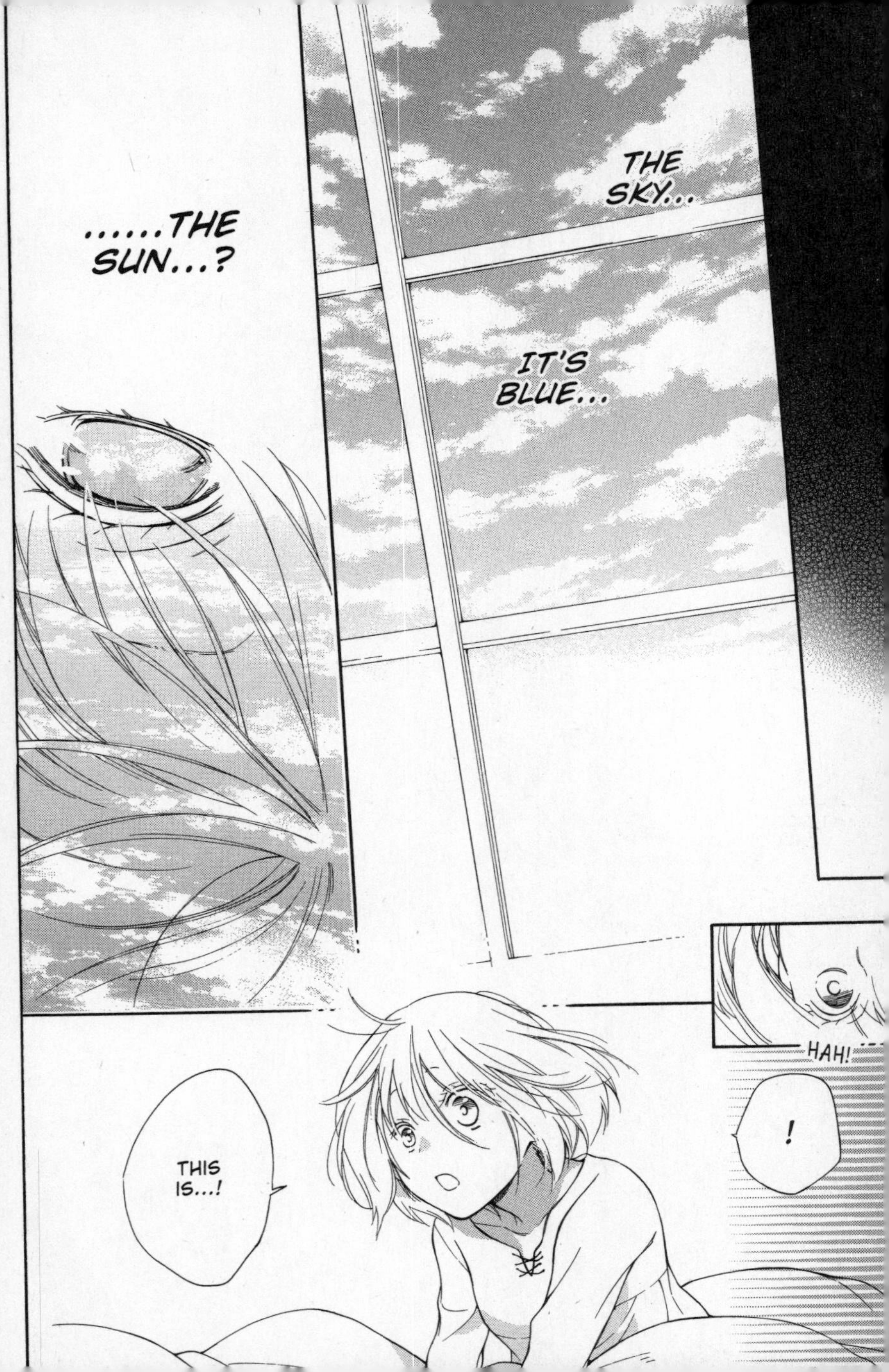
THE SKY...
IT'S BLUE...
......THE SUN...?
HAH!
!
THIS IS...!

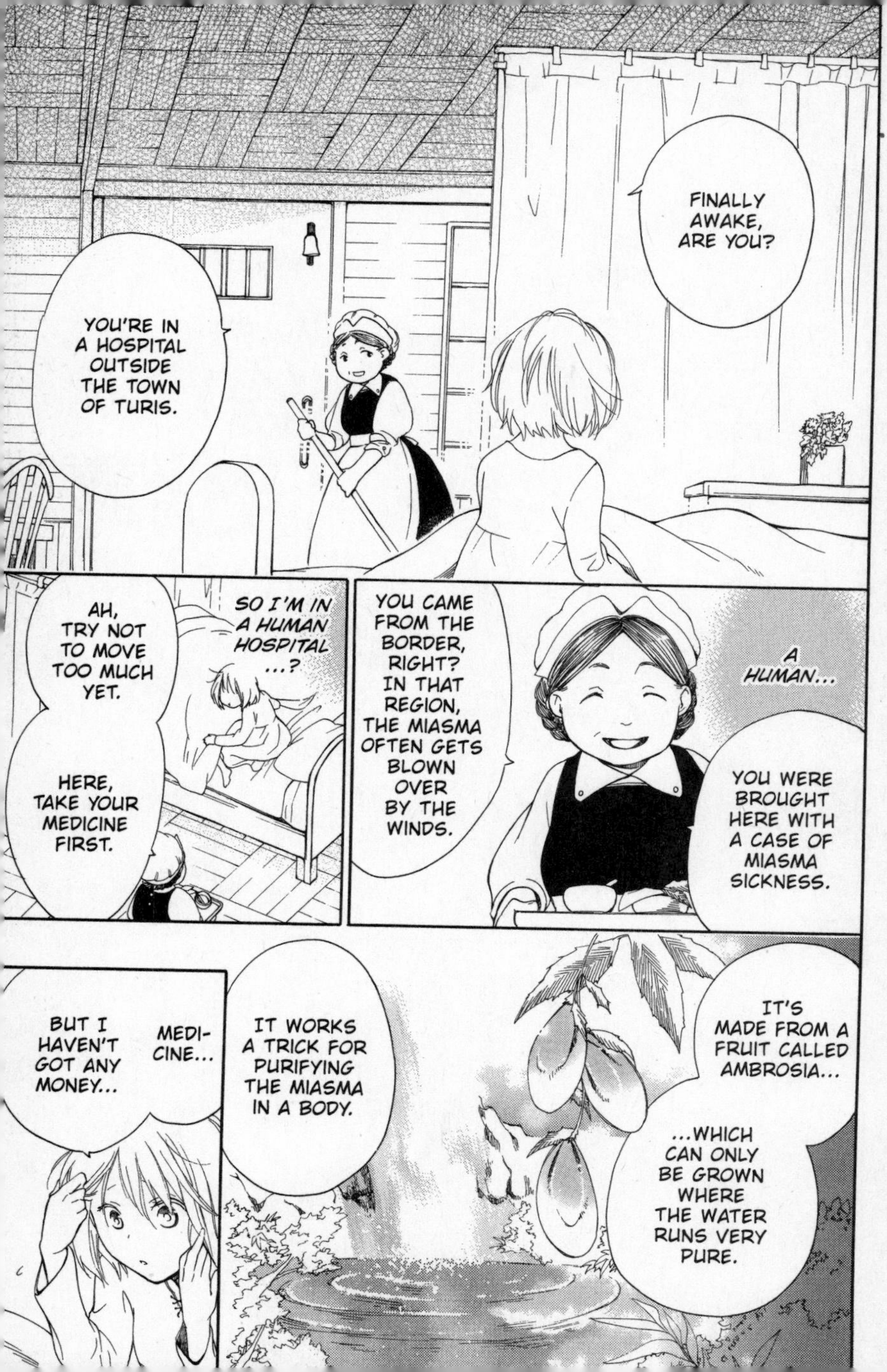
FINALLY AWAKE, ARE YOU?
YOU'RE IN A HOSPITAL OUTSIDE THE TOWN OF TURIS.
A HUMAN...
YOU WERE BROUGHT HERE WITH A CASE OF MIASMA SICKNESS.
YOU CAME FROM THE BORDER, RIGHT? IN THAT REGION, THE MIASMA OFTEN GETS BLOWN OVER BY THE WINDS.
SO I'M IN A HUMAN HOSPITAL...?
AH, TRY NOT TO MOVE TOO MUCH YET.
HERE, TAKE YOUR MEDICINE FIRST.
IT'S MADE FROM A FRUIT CALLED AMBROSIA...
...WHICH CAN ONLY BE GROWN WHERE THE WATER RUNS VERY PURE.
IT WORKS A TRICK FOR PURIFYING THE MIASMA IN A BODY.
MEDI-CINE...
BUT I HAVEN'T GOT ANY MONEY...

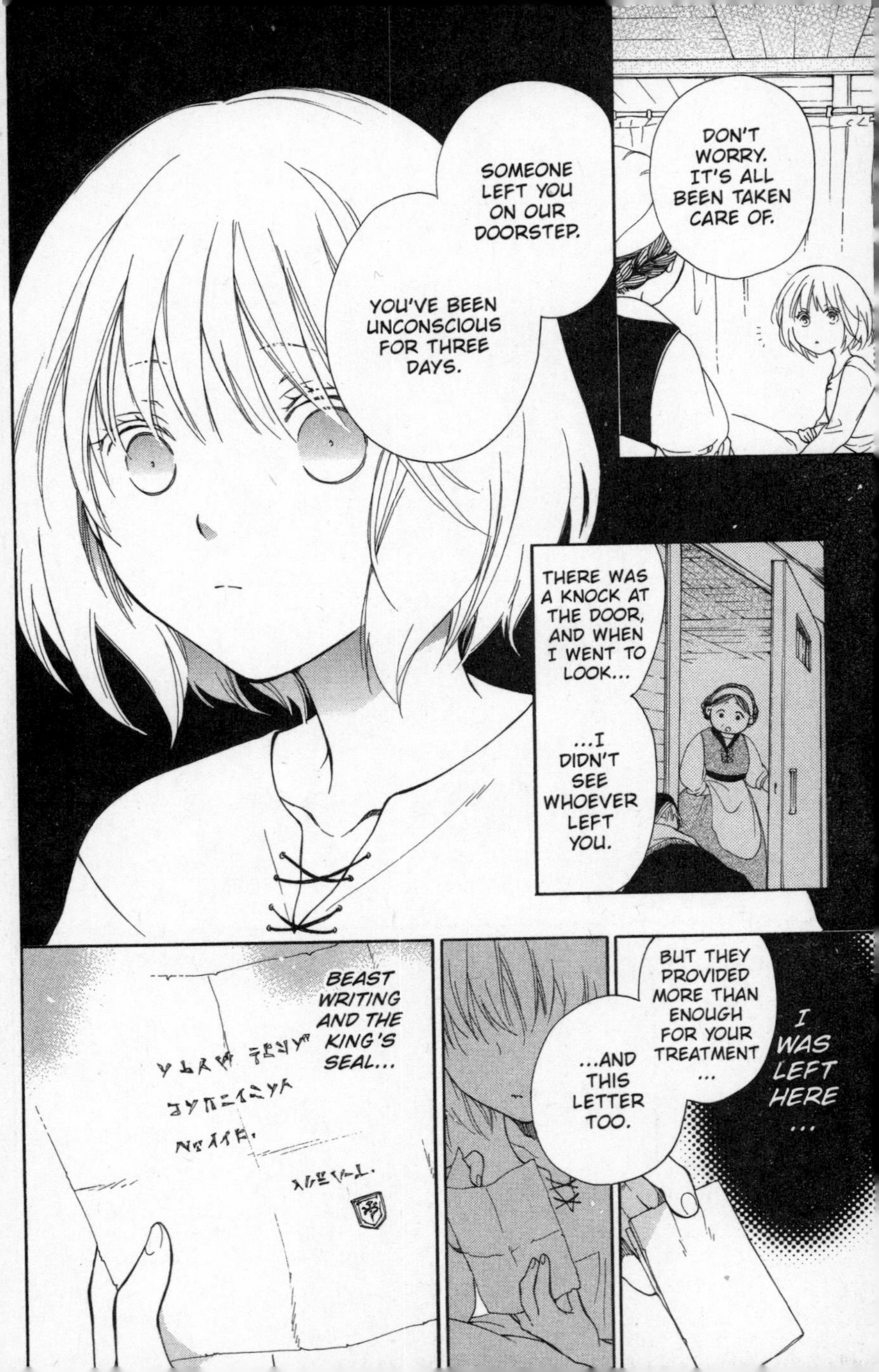
DON'T WORRY. IT'S ALL BEEN TAKEN CARE OF.
THERE WAS A KNOCK AT THE DOOR, AND WHEN I WENT TO LOOK...
...I DIDN'T SEE WHOEVER LEFT YOU.
SOMEONE LEFT YOU ON OUR DOORSTEP.
YOU'VE BEEN UNCONSCIOUS FOR THREE DAYS.
BUT THEY PROVIDED MORE THAN ENOUGH FOR YOUR TREATMENT...
...AND THIS LETTER TOO.
I WAS LEFT HERE...
BEAST WRITING AND THE KING'S SEAL...

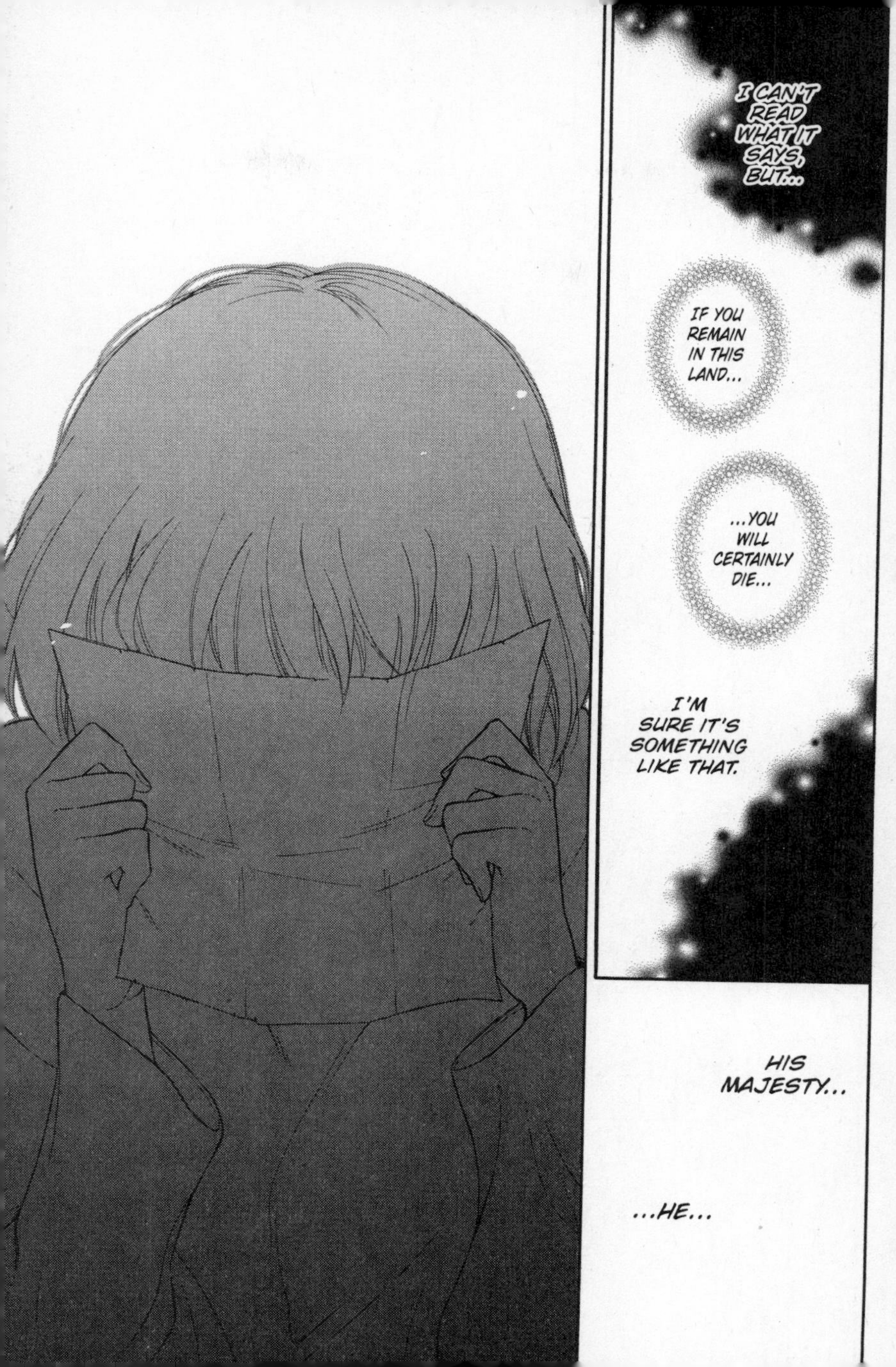
I CAN'T READ WHAT IT SAYS, BUT...
IF YOU REMAIN IN THIS LAND...
...YOU WILL CERTAINLY DIE...
I'M SURE IT'S SOMETHING LIKE THAT.
HIS MAJESTY...
...HE...

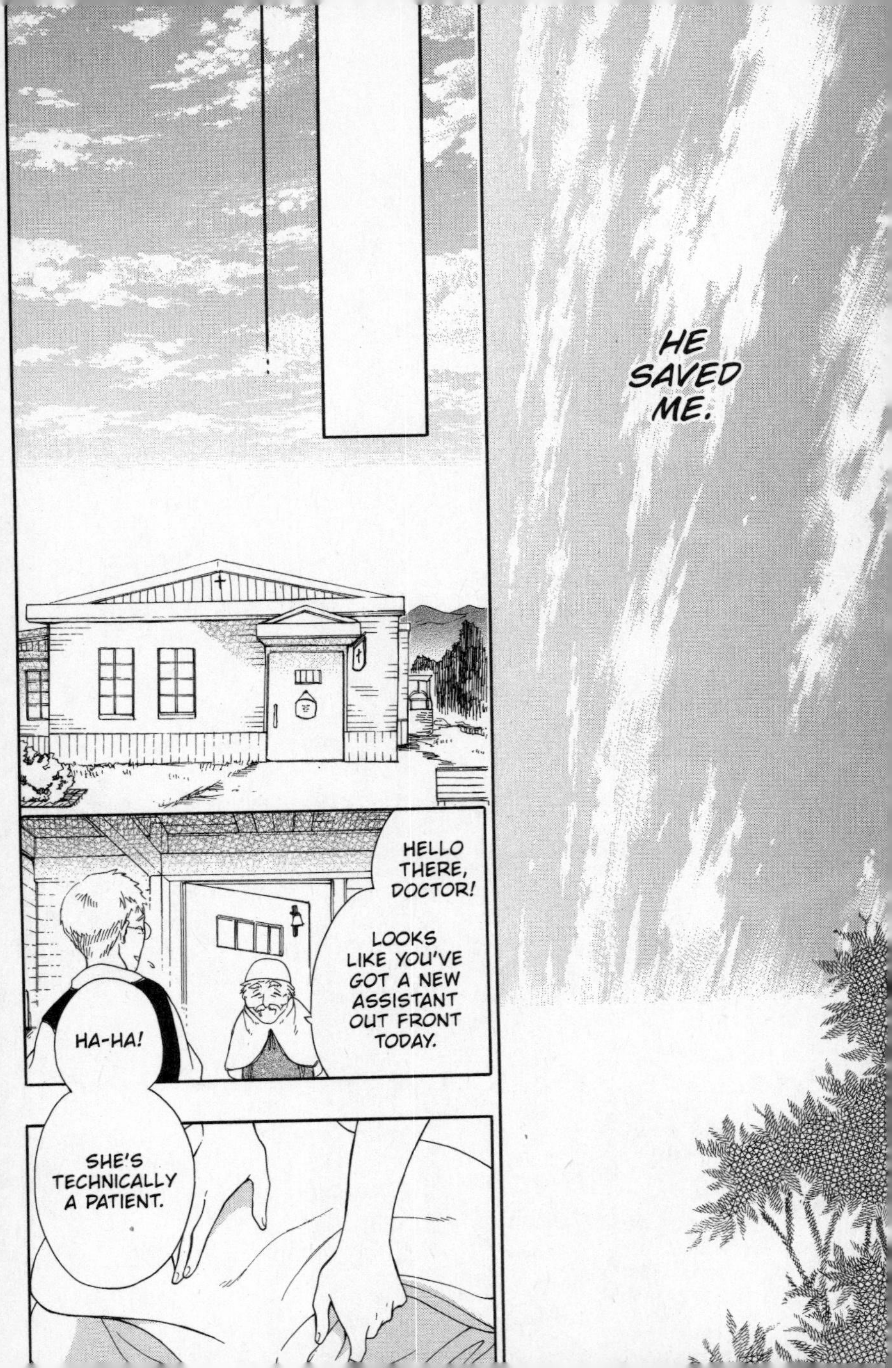
HE SAVED ME.
HELLO THERE, DOCTOR!
LOOKS LIKE YOU'VE GOT A NEW ASSISTANT OUT FRONT TODAY.
HA-HA!
SHE'S TECHNICALLY A PATIENT.

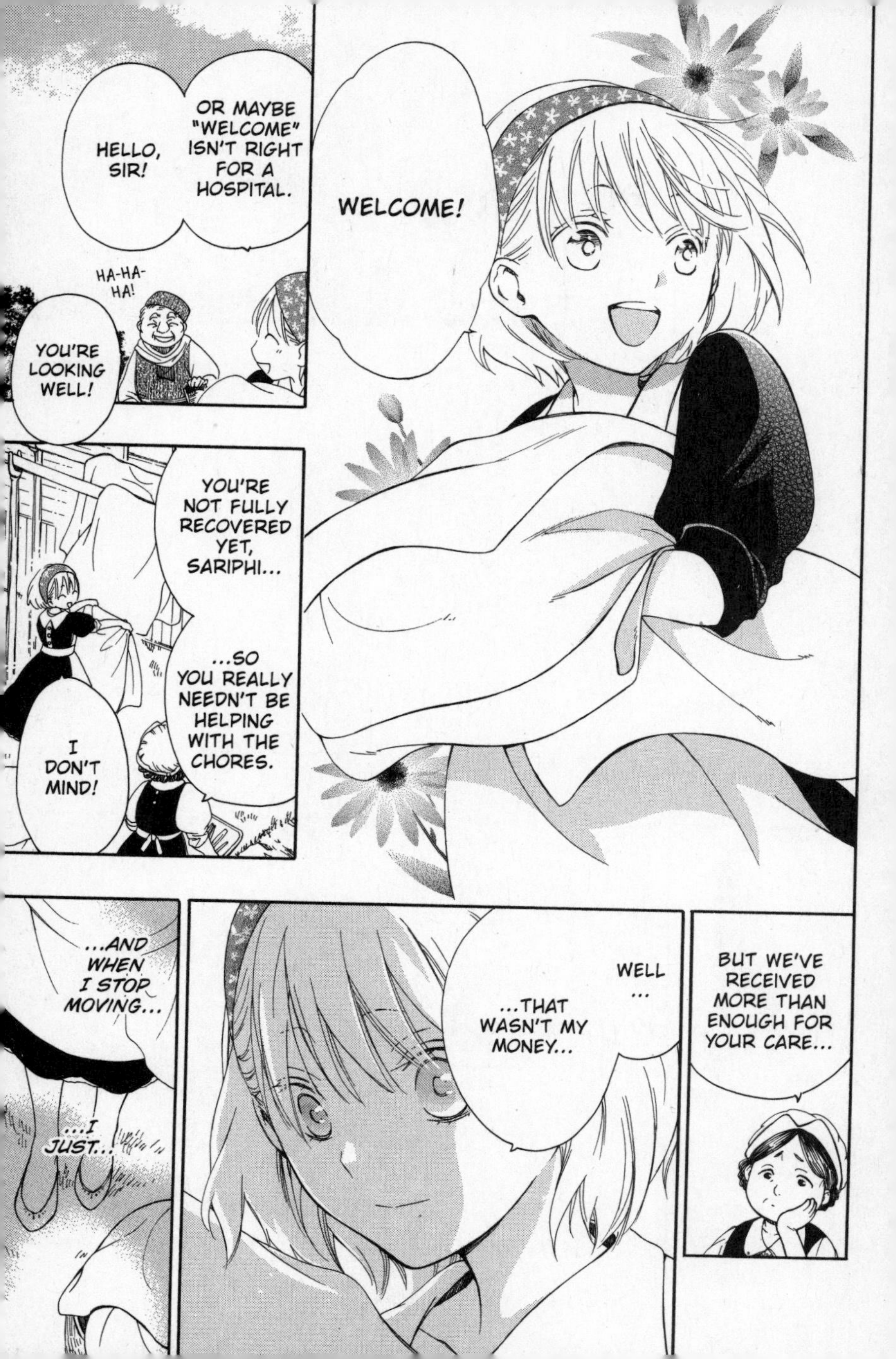
WELCOME!
OR MAYBE "WELCOME" ISN'T RIGHT FOR A HOSPITAL.
HELLO, SIR!
HA-HA-HA!
YOU'RE LOOKING WELL!
YOU'RE NOT FULLY RECOVERED YET, SARIPHI...
...SO YOU REALLY NEEDN'T BE HELPING WITH THE CHORES.
I DON'T MIND!
BUT WE'VE RECEIVED MORE THAN ENOUGH FOR YOUR CARE...
WELL ...
...THAT WASN'T MY MONEY...
...AND WHEN I STOP MOVING...
...I JUST...

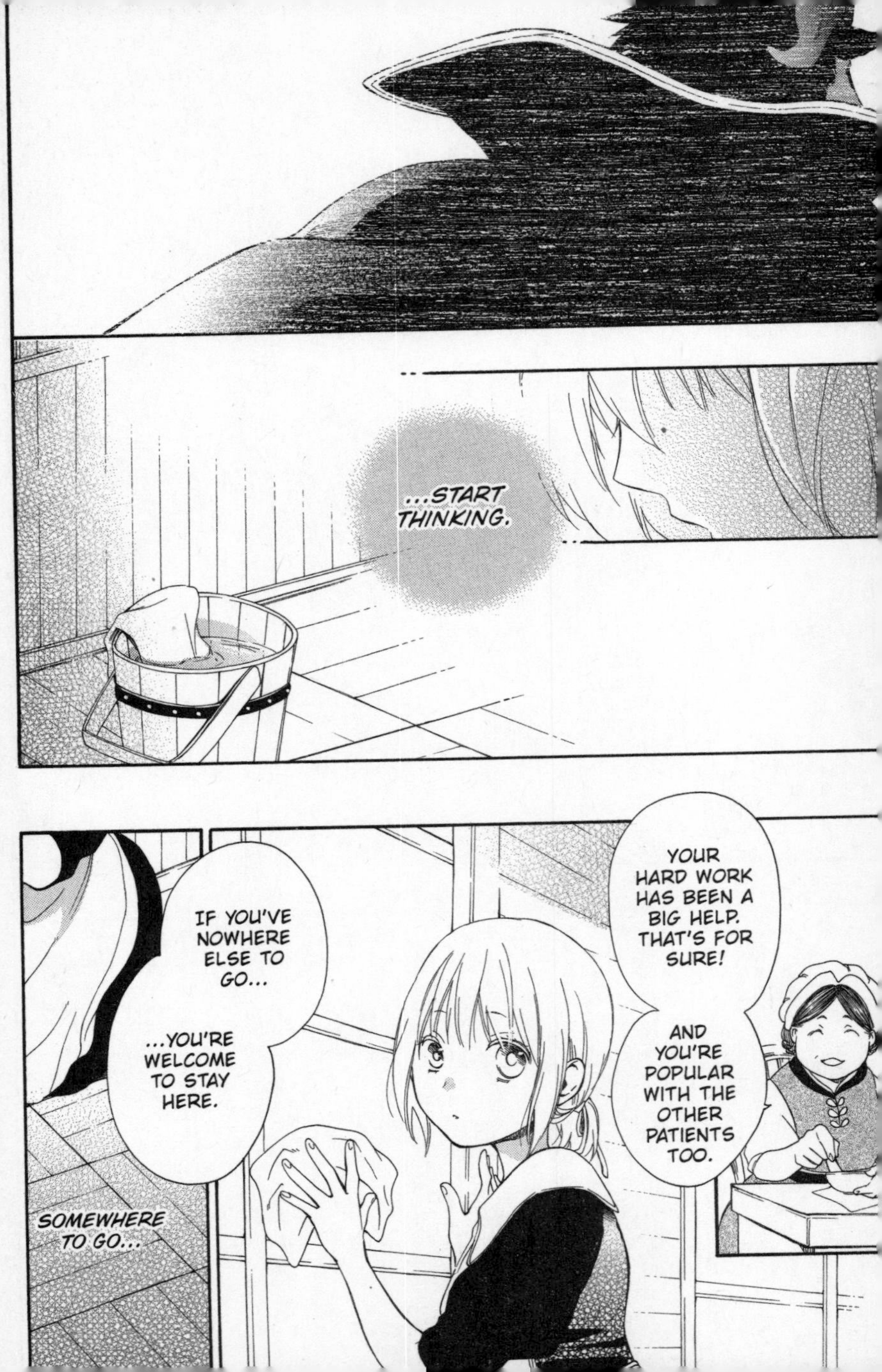
...START THINKING.
YOUR HARD WORK HAS BEEN A BIG HELP. THAT'S FOR SURE!
AND YOU'RE POPULAR WITH THE OTHER PATIENTS TOO.
IF YOU'VE NOWHERE ELSE TO GO...
...YOU'RE WELCOME TO STAY HERE.
SOMEWHERE TO GO...

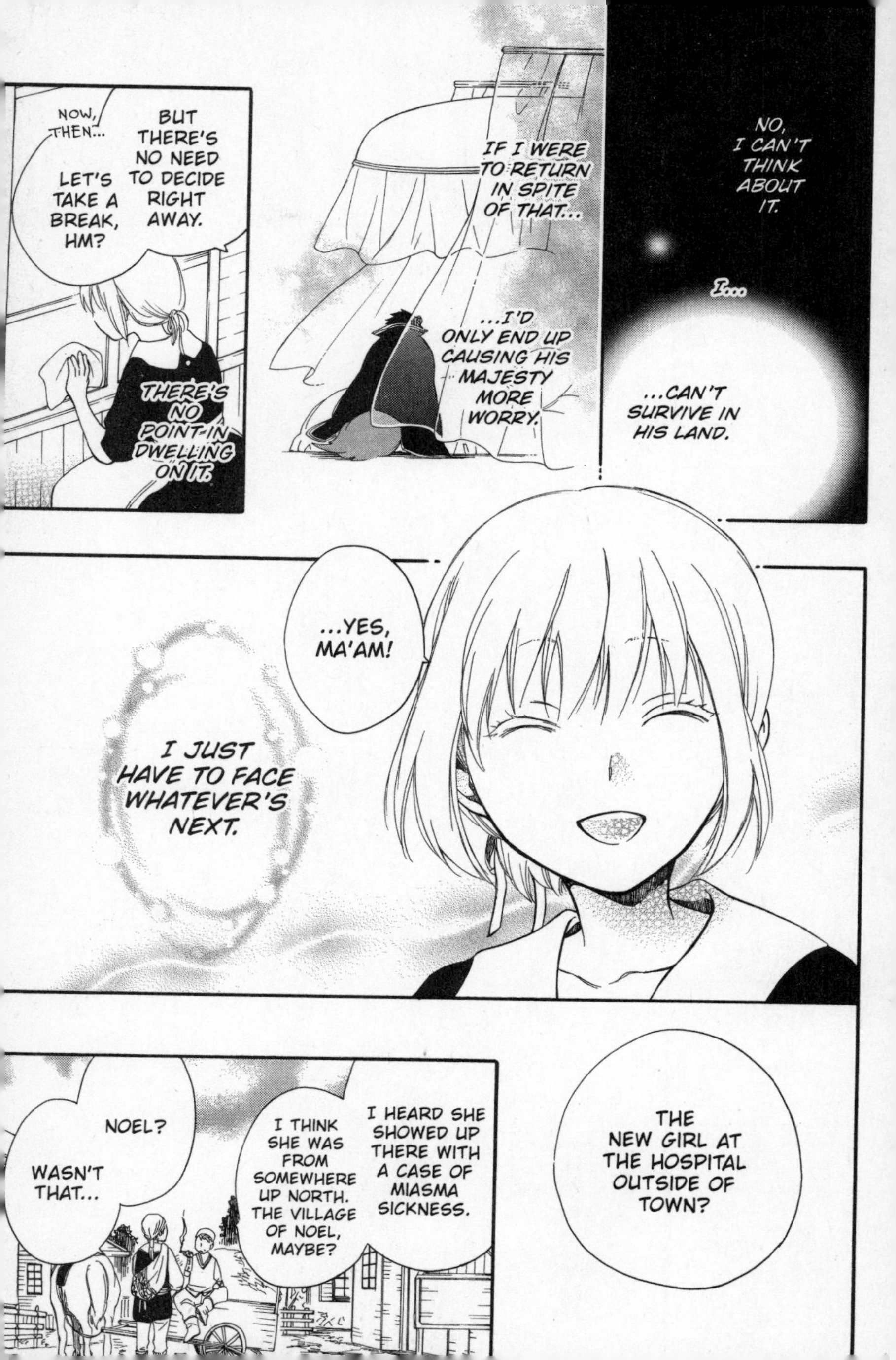
NO, I CAN'T THINK ABOUT IT.
I...
...CAN'T SURVIVE IN HIS LAND.
IF I WERE TO RETURN IN SPITE OF THAT...
...I'D ONLY END UP CAUSING HIS MAJESTY MORE WORRY.
BUT THERE'S NO NEED TO DECIDE RIGHT AWAY.
NOW, THEN... LET'S TAKE A BREAK, HM?
THERE'S NO POINT IN DWELLING ON IT.
...YES, MA'AM!
I JUST HAVE TO FACE WHATEVER'S NEXT.
THE NEW GIRL AT THE HOSPITAL OUTSIDE OF TOWN?
I HEARD SHE SHOWED UP THERE WITH A CASE OF MIASMA SICKNESS.
I THINK SHE WAS FROM SOMEWHERE UP NORTH. THE VILLAGE OF NOEL, MAYBE?
NOEL? WASN'T THAT...

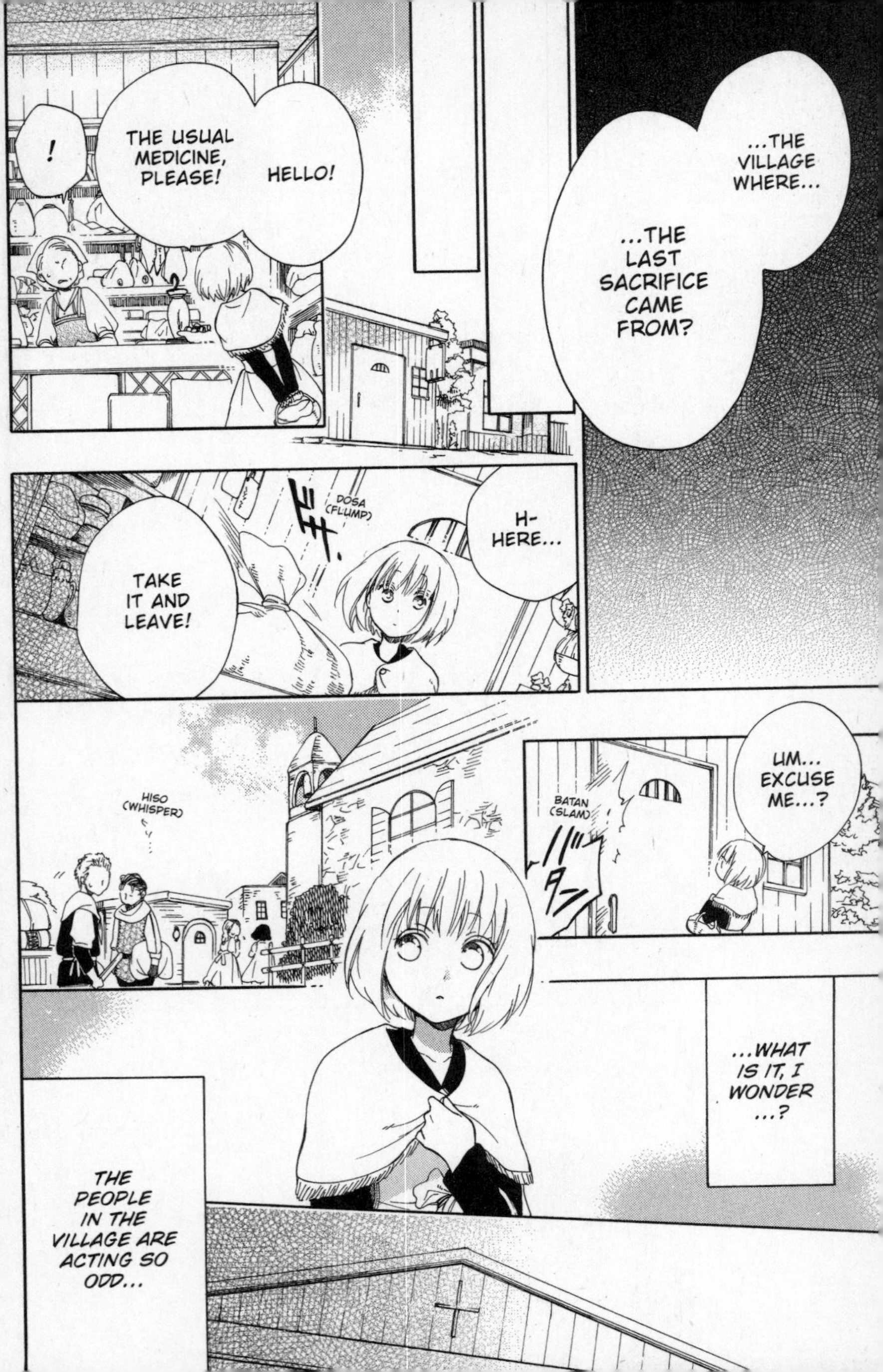
...THE VILLAGE WHERE...
...THE LAST SACRIFICE CAME FROM?
HELLO!
THE USUAL MEDICINE, PLEASE!
!
H-HERE...
DOSA (FLUMP)
TAKE IT AND LEAVE!
UM... EXCUSE ME...?
BATAN (SLAM)
HISO (WHISPER)
...WHAT IS IT, I WONDER ...?
THE PEOPLE IN THE VILLAGE ARE ACTING SO ODD...

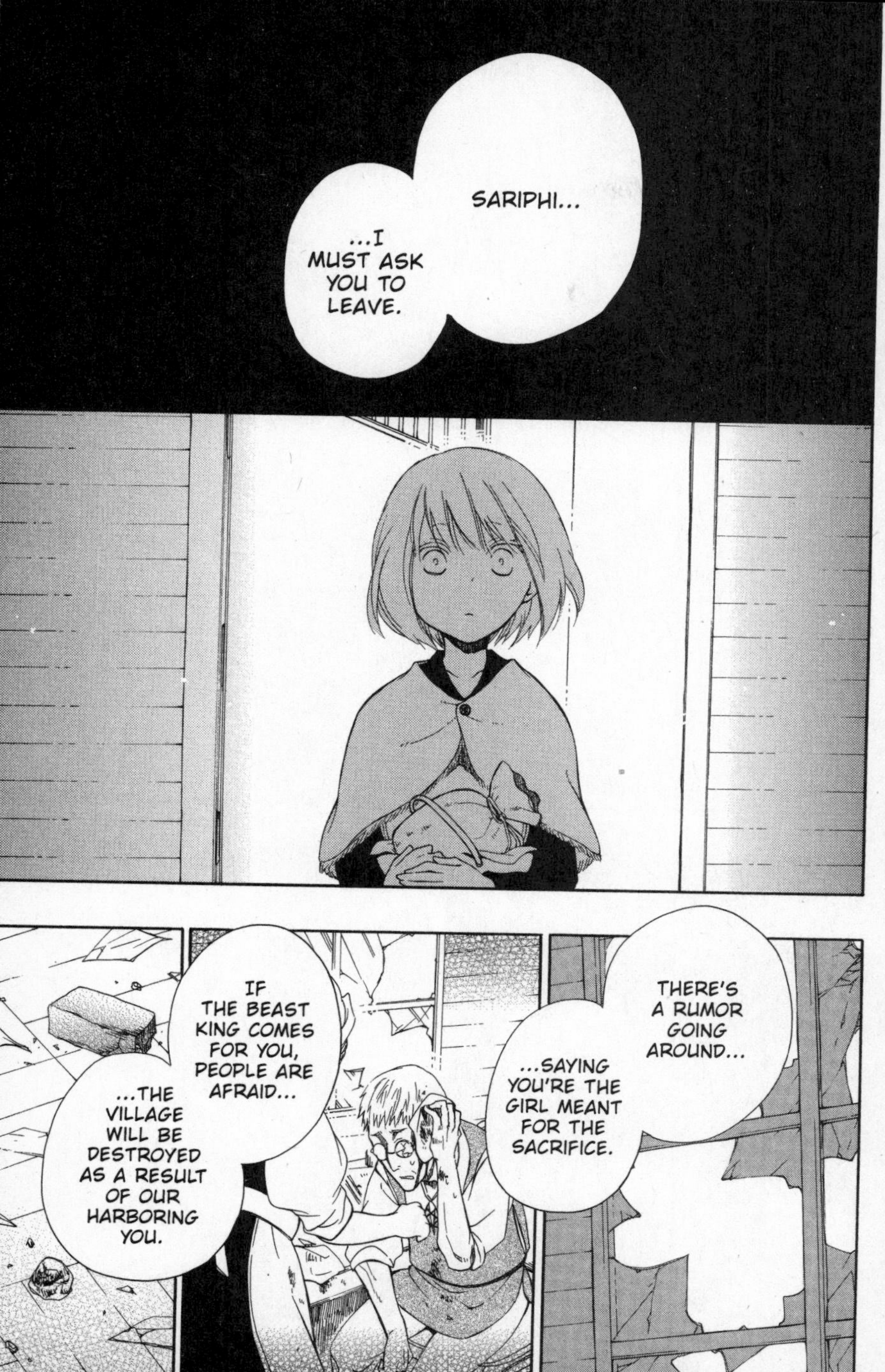
SARIPHI...
...I MUST ASK YOU TO LEAVE.
THERE'S A RUMOR GOING AROUND...
...SAYING YOU'RE THE GIRL MEANT FOR THE SACRIFICE.
IF THE BEAST KING COMES FOR YOU, PEOPLE ARE AFRAID...
...THE VILLAGE WILL BE DESTROYED AS A RESULT OF OUR HARBORING YOU.

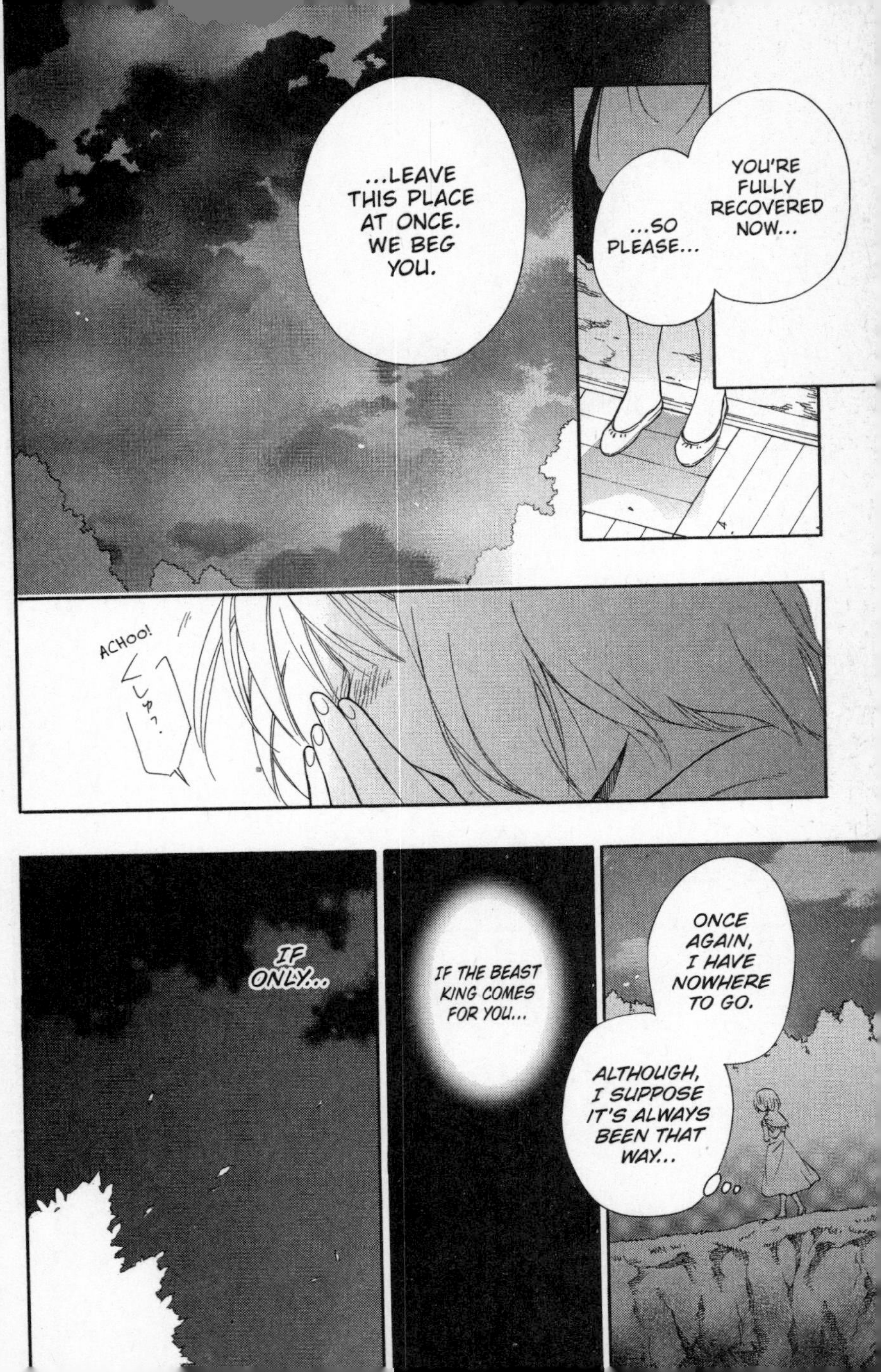
YOU'RE FULLY RECOVERED NOW...
...SO PLEASE...
...LEAVE THIS PLACE AT ONCE. WE BEG YOU.
ACHOO!
ONCE AGAIN, I HAVE NOWHERE TO GO.
ALTHOUGH, I SUPPOSE IT'S ALWAYS BEEN THAT WAY...
IF THE BEAST KING COMES FOR YOU...
IF ONLY...

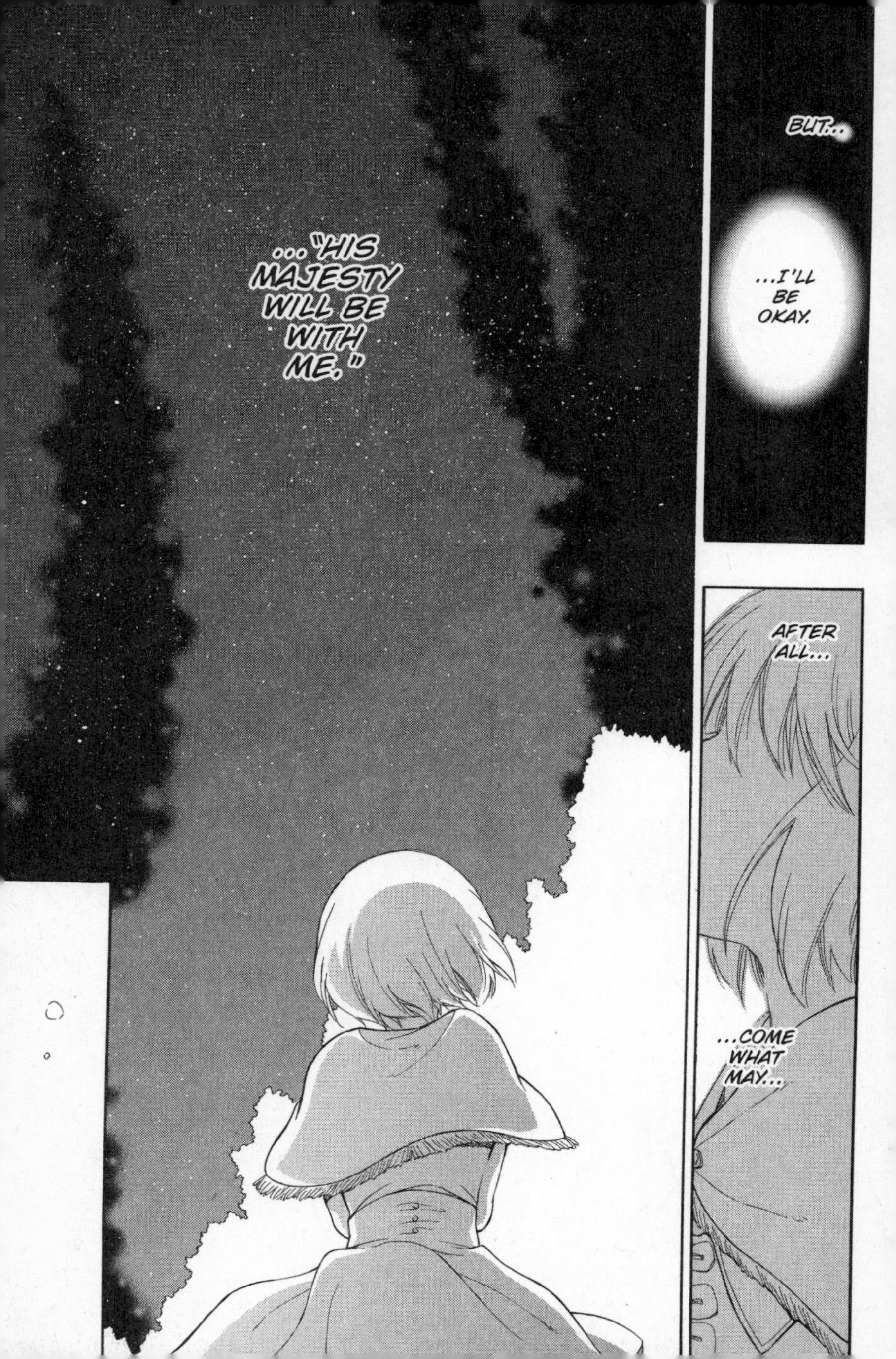
BUT...
...I'LL BE OKAY.
AFTER ALL...
...COME WHAT MAY...
..."HIS MAJESTY WILL BE WITH ME."

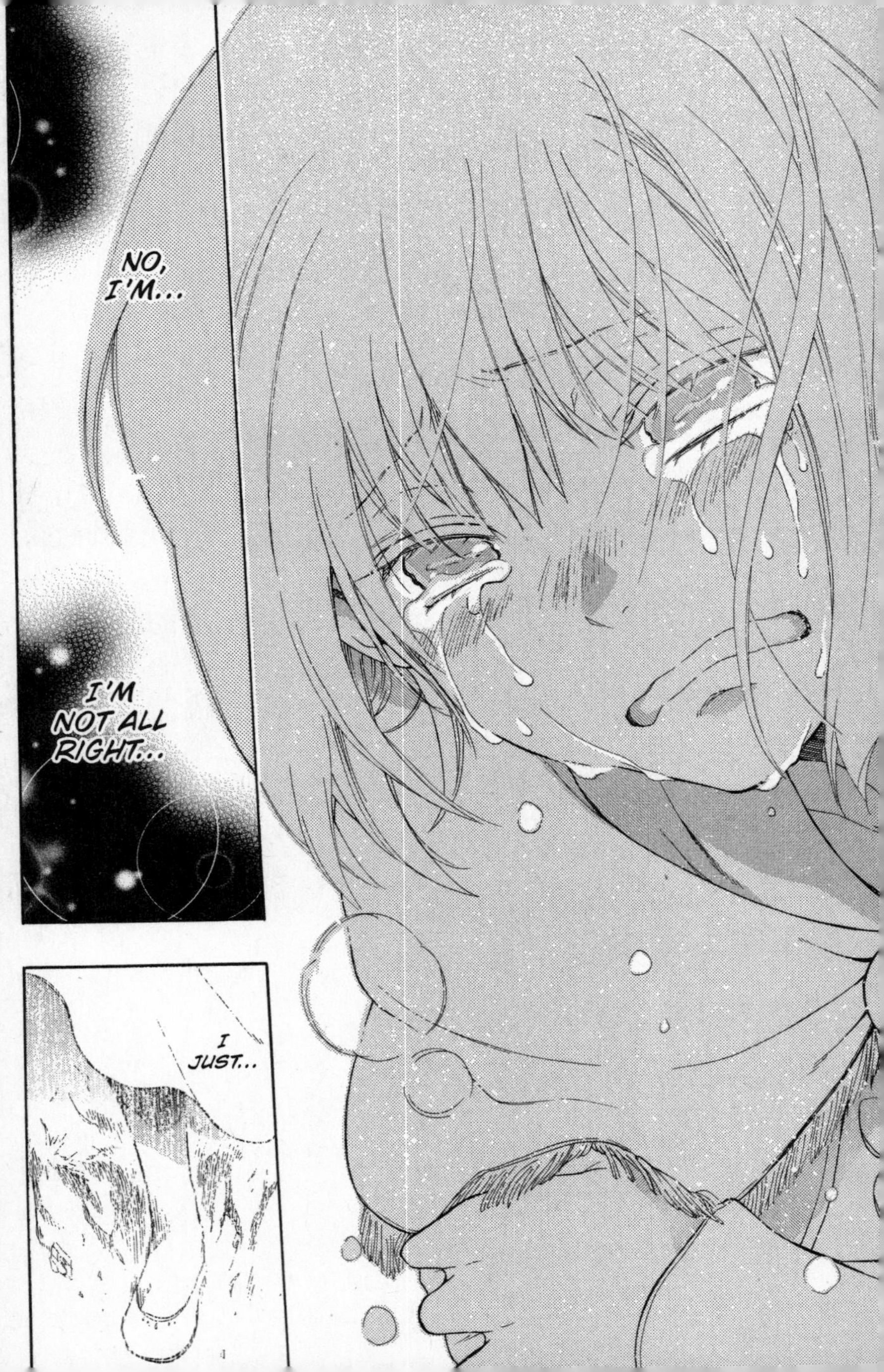
NO, I'M...
I'M NOT ALL RIGHT...
I JUST...

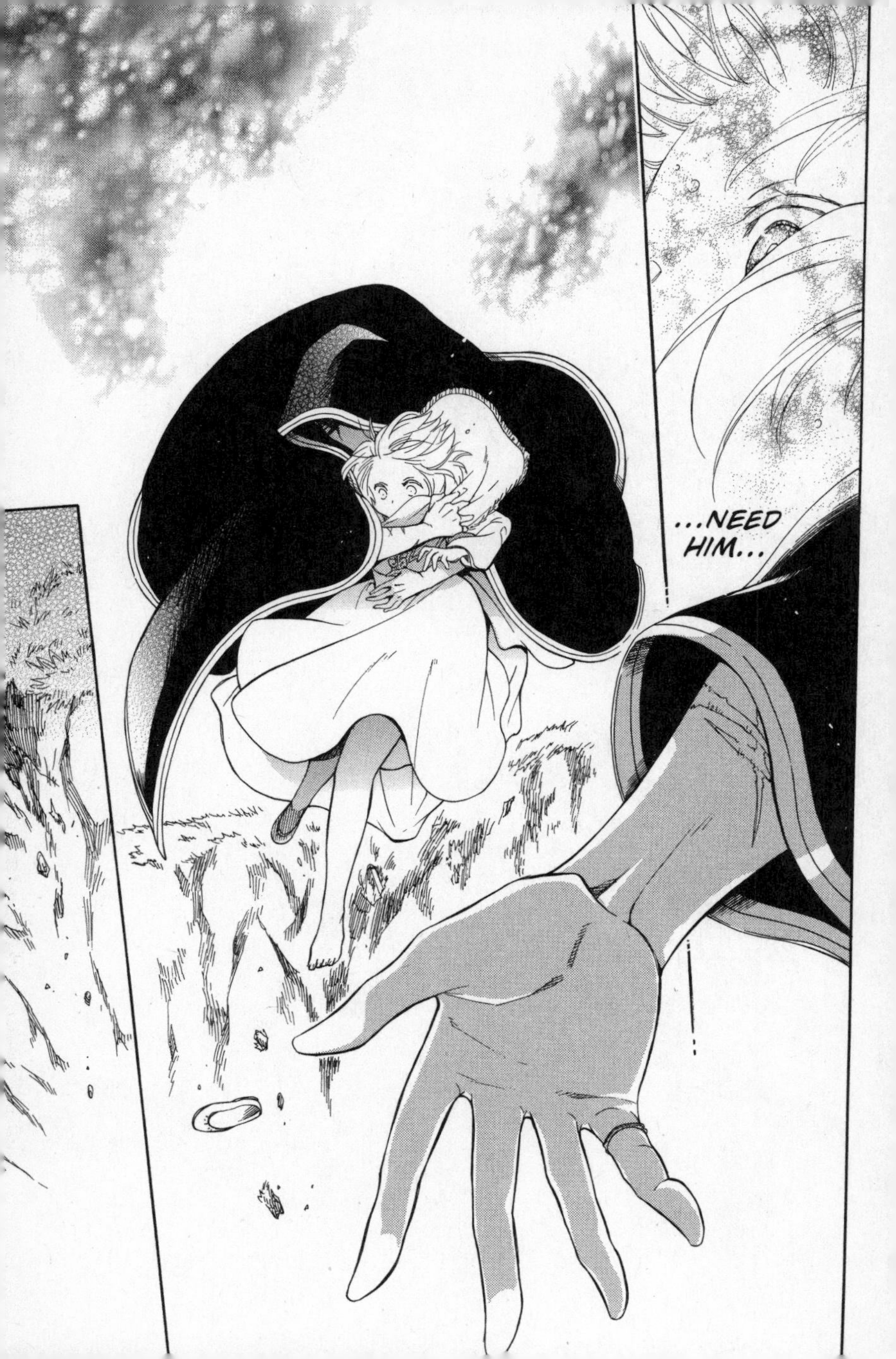
...NEED HIM...

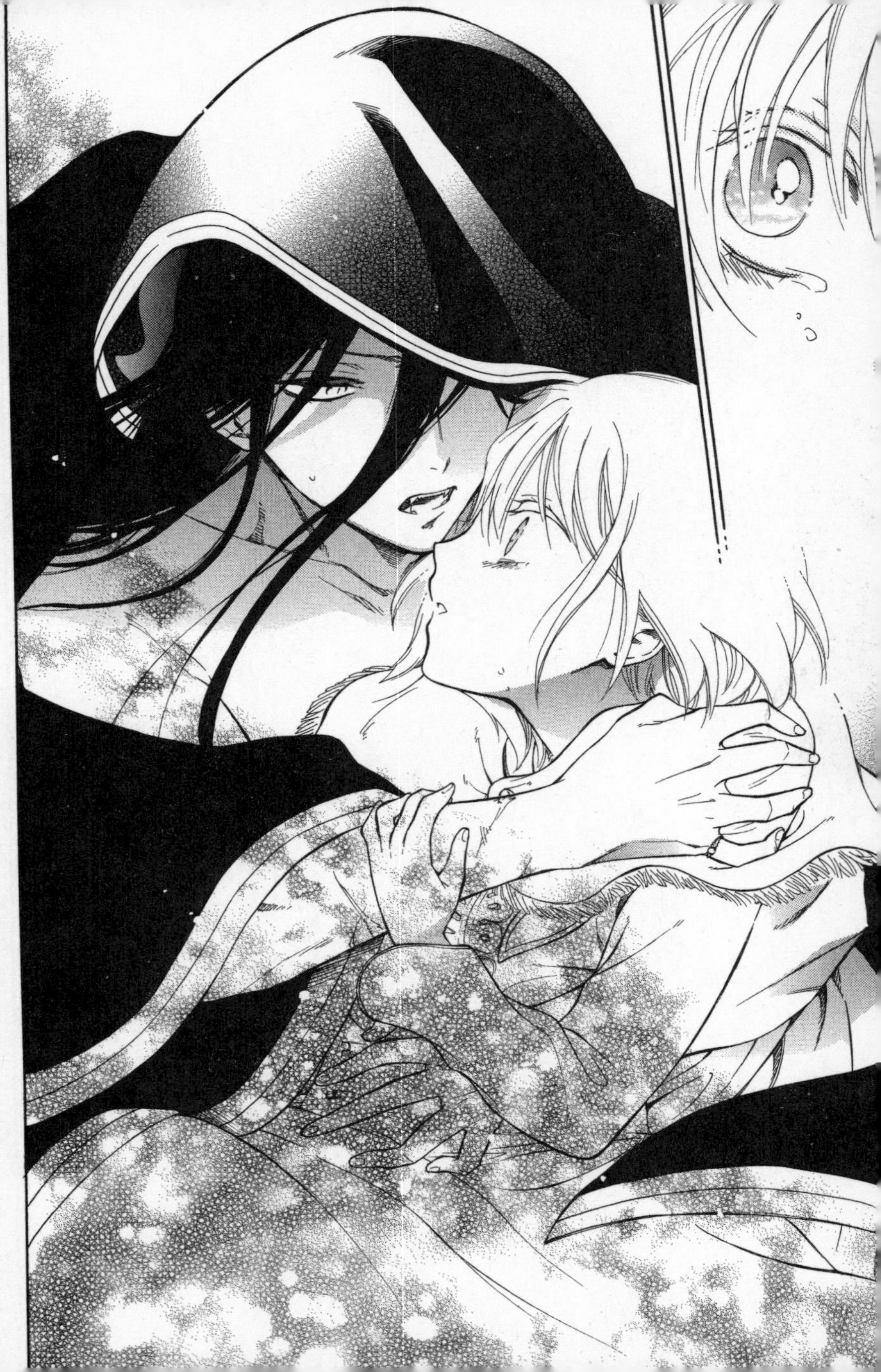

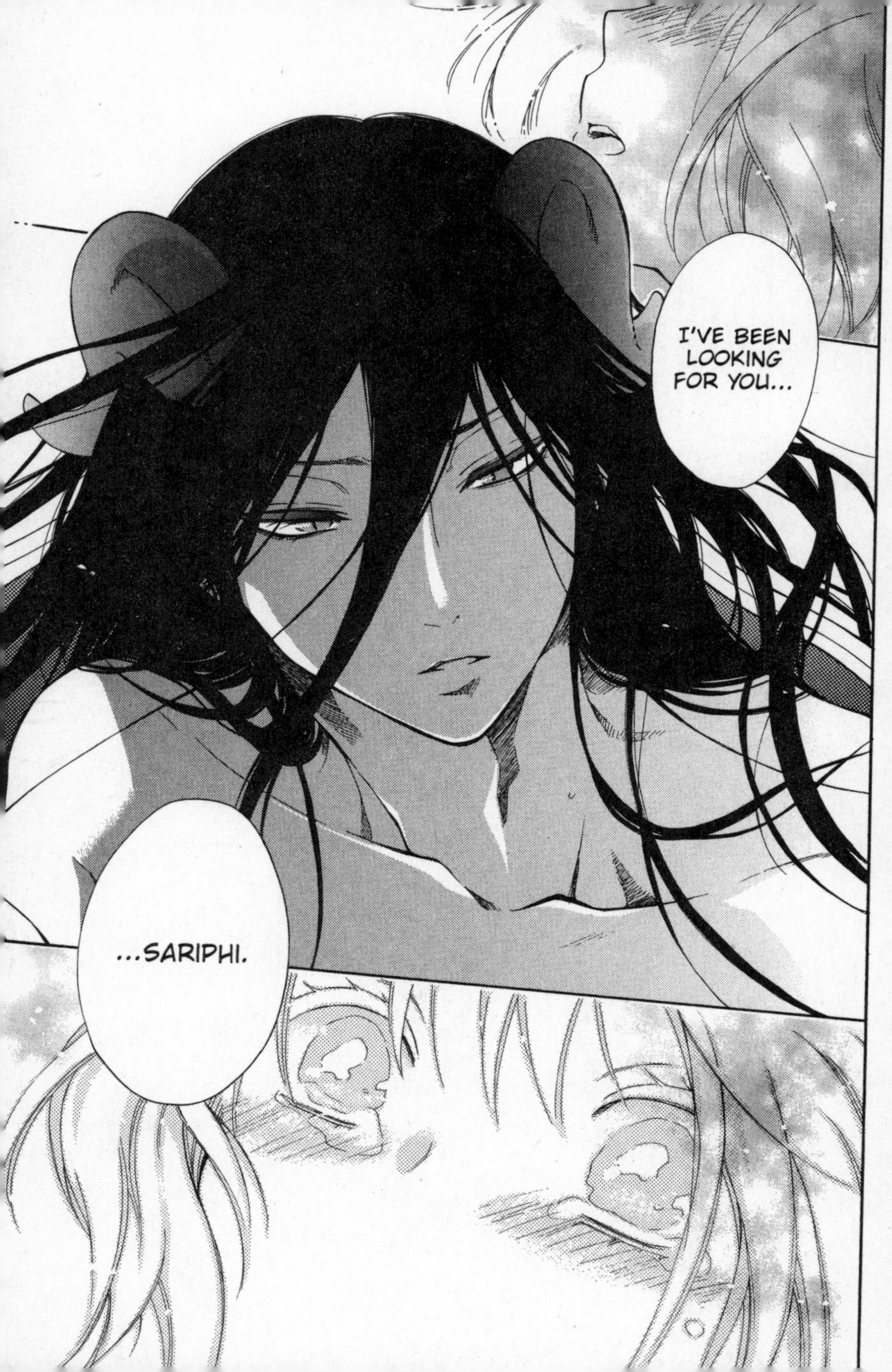
I'VE BEEN LOOKING FOR YOU...
...SARIPHI.

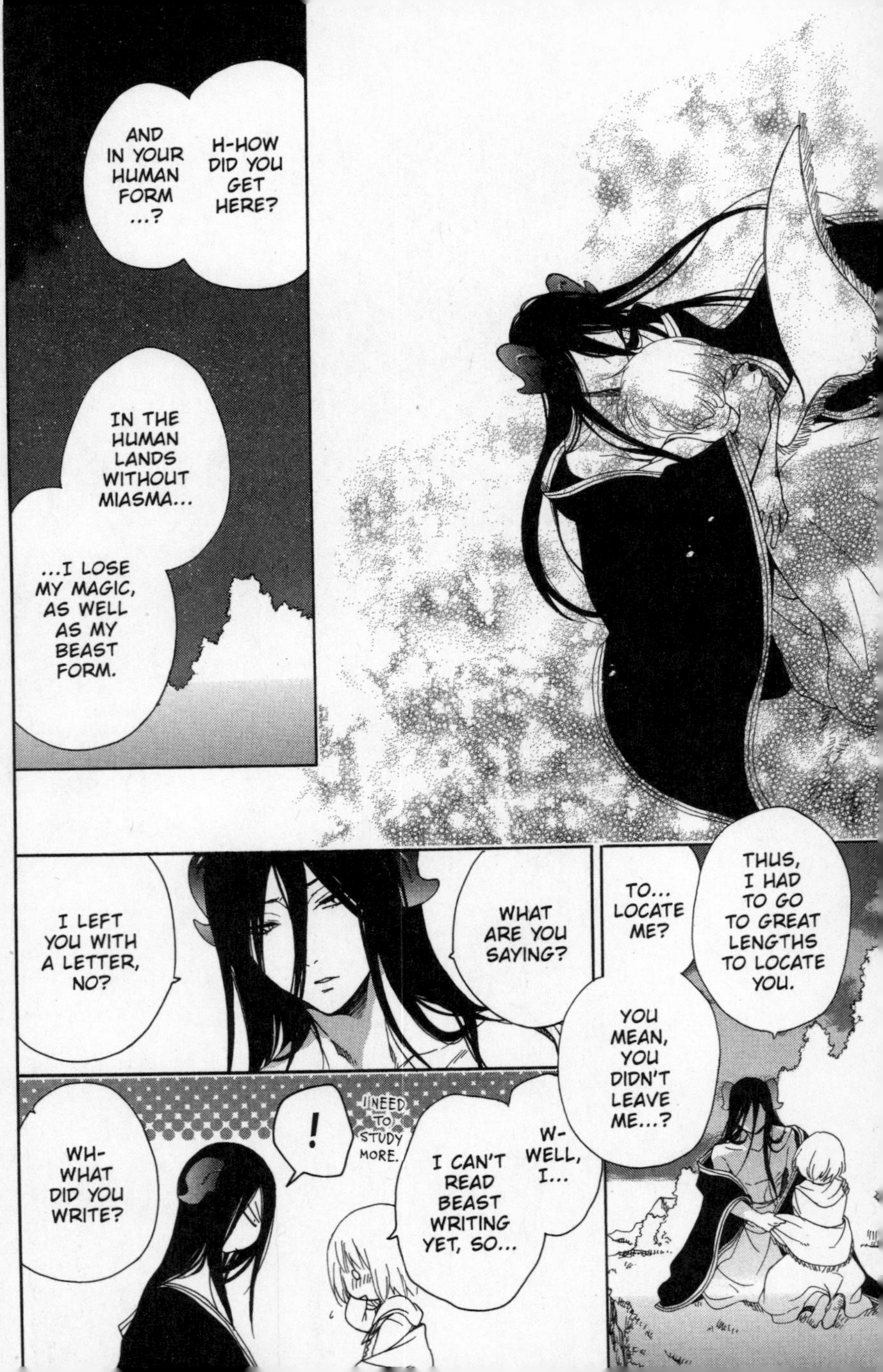
H-HOW DID YOU GET HERE?
AND IN YOUR HUMAN FORM ...?
IN THE HUMAN LANDS WITHOUT MIASMA...
...I LOSE MY MAGIC, AS WELL AS MY BEAST FORM.
THUS, I HAD TO GO TO GREAT LENGTHS TO LOCATE YOU.
TO... LOCATE ME?
YOU MEAN, YOU DIDN'T LEAVE ME...?
WHAT ARE YOU SAYING?
I LEFT YOU WITH A LETTER, NO?
W-WELL, I...
I CAN'T READ BEAST WRITING YET, SO...
I NEED TO STUDY MORE.
!
WH-WHAT DID YOU WRITE?

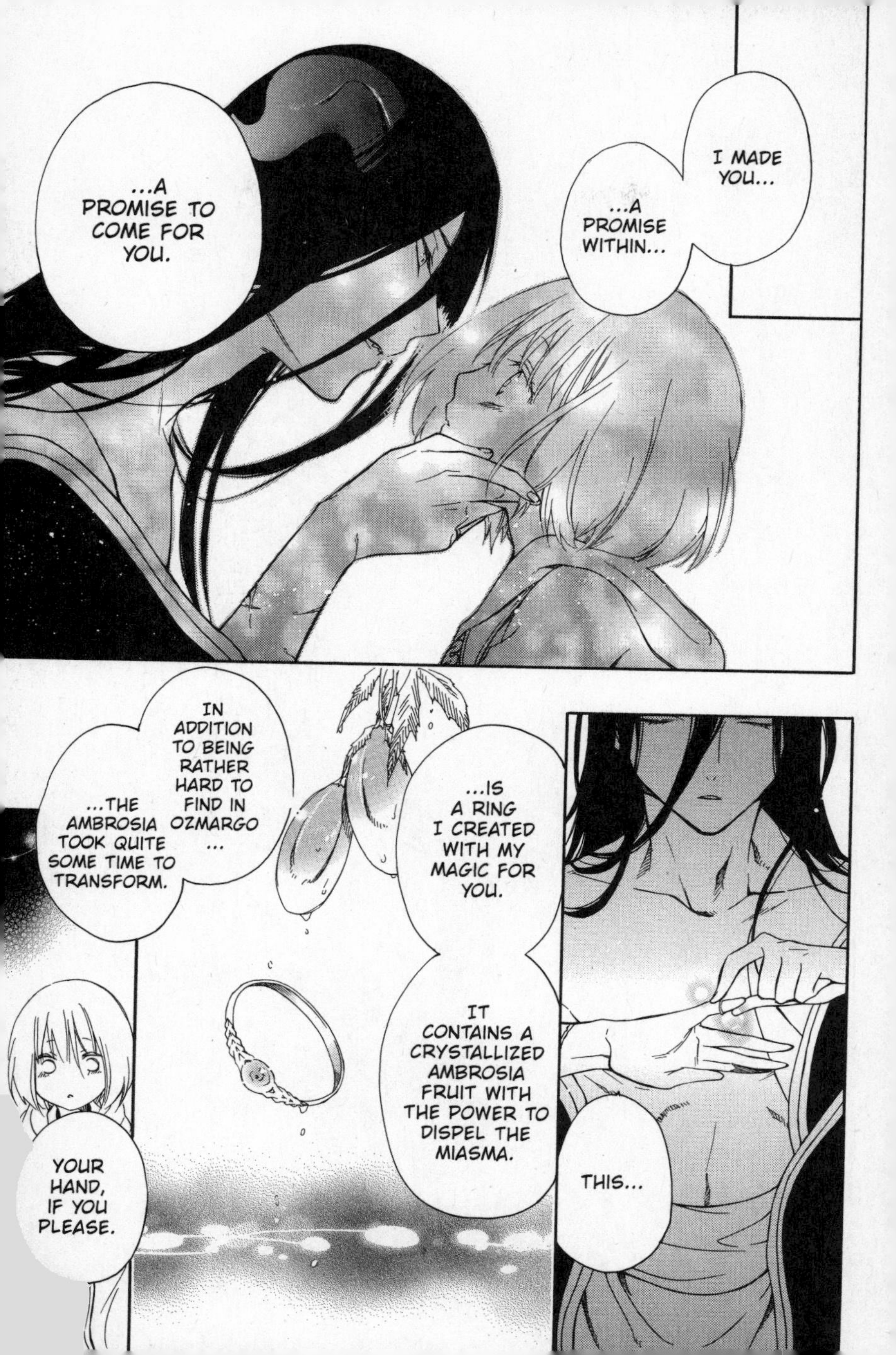
I MADE YOU...
...A PROMISE WITHIN...
...A PROMISE TO COME FOR YOU.
THIS...
...IS A RING I CREATED WITH MY MAGIC FOR YOU.
IT CONTAINS A CRYSTALLIZED AMBROSIA FRUIT WITH THE POWER TO DISPEL THE MIASMA.
IN ADDITION TO BEING RATHER HARD TO FIND IN OZMARGO...
...THE AMBROSIA TOOK QUITE SOME TIME TO TRANSFORM.
YOUR HAND, IF YOU PLEASE.

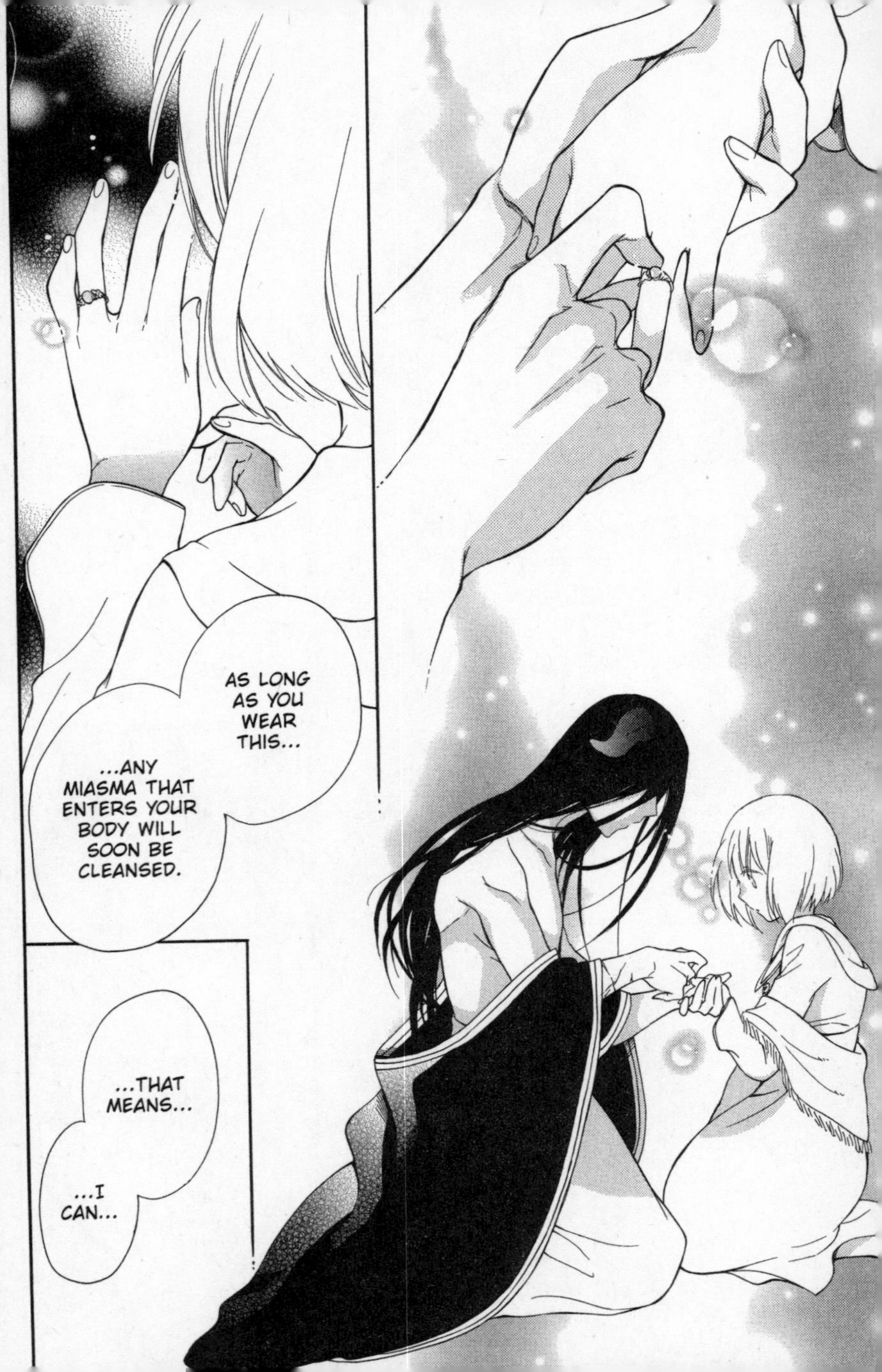
AS LONG AS YOU WEAR THIS...
...ANY MIASMA THAT ENTERS YOUR BODY WILL SOON BE CLEANSED.
...THAT MEANS...
...I CAN...

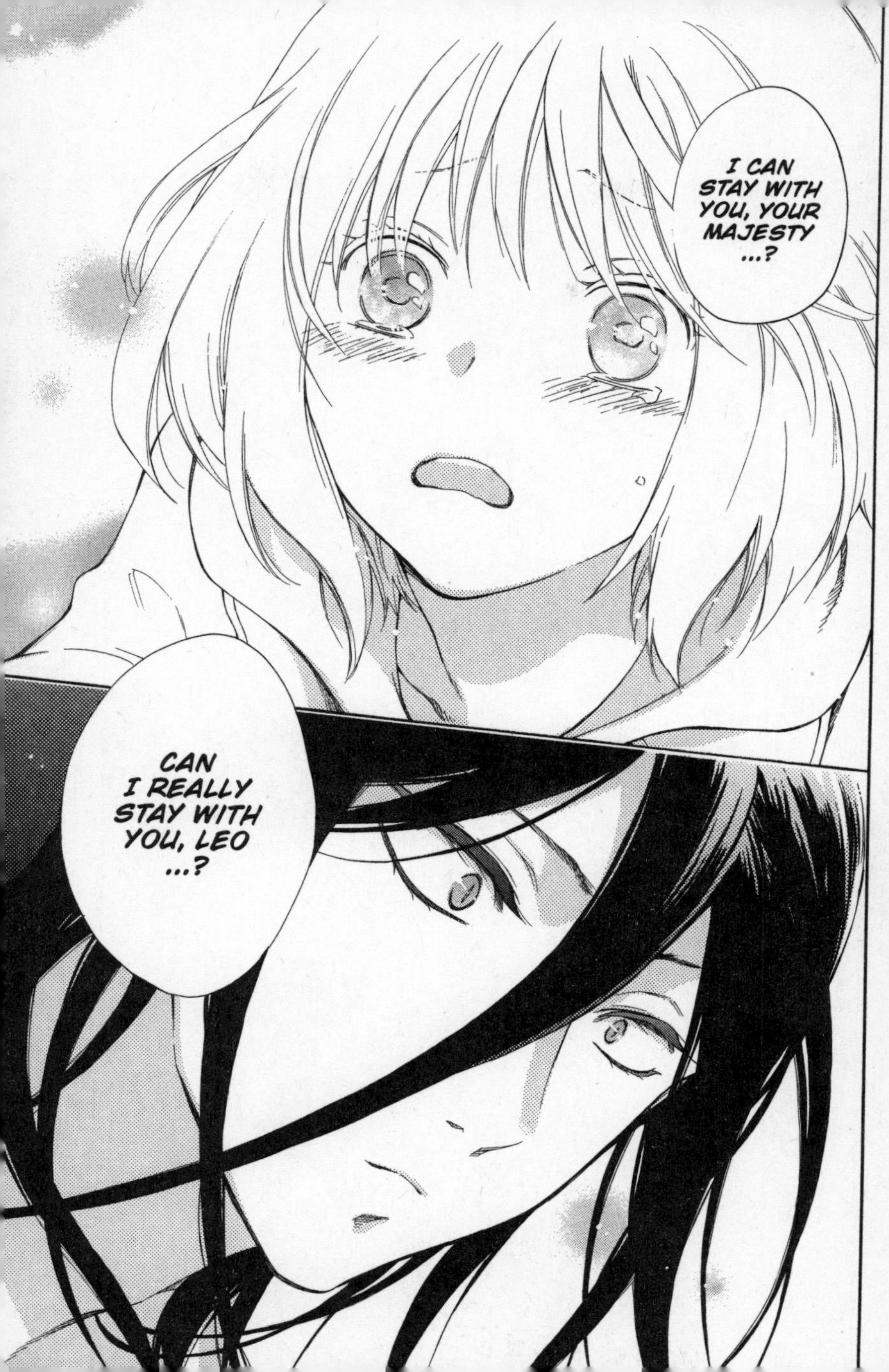
I CAN STAY WITH YOU, YOUR MAJESTY ...?
CAN I REALLY STAY WITH YOU, LEO ...?

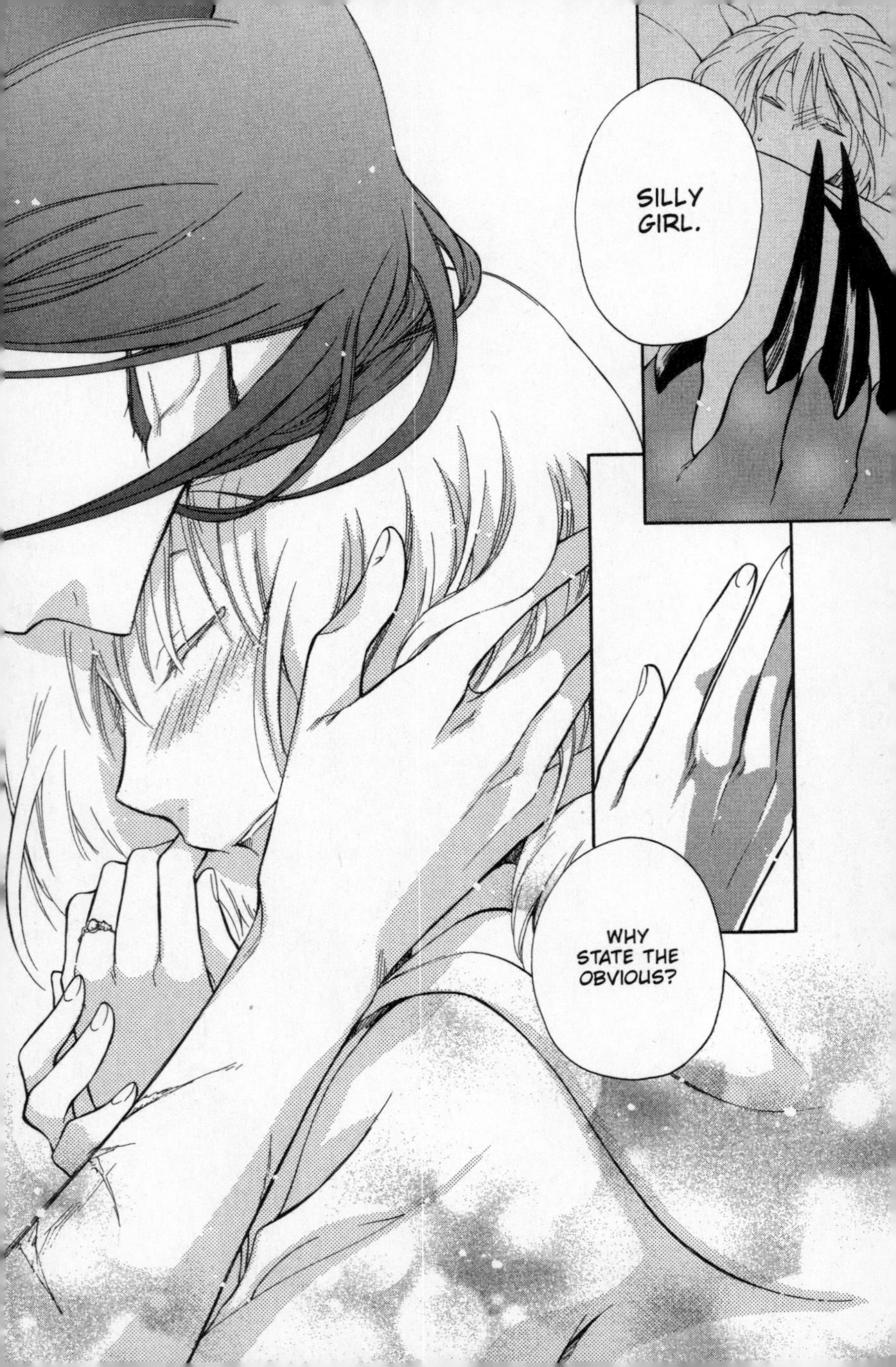
SILLY GIRL.
WHY STATE THE OBVIOUS?

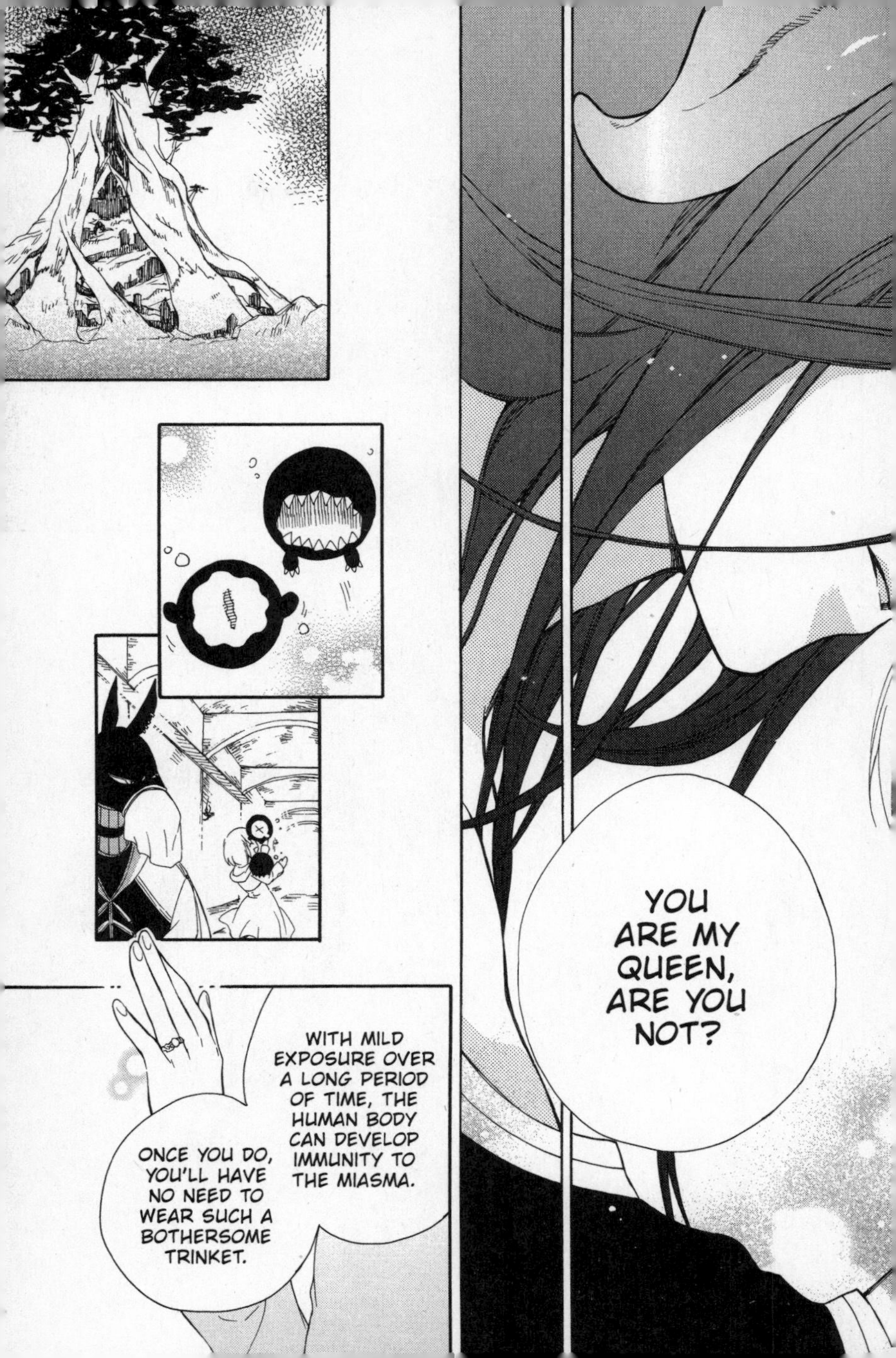
YOU ARE MY QUEEN, ARE YOU NOT?
WITH MILD EXPOSURE OVER A LONG PERIOD OF TIME, THE HUMAN BODY CAN DEVELOP IMMUNITY TO THE MIASMA.
ONCE YOU DO, YOU'LL HAVE NO NEED TO WEAR SUCH A BOTHERSOME TRINKET.

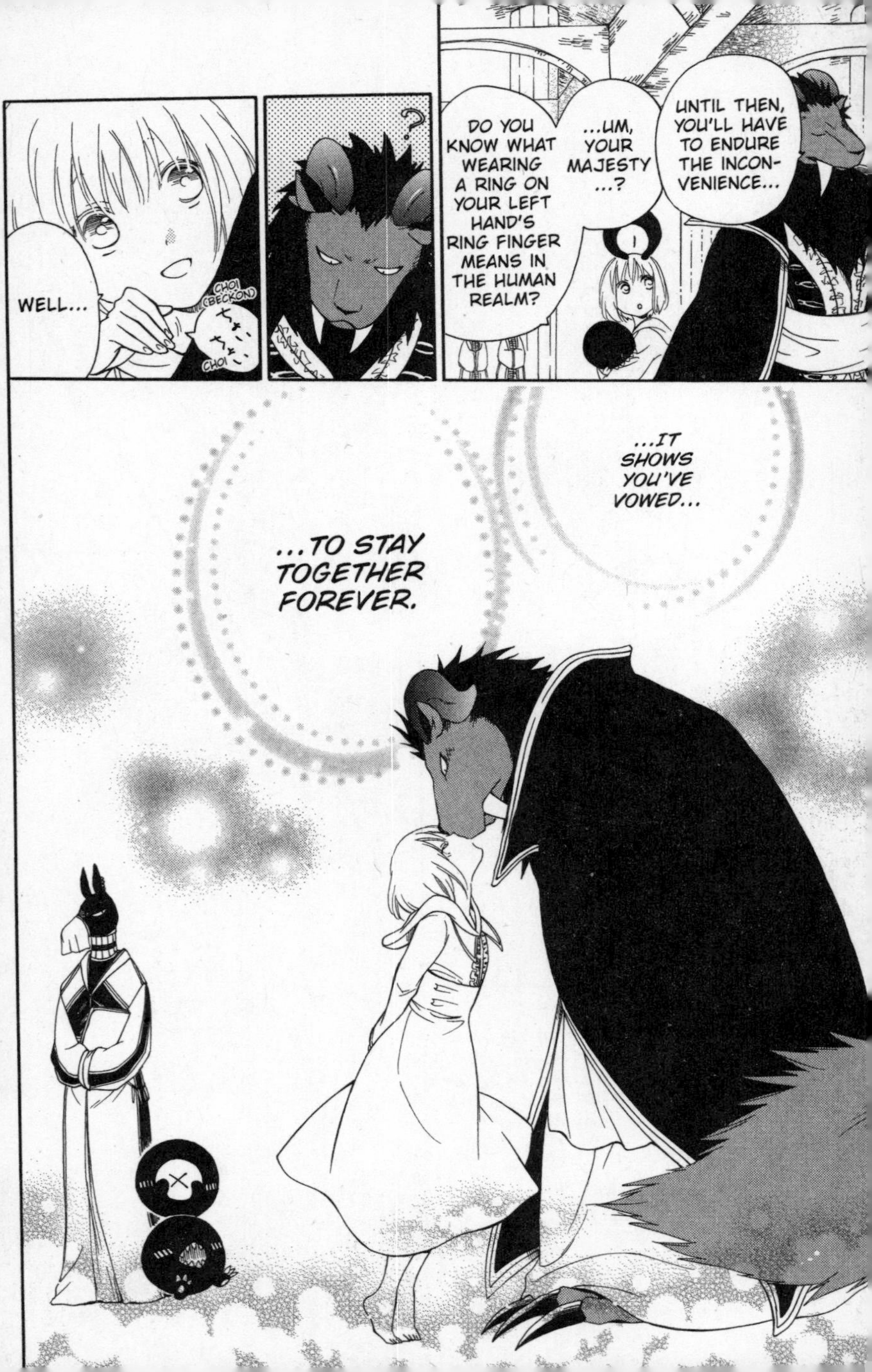
UNTIL THEN, YOU'LL HAVE TO ENDURE THE INCON-VENIENCE...
...UM, YOUR MAJESTY ...?
DO YOU KNOW WHAT WEARING A RING ON YOUR LEFT HAND'S RING FINGER MEANS IN THE HUMAN REALM?
?
CHOI (BECKON) ちょい ちょい CHOI
WELL...
...IT SHOWS YOU'VE VOWED...
...TO STAY TOGETHER FOREVER.

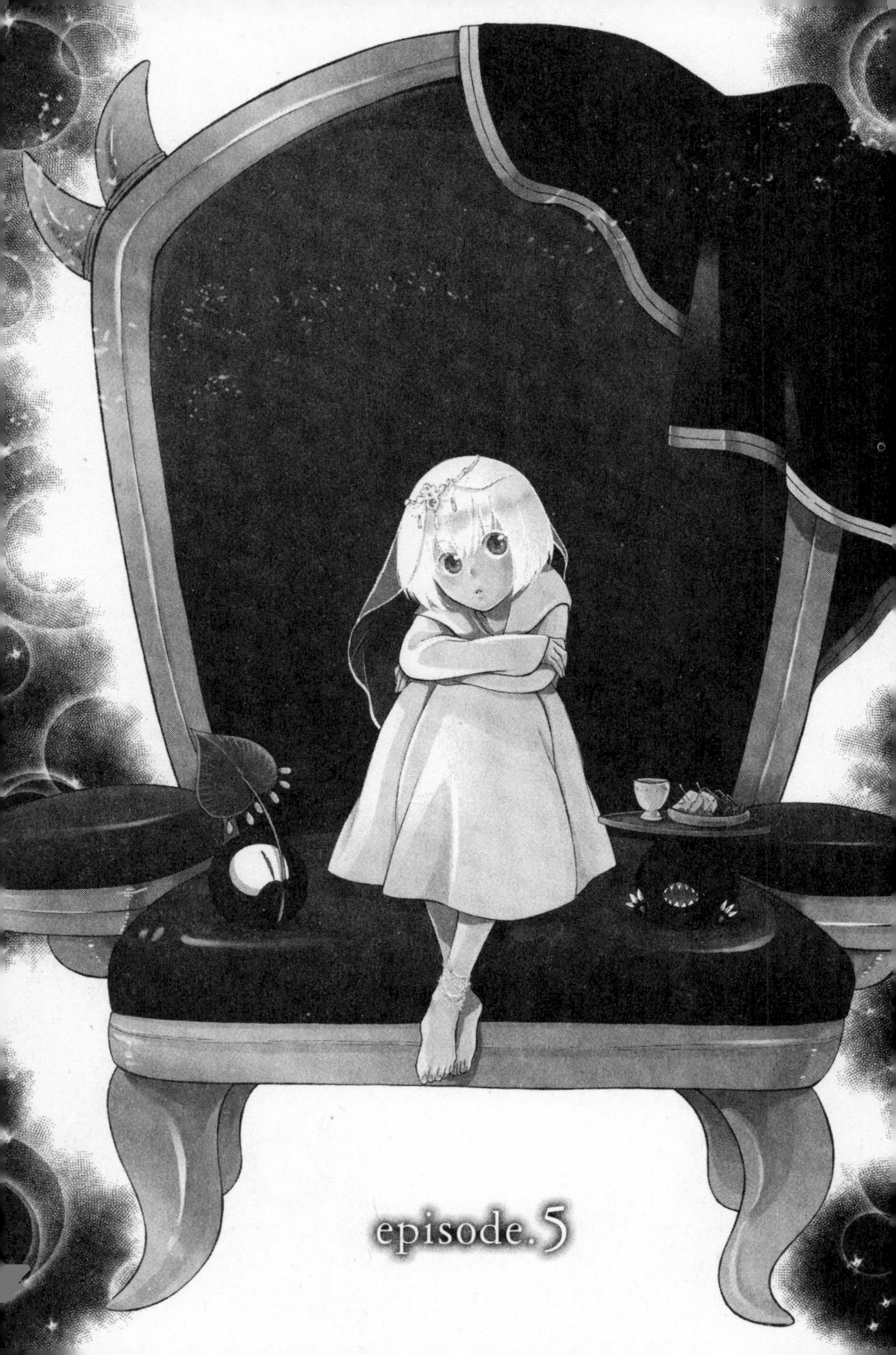
episode.5

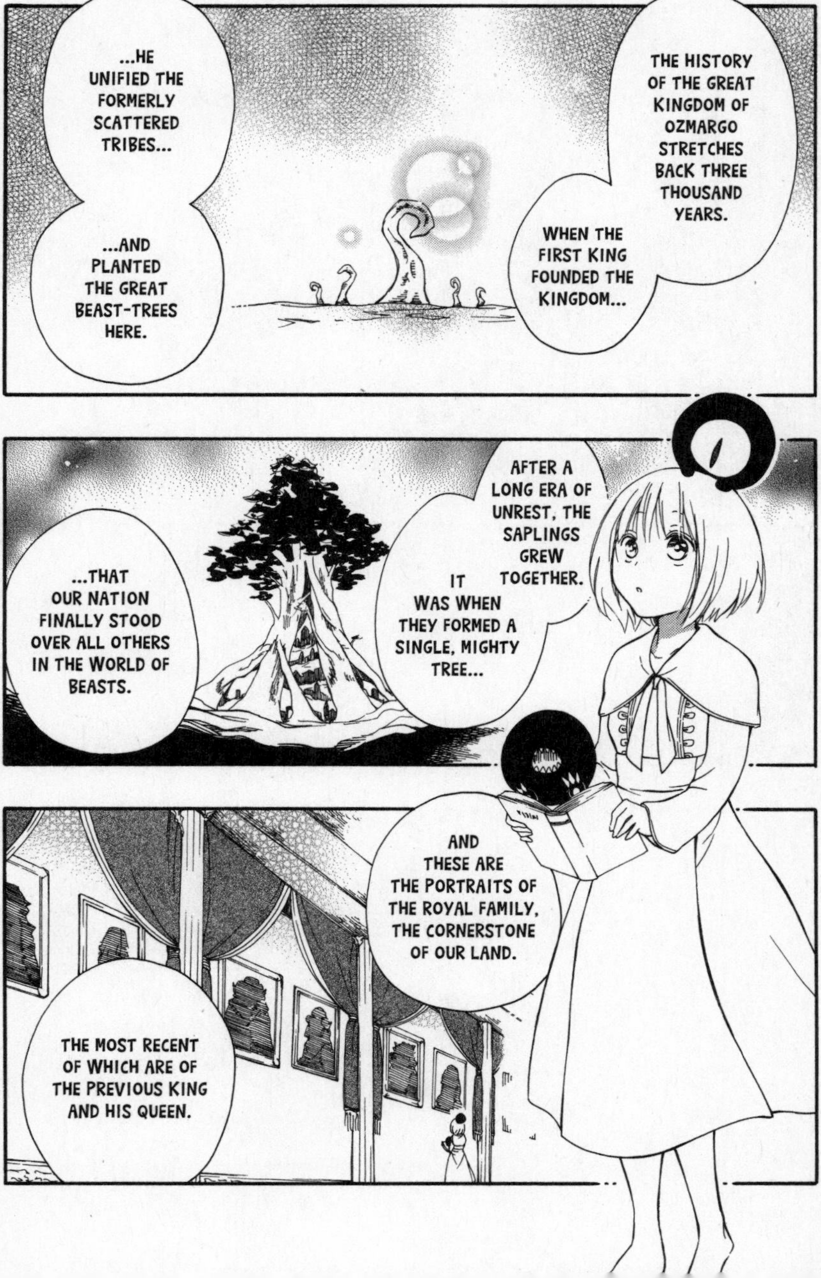
THE HISTORY OF THE GREAT KINGDOM OF OZMARGO STRETCHES BACK THREE THOUSAND YEARS.
WHEN THE FIRST KING FOUNDED THE KINGDOM...
...HE UNIFIED THE FORMERLY SCATTERED TRIBES...
...AND PLANTED THE GREAT BEAST-TREES HERE.
AFTER A LONG ERA OF UNREST, THE SAPLINGS GREW TOGETHER.
IT WAS WHEN THEY FORMED A SINGLE, MIGHTY TREE...
...THAT OUR NATION FINALLY STOOD OVER ALL OTHERS IN THE WORLD OF BEASTS.
AND THESE ARE THE PORTRAITS OF THE ROYAL FAMILY, THE CORNERSTONE OF OUR LAND.
THE MOST RECENT OF WHICH ARE OF THE PREVIOUS KING AND HIS QUEEN.

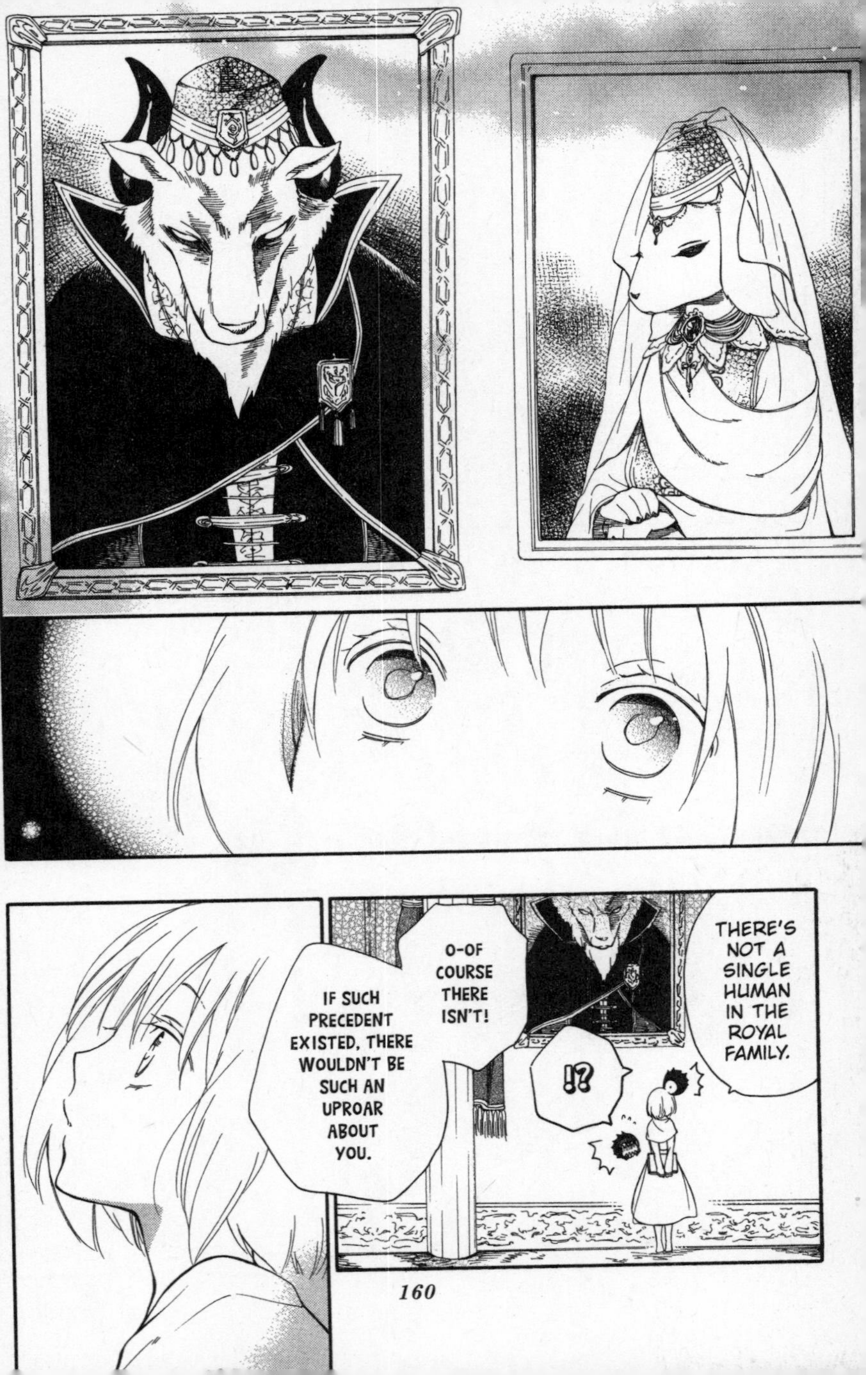
THERE'S NOT A SINGLE HUMAN IN THE ROYAL FAMILY.
!?
O-OF COURSE THERE ISN'T!
IF SUCH PRECEDENT EXISTED, THERE WOULDN'T BE SUCH AN UPROAR ABOUT YOU.

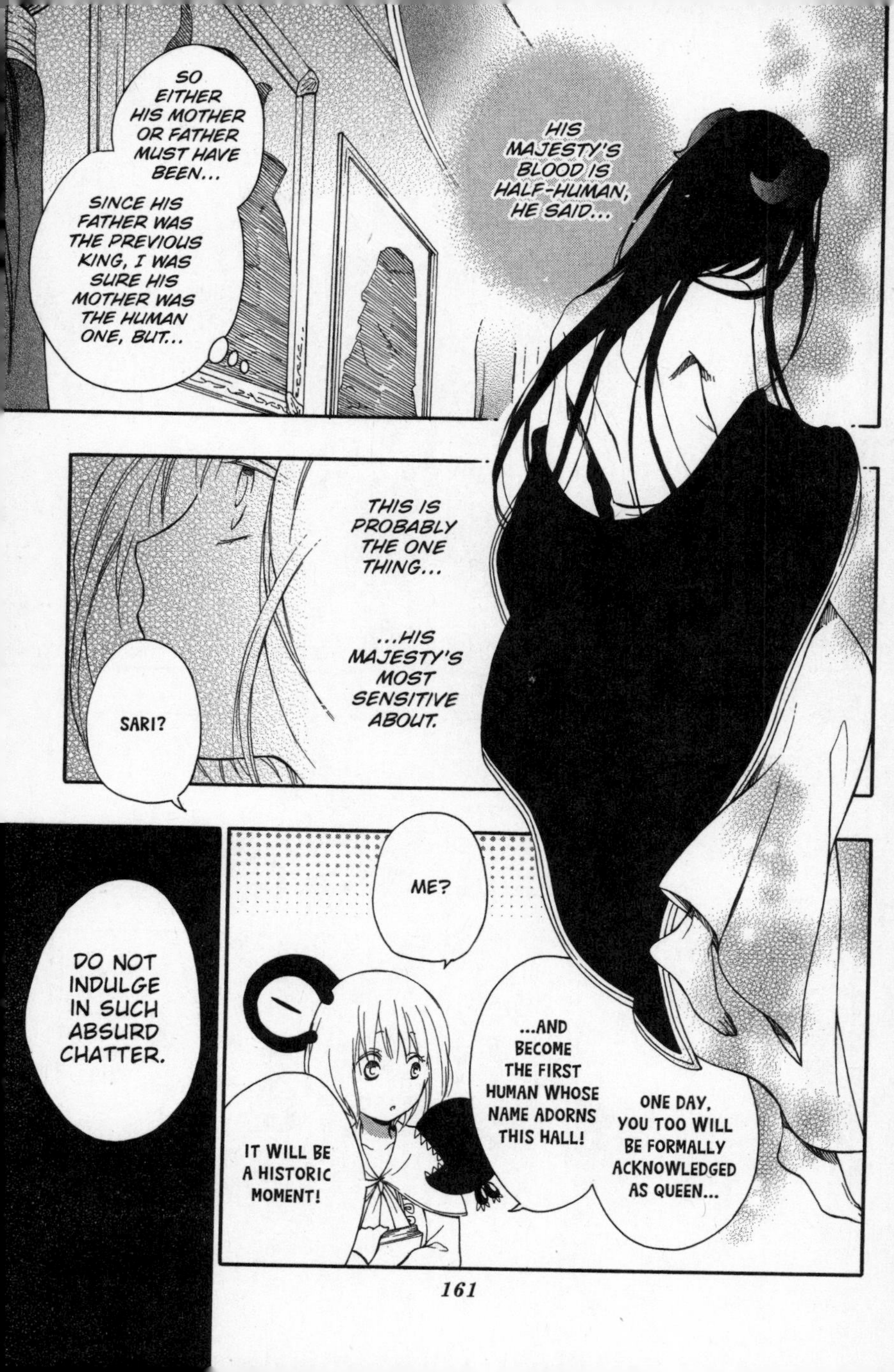
HIS MAJESTY'S BLOOD IS HALF-HUMAN, HE SAID...
SO EITHER HIS MOTHER OR FATHER MUST HAVE BEEN...
SINCE HIS FATHER WAS THE PREVIOUS KING, I WAS SURE HIS MOTHER WAS THE HUMAN ONE, BUT...
THIS IS PROBABLY THE ONE THING...
...HIS MAJESTY'S MOST SENSITIVE ABOUT.
SARI?
ME?
ONE DAY, YOU TOO WILL BE FORMALLY ACKNOWLEDGED AS QUEEN...
...AND BECOME THE FIRST HUMAN WHOSE NAME ADORNS THIS HALL!
IT WILL BE A HISTORIC MOMENT!
DO NOT INDULGE IN SUCH ABSURD CHATTER.

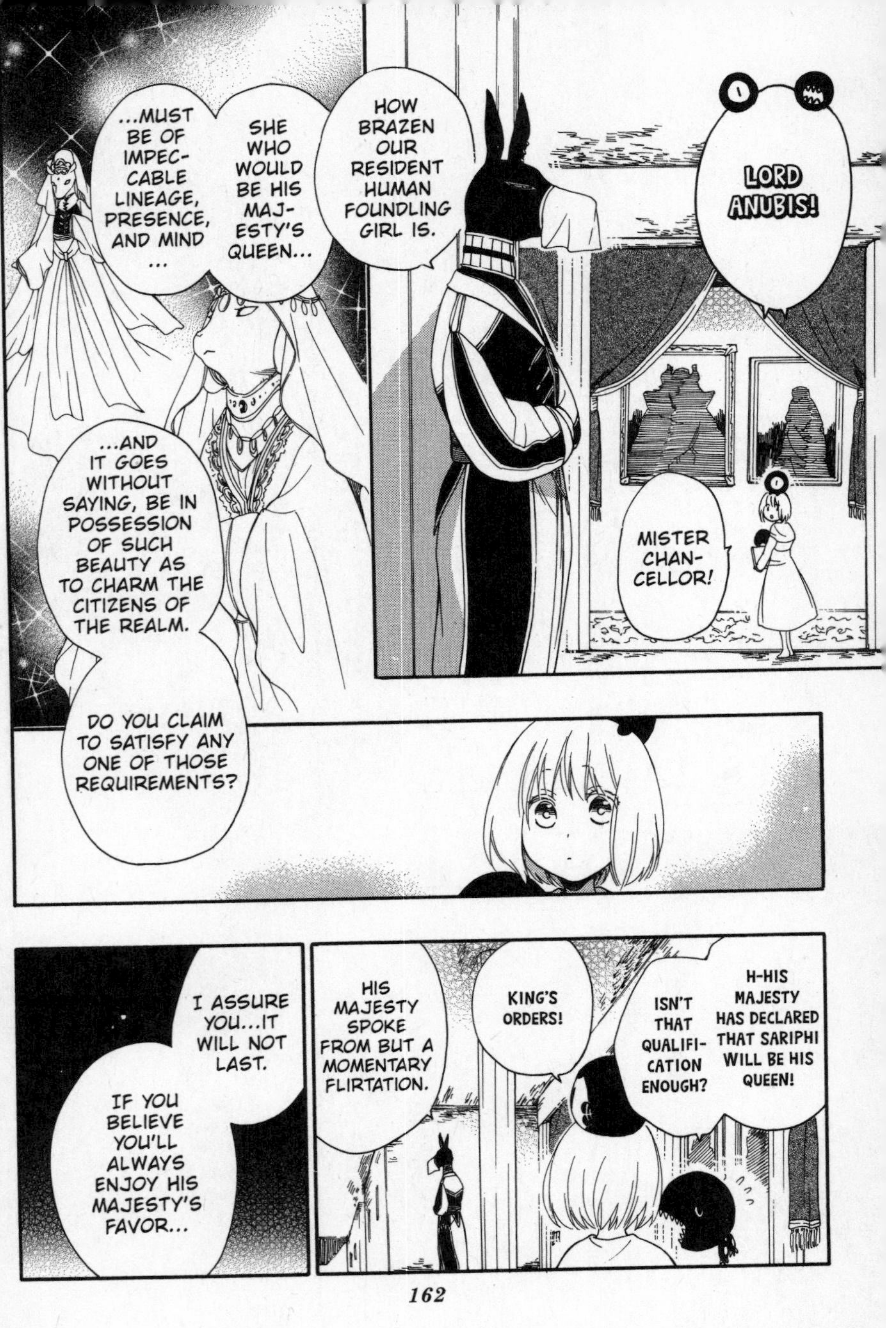
LORD ANUBIS!
MISTER CHANCELLOR!
HOW BRAZEN OUR RESIDENT HUMAN FOUNDLING GIRL IS.
SHE WHO WOULD BE HIS MAJESTY'S QUEEN...
...MUST BE OF IMPECCABLE LINEAGE, PRESENCE, AND MIND...
...AND IT GOES WITHOUT SAYING, BE IN POSSESSION OF SUCH BEAUTY AS TO CHARM THE CITIZENS OF THE REALM.
DO YOU CLAIM TO SATISFY ANY ONE OF THOSE REQUIREMENTS?
H-HIS MAJESTY HAS DECLARED THAT SARIPHI WILL BE HIS QUEEN!
ISN'T THAT QUALIFICATION ENOUGH?
KING'S ORDERS!
HIS MAJESTY SPOKE FROM BUT A MOMENTARY FLIRTATION.
I ASSURE YOU...IT WILL NOT LAST.
IF YOU BELIEVE YOU'LL ALWAYS ENJOY HIS MAJESTY'S FAVOR...

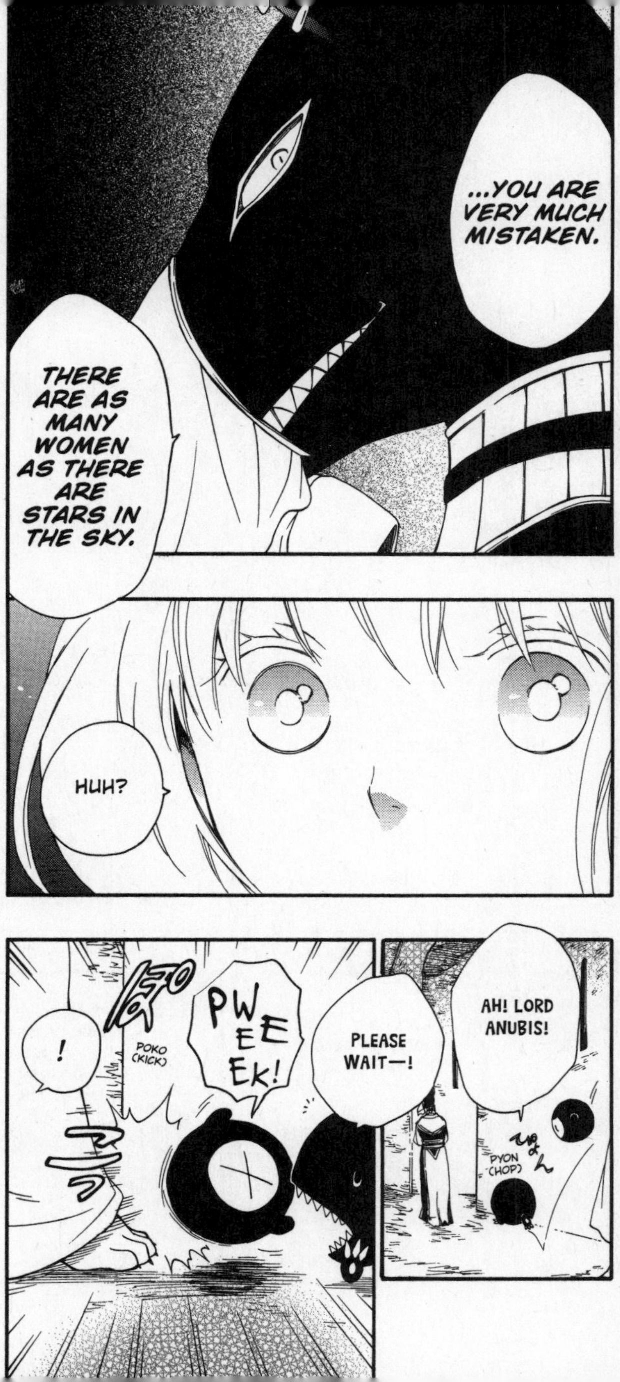
...YOU ARE VERY MUCH MISTAKEN.
THERE ARE AS MANY WOMEN AS THERE ARE STARS IN THE SKY.
HUH?
AH! LORD ANUBIS!
PYON (HOP)
PLEASE WAIT—!
PWEEK!
POKO (KICK)
!

(4)

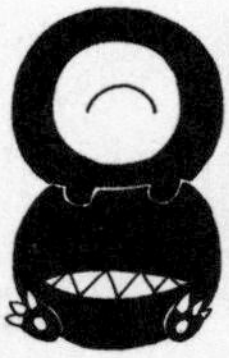

THE TONGUE-TIED CY AND THE CHATTY CLOPS COME FROM ME WANTING TO BRING TO LIFE THE OLD SAYING ABOUT HOW "THE EYES SPEAK MORE THAN THE MOUTH." THEY'RE SUPER-FUN TO DRAW.

WELL, ANYWAY, THANK YOU SO MUCH FOR READING SACRIFICIAL PRINCESS AND THE KING OF BEASTS! I MUST THANK MY EDITOR, TO WHOM I'M TERRIBLY INDEBTED, AS WELL AS MY VERY UNDERSTANDING FAMILY. THERE'S A LITTLE BONUS AT THE END, SO PLEASE READ THE WHOLE THING!

TOMOFUJI

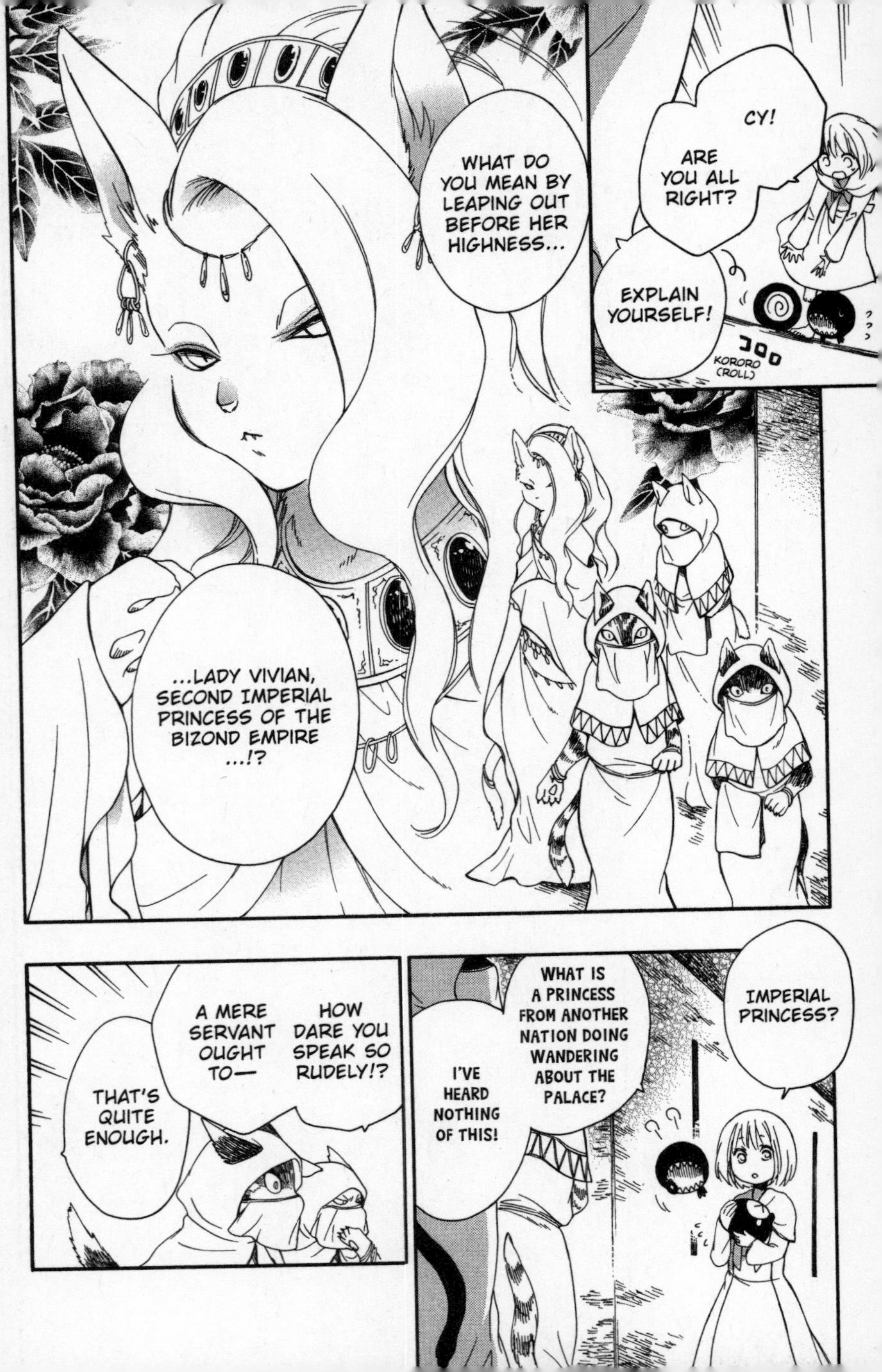
CY!
ARE YOU ALL RIGHT?
EXPLAIN YOURSELF!
コロロ
KORORO (ROLL)
WHAT DO YOU MEAN BY LEAPING OUT BEFORE HER HIGHNESS...
...LADY VIVIAN, SECOND IMPERIAL PRINCESS OF THE BIZOND EMPIRE ...!?
IMPERIAL PRINCESS?
WHAT IS A PRINCESS FROM ANOTHER NATION DOING WANDERING ABOUT THE PALACE?
I'VE HEARD NOTHING OF THIS!
HOW DARE YOU SPEAK SO RUDELY!?
A MERE SERVANT OUGHT TO—
THAT'S QUITE ENOUGH.

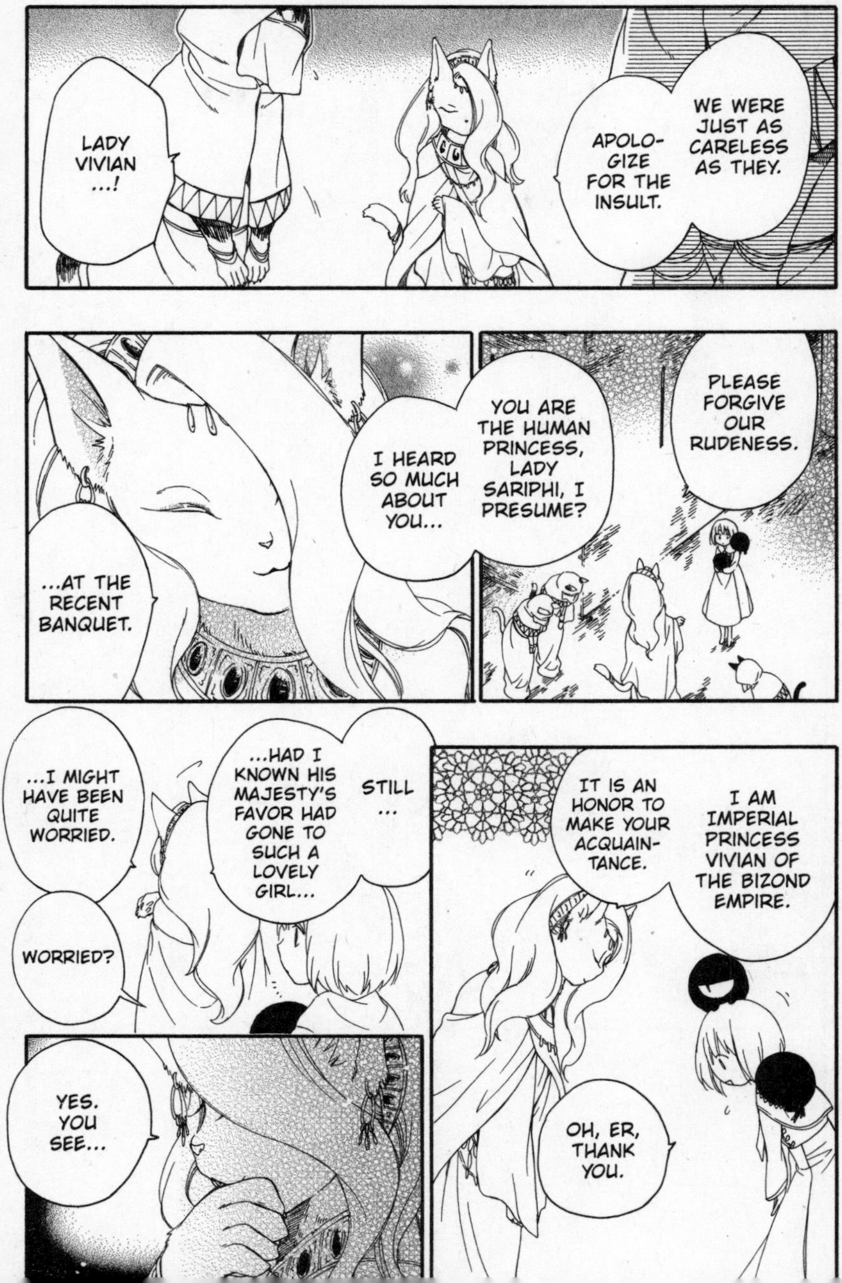
WE WERE JUST AS CARELESS AS THEY.
APOLO-GIZE FOR THE INSULT.
LADY VIVIAN ...!
PLEASE FORGIVE OUR RUDENESS.
YOU ARE THE HUMAN PRINCESS, LADY SARIPHI, I PRESUME?
I HEARD SO MUCH ABOUT YOU...
...AT THE RECENT BANQUET.
I AM IMPERIAL PRINCESS VIVIAN OF THE BIZOND EMPIRE.
IT IS AN HONOR TO MAKE YOUR ACQUAIN-TANCE.
OH, ER, THANK YOU.
STILL ...
...HAD I KNOWN HIS MAJESTY'S FAVOR HAD GONE TO SUCH A LOVELY GIRL...
...I MIGHT HAVE BEEN QUITE WORRIED.
WORRIED?
YES. YOU SEE...

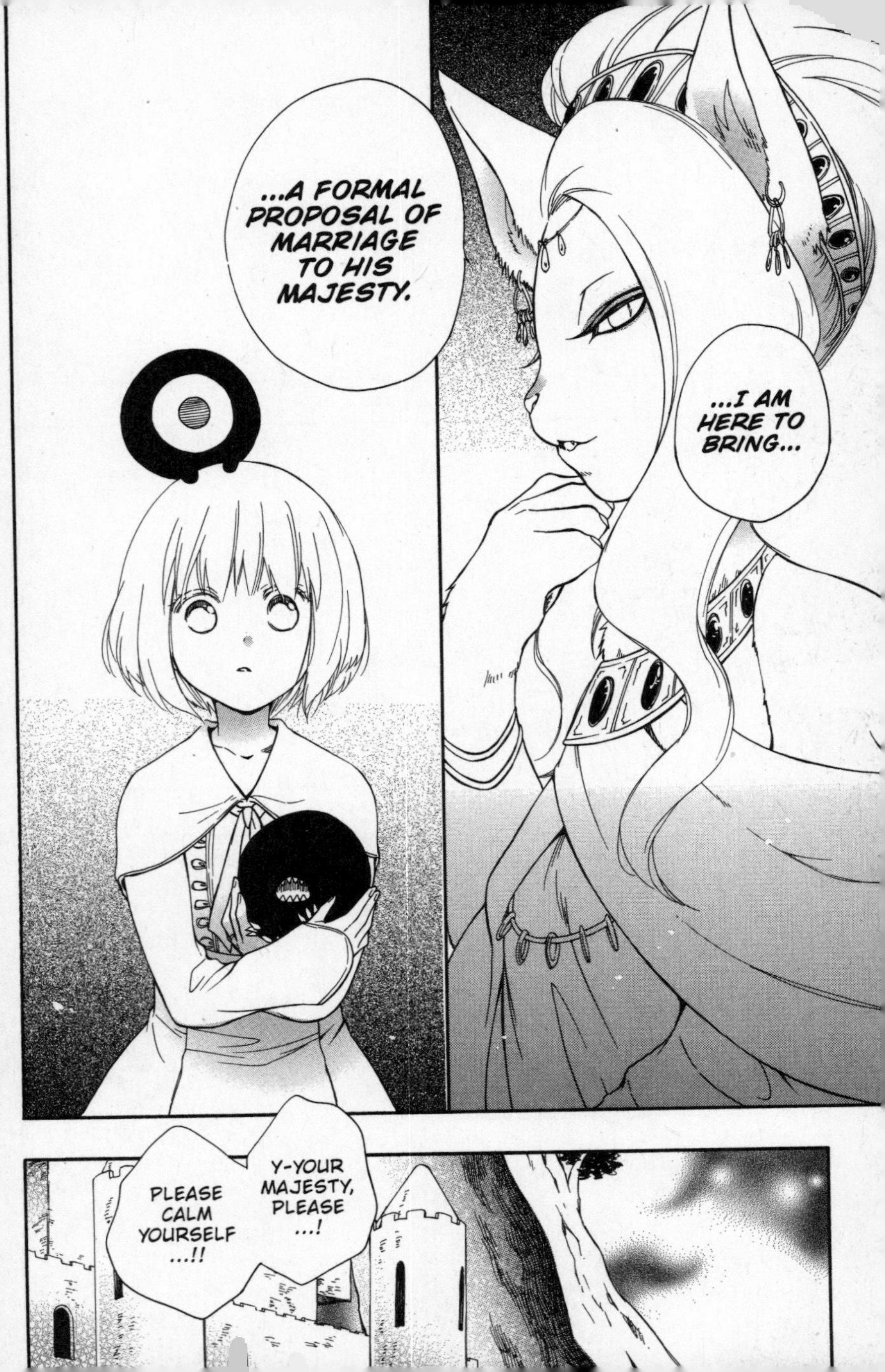
...I AM HERE TO BRING...
...A FORMAL PROPOSAL OF MARRIAGE TO HIS MAJESTY.
Y-YOUR MAJESTY, PLEASE ...!
PLEASE CALM YOURSELF ...!!

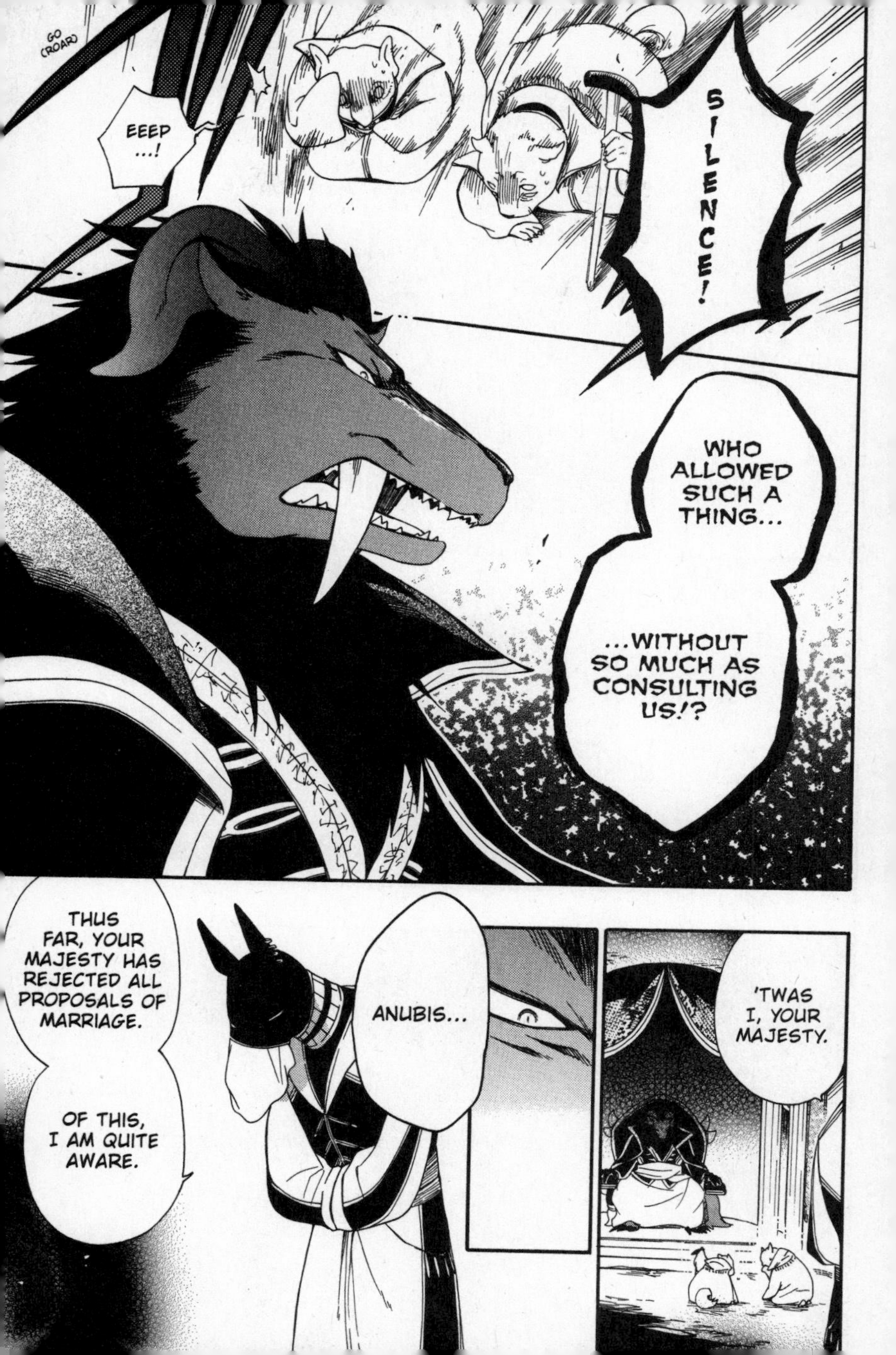
SILENCE!
GO (ROAR)
EEEP ...!
WHO ALLOWED SUCH A THING...
...WITHOUT SO MUCH AS CONSULTING US!?
'TWAS I, YOUR MAJESTY.
ANUBIS...
THUS FAR, YOUR MAJESTY HAS REJECTED ALL PROPOSALS OF MARRIAGE.
OF THIS, I AM QUITE AWARE.

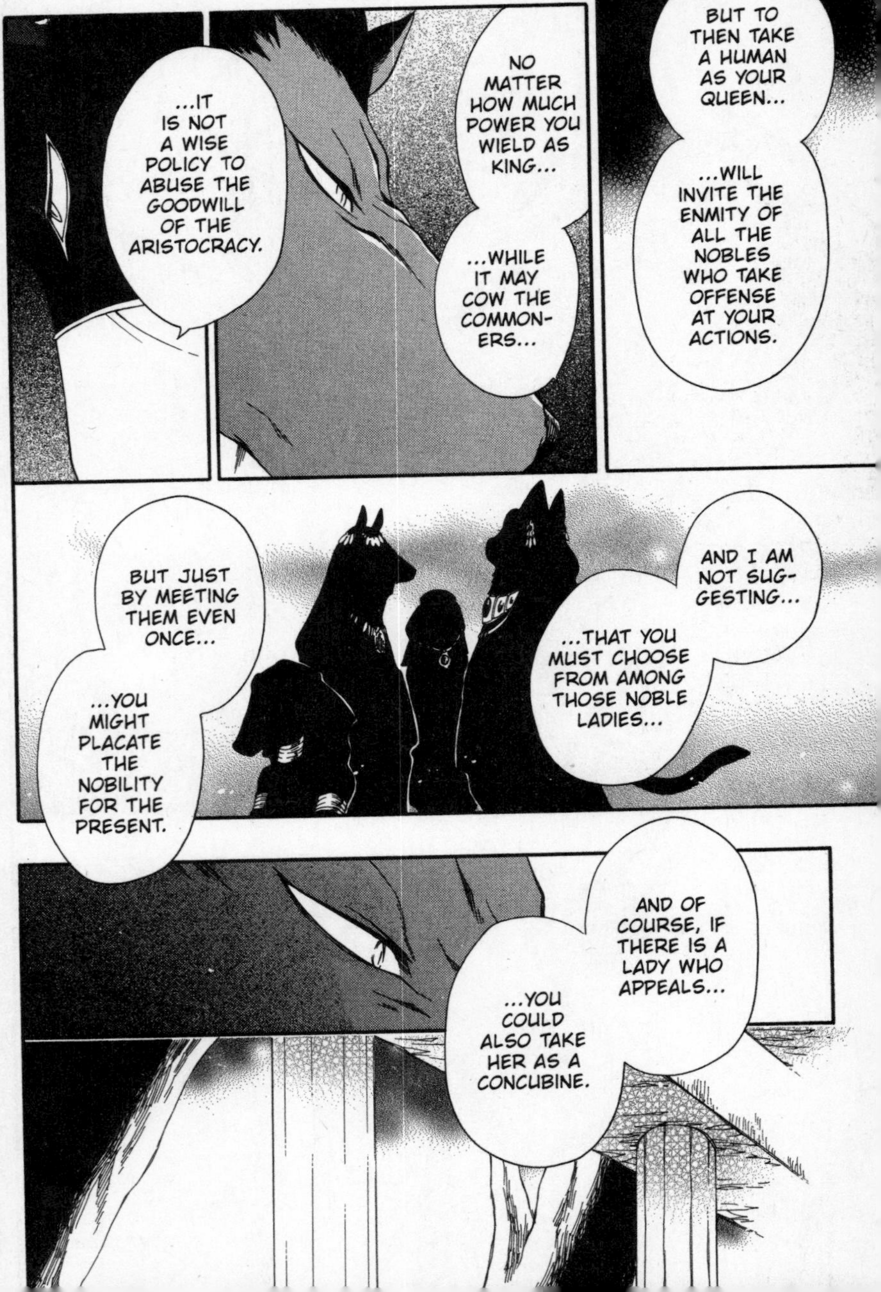
BUT TO THEN TAKE A HUMAN AS YOUR QUEEN...
...WILL INVITE THE ENMITY OF ALL THE NOBLES WHO TAKE OFFENSE AT YOUR ACTIONS.
NO MATTER HOW MUCH POWER YOU WIELD AS KING...
...WHILE IT MAY COW THE COMMON-ERS...
...IT IS NOT A WISE POLICY TO ABUSE THE GOODWILL OF THE ARISTOCRACY.
AND I AM NOT SUG-GESTING...
...THAT YOU MUST CHOOSE FROM AMONG THOSE NOBLE LADIES...
BUT JUST BY MEETING THEM EVEN ONCE...
...YOU MIGHT PLACATE THE NOBILITY FOR THE PRESENT.
AND OF COURSE, IF THERE IS A LADY WHO APPEALS...
...YOU COULD ALSO TAKE HER AS A CONCUBINE.

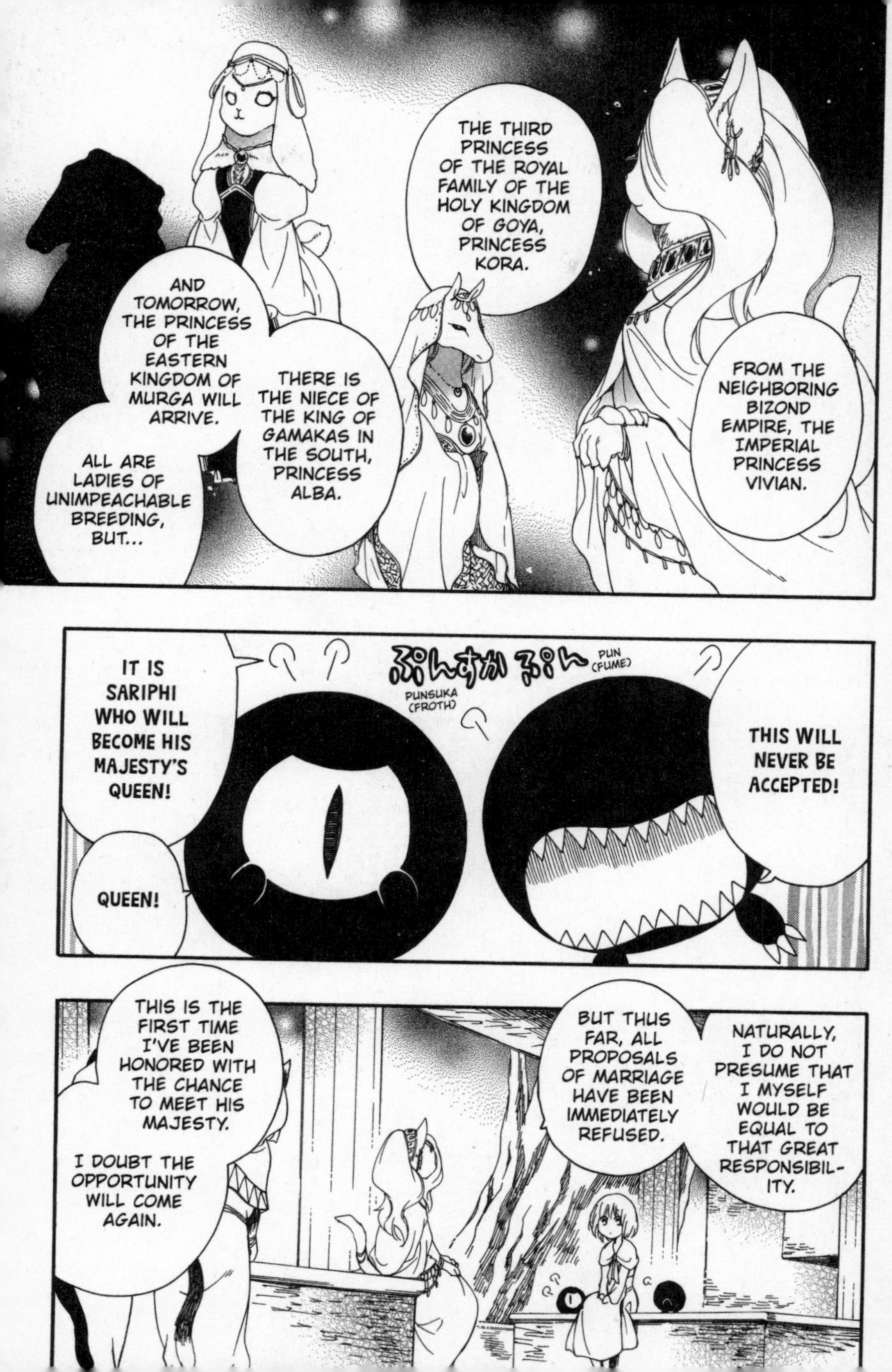
THE THIRD PRINCESS OF THE ROYAL FAMILY OF THE HOLY KINGDOM OF GOYA, PRINCESS KORA.
FROM THE NEIGHBORING BIZOND EMPIRE, THE IMPERIAL PRINCESS VIVIAN.
THERE IS THE NIECE OF THE KING OF GAMAKAS IN THE SOUTH, PRINCESS ALBA.
AND TOMORROW, THE PRINCESS OF THE EASTERN KINGDOM OF MURGA WILL ARRIVE.
ALL ARE LADIES OF UNIMPEACHABLE BREEDING, BUT...
THIS WILL NEVER BE ACCEPTED!
ぷんすかぷん
PUN (FUME)
PUNSUKA (FROTH)
IT IS SARIPHI WHO WILL BECOME HIS MAJESTY'S QUEEN!
QUEEN!
NATURALLY, I DO NOT PRESUME THAT I MYSELF WOULD BE EQUAL TO THAT GREAT RESPONSIBIL-ITY.
BUT THUS FAR, ALL PROPOSALS OF MARRIAGE HAVE BEEN IMMEDIATELY REFUSED.
THIS IS THE FIRST TIME I'VE BEEN HONORED WITH THE CHANCE TO MEET HIS MAJESTY.
I DOUBT THE OPPORTUNITY WILL COME AGAIN.

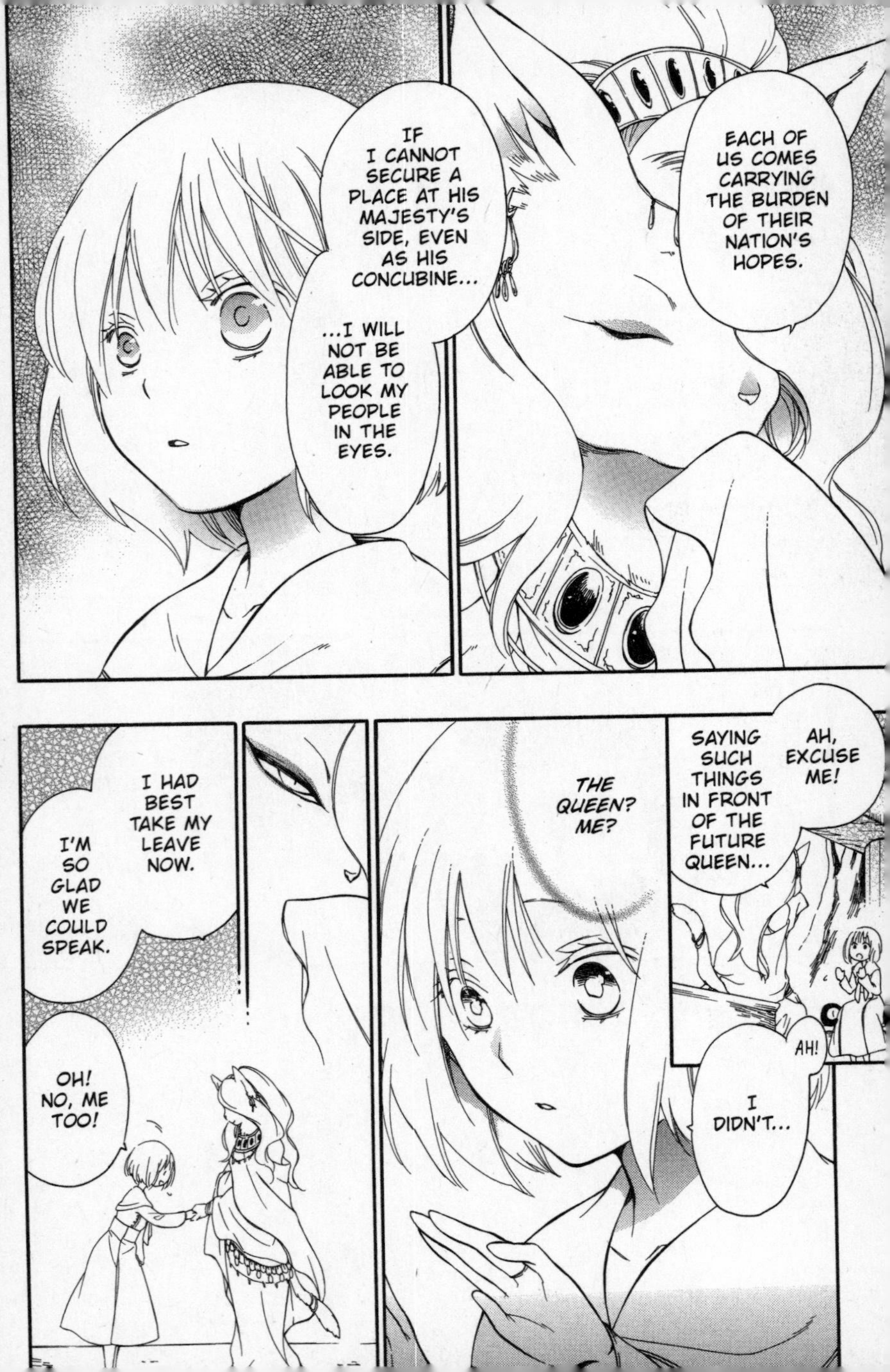
EACH OF US COMES CARRYING THE BURDEN OF THEIR NATION'S HOPES.
IF I CANNOT SECURE A PLACE AT HIS MAJESTY'S SIDE, EVEN AS HIS CONCUBINE...
...I WILL NOT BE ABLE TO LOOK MY PEOPLE IN THE EYES.
AH, EXCUSE ME!
SAYING SUCH THINGS IN FRONT OF THE FUTURE QUEEN...
THE QUEEN? ME?
AH!
I DIDN'T...
I HAD BEST TAKE MY LEAVE NOW.
I'M SO GLAD WE COULD SPEAK.
OH! NO, ME TOO!

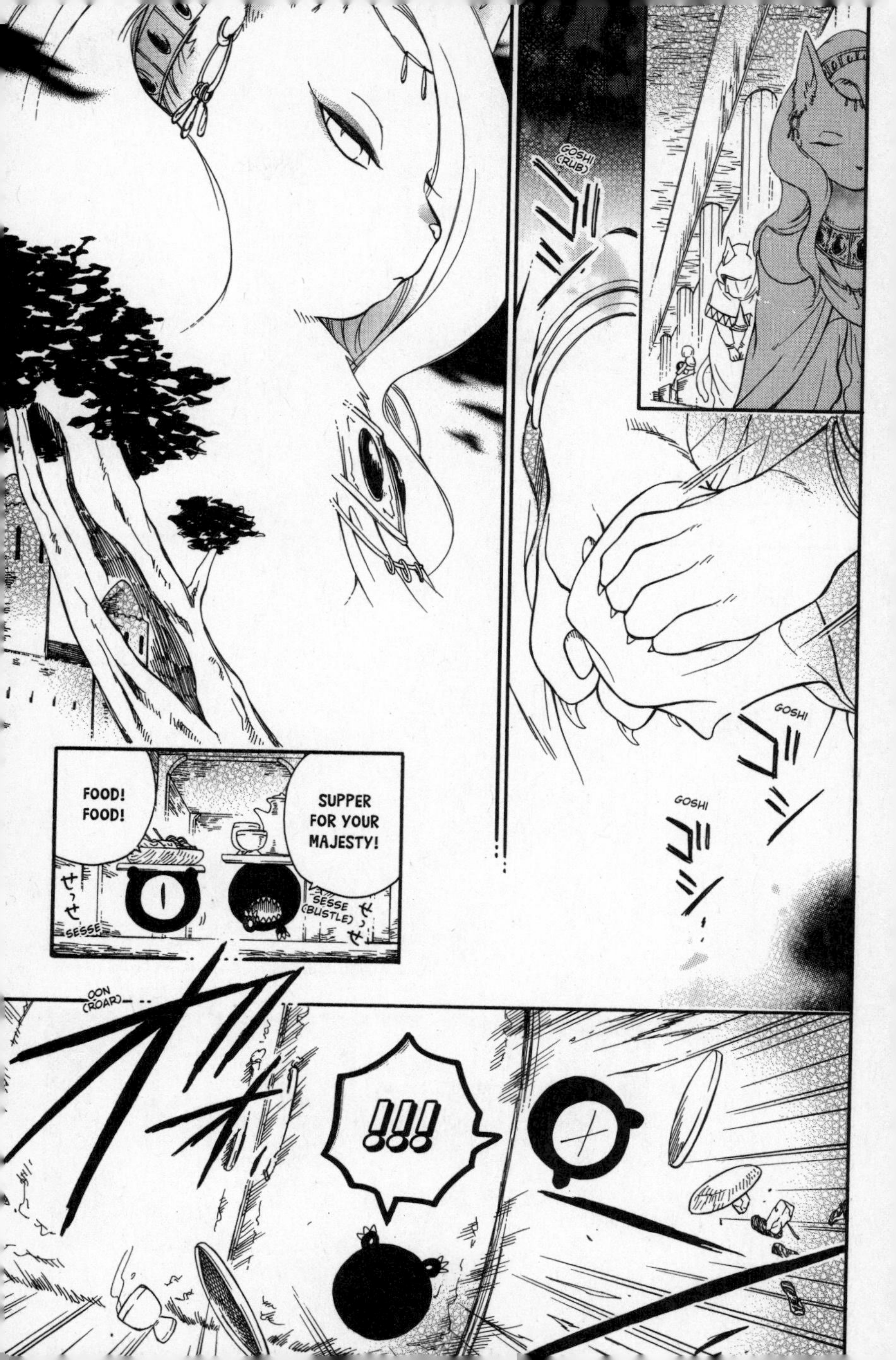
GOSHI (RUB)
GOSHI
GOSHI
SUPPER FOR YOUR MAJESTY!
FOOD! FOOD!
せっせ
SESSE (BUSTLE)
せっせ
SESSE
OON (ROAR)
!!!

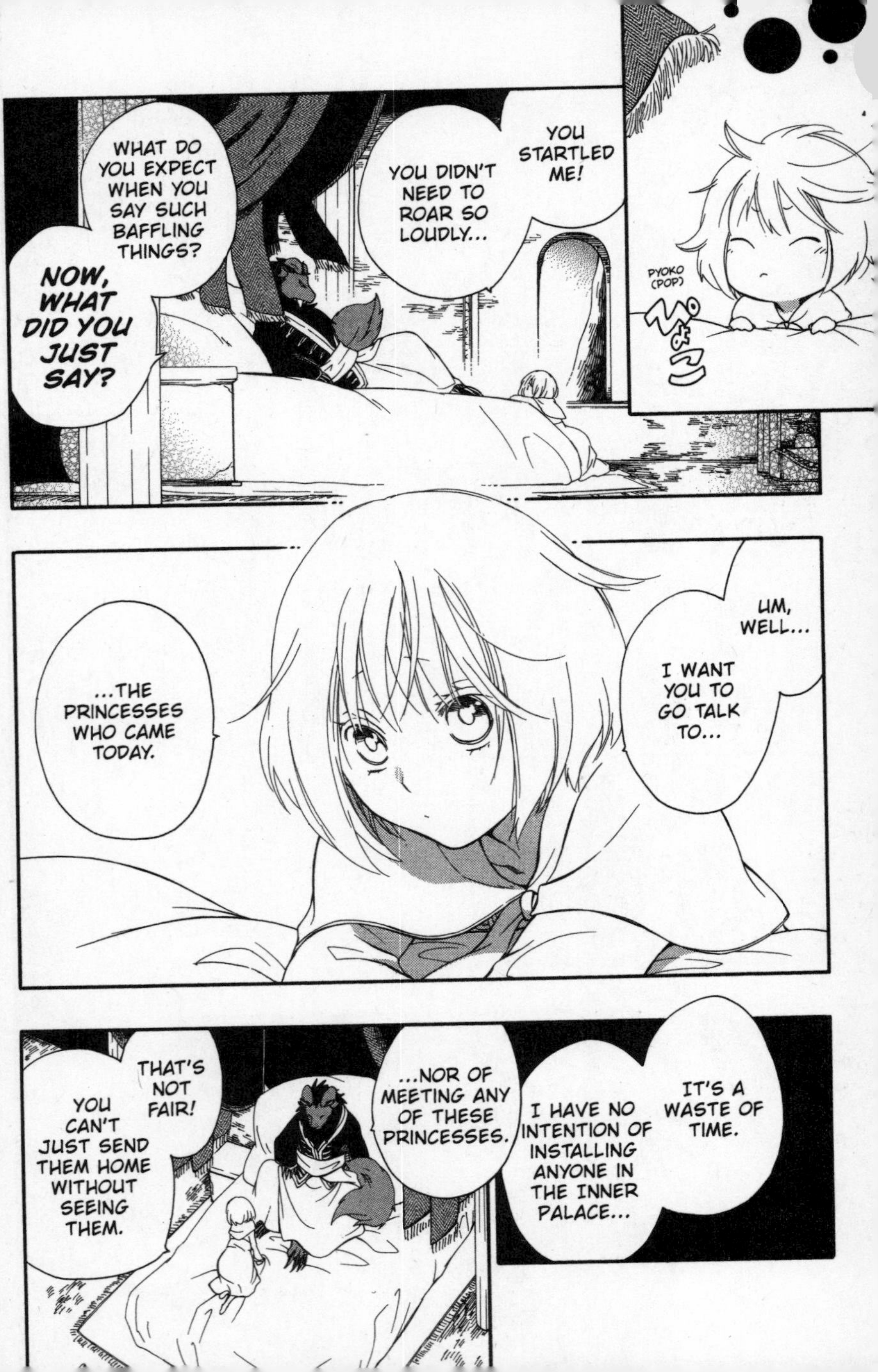
PYOKO (POP)
YOU STARTLED ME!
YOU DIDN'T NEED TO ROAR SO LOUDLY...
WHAT DO YOU EXPECT WHEN YOU SAY SUCH BAFFLING THINGS?
NOW, WHAT DID YOU JUST SAY?
UM, WELL...
I WANT YOU TO GO TALK TO...
...THE PRINCESSES WHO CAME TODAY.
IT'S A WASTE OF TIME.
I HAVE NO INTENTION OF INSTALLING ANYONE IN THE INNER PALACE...
...NOR OF MEETING ANY OF THESE PRINCESSES.
THAT'S NOT FAIR!
YOU CAN'T JUST SEND THEM HOME WITHOUT SEEING THEM.

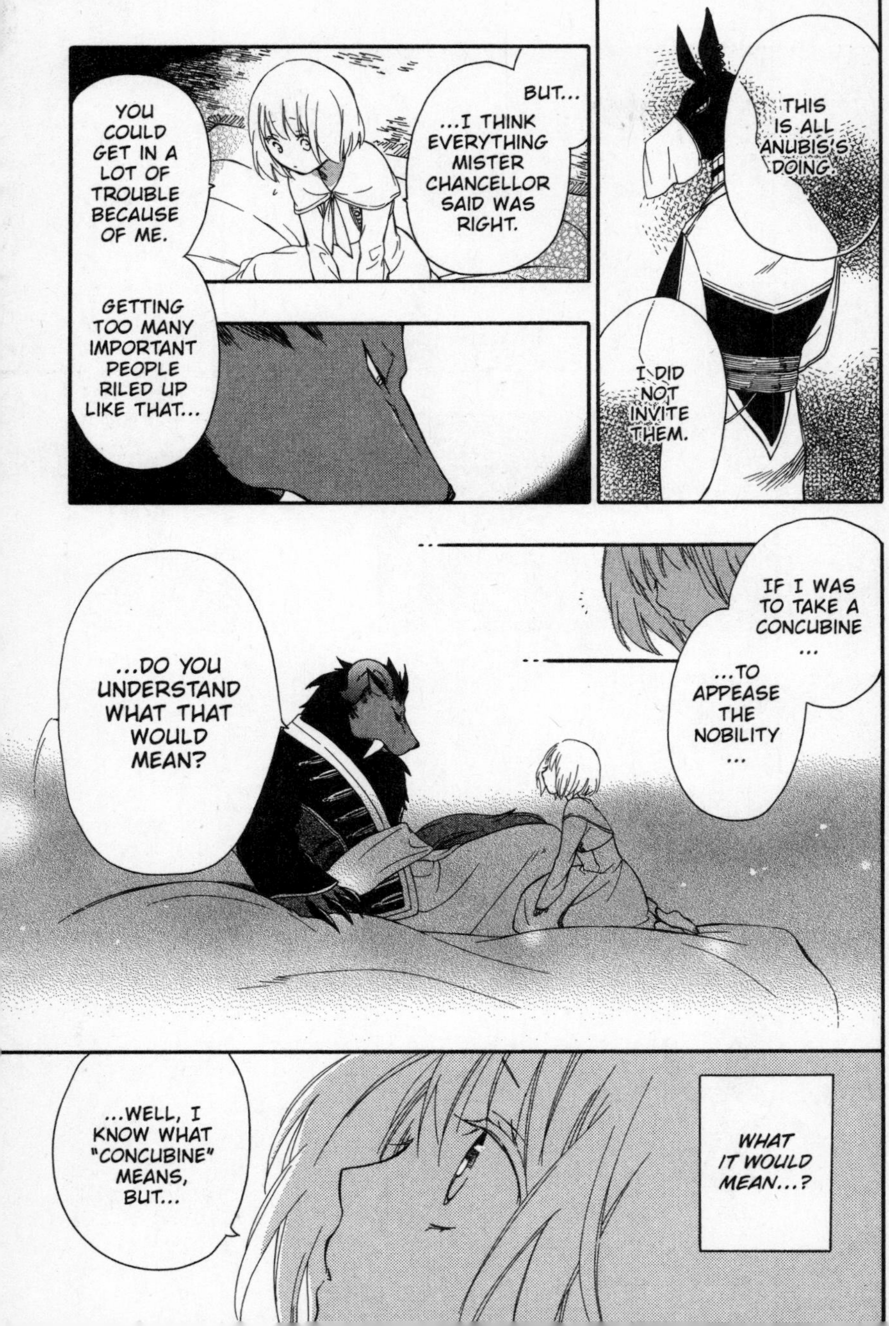
THIS IS ALL ANUBIS'S DOING.
I DID NOT INVITE THEM.
BUT...
...I THINK EVERYTHING MISTER CHANCELLOR SAID WAS RIGHT.
YOU COULD GET IN A LOT OF TROUBLE BECAUSE OF ME.
GETTING TOO MANY IMPORTANT PEOPLE RILED UP LIKE THAT...
IF I WAS TO TAKE A CONCUBINE ... ...TO APPEASE THE NOBILITY ...
...DO YOU UNDERSTAND WHAT THAT WOULD MEAN?
WHAT IT WOULD MEAN...?
...WELL, I KNOW WHAT "CONCUBINE" MEANS, BUT...

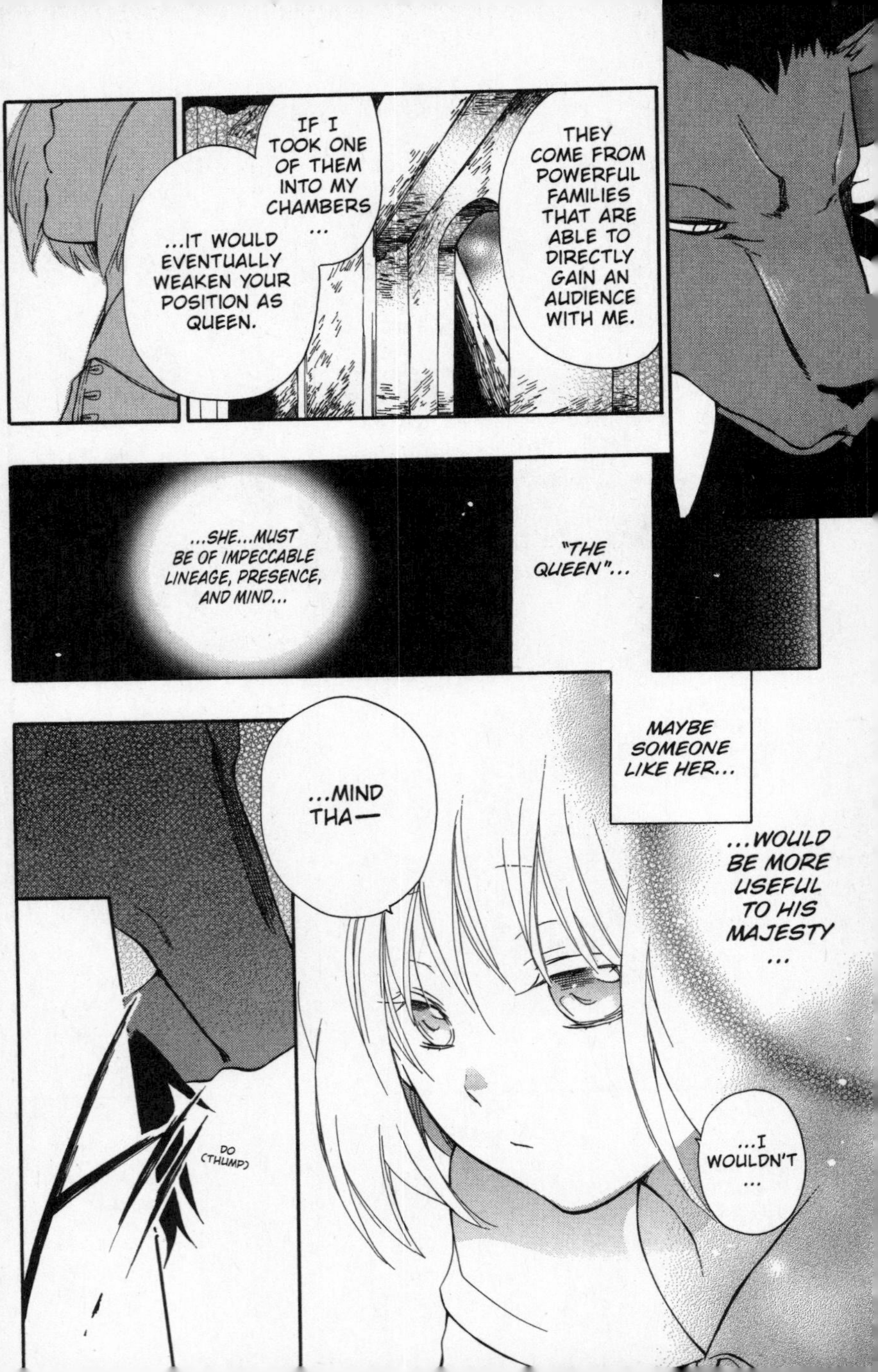
THEY COME FROM POWERFUL FAMILIES THAT ARE ABLE TO DIRECTLY GAIN AN AUDIENCE WITH ME.
IF I TOOK ONE OF THEM INTO MY CHAMBERS...
...IT WOULD EVENTUALLY WEAKEN YOUR POSITION AS QUEEN.
"THE QUEEN"...
...SHE...MUST BE OF IMPECCABLE LINEAGE, PRESENCE, AND MIND...
MAYBE SOMEONE LIKE HER...
...WOULD BE MORE USEFUL TO HIS MAJESTY...
...I WOULDN'T...
...MIND THA—
DO (THUMP)

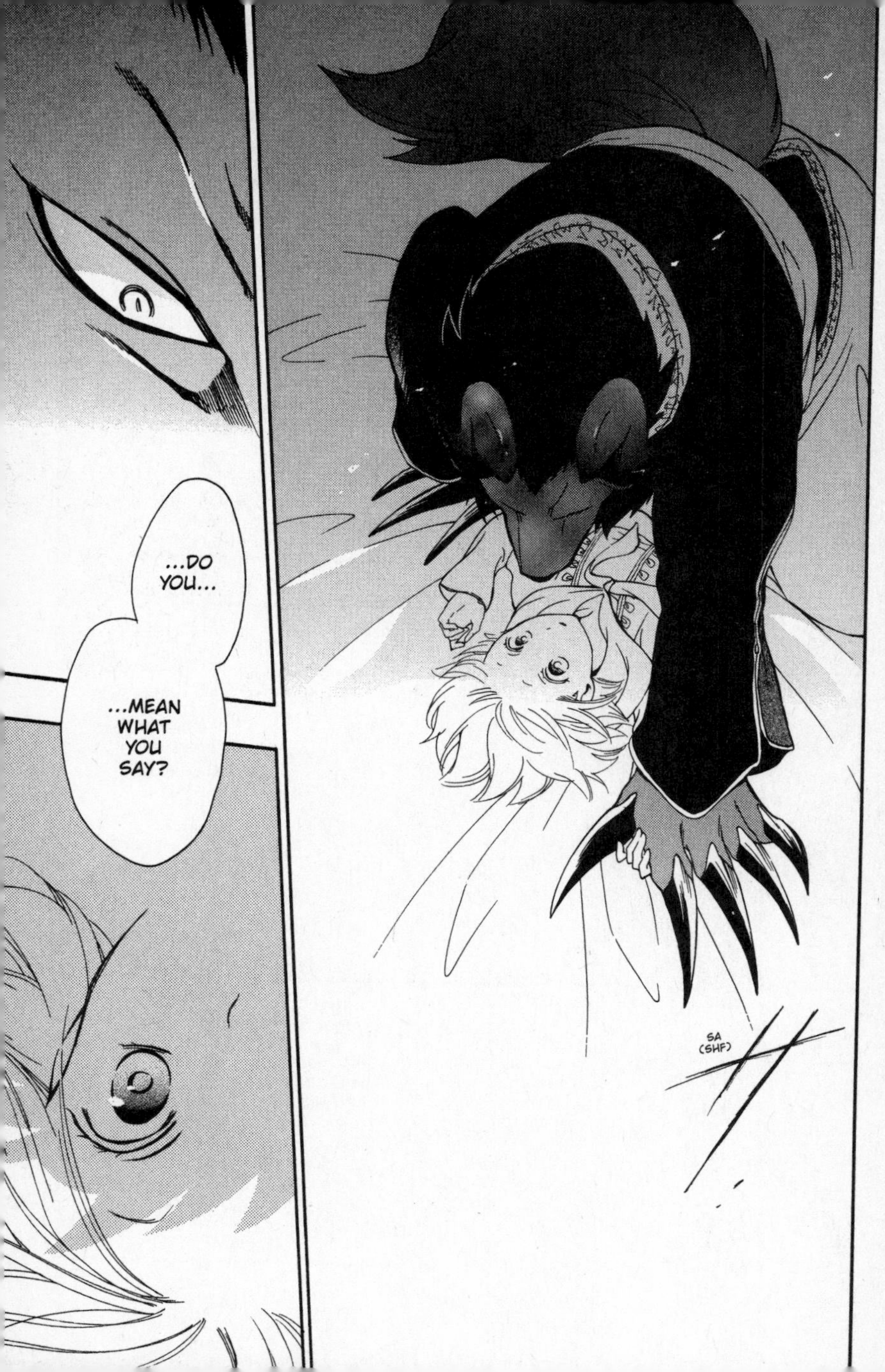
SA (SHF)
...DO YOU...
...MEAN WHAT YOU SAY?

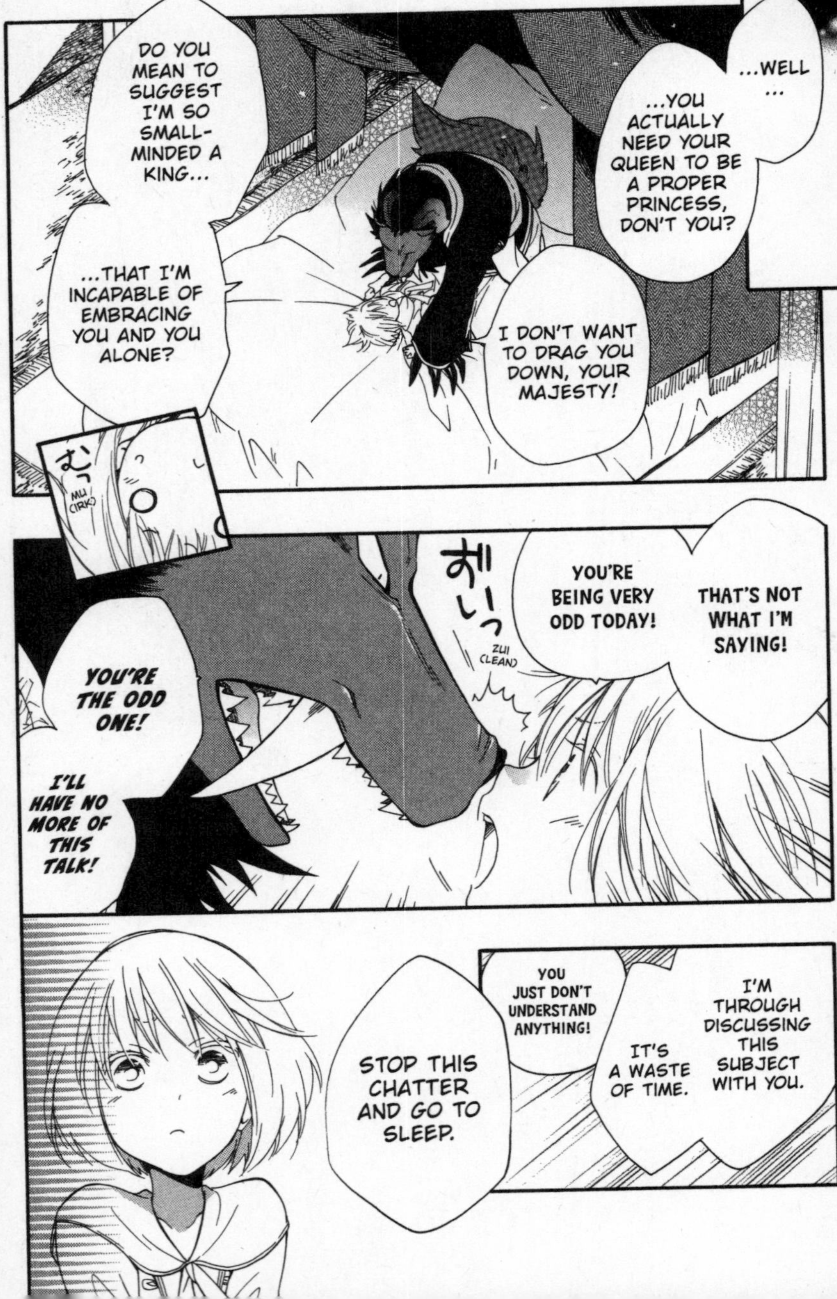
...WELL ...
...YOU ACTUALLY NEED YOUR QUEEN TO BE A PROPER PRINCESS, DON'T YOU?
I DON'T WANT TO DRAG YOU DOWN, YOUR MAJESTY!
DO YOU MEAN TO SUGGEST I'M SO SMALL-MINDED A KING...
...THAT I'M INCAPABLE OF EMBRACING YOU AND YOU ALONE?
むっ
MU (IRK)
THAT'S NOT WHAT I'M SAYING!
YOU'RE BEING VERY ODD TODAY!
ずいっ
ZUI (LEAN)
YOU'RE THE ODD ONE!
I'LL HAVE NO MORE OF THIS TALK!
I'M THROUGH DISCUSSING THIS SUBJECT WITH YOU.
IT'S A WASTE OF TIME.
YOU JUST DON'T UNDERSTAND ANYTHING!
STOP THIS CHATTER AND GO TO SLEEP.

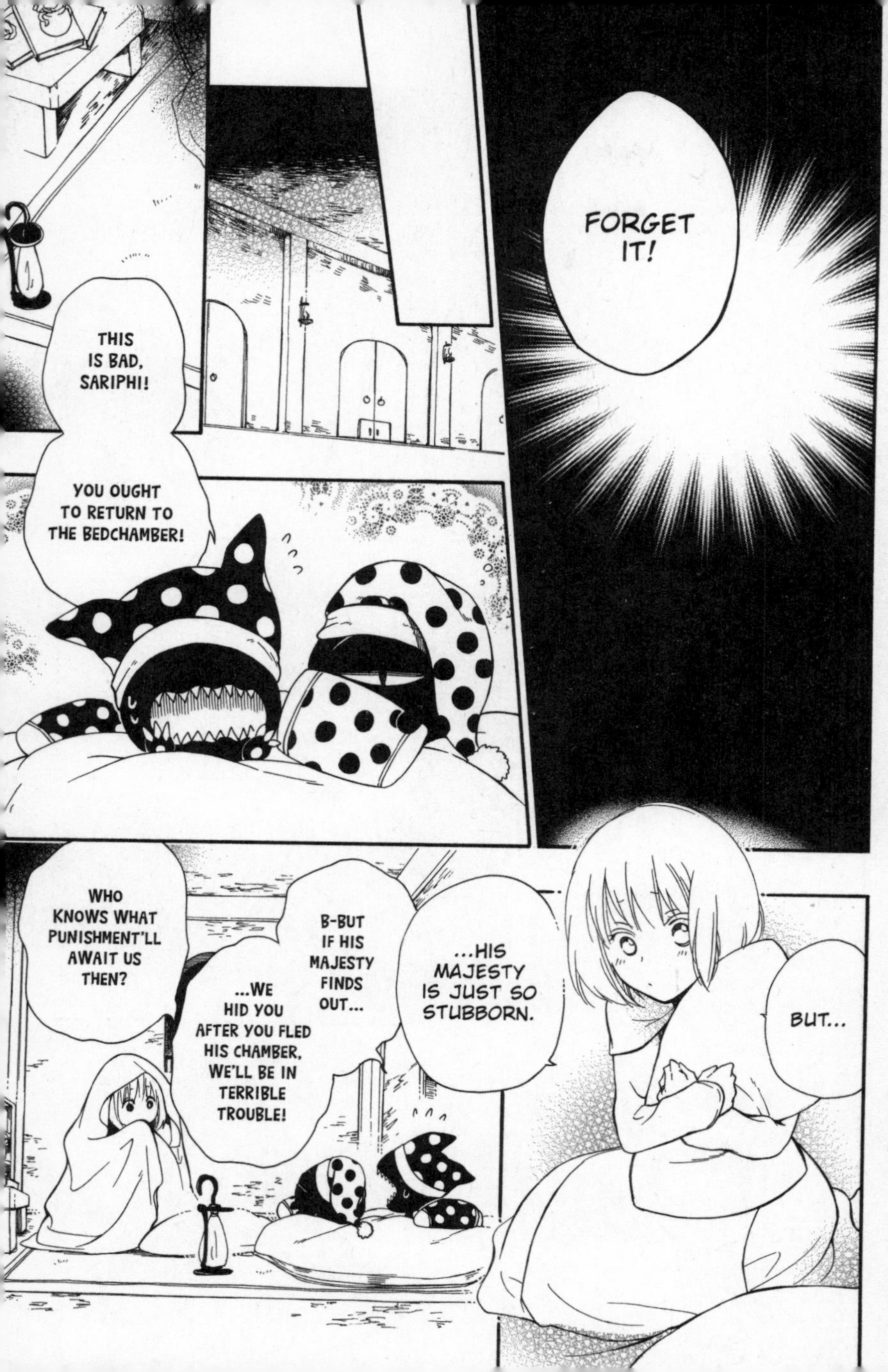
FORGET IT!
THIS IS BAD, SARIPHI!
YOU OUGHT TO RETURN TO THE BEDCHAMBER!
BUT...
...HIS MAJESTY IS JUST SO STUBBORN.
B-BUT IF HIS MAJESTY FINDS OUT...
...WE HID YOU AFTER YOU FLED HIS CHAMBER, WE'LL BE IN TERRIBLE TROUBLE!
WHO KNOWS WHAT PUNISHMENT'LL AWAIT US THEN?

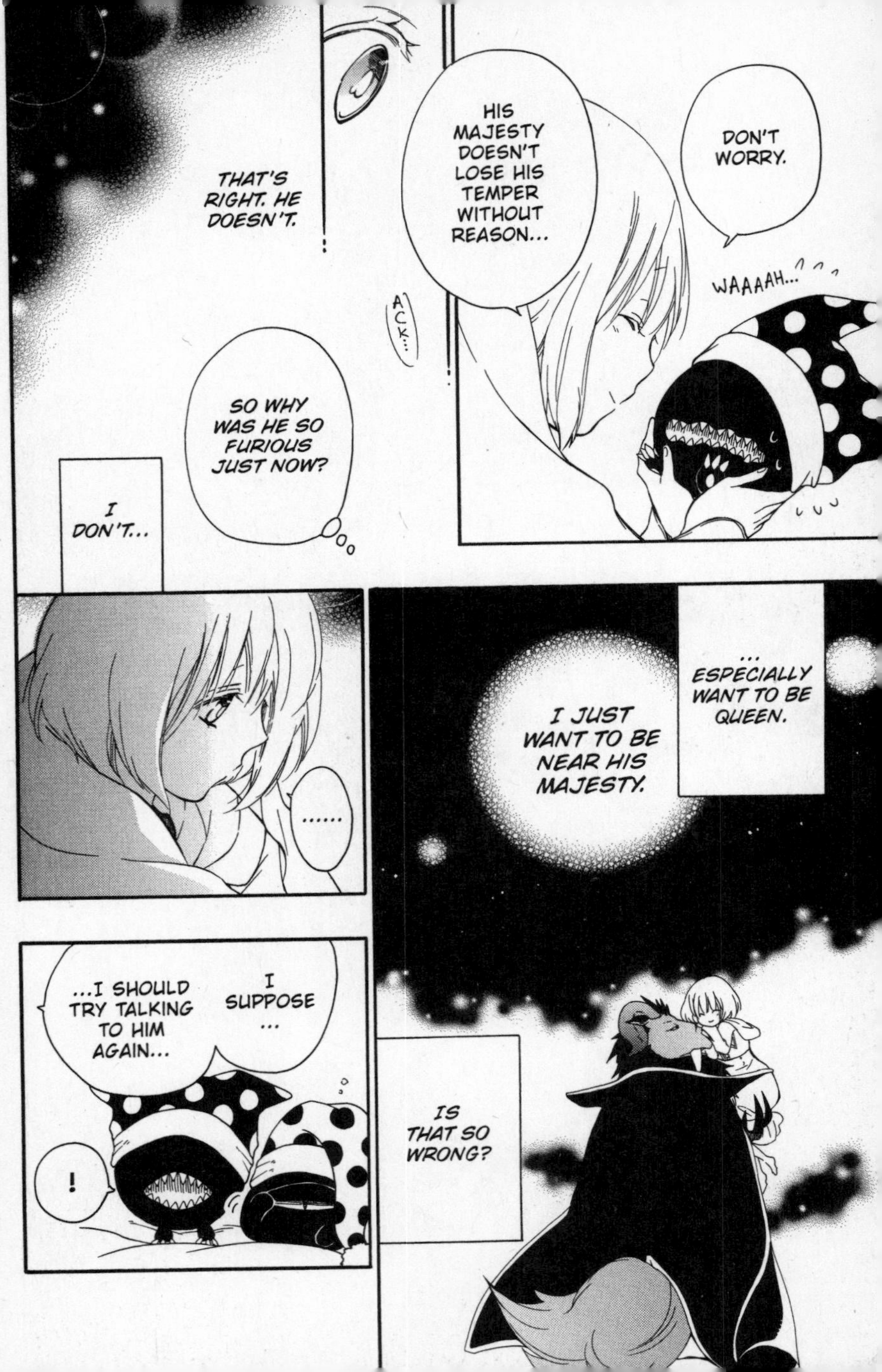
DON'T WORRY.
HIS MAJESTY DOESN'T LOSE HIS TEMPER WITHOUT REASON...
WAAAAH...
ACK...
THAT'S RIGHT. HE DOESN'T.
SO WHY WAS HE SO FURIOUS JUST NOW?
I DON'T...
...ESPECIALLY WANT TO BE QUEEN.
I JUST WANT TO BE NEAR HIS MAJESTY.
IS THAT SO WRONG?
......
I SUPPOSE...
...I SHOULD TRY TALKING TO HIM AGAIN...
!

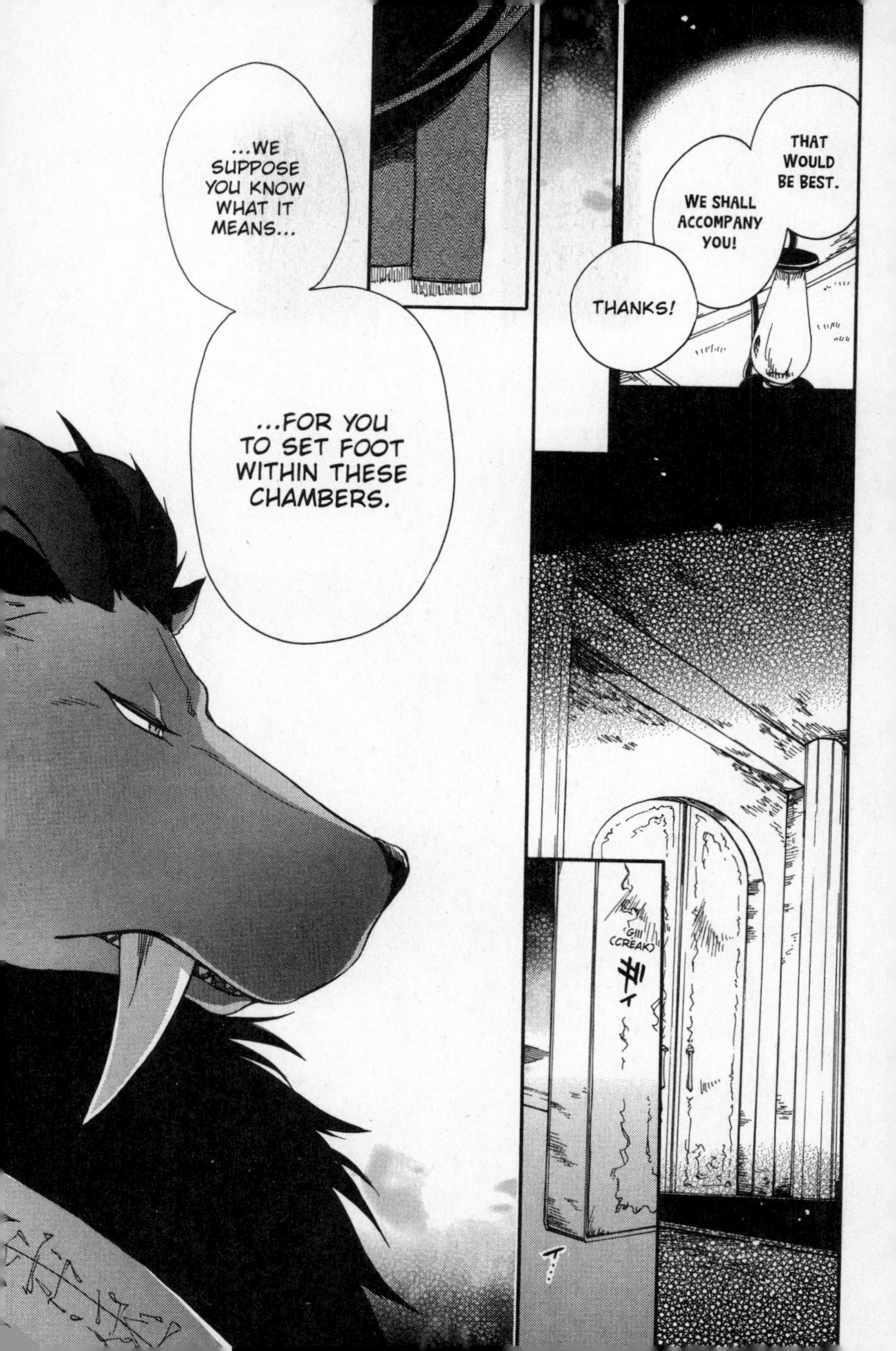
THAT WOULD BE BEST.
WE SHALL ACCOMPANY YOU!
THANKS!
GIII (CREAK)
ギィ
...WE SUPPOSE YOU KNOW WHAT IT MEANS...
...FOR YOU TO SET FOOT WITHIN THESE CHAMBERS.

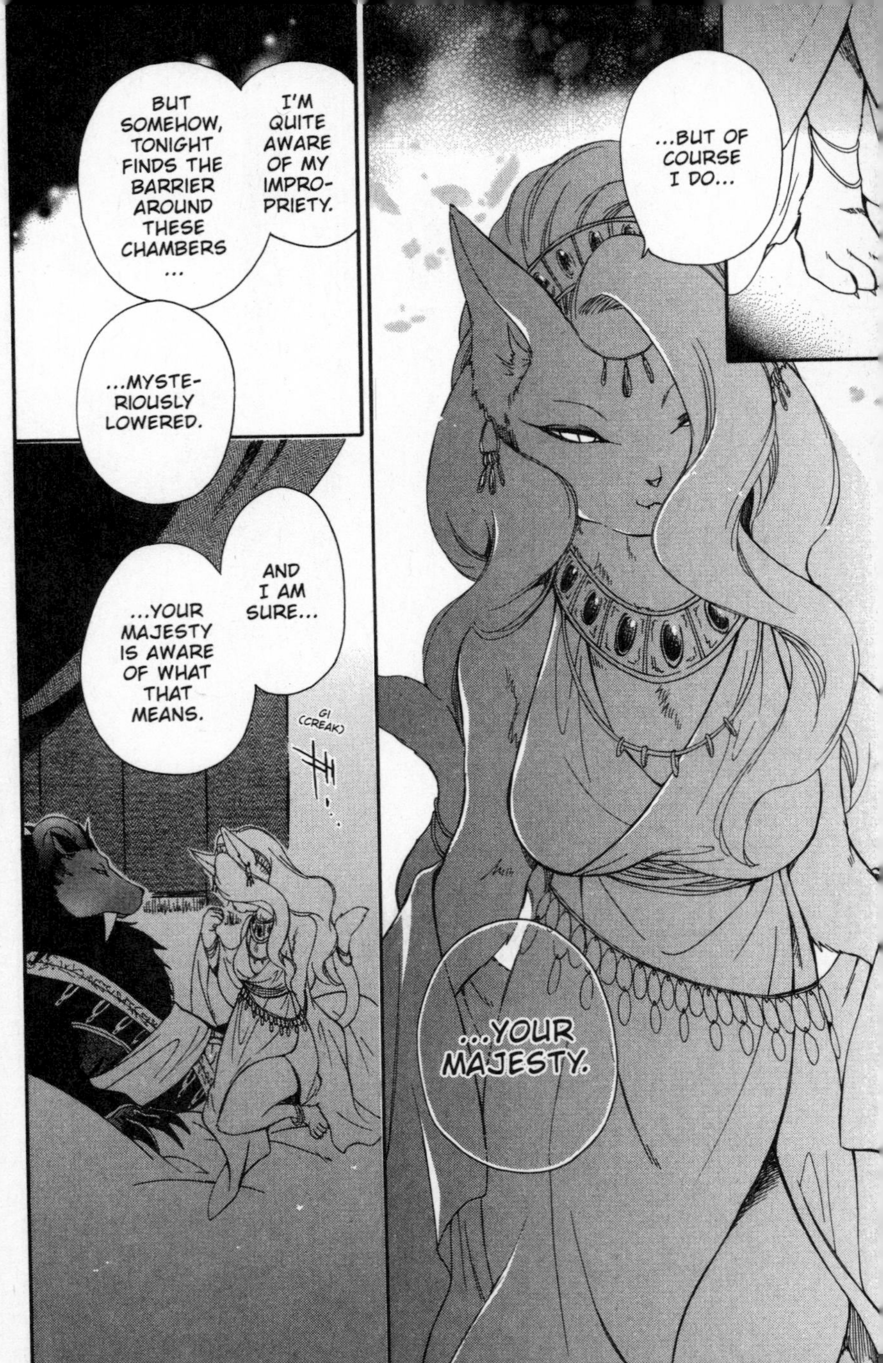
I'M QUITE AWARE OF MY IMPRO-PRIETY.
BUT SOMEHOW, TONIGHT FINDS THE BARRIER AROUND THESE CHAMBERS ...
...MYSTE-RIOUSLY LOWERED.
AND I AM SURE...
...YOUR MAJESTY IS AWARE OF WHAT THAT MEANS.
GI (CREAK)
...BUT OF COURSE I DO...
...YOUR MAJESTY.

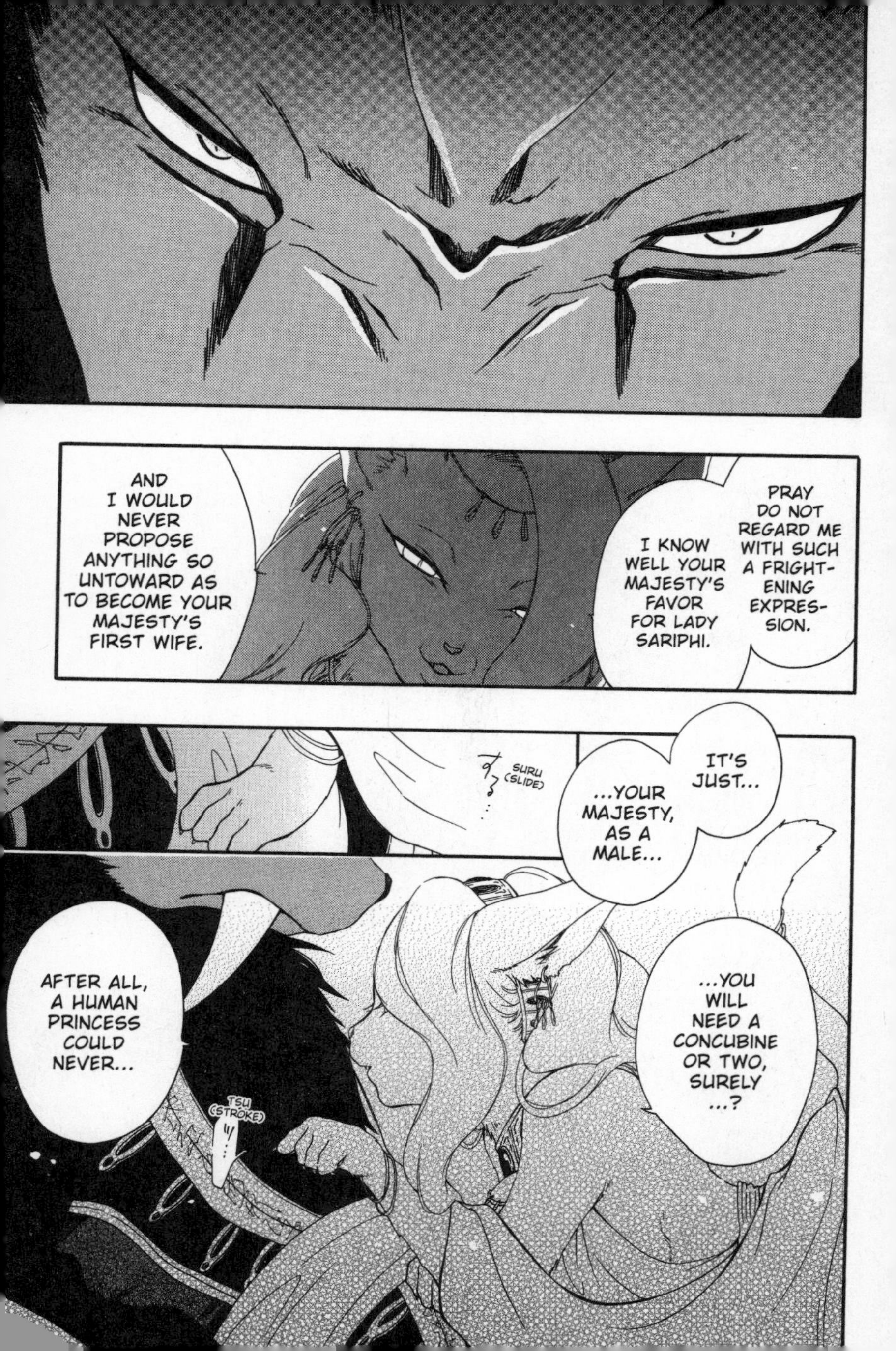
PRAY DO NOT REGARD ME WITH SUCH A FRIGHT-ENING EXPRES-SION.
I KNOW WELL YOUR MAJESTY'S FAVOR FOR LADY SARIPHI.
AND I WOULD NEVER PROPOSE ANYTHING SO UNTOWARD AS TO BECOME YOUR MAJESTY'S FIRST WIFE.
IT'S JUST...
...YOUR MAJESTY, AS A MALE...
SURU (SLIDE)
...YOU WILL NEED A CONCUBINE OR TWO, SURELY ...?
TSU (STROKE)
AFTER ALL, A HUMAN PRINCESS COULD NEVER...

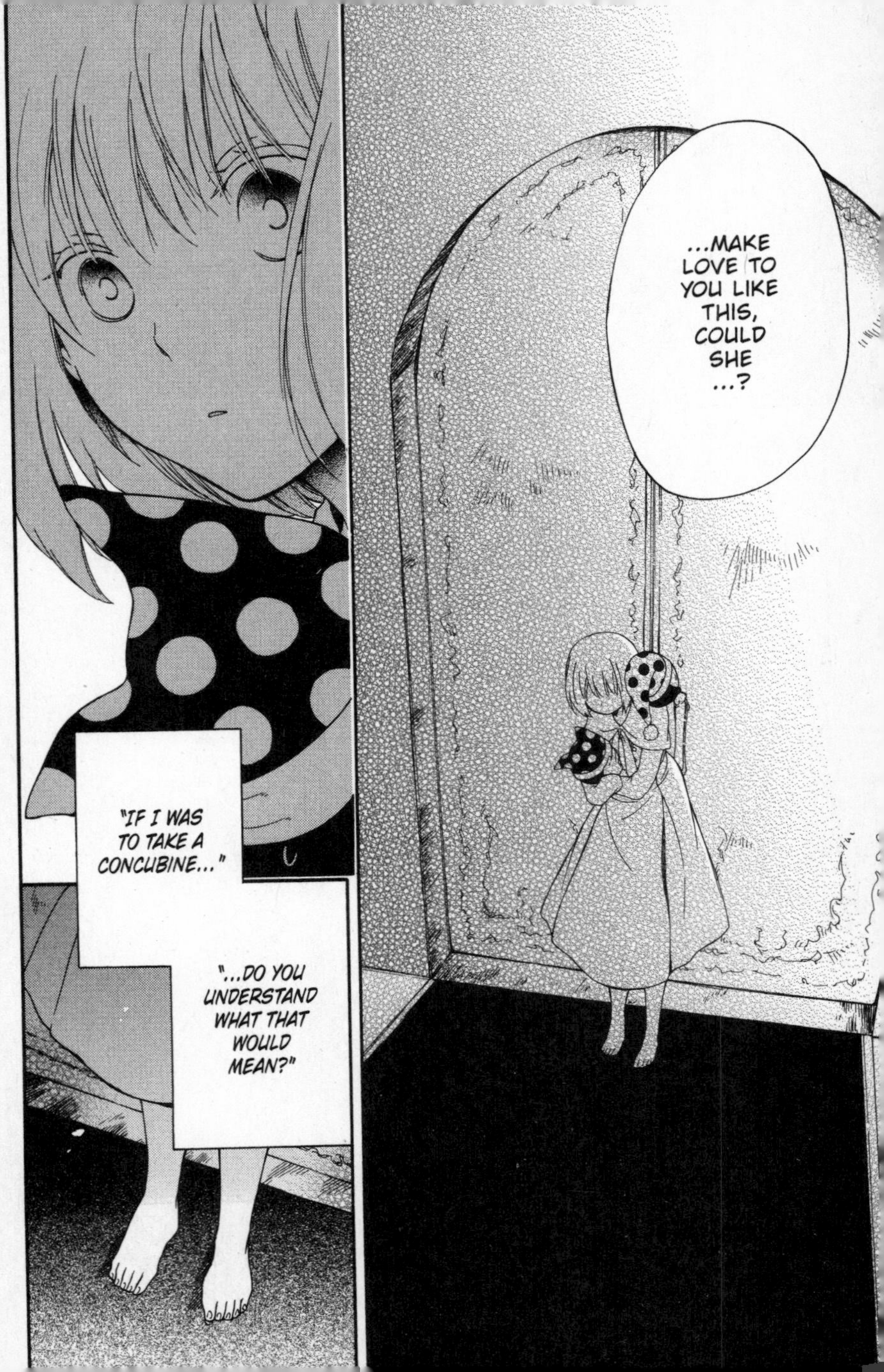
...MAKE LOVE TO YOU LIKE THIS, COULD SHE ...?
"IF I WAS TO TAKE A CONCUBINE..."
"...DO YOU UNDERSTAND WHAT THAT WOULD MEAN?"

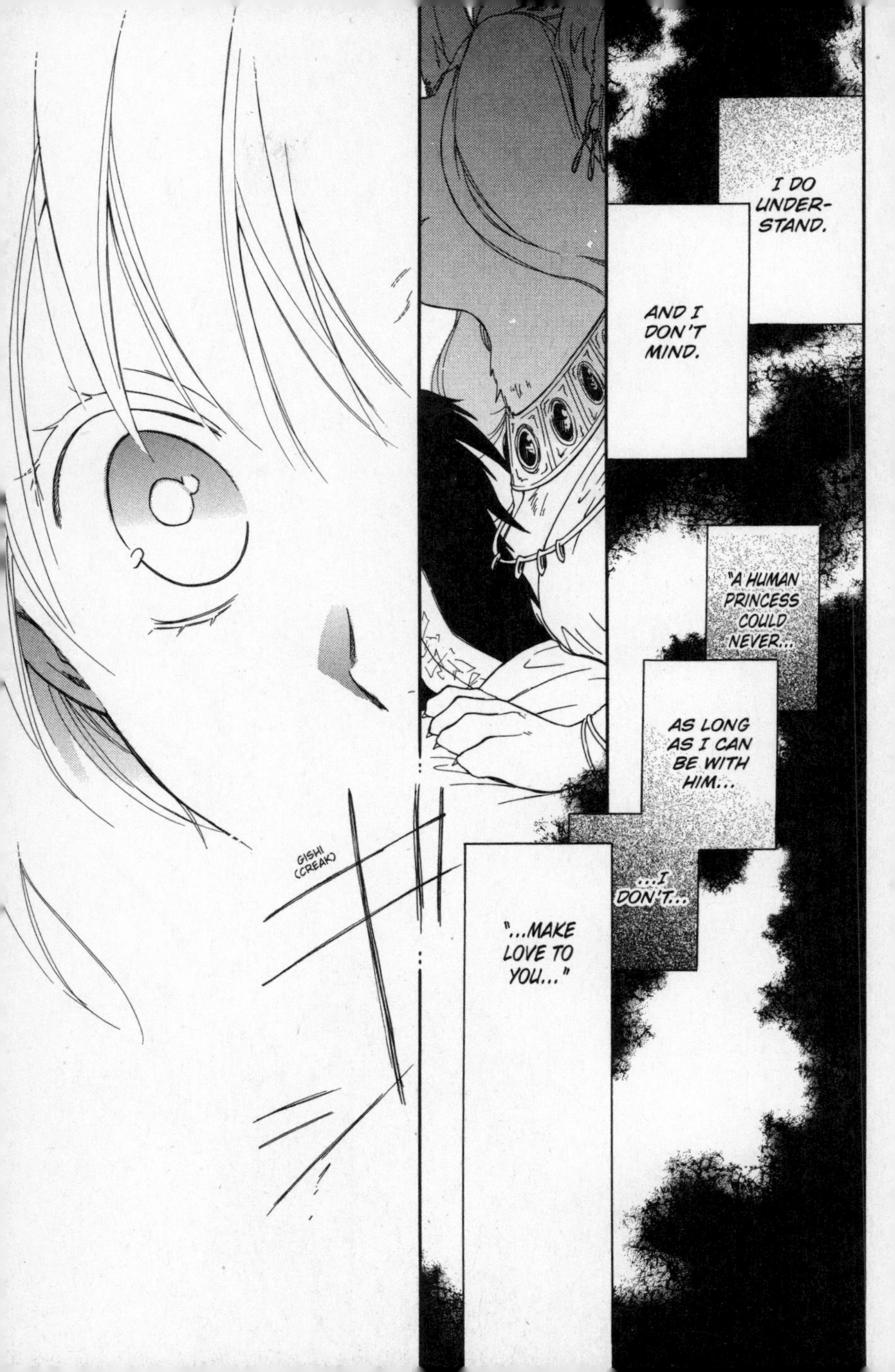
I DO UNDER-STAND.
AND I DON'T MIND.
"A HUMAN PRINCESS COULD NEVER...
AS LONG AS I CAN BE WITH HIM...
...I DON'T...
"...MAKE LOVE TO YOU..."
GISHI (CREAK)

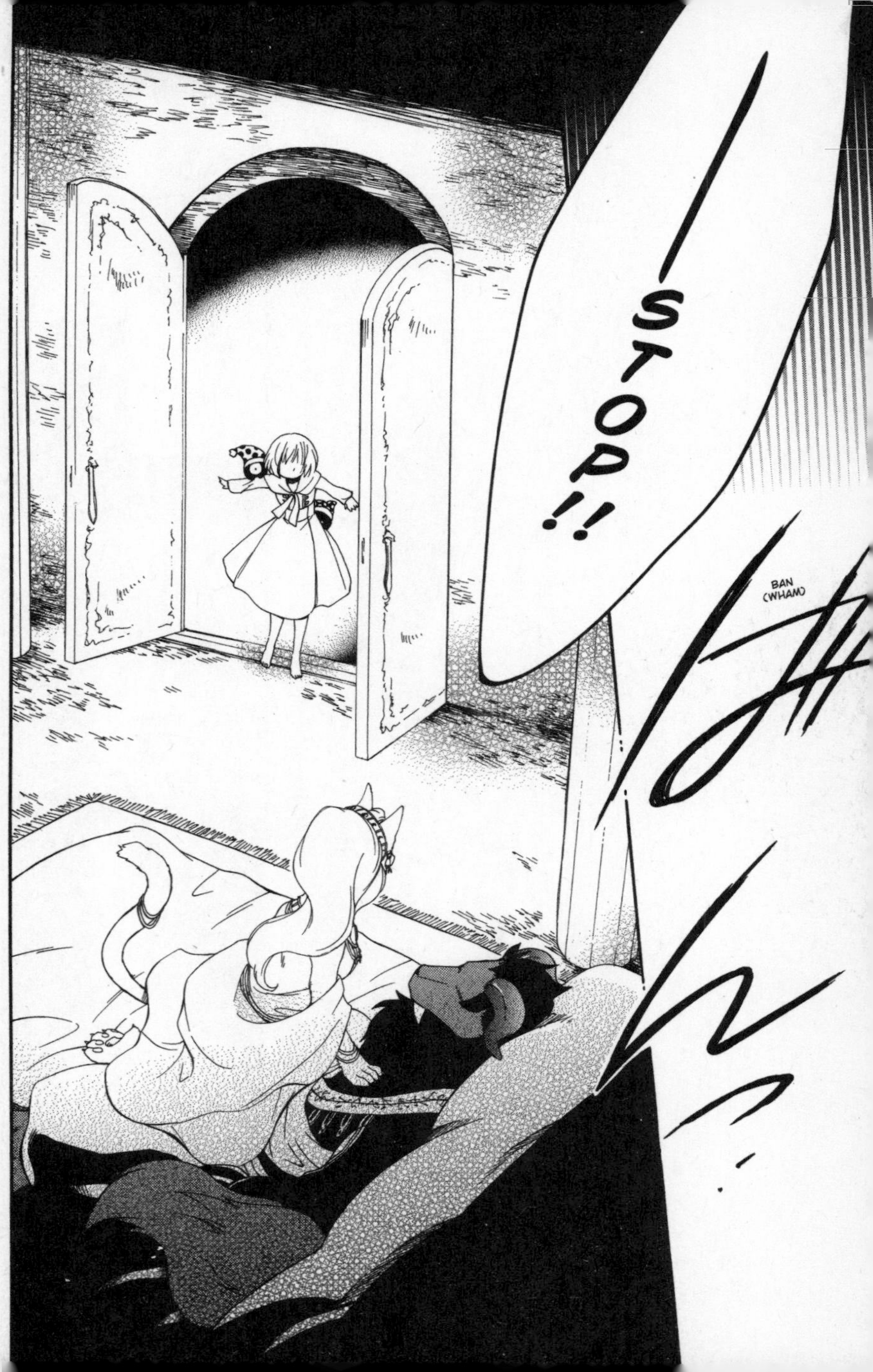
STOP!!
BAN
(WHAM)

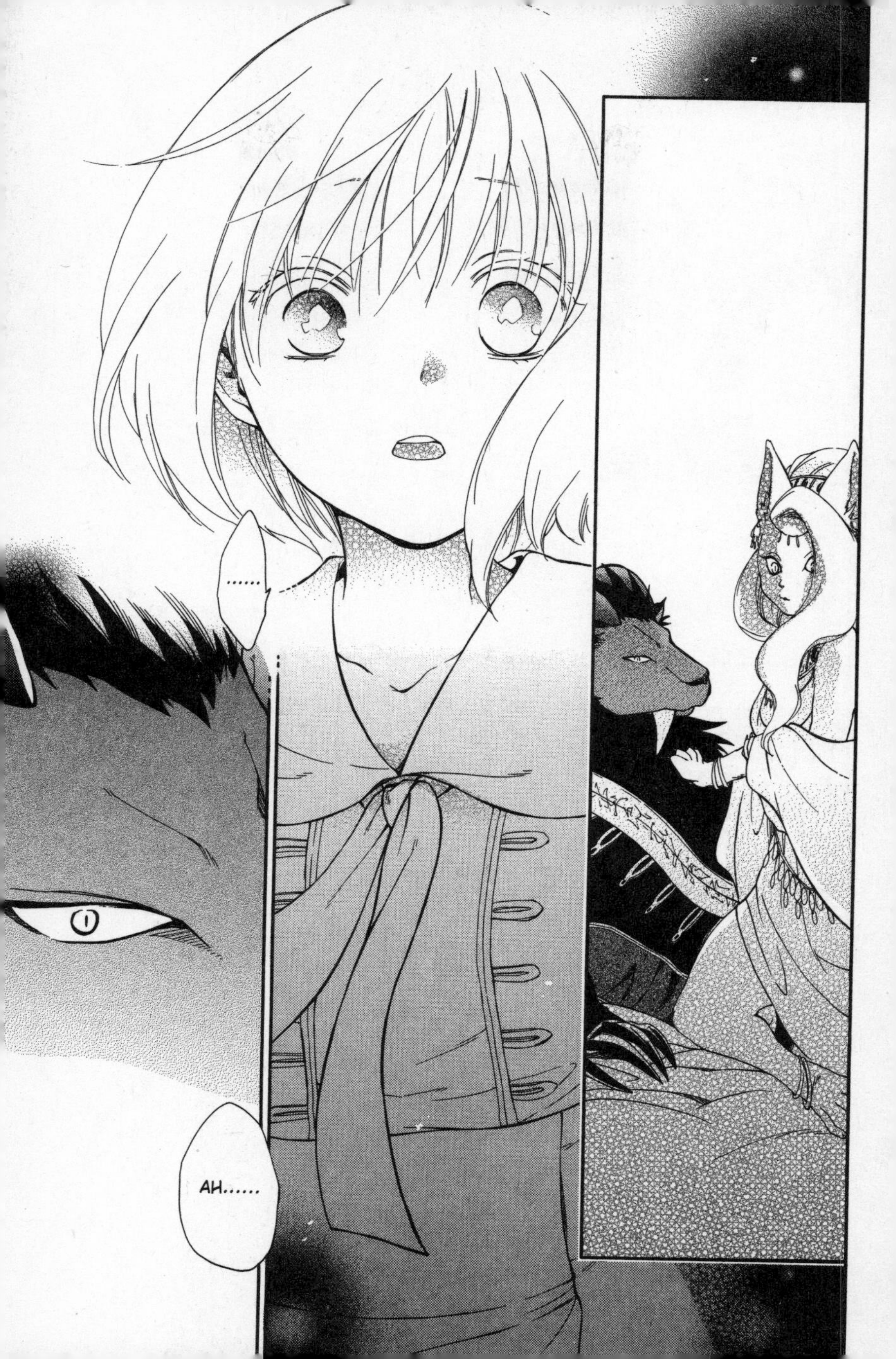
......
AH......

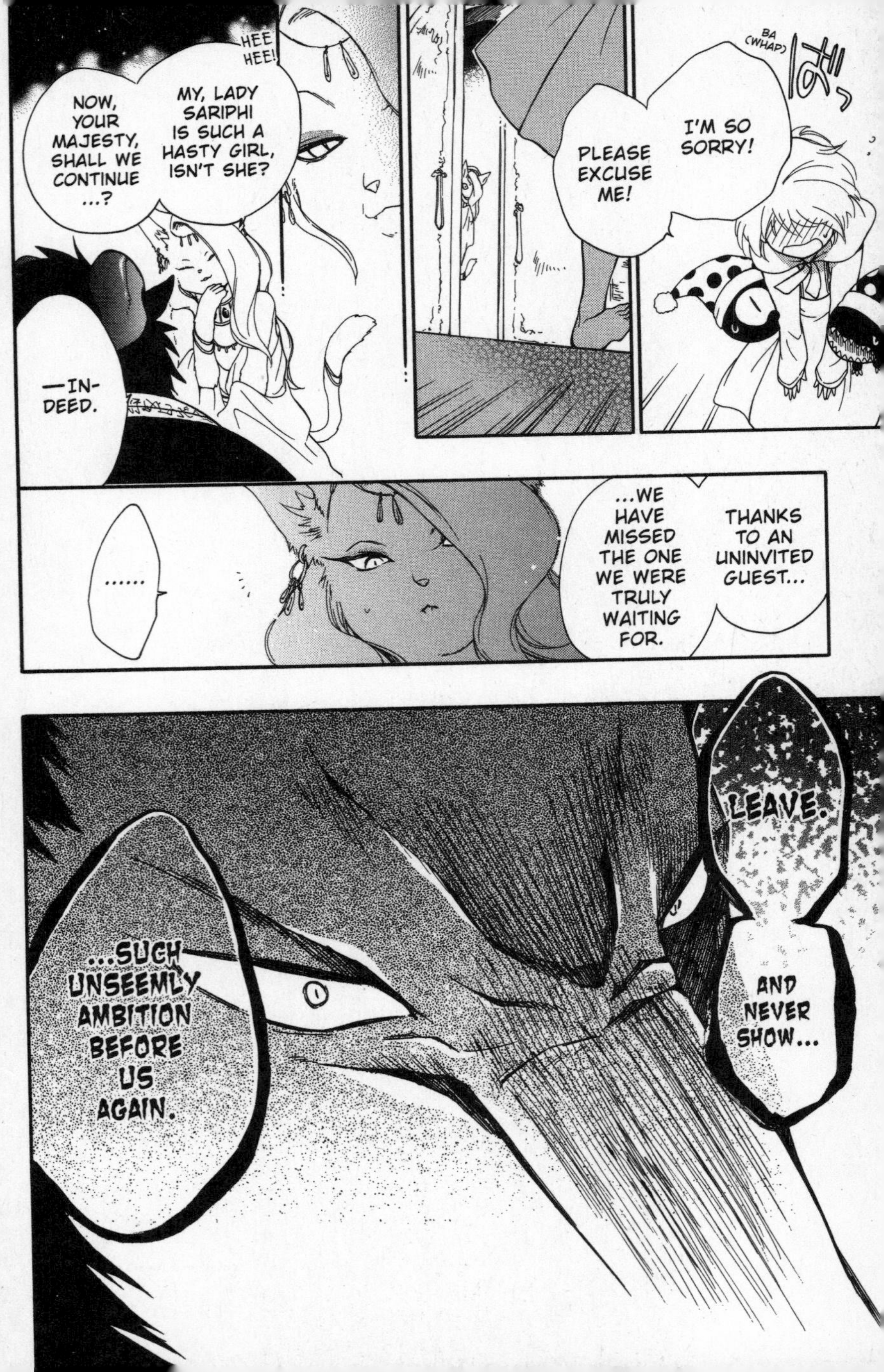
BA (WHAP)
ぱっ
I'M SO SORRY!
PLEASE EXCUSE ME!
HEE HEE!
MY, LADY SARIPHI IS SUCH A HASTY GIRL, ISN'T SHE?
NOW, YOUR MAJESTY, SHALL WE CONTINUE ...?
—INDEED.
THANKS TO AN UNINVITED GUEST...
...WE HAVE MISSED THE ONE WE WERE TRULY WAITING FOR.
......
LEAVE.
AND NEVER SHOW...
...SUCH UNSEEMLY AMBITION BEFORE US AGAIN.

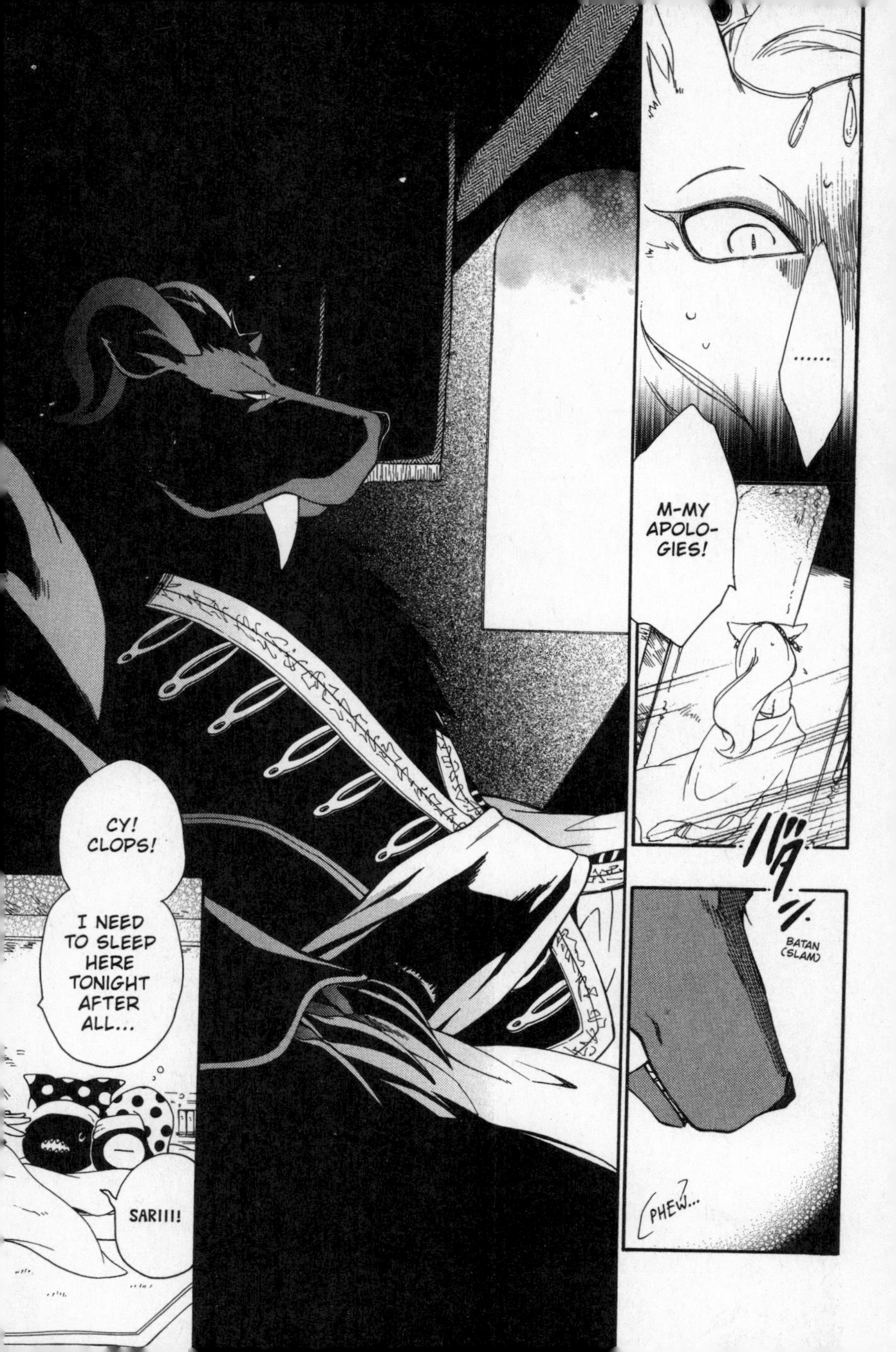
......
M-MY APOLO- GIES!
BATAN (SLAM)
PHEW...
CY! CLOPS!
I NEED TO SLEEP HERE TONIGHT AFTER ALL...
SARIII!

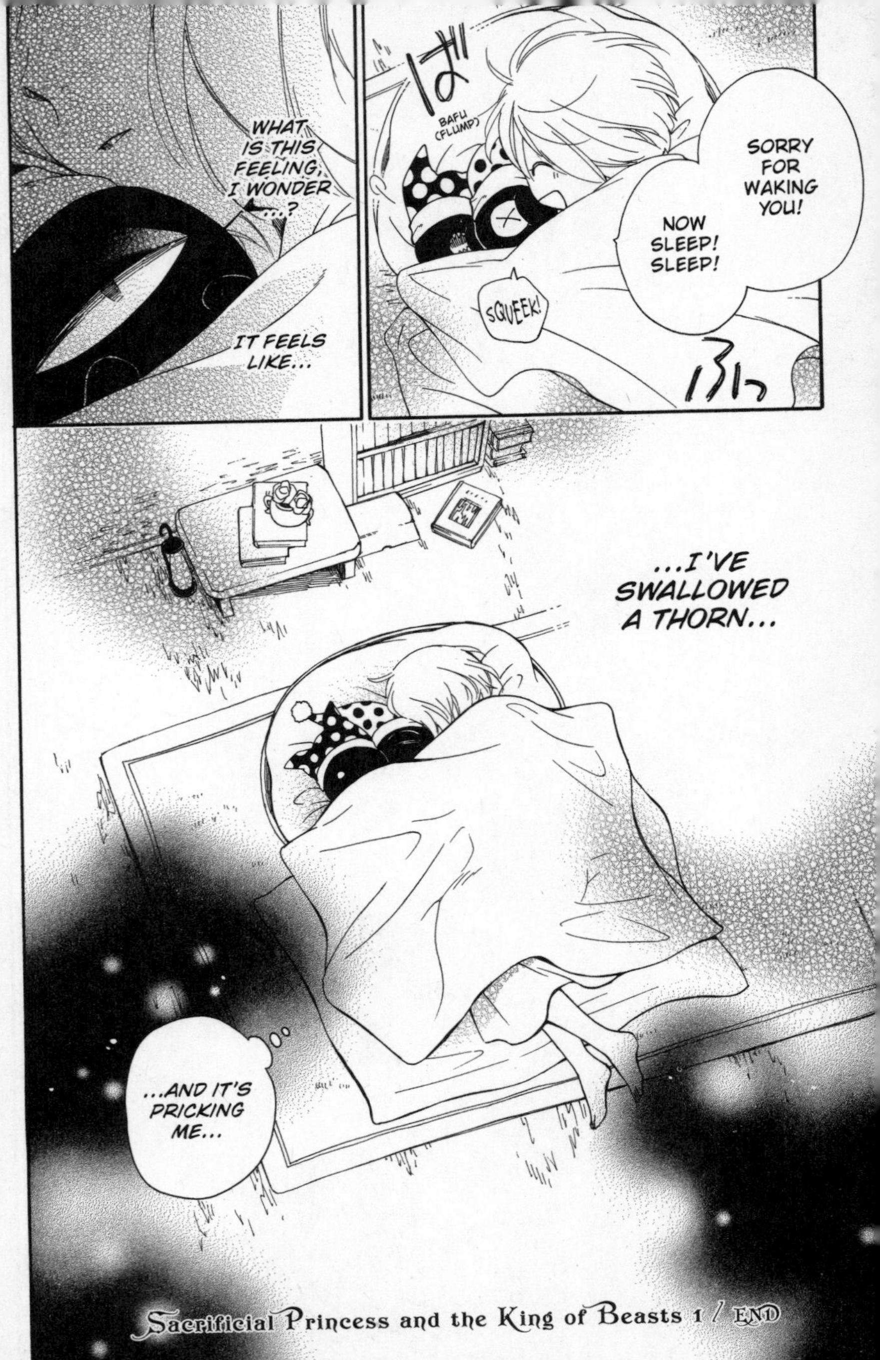
SORRY FOR WAKING YOU!
NOW SLEEP! SLEEP!
BAFU (FLUMP)
SQUEEEK!
WHAT IS THIS FEELING, I WONDER...?
IT FEELS LIKE...
...I'VE SWALLOWED A THORN...
...AND IT'S PRICKING ME...
Sacrificial Princess and the King of Beasts 1 / END

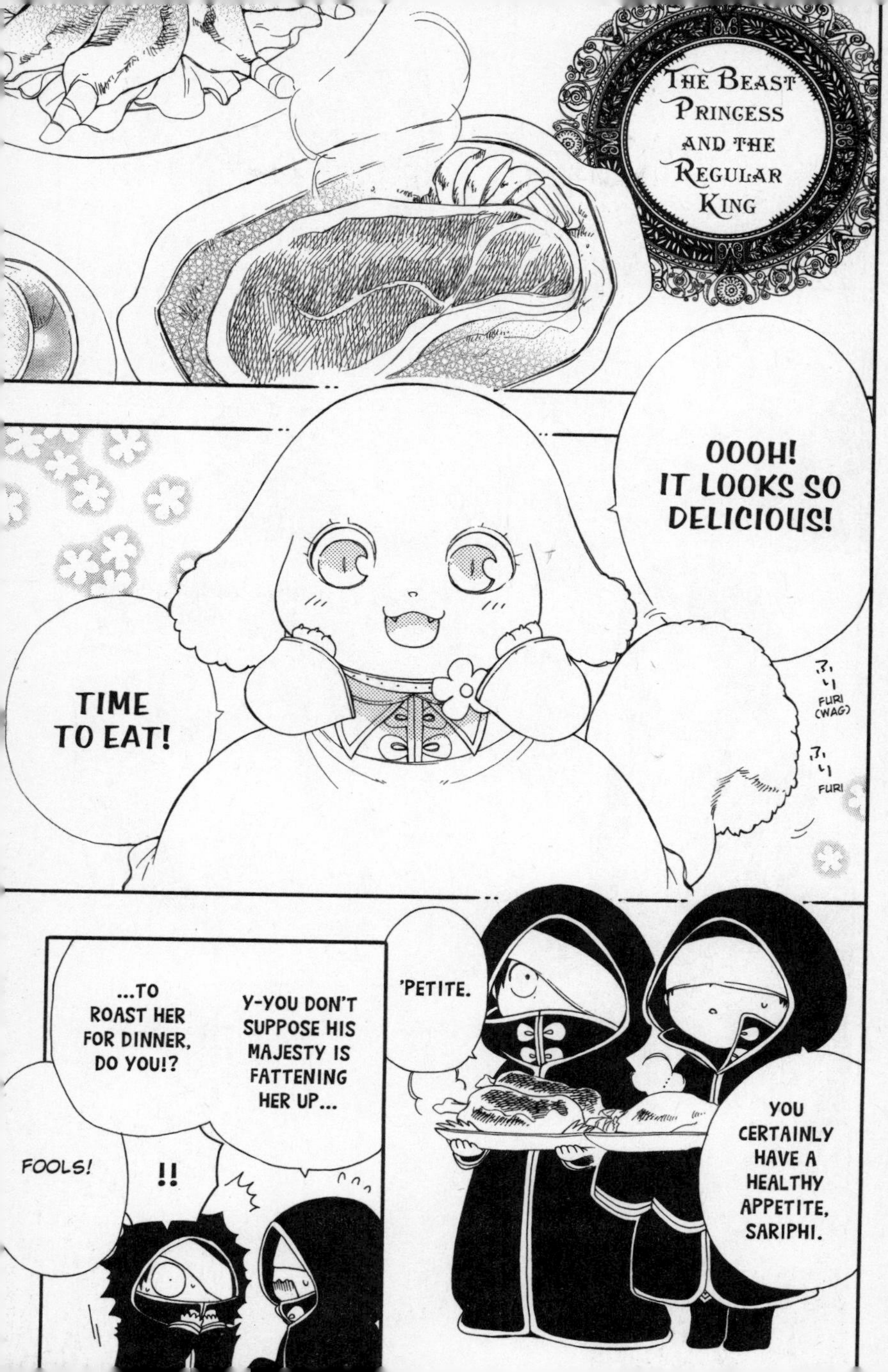
The Beast Princess and the Regular King
OOOH! IT LOOKS SO DELICIOUS!
ふり FURI (WAG)
ふり FURI
TIME TO EAT!
YOU CERTAINLY HAVE A HEALTHY APPETITE, SARIPHI.
'PETITE.
Y-YOU DON'T SUPPOSE HIS MAJESTY IS FATTENING HER UP...
...TO ROAST HER FOR DINNER, DO YOU!?
!!
FOOLS!

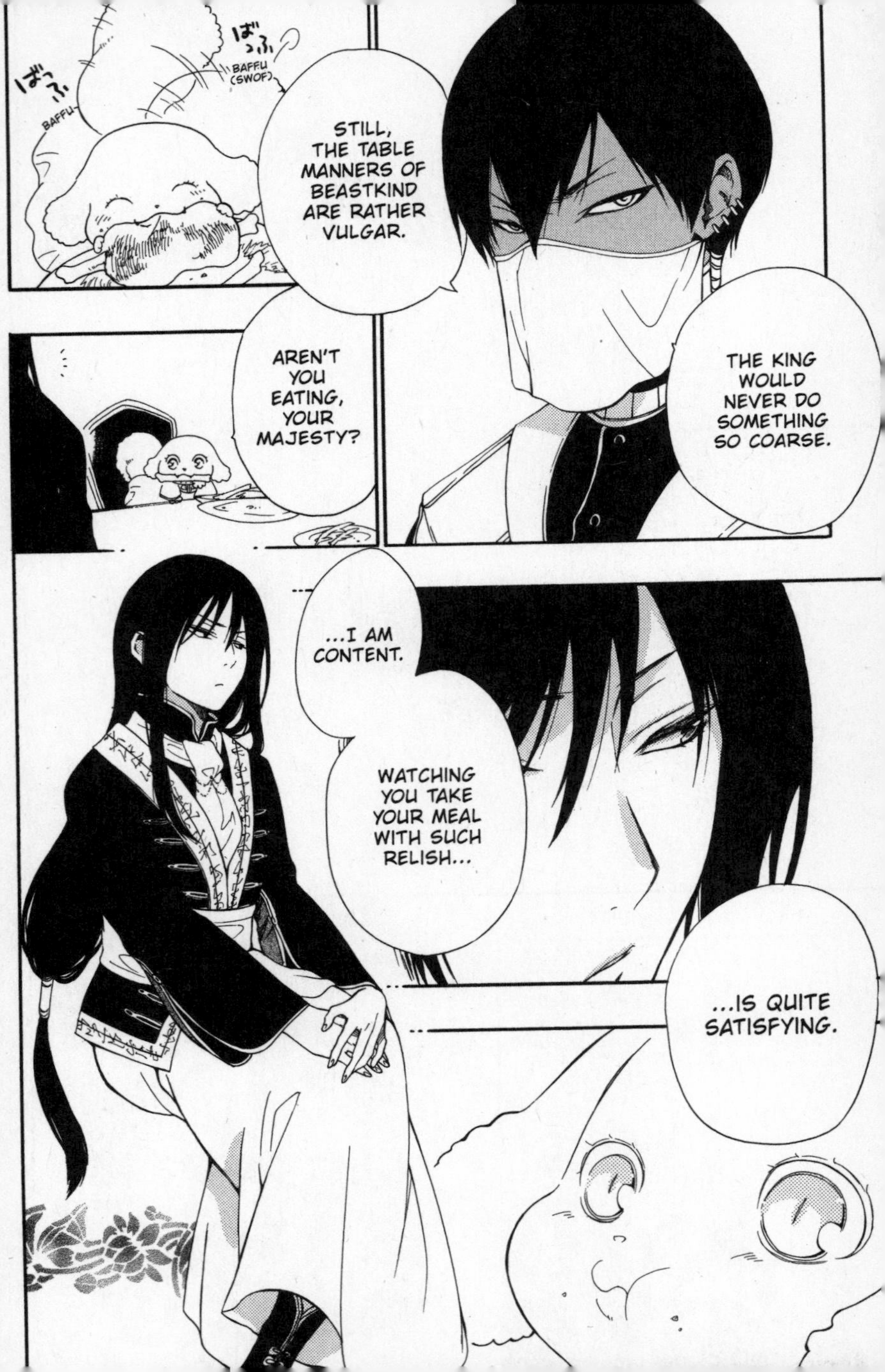
STILL, THE TABLE MANNERS OF BEASTKIND ARE RATHER VULGAR.
THE KING WOULD NEVER DO SOMETHING SO COARSE.
ばふ
BAFFU (SWOF)
ばふ
BAFFU
AREN'T YOU EATING, YOUR MAJESTY?
...I AM CONTENT.
WATCHING YOU TAKE YOUR MEAL WITH SUCH RELISH...
...IS QUITE SATISFYING.

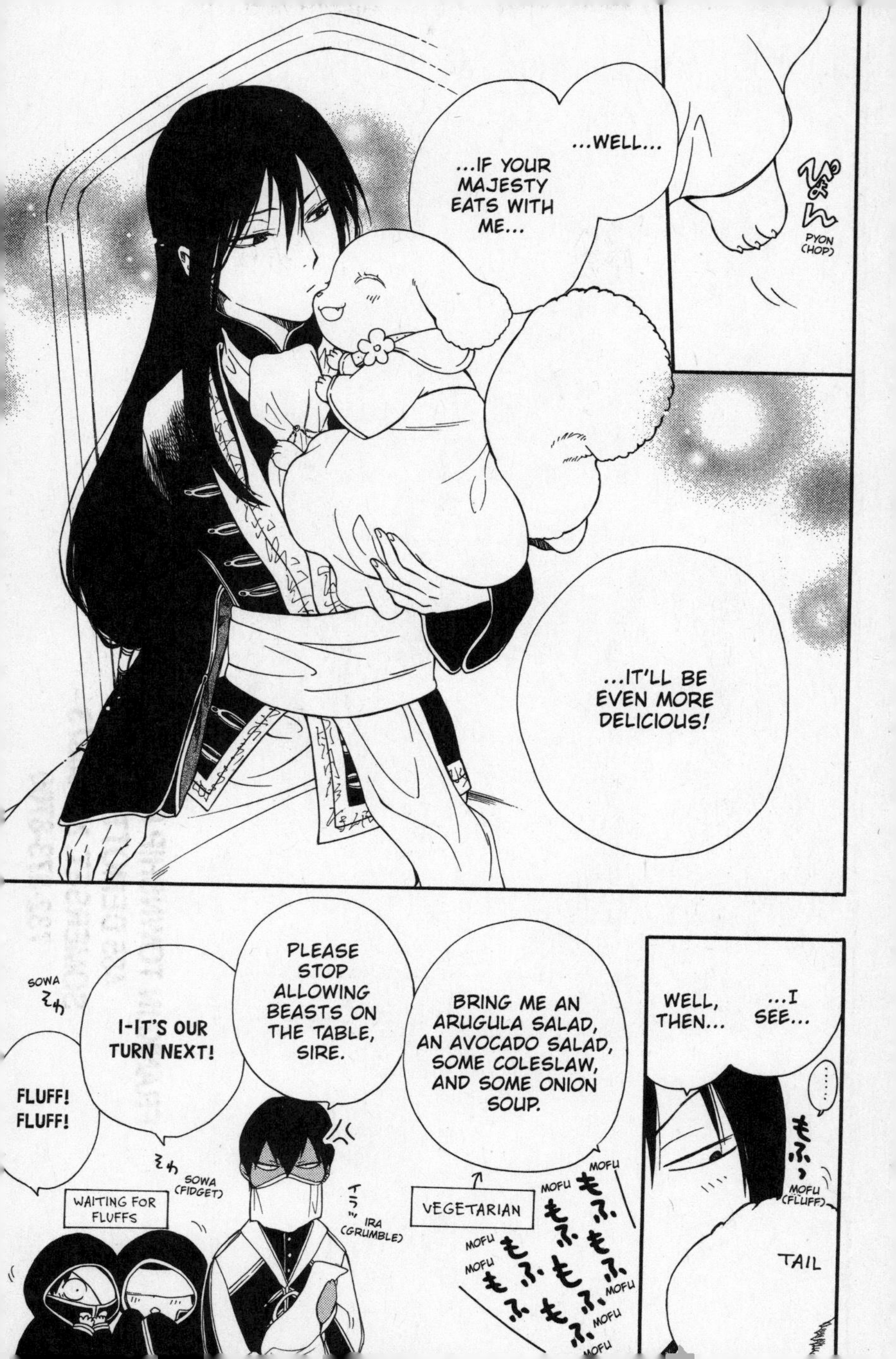

ぴょん
PYON (HOP)
...WELL...
...IF YOUR MAJESTY EATS WITH ME...
...IT'LL BE EVEN MORE DELICIOUS!
...I SEE...
WELL, THEN...
......
もふっ
MOFU (FLUFF)
TAIL
BRING ME AN ARUGULA SALAD, AN AVOCADO SALAD, SOME COLESLAW, AND SOME ONION SOUP.
VEGETARIAN
もふ もふ もふ もふ もふ もふ
MOFU MOFU MOFU MOFU MOFU MOFU
PLEASE STOP ALLOWING BEASTS ON THE TABLE, SIRE.
イラッ
IRA (GRUMBLE)
I-IT'S OUR TURN NEXT!
そわ
SOWA
FLUFF! FLUFF!
そわ
SOWA (FIDGET)
WAITING FOR FLUFFS

SACRIFICIAL PRINCESS AND THE King of Beasts

1

Yu Tomofuji

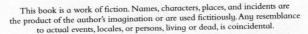

TRANSLATION: Paul Starr

LETTERING: Lys Blakeslee

This book is a work of fiction. Names, characters, places, and incidents are the product of the author's imagination or are used fictitiously. Any resemblance to actual events, locales, or persons, living or dead, is coincidental.

NIEHIME TO KEMONO NO OH by Yu Tomofuji
© Yu Tomofuji 2016
All rights reserved.
First published in Japan in 2016 by HAKUSENSHA, Inc., Tokyo.
English language translation rights in U.S.A., Canada and U.K. arranged with
HAKUSENSHA, Inc., Tokyo through Tuttle-Mori Agency, Inc., Tokyo.

English translation © 2018 by Yen Press, LLC

Yen Press
1290 Avenue of the Americas
New York, NY 10104

Visit us at yenpress.com ❅ facebook.com/yenpress ❅ twitter.com/yenpress
yenpress.tumblr.com ❅ instagram.com/yenpress

First Yen Press Edition: May 2018

Yen Press is an imprint of Yen Press, LLC.
The Yen Press name and logo are trademarks of Yen Press, LLC.

The publisher is not responsible for websites (or their
content) that are not owned by the publisher.

Library of Congress Control Number: 2018930817

ISBNs: 978-0-316-48098-7 (paperback)
978-0-316-48103-8 (ebook)

10 9 8 7 6 5 4 3 2 1

WOR

Printed in the United States of America